TORMENTED

A Gothic Tale of Vampires

MARK L'ESTRANGE

For Jude. This one is for you, big boy.

Chapter One

IT WAS LATE AFTERNOON, AND THE AUTUMN SUN WAS already on the wane. The wind was brisk, and whipped through the trees, shaking the loose leaves free, freeing them to flutter down to the ground.

As the sombre funeral procession emerged from the clump of trees which separated the local church from the graveyard, the horse that pulled the cart which housed the coffin, reared up, and let out a loud whinny.

The coffin slid back and was only prevented from sliding off the cart by the low ridge of the back plate which had been bolted into place.

The horse stopped, dead in its tracks, clearly not keen to walk on any further.

The driver of the cart jumped down, and immediately grabbed hold of its bridle, gripping it tightly with both hands. Fearing his horse may try to bolt, he leaned in closely and whispered words of comfort as he patted its flank in order to entice the beast to calm down.

Eventually, the horse relaxed, and moved forward.

The two gravediggers stood nearby, leaning on their shovels.

The first half of their labours already complete. The coffin held the body of the eldest daughter of Samuel Grant, a farm worker from the other side of the village.

She had only been a slight girl, barely five foot tall, so the size of the hole dug for her coffin matched, accordingly.

The procession walking behind the cart consisted of Samuel Grant and his wife, Sophie. Their youngest daughter Daisy. The four pall bearers, and the priest, Father John James.

Behind those gathered walked another man, who kept several paces behind the official party. He wore a long cloak and hood which came down over his face, and in his hand, he carried a dark brown leather bag.

The driver, still walking beside his horse, pulled it up when they were still several feet from the grave.

Two of the pallbearers climbed into the cart and released the back flap, sliding the coffin towards their colleagues who had positioned themselves on the ground at the back of the cart.

Together, the four men slid the coffin over the edge until the two on the ground had a firm hold of it, then the other two balanced the rear of the wooden box on the back of the cart, before jumping down and taking up their positions.

The four men worked in silence. They did not dress in Sunday best for the task, but remained in their working attire, knowing that this job would not be a clean one.

Together, they carried the coffin towards the grave, and placed it gently down on the soft earth.

Everyone gathered round as the priest began to say the prayers for the dead.

He knew them off by heart, having recited them many hundreds of times during his long career. But, even so, he still insisted on reading them from the pages of his book, like a novice.

As Father James spoke, from behind he could hear Sophie Grant crying.

Samuel wrapped his arms around both his wife and daughter and held them tightly to his chest. The two women sobbed into his shirt. Samuel raised his head to heaven in the hope that his own tears would not fall on his wife and daughter, he knew he had to be strong for them both.

Their grief being shared made it no less painful for any of them.

The priest continued with his sombre words. Both gravediggers knew from past experience that he was coming to the end of his prayers. Soon it would be their turn to take over and replace the dirt they had removed that morning.

The cloaked figure who had followed the procession in, still stood several feet behind the rest of the gathering, his head bowed, and his bag on the floor beside him.

Once the priest had finished, he turned back and looked over at Samuel.

Blinking away his tears, Samuel nodded his head.

Father James moved away from the grave and signalled for the bearers to place the coffin inside. As they settled their ropes under the coffin, in order to lift it into the hole, Sophie broke away from her husband and ran to the grave.

She fell to her knees and flung her arms over her daughter's coffin sobbing uncontrollably.

Samuel moved in and lifted his grieving wife off the floor. For a moment she fought against him, struggling to break free. But eventually she relented and allowed him to hold her once more.

Father James moved in closer to the couple. "Do not grieve my child," he said, comfortingly. "She is with God now, and free from all the danger and evil in this world."

Samuel looked at the priest and nodded his thanks.

He took his wife back to where their daughter was standing and held them both.

Father James signalled for the pallbearers to continue with

their task. He four men lifted the ropes which supported the coffin, and gently lowered it into the hole.

Once the coffin was out of sight, Samuel turned, taking his wife and surviving daughter with him, and set off for home.

Everyone else gathered at the gravesite watched them go.

As the three of them entered the clump of trees which surrounded the graveyard, Father James looked to the western sky. The sun was about to set, and from the east the sky had already changed to a dark grey hue.

He waited until the three mourners were out of sight, and earshot.

The pallbearers, still holding the end of the ropes, waited for his command before they took the strain and hefted the coffin back up, out of the hole.

They placed it gently back on the ground.

The mysterious cloaked figure moved forward to join the others.

One of the gravediggers came forward with an iron bar and, once Father James gave him permission, slid one end of it under the wooden lid of the coffin, and put all his weight on the other end.

The wood began to crack as the bar fought against the nails keeping the lid down.

Finally, it gave.

The gravedigger stopped and pulled the bar out, then placed it under the lid further down the coffin and used his weight as before.

This time the lid gave more quickly, already weakened by his initial effort.

He continued with his task until the entire lid was raised, then the pallbearers moved in and together they lifted the lid clean off the coffin.

The angelic figure of Mary Grant dressed in white, lay in situ, her eyes closed.

Suddenly, her eyelids shot open, revealing a glassy stare which turned the priest's blood to ice.

The pallbearers and the gravediggers all took a step back, and turned towards the cloaked figure, who moved forward and removed his cowl.

Mathew Hammond had what most people referred to as a stern countenance, with a short grey beard, and thick wiry hair of the same colour. His eyebrows too were abundant and bushy, and seemed to point downwards towards his nose, as if he wore a permanent frown.

He opened his bag and plunged his hand inside, removing a large wooden stake and a stout hammer.

Upon seeing the two implements, Mary Grant opened her mouth, baring two elongated canines, and hissed at the figure above her.

Before she had a chance to move, Mathew dropped to his knees beside the coffin, and raised the wooden stake high above his head, before plunging it into Mary's chest.

Mary screamed.

It was not the normal sound of a girl screaming, but a guttural, almost inhuman emanation which seemed to fill the very air around them.

Mathew brought the hammer down hard on top of the stake, driving it deeper into the hapless girl's chest. He swung it three more times until he could hear the point reaching the wooden base of the coffin.

The figure of Mary Grant lay, as she first appeared, with her eyes closed and the angelic look of a young girl at peace.

Mathew stood up and wiped the sweat from his brow.

He turned to Father James. "It is done!" he informed him.

The priest made the sign of the cross and signalled for the men around him to continue with their work.

The lid was positioned back on the coffin, with the top of the stake sticking out from the young girl's chest, and the nails were hammered back into place.

Mathew and Father James stood back and waited for the coffin to be lowered back into the ground, then the priest said the last of his prayers while the gravediggers filled the hole with earth.

Chapter Two

ONCE THE DEED WAS COMPLETE, ALL THE MEN PILED into the wagon, and were taken to the nearest inn, The Wild Boar, for a well-earned drink.

When they opened the door of the inn and stepped inside, everyone already there stopped their conversations and turned their heads to look at the newcomers.

Father James scanned the room for Samuel Grant, but to his relief, the man was nowhere to be seen. Although there were several of his friends and fellow workers scattered around the room.

They all know where the men had been, and, more importantly, what task they had undertaken.

None of them envied the new arrivals.

Mathew Hammond strode up to the bar and ordered an ale for the men, and a large claret for Father James.

The men had all been paid for their part in the ceremony, and well paid too. But Mathew felt that they deserved a little something extra for their efforts. At one point, he was afraid that they would take flight, leaving just him and the priest to compete the task alone.

Such a scenario had occurred on many occasions in the past.

Men were always keen to help when they saw the colour of the money being offered. But when it came down to performing the task in question, many of them turned tail and ran.

Some of these men were the biggest and the strongest in the district. Yet it seemed to make little matter when the coffin was opened, and they faced it for the first time.

Even though they were all well briefed before the event, Mathew could always tell from the look of bewilderment and disbelief in their eyes that they did not comprehend what he was saying.

The proof came when the lid was lifted.

Ideally, Mathew would have preferred to have his own crew to travel with. A reliable group of six or so men, all of whom knew what the job entailed and were satisfied to just get on with it.

He had requested such an arrangement on umpteen occasions, but his employers, the church, were more concerned with him keeping a low key for his investigations, and the sight of an entire group entering a district, in their minds, would attract far too much attention.

Instead, he had to make do with whomever the local priest felt that he could trust.

As it was, Father James had done well in gathering his helpers. At least none of them bolted when the moment of truth arrived.

Mathew and the priest took their drinks over to a spare table at the back on the room, while the rest of the men decided to stand at the bar.

The gentle hum of conversation returned slowly as everyone else turned back to their own groups.

Father James took a drink of his wine.

Mathew could see that the priest's hands were shaking. It was not surprising under the circumstances. Just like the hired help, when Mathew first arrived in a new district and presented his letter of introduction, most priests looked at him with vague distrust. If it were not for his letter, signed by the archbishop himself, Mathew was sure that he would be turned away, or thrown into jail.

Mathew slid his hand across the table and patted Father James on the arm. "You did very well today, Father," he informed him, encouragingly. "I've seen the most devout, senior members of the cloth crumble into a quivering mess upon seeing one of the undead rise. You should be proud."

Father James nodded. "Thank you, my son," he replied, keeping his voice low. "I only hope that God will see the necessity of our actions as righteous, for I must admit, I am struggling to accept what we were forced to do as being anything short of murder."

Mathew stopped his tankard from reaching his lips. "Murder?" he repeated.

Father James looked up to ensure that no one was listening in on their conversation.

The rest of the bar seemed to be engrossed in their own affairs, but even so, the priest felt that such a conversation was best had elsewhere than in a public house.

"Please keep your voice down, my son," he implored. "These good people are in enough of a stir without us adding to their worries."

Mathew shook his head and drank. He appreciated the difficult position the priest found himself in, but there was no use in pretending that nothing untoward was taking place.

"They'd have a damn sight more to worry about if we left matters unchecked," said Mathew, this time keeping his tone low for the priest's sake. "And how can you murder something which is already dead?"

Father James looked shocked by the man's words, but deep down he knew that there was some truth to them, and for that, he was grateful that the church had seen fit to send him help.

It had taken a long time for the priest to accept what was taking place in his own parish. Most of the stories he had heard he put down to rumour, speculation and weak-minded folk allowing what little imagination they had to run riot.

As a result of his hesitance, he knew that he had to shoulder the blame for all the disappearances which had ensued.

Then, when the bodies were discovered drained of every ounce of blood, the locals were sent into a blind fury.

They demanded action, but all he could offer them was prayer and faith that the almighty would hear them, and thus bring an end to whatever horror had taken over their town.

But it was not enough.

Mob-handed they began capturing anyone in the area whom they suspected and torturing them into making a confession.

Thomas Rudd, the poor simple-minded son of a local midwife was dragged from his bed and strung up, right in front of his poor mother while she screamed of his innocence. Joshua Campbell, a young labourer who had a bad reputation for leading young ladies astray, was thrown into a ditch and stoned to death. Simon Kent, an octogenarian who had spent most of his life living off the land, and to the priest's knowledge had never hurt a living soul, was burned to death having been barricaded in his tiny wooden hut in the woods.

Carnage rained.

No one was safe from the baying mob.

Yet still the disappearances continued.

It was fast becoming worse than the witch trials from the previous century. Father James still had the parish records from the time, and some of the atrocious and inhumane practices which were performed on women and young girls to try and force them to confess, still made his heart turn over at the very thought.

This latest excuse for justice was fast growing out of control, and Father James knew it, even if no one else of power in the vicinity accepted it.

Finally, the Militia were called in to quell the uprising. Colonel Drake, the officer in charge rounded up the leaders of the mob and gave them an ultimatum: Either halt their actions or face the noose.

Drake was a harsh man, but fair. He believed in giving people a chance, and if they were willing to let that opportunity slip by, then they deserved to suffer the consequences.

To the priest's relief, once the Militia were on side, the riots quelled, and normal life was resumed. There were no more disappearances, no more bloodless corpses, and as a result, the rumblings made by those who chose to take the law into their own hands, lessened until they became nothing more than a whisper.

Colonel Drake was eventually ordered to attend to troubles in another part of the country. He left behind a skeleton force to keep the peace and vowed to return if matters grew out of hand.

Over time, the local residents grew used to sleeping soundly in their beds, without having to worry that they, or their loved ones, might be carried away by some diabolical creature of the night, intent on draining them of their life blood.

Young Mary Grant had been the first victim in a long time, but as she was found without having had the blood drained from her, Father James managed to convince his congregation that her death was not related to those earlier cases. Doctor Harris was clearly not pleased by the assumption, but once Father James explained to him about the town being a powder keg jus wating for a spark to ignite it, he relented. The cause of death was heart failure, so in his opinion further investigation was unnecessary.

Even so, word of the death quickly spread, and Father James received word from the archbishop's office that the church was sending a specialist in such matters to carry out an investigation. But the night before he arrived, Mary Grant had been seen strolling through the woods by no less than three witnesses.

The following morning, once Mathew had arrived, Father James and the Militia soldiers led him to the poor girl's coffin. The lid was removed, and the body of the young girl was still in situ, looking as peaceful and angelic as she had in life.

But even so, Mathew had his suspicions, and upon investigation he found two slight puncture marks on the side of the girl's neck. Proof positive, so far as he was concerned, that whatever evil had plagued the area was still at work.

That was when he explained to Father James about his plan to ensure that poor Mary Grant could be allowed to rest in eternal peace.

Horrified as he was by the barbaric ritual, Father James eventually came around to believing that Mathew knew what he was talking about, having spent many years travelling throughout central Europe on his lonely quest to try and understand the genesis of this evil, and how to defeat it.

It had been an even harder task explaining their plan to Mary's father, but eventually he understood and came to terms with it. His one request was that they carry out their task after he had taken his wife and younger daughter out of earshot.

Now that they had dealt with one of the symptoms of this plague, Father James knew that they still had to face the cause, and he knew that even with Mathew by his side, that would be a herculean task.

Chapter Three

THE CARRIAGES BOUNCED ALONG THE WOODLAND
path, their wheels kicking up dust and pebbles as they went. In
the lead coach sat Lord Vincent Goddard, the fourth Viscount of
Hasterley, and his new wife, Corrine. They had only been
married a year, and first met in Paris while Vincent had been on
holiday with his daughters.

Corrine was his second wife. His first wife, Charlotte, died
whilst giving birth to their second daughter, Emily, nine years
earlier.

They were returning to Hasterley after the death of Vincent's
father, so that Vincent could take up his seat as the new
Viscount. His father's death had come about somewhat
suddenly and by the time word reached him in Paris, it was too
late for Vincent to return in time for the funeral.

Both his daughters were particularly upset at the death of
their paternal grandfather, as they had always been close, and
spent many enjoyable holidays with him when not accompa-
nying their father on his travels.

Vincent's youngest daughter was especially close to him and
had taken the news of his death very badly. She had suffered

some terrible nightmares since then, and Margaret, her nanny, had reverted to spending the night in a chair beside her bed, so that she was on hand to comfort the girl if such traumas took hold.

Margaret had been initially employed as Stella's nanny, but when Charlotte died in childbirth, she became more of a surrogate mother to both girls, but especially to Emily who had never known the love of her real mother.

Corrine turned to Vincent. "Is it much further?" she asked, excitedly. Corrine was a good deal younger than her husband, and this was her first time away from home.

"Not long now my darling," Vincent assured her, leaning in and planting a kiss on the end of her nose. "Once we pass through the woods you should be able to see the house in the distance."

Corrine smiled. She was thoroughly looking forward to taking up her new position as lady of the manor. To her, Vincent was a far better catch than all those young men her father paraded in front of her as potential suiters.

Vincent was strong, virile, and already settled in many of his ways, most of which Corrine found enchanting.

"Do you think your servants will like me?"

Vincent turned to her. "What a curious thing to say," he replied, furrowing his brows. "If they don't, they'll be out on their ears before morning," he promised her.

Corrine hugged his arm. "I know how important one's servants are in England. You treat them like family, and they stay with you all their lives. So, it is important to me that they like and accept me."

Vincent laughed. "You're right about that," he admitted. "Some of the household staff have been with my father for years, some have even been there since before I was born. But you've no need to worry my dear, I am sure that they will love you, as I do."

14

In the second carriage Stella, Emily, and Nanny Margaret rode together.

Emily was fidgeting and rubbing herself against the seat.

"What is the matter with you today?" asked Margaret. "You've been jumping around like a little cricket all day."

"It's this dress," the girl protested. "It itches. Why must I wear it when I have so many nice ones in my chest?"

Stella put down her book. "It's out of respect for our grandpapa," she informed her sister. "It will be expected that we show we are in mourning for his passing. You don't want the servants to think that we are being disrespectful, do you?"

Emily thought for a moment. "I suppose not," she agreed reluctantly, pulling a face. "But why did Papa have to buy me such an itchy one?"

"I am sure he did not do it on purpose," Margaret assured her. "New clothes often need to be washed before they settle, it won't always be like this, you'll see."

"I'm never wearing it again," Emily replied, defiantly.

"And what if I die?" asked Margaret. "Won't you want to mourn my passing?"

Emily's face dropped. "Do not say that, Nanny," she implored. "You must live forever."

Stella tutted. "No one lives forever," she insisted.

"Nanny will," Emily pouted, "won't you, Nanny?"

"I'll do my best if you promise to be a good girl and stop fussing over your dress."

Emily nodded, enthusiastically, then waited for Margaret to look back out at the passing countryside before she surreptitiously rubbed herself against her seat once more.

Up ahead, Vincent tapped his cane against the roof of his carriage and called for the driver to stop. The man did as he was instructed and went to climb down from his perch to open his master's door, but Vincent did not wait, and was already out of the carriage before the driver could reach him.

Vincent turned back and looked up at Corrine. "I'd like you to meet one of our oldest tenants, my dear," he said, pointing with his cane towards the two men in the field who, having seen the carriage pull up, had started to make their way towards it.

The two men removed his hats. Their clothes were soiled and wet with perspiration.

They stopped when they were about ten feet away from the Viscount and bowed their heads. "My lord," announced the elder of the two men. "It's good to have you back. We're all very sorry for your great loss."

"Thank you, Watkins, and how are things with you? Keeping the hall well stocked with vegetables I trust?"

"Bless you, yes, your lordship. Potatoes, turnips, carrots, enough for a feast."

Vincent smiled. "Good, that's excellent." He turned to his wife. "Corrine my dear, this is Ralph Watkins and his son Toby. Ralph and his family have been working the soil here since as far back as anyone can remember. Isn't that right Ralph?"

The man nodded, smiling up at Corrine. "Indeed, my lord, and proud to carry on the tradition if it pleases you."

"It does indeed, Ralph," answered Corrine, "and I'm sure we all look forward to enjoying the results of your hard work up at the hall."

Ralph bowed once more. "Thank you, your ladyship, we'll do everything we can not to let you down."

Vincent laughed. "Ralph is joking of course, my dear, he and his family have never let us down, and I'm sure they never will, aye Ralph?"

Vincent's driver held open his carriage door he climbed in.

Ralph and his son stayed beside the road, their caps still in their hands.

The carriage driver climbed back aboard and cracked his whip, urging the horses to move on.

Ralph and Toby smiled and bowed as the second carriage

rolled past, only Emily waved to them, the other two women busied themselves with reading.

When the carriages were far away enough to be safe, Toby turned to his father. "You didn't say anything about…"

Before he had a chance to finish, his father cut him off. "That's no for us to say lad."

"Everyone's talking about it down at the inn," Toby insisted, feeling rebuked.

"That still don't make it our business to go spreading gossip, let's leave that to others. And what's more, there are those much better placed than the likes of us to be advising the master on what others may be saying. We're best out of it, understand?"

Toby nodded, and Ralph clapped his son's shoulder to show that he was not angry with him.

"They were nice and friendly," said Corrine cheerfully, "and you seem to have a very good relationship with your tenants if they are anything to go by."

Vincent turned to her, holding her close. "You see," he replied triumphantly, "I told you they would like you. But to be honest, there are some who owe us allegiance who are not so congenial. I'll do my best to keep you from them, I don't want you getting upset."

"Really." Corrine sounded startled. "Well, I hope if I do meet them that they will at least moderate their manner in the presence of a lady."

"They better had," demanded Vincent, "or they'll have me to answer to."

As the carriages emerged from the last clump of trees which formed part of the surrounding wood, Mandrake Hall came into view for the first time. It was still over a mile away, but the land around it was mostly flat, so at least it could be seen.

Vincent pointed to it. "Your new home, my darling," he announced proudly.

Corrine held onto the open window of the carriage and gazed out at the enormous structure which seemed to rise from the land like some huge monster, ready to gnaw away at anyone, or anything, which dared to cross its path.

It appeared far more eerie than Corrine had imagined, even in the daylight, but she put that down to her imagination running wild.

She turned back to Vincent and smiled. "It's magnificent," she said enthusiastically. "But it is so big, just for us. I will get lost on my way to the dining room, you'll have to send out a search party for me."

Vincent laughed, heartily. "Not to worry, you'll grow to love it just as I have, and before you know it, you'll be able to navigate your way around without even having to ask any of the servants."

Corrine sat back in her seat. She grabbed her husband's hand and squeezed it.

"Oh Vincent, you have made me so happy. I will do whatever it takes to be a good wife to you, and a mother for Stella and Emily, if Nanny Margaret allows me."

Vincent leaned down and rubbed her stomach. "And soon, I trust you will provide me with a son and heir to carry on our proud name."

Corrine placed her hand over his. "He will be the most handsome man in all of England, after his father of course."

Chapter Four

THE PATH WHICH LED TO THE HALL WAS LONG AND
winding and stretched around the perimeter of the grounds, and
past the lake. As they neared the embankment, Corrine noticed
a large stone structure which sat alone, across from the water.

"Oh, what is that?" she asked, peering through the window
as they approached. "It looks like such a lonely little building, all
by itself. Is it where your servants live?"

Vincent laughed. "No darling, that is the Goddard
mausoleum, the final resting place for all of us. We will have to
visit there soon to pay respects to my father as we missed his
funeral."

"I see," replied Corrine. "I'm sorry, I did not mean to be
disrespectful."

"I'm sure my ancestors won't take it to heart."

"I have never seen one like it before. Is it usual to have one
in the grounds?"

Vincent nodded. "Most great houses have one built when the
house is being constructed," he explained. "I've known some
families who have even had to have theirs added to due to the
large number of deaths in the family."

"Hopefully ours will not see any new additions for many years to come," Corrine offered.

Vincent kissed her.

As the carriage pulled up outside the main entrance to Mandrake Hall, an elderly man climbed down the stairs to meet it. He was closely followed by four strapping lads, all dressed in identical attire.

This time, Vincent waited for the driver to come around and open his door before he jumped down. He held out his hand to the old man. "Jasper, you old war horse, how are you?" he asked cheerfully.

The old man shook his hand and bowed. "Very well thank you, your lordship. All the staff wish me say how sorry we are for the loss of your father. He will be greatly missed."

"Thank you, that's very kind." Vincent turned back to the carriage. The driver had now lowered the small set of steps to allow Corinne easy access to the ground, and he waited at attention by the open door to assist her.

Vincent waved the man off, and moved forward himself, offering up his hand.

Corrine pulled back her dress and took his hand while she navigated the steps.

Vincent waited for his wife to reach the floor before speaking. "I would like to present my wife, the lady Corrine," he said, smiling proudly.

Jasper bowed once more. "I am most honoured your ladyship."

"Jasper has been with our family since before I was conceived," explained Vincent. "This place wouldn't run a day without him."

Jasper blushed.

"I am very pleased to make your acquaintance, Jasper," said Corrine, smiling.

"Thank you, your ladyship, I have taken the liberty of assembling the staff in the grand hall so that I may introduce them to you."

"You are most kind," replied Corrine. "I hope they won't be offended if I do not remember all their names at once."

Jasper shook his head, reassuringly.

"And while you are becoming acquainted with our staff, I'll have some sherry in the drawing room," said Vincent. "The road was particularly dry for the last hour or so."

"Yes, sir," replied Jasper, "and I have arranged for some tea for the ladies to be served once the introductions are complete."

Corrine thanked him.

The four men who had accompanied the old retainer were already busying themselves removing the cases and trunks from on top of the carriages.

The driver of the second coach was assisting Margaret and the girls down, so that they could join Corrine and their father.

Jonathan, one of the servants assisting with the luggage, gazed fondly after Stella as she sashayed towards the main entrance to the hall. He had just taken up employment at Mandrake the last time Stella had visited her grandfather. He had noticed her then and was almost sure that she had given him a knowing smile when she met his gaze.

As a mere servant, Jonathan knew better than to approach Stella with romantic designs. But even so, he allowed himself to fantasize that if his feelings were reciprocated, she might concoct a plan to catch him alone one day. He knew from some of his fellow servants at other houses that such things happened. Many of his counterparts had enjoyed secret liaisons with the mistresses of the house, or on occasion, visiting guests after a party or ball.

When he listened to such tales, Jonathan always felt awkward that he did not have one to offer. But he was still only in his early twenties, and the only girls he had ever gone with had been housemaids, or the occasional tavern maid.

He knew that women fancied him. Enough of them had said it in the past. But Stella was, in all ways, out of his league, and he knew it. There was no way that the master would ever condone a relationship between them, so Jonathan had no sights set on wooing the Viscounts eldest daughter.

But, if she ever wanted to gain some experience of the pleasures of the flesh before being married off to some fat, old member of the aristocracy, then he was definitely the man for the job.

He just had to make sure that Stella knew it, without risking his position.

"Hey, are you going to help with these or what?"

Jonathan turned round. Clive, one of his fellow servants was standing beside him holding a trunk from one of the straps.

"Sorry," Jonathan apologised, smirking. "I was just wool gatherin'."

Clive shook his head. "And you'd best keep thoughts like that inside your head, else you'll be out on your ear without so much as a reference to keep you warm."

Jonathan laughed. "I know, but a man can dream."

As the family entered the main foyer, Corrine could not help but gaze up in wonder and awe at the marvellous ceiling. The painting put her in mind of some of the great cathedrals and palaces she had visited in France. It was hard for her to believe that she was now the mistress of such a wonderful property.

The servants standing just inside the doorway, helped the family with their travelling cloaks, and hats.

"Now then young lady," said Margaret, looking down at Emily. "I believe it is time for your nap, otherwise you'll be falling asleep at supper this evening."

Emily pulled a face but knew there was no point in arguing.

Corrine noticed the young girl's disappointment. "Oh, that's a pity," she said. "I was hoping you could help introduce me to the staff. Jasper has them lined up for me to meet."

Emily pulled at Margaret's hand and jumped up and down, excitedly. "Oh, please let me go," she implored. "Mama needs my help, I can have my nap after."

Vincent smiled.

He still loved to hear his girls calling Corrine their mama.

When he and Corrine were first engaged, he sat down with Stella and Emily and explained to them, separately, about his plans to marry. He was cautious about broaching the subject of how the girls should address his new wife. Stella had been ten when her mother died, so naturally she still remembered her with affection, whereas poor little Emily never had the chance of knowing her.

Stella, being a modest and considerate daughter, asked Vincent how he would prefer her to address Corrine. When he suggested that Corrine would love to be called Mama, Stella agreed without hesitation.

Emily, as a very young girl, had often questioned why Margaret was not her mother, and had even asked at one point if she could call her that. But Margaret explained to the little girl that until, or unless, her father remarried, it would not be right for her to address anyone else in such a way.

Therefore, when Vincent approached his youngest daughter, she was overjoyed at the prospect of having a new mama and told him so in gushing terms.

Margaret glanced over at Vincent, who nodded his assent. "Go on then," she smiled. "Just don't overexcite yourself or you won't be able to sleep, afterwards."

Emily swapped Margaret's hand for Corrine's, squeezing it tightly. "Come, Mama," she urged. "Don't be afraid, they're all very nice. Jasper is especially kind."

The old man blushed slightly and bowed to the little girl.

Before Corrine could say anything further, Emily was pulling her along the polished floor towards the grand hall, evidently thrilled to be the one to introduce her to the staff.

Watching them go, Vincent called out. "Careful, you'll have your mama's arm off at that rate." But they were already through the door before either could acknowledge him.

Jasper led Vincent, Margaret, and Stella into the front parlour.

A maid was busying herself setting out the china for their tea.

She looked up and curtseyed when she saw them enter.

Vincent and the ladies took their seats, while the maid ensured that everything was laid out in the correct order for the tea. Once she was satisfied, she curtseyed once more, and left.

"I think we should all go and visit my father's coffin tomorrow, while he is still lying in state. We need to pay our respects before his coffin is placed in its concrete enclave. Can you arrange that, Jasper? Shall we say eleven o'clock?"

Jasper bowed, instinctively, but when he rose, there was an unmistakable look of alarm in his eyes which, thought he tried, he could not disguise.

Fortunately for him, no one else noticed it.

"I will send word for Doctor Harris, so that he is aware of your lordship's intentions."

Vincent turned in his chair. "Why on earth do we need the doctor to be present?" he asked quizzically. "It's a little late for his intervention."

"Father, please," Stella reprimanded him.

"I just thought it might be prudent to have the physician who was present when he passed to be on hand in case your lordship had any questions."

Vincent mulled over the prospect. "Well, it can't do any harm I suppose. Very well Jasper, I'll leave that in your capable hands. Now, what about my sherry?"

The servant poured his master a large glass of his favourite sherry and carried it over to him. Just then, another servant appeared with a trolley, upon which were plates of sandwiches, cakes, and biscuits. She unloaded the trolley onto the table where the previous girl had set out the tea service.

From the bottom shelf, the girl retrieved a large pot of tea. It was so heavy that she needed both hands to lift it, but as it only had the one handle, she used her apron to protect her fingers from the heat as she placed them under the spout to assist her.

Once she was ready, the girl asked if she may pour the tea.

Margaret assented, and the girl began the task.

While the ladies enjoyed their refreshments, Vincent opted for another glass of sherry. After a long coach journey, Tea just did not hit the spot in the same way as a fine amontillado.

As the ladies finished their tea, Corrine and Emily entered the room.

"Oh, tea," cooed the little girl. "Smashing, I'm very thirsty from our journey."

She purposely avoided Margaret's gaze and glanced up at Corrine.

Corrine knew this game very well, the little one was forever pitting her against both her nanny and her father, feeling that she was an easy touch when it came to avoiding something she did not wish to do.

Such as go for her afternoon nap.

Corrine, for her part, ensured that she did not encroach on Margaret's territory.

She crouched down beside Emily, and said, gently. "Perhaps if you ask Nanny very politely, she will allow you some cake before your nap, so long as you don't spoil your appetite for supper."

Emily slowly turned her head towards Margaret.

"Come on then you little terror, one cup and one slice of cake, then it's nap time, no arguments." She wagged her index finger at the girl, whose smile spread across her face.

Fresh tea was ordered, and Corrine took a seat on the couch

opposite to Stella and Margaret. Emily joined her having selected her choice of cake.

"I've decided to visit my father in state tomorrow after breakfast," Vincent announced. "I think it would be fitting if you all accompanied me. What do you say?"

The maid carrying the fresh tea, stumbled and almost dropped the pot.

She looked up, red faced, and apologised.

Vincent turned back to his family. "So, what do you all think."

Everyone agreed it would be right and proper for them to pay their respects.

Margaret questioned whether it might be too upsetting for Emily, but the little girl insisted that she wished to see her grandpapa one last time, so Vincent assured the nanny that it would be fine.

As the maid left the room, she glanced up at Jasper who was standing by the door. He shook his head as if warning her not to say anything to anyone, and she understood, perfectly.

Chapter Five

RALPH WATKINS AND HIS SON TOBY SAT IN THE SNOOK of the Wild Boar enjoying a well-earned pint of ale. The bar was almost full, as was usual at this time of day, with the local farm workers and labourers scattered around the tables, enjoying their pre-supper libation, and discussing their days work.

There was a large fire in the hearth and the heat which emanated from it filled the entire bar with its warming glow. The sound of logs crackling as the hungry flames licked against them, helped to drown out the mumbled conversations from the patrons scattered around the bar.

Toby glanced over at his father. He could tell from the dour expression on the old man's face that his thoughts were troubled by something. What's the matter pa?" he asked, concerned. "You look as if you've just lost yer last penny."

Ralph nodded and took another sip of ale.

He looked around him before answering. "Everyone around these parts should be worried now that the laird has returned."

Toby frowned. "What d'yer mean?" he asked curiously.

"All that business we had 'ere with them murders, and disappearances, it all 'ad something to do with the laird's father an' those people he had staying up at the hall, you mark my words."

Toby sat back in his chair. "Yea, but no one's seen hide nor hair of 'em since the laird passed away. They've moved on now, everyone says so. Besides, we 'aven't had any killings the likes of those since, so what makes yer think they'll start up again?"

Ralph signalled for his son to move in closer. "You heard about young Mary Grant?"

Toby frowned. "Yea, but she died of something natural, the doc told everyone."

"And you believed him? Well, I heard from old Colin Sedgwick that after Samuel had taken his family away, Father James let that Mathew Hammond stab the young girl's body with a wooden stake. Hammered it clean through to the floor accordin' to Sedgwick."

Toby pulled a face. "He stabbed the girl's dead body after it were already laid in its coffin?"

Ralph nodded.

"But what for, she was already dead?"

Ralph shook his head. "Sedgwick reckoned she sat up when they lifted off the lid. He was still standin' back at his cart, so 'e couldn't see everything, but he swears he saw young Mary's head and shoulders poking up from her coffin."

Toby swallowed hard. "An' you believe him?"

"I do. Colin Sedgwick may be an old drunk, but I've known him since we were kids, an' he has no reason to lie to me. You should 'ave seen the look on his face when 'e was telling me. It was like the blood had drained from him."

Toby rubbed his hand across his mouth, before taking another long swig from his tankard. Then asked, "An' you reckon that has something to do with the laird returning to take up residence at the hall?"

"Well, it all seems a little too coincidental fer my taste," replied Ralph. "Things round here have been an awful lot quieter since the laird died, now just before 'is son returns, we 'ave us another suspicious death. All I'm saying is it makes you think, boy."

"Have you told anyone else about this?"

Ralph shot his son a stern look. "No, I 'ave not, it's not my business to be messin' with such things, an' neither is it yours." He tapped the side of his nose with his index finger. "So, you make sure you keep this to yerself. I'm only tellin' you as a warning to make sure you keep yer wits about you, understand?"

Toby nodded. "Not sure I'd even recognise one of them if they walked in this pub, they didn't exactly mingle with the townsfolk while they were guests of the laird."

Ralph leaned in. "Just you be wary of strangers an' keep yerself to yerself, no use in tempting fate."

They drained their glasses.

"Time for another?" asked Toby.

Ralph shook his head. "Your mother will be wondering where I am."

Toby nodded. "Tell her I'll be in a bit later, save me some stew."

Ralph stared at his son, perplexed. "And where are you thinking of going at this time of night, other than home fer yer supper, and' bed?"

Toby shrugged. "I just fancy another tankard. Then I thought I might check the traps on the right side of the woods. There's bound to be something there mum can use for tomorrow night's supper."

Ralph finished his drink and slid his tankard across the table towards his son.

"You just be careful out in them woods," warned Ralph.

Toby laughed. "There'd have to be an entire gang of them to give me any trouble," he boasted.

Ralph clapped him on his back as he stood up from the table.

In truth, Toby was big enough to take care of himself, and then some, so Ralph was not seriously concerned.

A couple of the regulars called out to him as he made for the door. Ralph turned back and waved to them, before leaving.

Toby returned to the bar for his refill. While he waited, he spotted a very sullen-looking Colin Sedgwick tucked away in one of the alcoves of the inn, away from the main crowd and the fire.

Toby carried his ale over to where Colin sat, staring into his mug.

"D'yer mind if I join you?" asked Toby, preparing to sit down in anticipation of his friend's response.

But Colin merely continued to watch the surface of the liquid in his mug slosh from side to side as he gently rocked the vessel.

"Colin." Toby raised his voice, but not loud enough to draw attention.

Colin looked up, shocked to see his friend sitting next to him. "Oh, Toby, didn't see you there, how are yer doin'?"

"Better than you by the look of things. What's the matter, you look miles away?"

Colin did not answer. He merely shook his head slowly and took a drink from his cup.

It was obvious to Toby that his friend was in some distress, and from what his father had told him earlier, he suspected that he knew the reason why. In all the years Toby had known him, Colin had never been the most gregarious or jovial sort. Even so, it was unlike the farmer to be so distant and unresponsive.

Toby leaned in. "Is this about that business with the young Grant girl?"

Colin looked up, a shocked expression on his face as if he had just been slapped.

His hands shook, and he almost capsized his cup.

Toby checked around them to see if anyone had noticed his

friend's sudden discomfort. But most appeared to be lost in their own conversations, and unaware of the man's behaviour.

Toby turned back to his friend. In a low whisper he said. "Was it really that bad? You look like you've seen a ghost?"

Colin looked at him.

His eyes bore the weight of someone with a heavy heart.

Shaking his head, he replied. "I don't care who believes me or not, I saw that young lass sit up in her coffin and watched while that friend of Father James thrust a huge wooden stake into her. I keep seeing it over and over, every time I close me eyes, the scene replays right in front of me as if I were still there."

He took a swig from his cup and wiped away the froth from his lips.

Toby thought for a moment, then said. "So, who doesn't believe you? I know you're a man of 'is word, pa does too."

Colin gazed about him at the other patrons. "There's more than a few amongst this lot think I'm talking barmy. Even me own missus accused me of being in here that night instead of where I told her I'd been. Even after I showed her the money Father James gave me for my help. I wish I'd never agreed to it, and that's a fact."

"With all the funny things been going on around 'ere since before the laird passed away, nothing surprises me anymore. You must 'ave heard the rumours?"

Colin turned to look at him. "Aye, of course I 'ave, but I took most of 'em with a pinch of salt. All that business about black magic rituals, an' trying to raise spirits from the dead, it's all nonsense, 'as to be."

"Then what about the disappearances, and the bodies which were found with all the blood drained from 'em," Toby reminded him. "Those were real enough."

Colin thought for a moment while he took another swig from his tankard.

After a while, he nodded, but Toby could see that his friend was still very reluctant to accept the facts.

"Now you've seen proof for yerself, surely you can trust yer own eyes?"

Colin kept his head down. "I think I'd've preferred it if I'd remained in ignorance," he admitted, sheepishly.

"So, tell me what it is that bothers you more, the fact that you've seen the evidence yerself, or the fact that some people still don't believe you?"

Colin glanced at Toby sideways. "If I'm being honest, I don't know which is worse. There's something strange going on around this place, an' too many folks are burying their 'eads in the sand, pretending it's not so. Aren't you afeared of where it might end?"

Toby smiled. "I'm like me pa, I keep me head down an' do me work. If there's anything wrong with people, we have the doc for that, an' if it's their mind that's ill, we have Father James. Either way, like me pa says, it's none of our concern."

Colin kept his gaze fixed on his friend. "Yer wouldn't say that if yer had seen what I saw, an' once yer've seen it, yer can't unsee it, it's always with you."

Toby drained his mug.

Rising from his seat, he clapped Colin on the back. "So, I take it if Father James comes calling again an' asks for your help you'll refuse, regardless of 'ow much he's payin'?"

Colin did not rise to the bait.

Instead, he kept his head down and merely shrugged.

Chapter Six

When he left the inn, Toby set off for the woods on the outskirts of the town. The land still belonged to the Viscount, but the old laird had always turned a blind eye to his own tenants carrying out a little poaching, so long as they did not try and take advantage of his good nature.

So far as Toby was concerned, the deal would continue with the new laird, even if they had not officially discussed the matter.

The laird would have plenty to occupy his time now that he had returned to take up his father's old office and the last thing on his mind would be a couple of stray rabbits.

The sun had long since sunk below the horizon and the autumn wind was picking up. Toby buttoned up his coat and turned his collar up to protect his neck. The walk to the right side of the woods where he laid his traps would only take him around ten minutes, but as it was in the opposite direction of his home, he knew that the cold would be biting by the time he reached his parent's cottage.

But it would be worth the journey if his traps bore fruit. All he needed was a couple of rabbits for his mum to make her famous rabbit stew for tomorrows night's supper. His mouth watered at the thought of it and his stomach growled in support.

Toby veered off the main road as the woods came into sight.

He knew that if he cut across the field, he could save himself valuable time in reaching his destination. It was a clear night and bright stars covered the sky.

As Toby approached the mass of trees at the edge of the wood, a sudden feeling of being watched flooded over him. He spun around and glared into the distance, but he could not see anything untoward.

He was too far away for any light coming from the inn to assist him, and as there were no cottages in the vicinity, the only light he could rely upon was that of the half moon, which hung lazily above him.

Toby strained in the darkness to make out any movement, or distinct silhouettes created by a potential pursuer, but after a moment he convinced himself that it had only been his imagination, no doubt assisted from his discussion with Colin back at the inn.

He waited a moment or two longer before continuing on his way.

As much as he hated to admit it, even to himself, the uneasiness he had experienced from thinking that he was being followed still hung over him like a dead weight suspended by a weak rope.

He chided himself as he continued on his way.

Although only nineteen he was already considerably taller than his father, and a life of manual labour had given him a broad back and arms the size of kegs. He could arm-wrestle any man in the village without breaking sweat and had broken up many a fight without effort.

Yet here he was beginning to wish he had headed home with his dad after his first drink.

The shiver which ran through him seemed to come from inside as opposed to being caused by the wind which gushed through the trees.

Toby picked up his pace.

Entering the mass clump of trees at the edge of the wood, Toby began to feel comforted by the camouflage they offered him. Being an experienced poacher, even at his size, Toby was able to use the protection of the trees and general foliage to stay hidden while he lay in wait for his prey.

Oddly enough, on this particular occasion, Toby felt no relief from the protection the woods offered him. Feeling his anxiety grow, he stopped in his tracks, and listened for any sign of someone approaching. But above the sound of the wind whistling through the trees, all he could hear was the distant cry of a fox, calling for a mate.

His throat was parched, and Toby swallowed hard to try and relieve it, but to his dismay he found he could not create enough saliva to make it worth his while.

The area where he had set his traps was close at hand, and he decided to ignore the childish imaginings which appeared to have taken over his reason and attend to the task at hand.

"Hello."

The voice came out of nowhere and seemed to defy Toby's power of perception to the extent that he could not immediately ascertain which direction it came from.

In his haste to turn around, Toby caught his foot in some overgrown weeds, and before he had a chance to correct his balance he fell headlong, hitting the ground with a loud thud.

He heard laughter echoing around him as he tried frantically to untangle himself from the twisted foliage.

His impatience grew as the weeds which entrapped him refused to give.

Finally, Toby managed to stand and using a nearby tree for

balance he kicked himself free, wrenching the ties that bound him out of the ground by their roots.

He stood for a moment, breathing hard. He could feel the perspiration caused by his efforts streaming down the inside of his vest.

It took him a moment for his frustration to pass, then he remembered the voice he had heard emanating from the darkness before he fell.

Still holding the branch which he had used for stability, Toby looked around him, desperate to locate its owner.

"Are you alright?"

Toby spun round.

The owner of the voice stepped out from the shadows.

Toby was immediately taken with her beauty. She was not a local girl, at least he had never seen her before, and he prided himself that he knew all the girls for miles around.

He estimated she was about his age, or possibly a bit older. She had long dark hair which cascaded over her shoulders. It was cut with a fringe, which framed her face perfectly, showing off her gorgeous complexion and beautiful deep-set piercing blue eyes.

Before he could answer, the girl repeated her question.

Realising he was still holding the stick, Toby dropped it, afraid that the girl might think he needed protection from her. "Oh, I'm fine thank you," he stammered.

"Did I frighten you?" she asked teasingly.

"No, not at all," Toby assured her. "Nothing frightens me, not even when I was small."

The girl smiled. "Well, that's good to know," she said, moving closer.

It was now that he noticed she was dressed in, what appeared to be, a nightshirt. It was full white, and flowed down to her ankles, where he noticed she was not wearing any shoes.

Her bare feet crunched the twigs below them as she took another step towards him.

Toby felt an overwhelming urge to move back, but he stopped himself.

What self-respecting man would be afraid of a girl.

The last thing he wanted was for her to think him a coward, or, worse still, someone who was afraid of talking to women.

By now, they were barely a couple of feet apart.

The night wind billowed her shirt out, revealing her slim legs up to the knees.

Toby could not help but stare.

When he realised what he was doing, he looked up, ashamed for his actions.

But the girl merely smiled back at him, her eyes twinkling in the moonlight.

The absurdity of their situation suddenly occurred to Toby.

Why was this girl out here in the middle of the woods in nothing but her nightdress, with her feet bare, talking to a complete stranger who could-should he desire-overpower her in an instant and have his way before she even had a chance to summon help?

It made no sense!

Yet, here she was, standing opposite him, wearing next to nothing, and looking absolutely gorgeous to boot.

All of a sudden, Toby did not care why she was there, he was just glad that she was and that no one else was around to disturb their meeting.

Toby felt himself tongue-tied.

This never usually happened to him when it came to girls, regardless of the circumstances, but he felt that he had to say something before the pause in their conversation became awkward.

"Doesn't that hurt?" he asked, pointing down to her bare

feet. I was not much of an opener, but it was all he could think of.

The girl shook her head, smiling. "No, I have very strong feet," she informed him. "I prefer to keep shoes off my feet whenever possible, I find them very restricting."

Toby nodded, dumbly.

He shivered as a sudden breeze picked up. "Aren't you cold?" he asked, moving to take off his jacket to cover she shoulders.

The girl put out her hand to stop him. "No thank you, I'm fine, really. I love the night air and feeling he wind blow through my hair. It's so invigorating."

"Oh, right then, I see. Have you come far?"

"Not really, at least not tonight. I live on the other side of the wood. I've watched you working in the fields with your father. You're very handsome."

Toby felt himself blush at the compliment.

Looking at the girl, he desperately wanted to move in and put his arms around her. To taste those luscious lips against his. To smell her beautiful hair and feel the warmth of her body pressed against him.

But there was something stopping him, and he was no sure what it was.

After all, the girl had approached him, and she was making it perfectly clear that she liked him. So, even if he misjudged the situation and she pushed him away, slapping his face for good measure, what was the harm?

Yet he still could not bring himself to make the next move.

"Do you like me?" the girl asked, shattering his reverie.

Toby nodded. "Yes, very much, you're very beautiful," he blurted out, immediately feeling foolish for his lack of fortitude.

The girl tilted her head to one side. "Would you like to kiss me?" she enquired coquettishly.

This time Toby did not wait to answer.

The girl had made her feelings quite plain, and even if this were some sort of joke at his expense, he did not care.

Toby moved in and placed his hands on either side of her face and drew her towards him. Their mouths met, and they began to kiss passionately.

The touch of her skin was like ice to him, and Toby found it hard to believe that the girl really did not feel the cold.

Their eager tongues glided against each other, and Toby slipped his hands down her body taking in every curve, until they came to rest on her buttocks.

Toby squeezed her cheeks; the soft compliant flesh filling his large hands.

He could feel his erection growing, pushing against his trousers, demanding release.

The girl traced a hand down his body until she reached between his legs. There she cupped his manhood, gently rubbing her palm against it, teasing it with a promise of more to come.

Toby moaned out loud.

Lost in his lustful fantasy, he did not hear the rustling in the trees which surrounded them. Nor did he detect the shadowy figures which loomed out of the shadows, forming a circle, closing the pair of them inside.

Oblivious to the eyes boring into him, Toby tilted back his head as the girl began to kiss his neck. He felt the wet trail her tongue made as it slid over his bare flesh.

Toby let go of her bottom and slid his hands around to the front, grabbing the girl's hand as he lifted the waistband of his trousers away from his body, he slid her hands inside so that she could wrap her soft fingers around his penis.

He could feel a sharp sting as the girl nibbled the side of his neck.

As she sunk her fangs into his flesh, Toby let out a scream

that was more surprise than fear, his mind unable to comprehend what was happening.

His body went rigid as the girl drank from his jugular vein.

He could no longer feel the tender touch of her fingers encircling his erection.

Toby's body sagged, and went limp, but the girl managed to support his weight as she drank.

When she was done, she stepped back and let him crumple to the floor.

Then the rest of the group converged upon him to enjoy their fill.

Chapter Seven

FATHER JAMES RUBBED HIS HANDS TOGETHER vigorously to help keep out the night's chill, although in truth, if he were being honest, the main reason for his shivers was the task at hand which he and Mathew Hammond were about to embark on.

Even though the priest knew that their endeavours had been officially sanctioned by the church, he could not help the deep-rooted feelings of unease which had burrowed inside him, ready to erupt whenever he was called upon to assist Hammond and his crew.

I was not just the priest who felt anxious that night, even the horses were jumpy, pulling at their tethers as if trying desperately to escape. One of Hammond's crew went over to them and tried to calm them down, whilst also ensuring that their reins were secure.

He last thing any of them wanted was for their animals to bolt off into the darkness, possibly never to be seen again.

Two of the helpers climbed the stairs of the sepulchre holding torches to light the way.

Mathew turned to Father James and held out his hand.

Reluctantly, the priest took out the key for the door, and placed it inside Mathew's outstretched hand. Mathew thanked him and followed his helpers up the stone steps.

The second he placed the key inside the lock a mighty gust of wind whipped through the surrounding trees, causing the horses to frantically start whinnying and straining against their binds once more.

Mathew called down to the man who was still trying to calm them, but he could see that the poor man was already doing all he could to pacify the beasts.

Mathew turned the key and the locking mechanism reluctantly grinded in submission as it gave way. He pushed the main door open then stood back to allow his men carrying the torches to enter first.

The stone room was the size of a large stable, and within it they saw stone shelves on either side, several of which held a concrete coffin which encased a wooden version within.

The details of those enclosed within the coffin were etched on to the stone sides of each base, and in the middle of the room sat a large alter, upon which was another concrete coffin, this one revealing the details of the late viscount.

The torchbearers placed their lights in the holders scattered around the room, and from them lit further ones to assist their master with his task.

Once the inside of the cavern was properly lit, Father James entered, closely followed by two more of Mathew's crew.

The priest almost stumbled as he crossed the threshold although there was no stone step or obstruction in his path. One of the men behind him reached out and grabbed his arm, managing to steady him before he fell.

Father James held onto the man's arm for a moment to regain his composure, thanking him for his able assistance.

The inside of the sepulchre was gloomy despite the torches, and the air had a musty odour of things long since untouched or cleaned. There was a distinct cloud of dust which hovered in the air at about waist height, evidently kicked up by the men as they entered the tomb.

Father James removed a hankey from his pocket and coughed into it, expelling the stale air which had lodged in his throat.

His nerves had not been good for some time, and on the recommendation of Doctor Harris, he had started imbibing a strong tincture before retiring, to assist him in falling to sleep. As someone who had made a habit of retiring early, Father James had discovered that on those evenings when this was not possible, his body began to crave the tincture once it was passed a certain hour.

Tonight, was such a night.

Upon receiving word from Jasper earlier in the day that the Viscount was intending to visit his father to pay his respects, Mathew was adamant that they should inspect the late viscount's burial chamber to ensure that there was no evidence of tampering.

At the time of the viscount's death, although it was suspected by many of the locals that he had been killed by one of the strange group of exotic guests he had invited to the hall, Doctor Harris had found no evidence of anything suspicious on his body, save for two tiny pin pricks on the side of his neck.

When it subsequently came to light that several deaths in the locale had all left their victims with the same telltale marks, the doctor reported his findings to Father James, in the hope that there might be some spiritual reason behind them along the lines of stigmata.

It was not until the church sent Mathew Hammond to the scene that any relevance was placed on those marks. By then, there had already been several deaths, as well as some unexplained disappearances where the victims were subsequently seen at a later date roaming the woodlands, only to disappear once more.

After the militia had subdued the riots which followed, Mathew took Father James into his confidence and explained his suspicions concerning the telltale marks.

Since then, every time someone else in the locale died, Doctor Harris checked for the marks. If they were discovered, he would inform Father James, who in turn told Mathew, and after the individual was laid to rest, Mathew and his team would carry out their ritual in an attempt to free the victim's soul.

They carried out their horrendous task under a cloak of secrecy, only involving outsiders when necessary, and paying them handsomely for their silence.

But word eventually broke out, and although Father James initially denied such ungodly actions, eventually he feared for the sanity of many of his parish and divulged such information as he felt was necessary to make them understand.

At the time of the late viscount's entombment, out of respect for his title and position, it was agreed that rather than carry out the ritual on his corpse, his coffin would be encased in concrete before being laid in state, so that if he were one of the undead, he would not be able to escape and spread his contagion.

But now that the new laird had arrived, Mathew insisted that they inspect the departed viscount's remains to ensure that he did not pose a danger to anyone else in the town.

As the group huddled around the concrete tomb, Mathew turned to Father James and asked for his permission to give the order to have the lid removed. The request was more by way of convention out of respect for the priest's position in the town. But no one present was in any doubt that should Father James refuse, the ritual would proceed regardless.

Mathew instructed his crew to begin.

Four of them took up position at each corner of the lid, while the other two stood nearby, holding their torches aloft to afford their colleagues as much light as possible.

The four men took the strain, then on command from

Mathew they hefted the weighty lid off, and carried it to one side of the structure, where they placed it against one of the shelves for support.

Inside the concrete frame they all gazed at the carved wooden top which covered the corpse of the late viscount.

Even in the poor light it was obvious to everyone in attendance that the lid had been dislodged, and splinters of wood were scattered around the area as a result of the pressure placed against it from within.

Upon instruction, the men removed the lid of the coffin, and lifted it to one side, letting it rest between the concrete enclosure and the wooden structure.

In the flickering light of the nearest torch, they could all see the deep gouges made in the wood on the underside of the lid.

Father James pulled back in shock and revulsion.

For a brief moment, he was under the impression that the old laird must have been buried alive, and once he awoke, had tried desperately to free himself from his wooden confines.

But then he realised that the evidence of the laird trying to escape had a different, and altogether more sinister, meaning.

The laird had returned as one of the undead, and it was only due to the weight of the stone lid which sat on top of his final resting place that he was prevented from emerging and scouring the countryside looking for fresh victims.

Without saying a word, Mathew opened his bag and removed a large wooden stake.

Father James rushed forward and placed his hand on the man's arm, his expression a mixture of revulsion and desperation. "Is this absolutely necessary?" the priest begged.

"You know what must be done," Mathew insisted. "These rituals care nothing for rank nor favour. Once someone has become a creature of the night, there is only one course of action that the church condones."

The priest turned his head to look at the corpse.

Beads of perspiration ran from beneath his hat, dribbling down his face.

In the torchlight he appeared to have aged significantly.

Mathew felt sorry for the old man. To him this duty was merely a matter of procedure and edict, but he knew that for the priest, it was something which went against everything he believed in and held sacrosanct.

Had it not been for the letters from the archbishop Mathew had presented when he first arrived, Father James would never have allowed such immoral practices to take place.

"Come on, Father," said Mathew. "We need to get on."

The priest turned back to face him. "But what are we to do tomorrow when the new laird visits his father? He will demand an explanation for such sacrilege, and when he does, what am I to tell him?"

His question was almost rhetorical as he looked away and gazed into space as he spoke.

As much as Mathew sympathised with the man of God, his duty compelled him to focus his attention on the deed at hand, and not allow himself to be waivered by pleadings or arguments from anyone.

"Perhaps you should tell the new laird the truth," suggested Mathew. "After all, this is his land, his estate, doesn't he deserve to know what's been going on?"

Father James looked ashen faced at the suggestion. "And how am I supposed to tell him that it was his father who started all this? Him and those strange people he had visit him just before he died."

"Does he not deserve to know the truth?"

"Maybe, but knowing him as I do, he'll never believe it. He'll think there's a conspiracy abound and that his father is being blamed simply because he was the laird. I could make life very awkward for the rest of us who have to live here."

Mathew shook his head. "Well, the way I see it, by tomorrow

morning he's going to know something fishy is going on, so why not just grab the bull by the horns and tell him? I can corroborate your story, so can anyone else who has suffered a loss as a result."

The priest looked unconvinced by Mathew's argument.

Either way, he was right about one thing, the laird was going to demand an explanation when he sees his father's corpse with a wooden stake plunged through his heart tomorrow.

Father James peered in at the dead body.

The laird, for all the evidence of his trying to escape his sepulchre, seemed to be at peace now, and the priest wondered if they could cover up his earlier endeavours by replacing his coffin lid, so that the following day, the new laird would be none the wiser.

He turned back to Mathew to voice his recommendation.

Suddenly, he felt a hand grab him by the wrist. The grip was so strong that Father James was unable to extricate himself no matter how hard he pulled.

He looked back.

To his horror, the dead laird had opened his eyes and was grinning up at him, like a fox about to ravage a chicken.

Father James screamed.

The men surrounding the coffin did not have to wait for instruction. They leapt into action, using their weight to hold the undead corpse in situ, while attempting to free the priest.

The laird seemed reluctant to release his capture, almost ignoring the other men who forced him back. His eyes shone brightly with a glassy stare that seemed to bore straight through the hapless priest.

He opened his mouth and bared his sharp white fangs, hissing at Father James as he did so.

The priest continued to try and extricate himself from his captive, but no matter how hard he tried, the laird refused to loosen his grip.

In spite of the four men forcing him back down, the undead viscount began to rise slowly, into a seated position.

He turned in his coffin and stared at the priest with hungry eyes.

From out of the shadows a wooden stake flew through the air, its sharpened point plunging into the laird's chest.

The laird screamed out in agony, although it was believed by those standing around the coffin that a risen corpse could no longer feel pain. Even so, the cry that emanated from it was fierce and pitiful in equal measure.

As the corpse slid back down into position, it finally released the hold it had on Father James.

Taking his mallet, Mathew hammered the stake down several times until he could feel the point protruding through the back of the corpse and hitting the wooden base beneath it.

For a moment, the scream the laird had made seemed to echo throughout the stone cavern, and Father James slapped his hands against his ears for protection.

He knew now that there was going back.

Come the morning, he would have to offer the viscount a full explanation regarding the events of the past few months, as well as his father's involvement in it.

Chapter Eight

AFTER BREAKFAST, VINCENT, CORRINE, MARGARET, and the girls prepared themselves to go and pay their last respects to Vincent's father in the family burial tomb.

The journey was only a short one, so being such a bright, sunny day, they decided to walk to the tomb. The crisp autumn leaves crunched loudly beneath their feet as they all made their way along the path.

Jasper, and two of the younger servants, accompanied them on their way.

The two younger men could not help but notice the look of anguish on the older servant's face as they walked. One of them asked him if everything was alright, but he merely brushed the question away with a wave of his hand, without answering.

Margaret kept hold of Emily's hand as they walked. Although the little girl had already promised to be good and not run on ahead, as was often her way whenever the family took a stroll, the nanny thought it best to err on the side of caution, rather than risk upsetting the Viscount.

Stella kept her head down and clutched the two bunches of wildflowers she had picked before breakfast. One was for her grandfather, and the other for her mother who was also laid to rest in the family vault.

As they turned the bend in the road and the edifice came into view, Vincent could see the hunched-over figure of Father James waiting outside it.

"I wonder what he wants?" asked Vincent.

"I'm not sure," replied Corinne. "I take it you did not ask him to attend for any reason?"

Vincent shook his head. "No, but now I think of it, it might be a nice idea to have him say a prayer over my father while we're there, as we missed the funeral."

The walked on a little further.

Then Corinne asked. "But, if you did not invite him, how did he know that we were going to be here this morning?"

Vincent shrugged. "I'm not sure, but that's a very good question." He leaned down to whisper in her ear. "Perhaps he received word from above."

Corinne slapped his arm, playfully.

Seeing the family approach, Father James dismounted his stead, and secured it to the nearest tree. He remembered how jittery the horses had been the previous night when he and Mathew first entered the tomb, so the las thing he wanted now was for his beast to gallop away out of fright.

Even as he secured the rein, his horse began to buck and whiney.

He managed to calm it down with a gentle pat and a few soothing words.

Father James had often heard it said that animals were extremely sensitive to unseen dangers, and after last night he believed it. Whatever had spooked the horses then, his own mount still feared it, now.

The priest had hopes that after Mathew performed his ritual all the danger would be gone, but his horse's behaviour led him to suspect that something was still not quite as it should be.

He said a silent prayer to protect himself and all those present from whatever danger may still lurk within the concrete sepulchre. Even though the rational side of his intuition told him that if there were anything to fear, it would surely have shown itself the previous night in an attempt to stop the men carrying out their deed.

All the same, he repeated the words of his prayer under his breath once more.

As the viscount approached, he held out his hand. "Good morning, Father, what a pleasant surprise."

Father James shook his hand and smiled and bowed as he greeted the rest of the party.

Vincent introduced him to Corinne, and the priest kissed her glove.

"Have you come to pray with us?" she asked.

The priest immediately felt his face flush. "Regrettably, time is pressing on me this morning. He looked over towards Jasper, and the old servant shook his head, solemnly.

Last night, after the events at the tomb, Father James returned the key to Jasper and informed him of Mathew's idea to tell his master about recent events, leading up to the reason behind their visit to the family vault.

The old man was horrified at the prospect, and he did not keep his thoughts to himself. The two of them stood outside in the cold night air, away from prying ears, and argued late into the night over the subject.

Eventually, Jasper had to concede that there was no way of covering up what Mathew and his crew had done to the late viscount, especially as Vincent would demand to know why his father had been locked in his coffin when he should still be lying in state.

Had the viscount died tragically as the result of an accident, or been mauled to death by mad dogs, then perhaps an argument could have been made to Vincent that it was thought best to keep his father under cover for fear of frightening the girls.

But as it was, Vincent was already aware of how his father died, so it was too late now to concoct such a tale.

As a result of their conversation, Jasper barely closed his eyes that night.

The following morning all the other servants could see that the old man had something pressing on his mind, but any mention of the fact resulted in him reminding the enquirer to concentrate on their job, and not involve themselves in his business.

Jasper had spent all morning trying to come up with a plausible explanation to offer the viscount once the tomb was opened. But he was at a loss to find an excuse that might hold water.

The young viscount was no fool and any lie would need to be clarified with the strongest of evidence before he accepted it as the truth.

Now that they were finally at the vault, Jasper knew that the time for lies and excuses had passed.

The sight of Father James waiting by the entrance did give him a modicum of hope.

For now, at least, he would not be left to explain the situation to his master alone.

Initially, when the two of them spoke, Father James had asked Jasper to bring the viscount to the church to allow him to explain matters within the confines of God's house. In his mind, Father James believed that Vincent would be less likely to rant and rave and demand answers if they were on holy ground.

But as soon as he mentioned his plan, the priest could see how the prospect weighed down on the poor servant, and he immediately felt guilty for placing the task on his shoulders.

Therefore, he suggested that he meet the family at the tomb

when they arrived, then he and Jasper could support each other in their explanation.

The old servant still had his doubts over the proposal, but by then he could see that the priest was adamant in his conviction, so reluctantly, he let the matter drop.

Now that the time was at hand however, Jasper could feel his frail frame start to shiver.

Father James looked into the viscount's eyes and asked, solemnly. "If I could just have a moment of your time my lord."

Vincent frowned. "What, right this minute? We're about to go and pay our last respects to my father. Can't it wait?"

The priest shook his head. "Were that it could my lord, but I feel the matter has a moment of urgency which will not wait."

Vincent turned to glance at Corinne, a bemused expression on his face.

Although he was not as well acquainted with the priest as his father had been, he knew from his correspondence that Father James was a man who took his holy vocation extremely seriously, and he was by no means accustomed to waste time. Therefore, whatever he had to say Vincent knew that it must be serious and necessary.

"May we speak here?" Vincent asked.

Father James blushed even deeper. "I think under the circumstances it would be better to speak away from the ladies," he suggested.

Vincent sighed, deeply, then he turned to his wife. "My dear, as it's such a lovely morning would you and Margaret take the girls for a turn of the grounds? I'll see you all back here, presently."

Having heard the priest's recommendation and seen the strange look in his eyes as he spoke, Corinne merely nodded and untangled her arm for her husband's.

The four of them moved off, with little Emily skipping along beside her nanny.

Stella threw her father a quick glance as she passed. Vincent could tell that she had questions, but she could doubtless sense from the situation that right now was not the time to ask them.

They waited until the four females were out of earshot.

"Now then, what is all this about, Father? Why shouldn't my wife and daughters be privy to what you have to say?"

"I am afraid that it concerns your late father, and though I would do anything within my power to keep the truth from you, I am afraid that the time for secrets has come to an end."

Vincent turned back to his servants.

The three of them had stayed where they were as they had not been instructed to accompany the ladies.

"Jasper," called Vincent. "Have you any idea what's going on?"

The old man cleared his throat and walked forward, passing the two younger men so that he could stand before his master. "I am afraid I must confess that I do your lordship."

Vincent pulled back. Evidently shocked by the old man's revelation.

He turned back to Father James. "Well, don't just leave me here in suspense, what is it you have to tell me that cannot wait?"

Jasper took his cue, and climbed the steps of the vault, removing the key from his pocket. Once at the top, he turned for a moment and glanced behind at his master, then turned the key and pushed open the main door.

The two younger servants followed on and assisted the old man in his task.

Vincent planted his fists on his hips.

Father James could tell from his demeanour that the viscount was losing his patience with them, so he touched him on the elbow and indicated for him to follow his servants into the vault.

Vincent did not wait for the priest, but instead ran up the

stairs two at a time to join his retainers. Father James followed behind, taking care as his trembling legs took each step one at a time.

Once they were all inside, it took a moment for their eyes to adjust to the semi-darkness. Sunlight came streaming in through the lofty windows which encircled the stone structure, affording them just enough light to make out the stone coffins on either side of them.

Before Father James had a chance to explain further, Vincent noticed that his father's coffin already had its stone lid in place.

"What is the meaning of this?" he demanded, looking from the priest to his servants, expectantly. The two young men who had attended at Jasper's behest, both looked down at the floor, red-faced. They had both been in service with the late viscount and knew from local gossip the stories which surrounded his death.

But neither felt it their place to answer their master's question.

"Why has my father's coffin been closed when I specifically wrote to say I wished him to remain in state until after I could pay my respects?"

Father James moved forward. "That was what I wished to explain to you your lordship. I can assure you that your father was entombed with the utmost respect and solemnity, but further actions were deemed necessary in order to protect your noble house and the surrounding area."

Vincent looked at him, his lips curled back. "What in God's name are you talking about man? You try my patience." He pointed to his father's coffin. "Why has he been covered up?"

Father James took a deep breath. "In order not to upset you on your long journey, the details of your dear father's demise were distorted, somewhat."

"I've heard just about enough of this nonsense," Vincent

snorted. "Remove the lid at once," he demanded, pointed at the two young servants.

The men, suddenly snapped from their reverie, glanced over as Jasper.

"Don't look to him!" Vincent yelled. "Do as I say, now!"

Chapter Nine

THE TWO YOUNG SERVANTS SPRANG INTO ACTION upon hearing their master shout his orders.

Keeping their voices down so as not to irritate the viscount further, the two men whispered instructions to each other whilst trying to discover how best to dislodge the stone tablet from the grave, without sending it crashing to the ground.

As he looked on, Father James began to wish that he had taken up Mathew's offer to accompany him to see the viscount. His strength would certainly have come in handy right now.

Jasper, for his part, moved in to assist his two underlings, but his condition and general frailty made it obvious to everyone else that he was not up to the challenge.

Eventually, out of frustration at watching the two younger men push and strain against the stone cover without making much progress, Vincent moved forward and added his own weight. He ordered the men to move to one side of the coffin so that they could all exert their force in the same direction.

Jasper, fearing the outcome, advised his master that the concrete lid would no doubt shatter if not lowered to the ground, slowly, but Vincent waved his concerns aside and instructed the tow servants to put their backs into it.

Jasper moved behind and stood next to the priest.

Both men exchanged a glance which conveyed each other's concern at the inevitable outcome.

He three men managed to move the weighty cover just far enough so that it balanced on its support, without toppling over.

The viscount ordered the men to stand back while he peered in over the top at the wooden coffin below. The outside of the lid was still intact, having been secured in place the previous night by Mathew's men.

Vincent surveyed the outer lid and placed his hand against the wood, running it along the edge as if to check for interference.

Once he was satisfied, he turned to look at Father James. "No sign of violation here at least," he barked, but there was clearly no relief in his voice.

The priest bowed his head, unable to hold the viscount's gaze.

The laird knew instinctively that there was more to the situation than either the priest or his faithful servant wished to divulge. But he was determined to reach the bottom of it, whatever the case.

"Right," he continued, looking back at the young servants. "You two, help me to place this thing on the floor," he indicated towards the concrete lid with a nod of his head as he spoke.

The two young men looked at each other, then back to Jasper.

The old servant nodded his head, sombrely.

The three of them took the strain, then on the viscount's order they hefted the mighty stone slab off the coffin and carefully placed it on the floor.

They all stood up gasping from the strain.

Both young servants had perspiration running down their faces as they leaned back against the nearest set of shelving.

Vincent took another chance to survey the wooden coffin now that the stone tablet had been removed. He placed a hand on the middle of the lid and looked for a moment as if he were saying a silent prayer for his father.

The solemnity of the moment was not lost on Father James, and he too lowered his head and held his hands together in front of him.

As they all waited, Jasper could feel the tension of the moment start to gather momentum in his chest. Having heard from Father James about what he and Mathew had discovered the previous evening, as well as their subsequence course of action, he was dreading the moment when the lid of the coffin was removed to reveal the ravaged condition of the old laird's remains.

As the time grew closer, the old servant could hear the blood pounding in his ears.

Eventually, Vincent raised his head and called out to the young servants to find something to prise open the lid of his father's coffin.

The two men nodded and made their way towards the far end of the sepulchre where some of the tools Mathew's men had used the previous night were still lined up against the wall.

Although it was still only morning, a dark cloud seemed to obscure the sunlight, and the inside of the tomb suddenly became murky and black. It was too dark now to see anything clearly, so Vincent took down one of the torches from its perch and lit it using the stone and flint left on the window ledge by the doorway.

He brought the torch over as the young men began work on loosening the nails which held the coffin lid in place.

In spite of themselves, both Father James and Jasper moved in closer as if eager to see what the open coffin would reveal.

The nails prised up relatively easily as most had merely been driven back into their original holes the previous night. The two servants worked diligently so as to cause the minimum of damage while carrying out their task.

They managed a complete circle without splintering the wood.

Once they were satisfied that the lid was free of its confines, they stopped worked and looked to their master for instruction.

Vincent nodded his ascent.

The two men glanced at each other so as to time the lift as carefully as possible. As they heaved off the wooden lid, Vincent moved in closer with the torch. Before he stared in at his father, he noticed the deep gouges on the underside of the cover.

Vincent pulled back in disgust, unable to make sense of what he was looking at.

He turned to face Father James. "What is the meaning of this?" he demanded. "How can there be such damage to the inside of my father's coffin? Are you telling me he was still alive when you buried him?"

Father James held up his hand to calm the viscount down.

Vincent turned back for another look, still unable to process what he had seen.

As he moved in closer, it was only then that he saw the stout shaft of wood protruding from his father's chest.

The two servants that were holding the coffin lid in place, both glanced over the top and saw what their master had reacted to.

One of them screamed and let go of the lid.

The other man, unable to balance the heavy wooden structure on his own, fell backwards, dropping the lid which crashed down onto the stone floor.

Vincent's eyes opened wide in a look of shock and disbelief.

He too staggered backwards, almost dropping his torch on himself.

Seeing his master's distress, Jasper moved in and secured the lighted flame from him, to prevent it from burning him or setting the place alight.

Vincent grabbed the old man's tunic to steady himself. His head swam as if he were about to faint. He stared at the ground for a moment, shaking his head as if by doing so he would dislodge the awful memory of what he had just witnessed.

"Are you alright, my lord?" asked Jasper, with genuine concern in his voice.

Vincent slapped a hand against his forehead and took in several deep breaths to help clear his head. He knew he had to look again, even if only to convince himself of what he thought he had seen.

"Replace the cover."

It was Father James who barked out the order to the two young men.

The pair of them exchanged glances, almost as if daring the other to run from the place and never return.

"Now!" demanded the priest.

Regaining his composure, Vincent stood up. His breathing was still laboured, but now it sounded as if it had purpose. "No!" he shouted. "Leave it where it is."

The two servants obeyed, without question.

Vincent released his faithful retainer's sleeve and reached over to take back the torch.

"My lord, are you sure?" asked Jasper, his voice trembling.

Vincent did not answer.

Instead, he moved in once more to glance over at his father's corpse.

Holding the torch firmly in his grasp, Vincent grabbed hold of the side of the open coffin for balance, before peering in once more at the horror awaiting him.

It had not been a figment of his imagination, after all.

His mind raced with a myriad of questions as he stared down

at his father.

How was it possible that they buried his father without ensuring that he was dead?

How did he make those deep scratches in the wood unless he were still alive?

Who had dared to shove a wooden stake into his heart?

Vincent could feel his anger rising in his chest.

He turned slowly to look at Father James, his face flushed with anger. "Who is responsible for this unholy desecration?" he demanded, his knuckles turning white as they gripped the wooden side of the coffin.

Father James crossed himself and clasped his hands together as if he were about to begin a sermon. He eyed the two young servants who were still standing behind the coffin, looking on, nervously. They had both already witnessed more than he would have wished as young men like old women in his experience, were equally as likely to spread gossip and malicious rumour.

But it was too late to turn the clock back now. They had seen what they had seen, but the priest was adamant that he did not wish to explain matters any further in front of them.

Still, they were not his servants, as such, he had no sway over them, so it was down to him to persuade the viscount to send them away before he began his explanation.

Father James was sure that he could convince Vincent to swear the men to silence with the threat of them losing their positions.

"Well?" The fire in Vincent's eyes still raged as he spoke.

Father James took in a deep breath. "My lord," he began, "perhaps we could speak together in private."

Vincent switched the torch to his other hand as he let go of the coffin, confident in his balance. He shot out his hand to grab hold of the priest's cassock, but as he did so, Jasper intervened and tried to stand between them to offer his assertion that his master would do well to heed the priest's suggestion.

In his anger, Vincent swept the old man aside.

Jasper fell backwards, losing his balance, and collided with some of the stone shelving which housed the final resting places of the family.

The back of his head glanced off the corner of one such structure, and Jasper collapsed onto the floor, clutching his chest, blood pouring from the back of his head.

Realising what he had done, Vincent went to the old man and offered him his arm for support. "Jasper, forgive me, I did not mean to push you so hard."

Jasper's eyes flickered as he attempted to focus on his master. "Forgive me my lord, it is my clumsiness that's to blame, I'll be fine in a minute."

"Of course, you will," Vincent assured him, but he could not disguise the concern he felt for the old man. He shouted back at the young men. "Come here, both of you, help him to his feet, be quick about it."

Both men ran around the sepulchre and came to their mentor's aid.

Vincent stood back so that they could take a firm hold of the old man as they lifted him back to his feet.

They hoisted Jasper up, but he immediately began to slump once more, so they each supported him under his arm so that they could balance his weight between them.

"Jasper. Jasper, can you hear me?" Vincent asked, holding the man's jaw in his hand.

But here was no response.

"Carry him to the hall, and send for Doctor Harris, immediately," Vincent demanded, moving backwards to give the men ample room.

Although the old servant was mainly skin and bone, the two young men struggled to support his weight as they carried out their master's orders.

Chapter Ten

THE VISCOUNT AND THE PRIEST WATCHED AS THE young servants carried Jasper outside into the morning air. Vincent felt the urge to follow them to ensure that they carried out his orders, as Jasper was a loyal servant who had served the family since before Vincent was born.

But he decided that the matter at hand was more pressing. Vincent desperately needed to know what had happened to his father in his absence, and why such an unholy desecration had been allowed to take place.

He trusted Jasper and knew in his bones that he would never have allowed such an atrocity to take place had he been able to prevent it. The question was, why had Jasper not sent word to Vincent at the time to inform him of what was taking place?

Some other force was at work here, with an authority so high that it had managed to scare the old man into silence.

Save the king, only one other entity had the necessary clout to place such a burden of fear in people, and that was the church.

Father James was involved, there could be no doubt, and

Vincent was determined to elicit the truth from him, no matter what.

As the servants moved out of sight past the entrance to the tomb, Vincent turned to face the priest. "Now then, perhaps you'll be good enough to explain what exactly has gone on here."

Father James cleared his throat. "You deserve a full explanation my lord and believe me when I say I have no qualms about giving you the details. But, if I may, I would like you to come with me and meet someone, someone whom the church has ordained worthy to deal with this situation. He is waiting for us at the church."

Vincent looked perplexed. "And he can explain why my poor father was treated with such disrespect?" He pointed back at the coffin.

Father James nodded. "I can assure you my lord that he will be able to answer all your questions and satisfy any doubts or concerns you might have at this moment."

Vincent took in a couple of deep breaths while he considered the priest's recommendation. He was far from happy, but he had to admit, if only to himself, that his curiosity was overwhelming.

If the church was involved in such desecration, there had to be a good reason for it. So, unless Father James had gone mad or switched over to devil worship, Vincent knew that there would be an explanation waiting for him back at the church.

"Alright Father," he replied, evidently still not convinced, but at least willing to listen to what the man back at the church had to say. "But first, help me to place the lid back on my father's remains. He's been defiled enough without leaving room for rats to have their way."

Together they lifted the wooden cover back onto the coffin. Vincent hammered some of the nails back into place, just enough to block up any gaps.

He extinguished his torch as the two of them made their way back out into the daylight. The sun was bright and hurt his eyes after being in the semi-darkness of the tomb. Vincent shielded his eyes and closed the door behind them, taking the key from Father James so that he could secure it.

"Papa."

Vincent turned to see Corrine, Margaret and the girls standing at the bottom of the steps.

The two men climbed down to their level.

"Is everything alright, Papa?" asked Stella, still clutching the flowers she had brought with her that morning.

Vincent attempted a smile. "Nothing to worry about," he assured them all. "Just a little damage caused by some mischievous rodents. It won't take long to have it rectified."

Father James looked down to avoid having to make eye contact with the women. Vincent's quick thinking may well have helped to conceal the truth, but the priest had never been comfortable with lies, even when they were employed to save another's feelings.

"May we still go in and pay our respects?" asked Stella, looking past her father at the locked door. "I've been carrying these flowers all morning and I would dearly love to place them next to Mama and Grandpapa's graves and say a few prayers."

"Me too, Papa," squealed Emily, holding up the flowers which she had picked during their walk.

"I'm afraid that won't be possible right now," Vincent informed them. "Perhaps later, or tomorrow, we'll see."

"But, Papa," Emily pouted, "my flowers will be dead by then."

"I said no!" Vincent shouted, his temper getting the better of him.

He instantly regretted his action as his youngest daughter buried her face in Margaret's dress and began to sob, uncontrollably.

He looked at Corinne and Stella, and expression of apology on his face.

Both women knew that Vincent had a temper which often raised its head without warning. But this was the first time either of them could remember him yelling at his youngest daughter.

Vincent walked over towards Margaret, who was busy comforting the little girl.

"You overindulge her," Vincent chided.

Margaret blushed. "She's only seven my lord," she snapped defiantly, as if replying to a stranger who could not possibly know the child's age.

The nanny was not in the habit of answering her employer in such a manner and as such, her remark took Vincent by surprise.

For a moment, his face clouded over, and Margaret held little Emily tight against the folds of her skirt for fear that her father was about to unleash a torrent of reprimands. Like the other two women, she too knew that it was not wise to provoke the viscount when his anger was on the ascent, and she quickly regrated the sharpness of her words.

"My apologies your lordship, my words were ill chosen." Margaret attempted a half-curtsey without dislodging Emily from her protection.

Vincent nodded and ruffled the back of Emily's hair to show that he was no longer angry with her. But the little girl was having none of it. She clung rigidly to her nanny's skirt and refused to let go, or even turn to face him.

Father James cleared his throat to help avoid an uncomfortable silence.

Vincent looked up and saw the strained expression on the priest's face.

Clearly, he wanted them to leave for the church as soon as possible, as did Vincent. He would be very interested to hear what this representative of the church had to say about the treatment of his father's remains.

"Yes, of course," said Vincent thoughtfully. He considered for a moment what his next step should be. He realised now that it would have saved time if he had ordered one of the young servants to send for his horse when they reached the hall, it was too far to walk to the church. Plus, he wanted to make sure that Doctor Harris had been sent for, as instructed.

Knowing Jasper, if he had regained his composure by the time they had reached Mandrake, he would have ordered the servants not to ride out for the doctor and insisted that he was perfectly fine. Well, fine or not, Vincent wanted the old man examined after his nasty fall in the crypt, especially as he was to blame for it.

The old servant could demand obedience from the rest of the staff, but he would not be able to refuse Vincent.

"Father, I need to fetch my horse and check on how Jasper is feeling. Perhaps you could ride to the church, and I'll join you there, later?"

"What's happened to Jasper?" Emily had forgotten her crying and turned around at the mention of the man's name. She had a fondness for him ever since she had fallen and grazed her knee a few years earlier, and Jasper had insisted on carrying her in from the grounds to have it treated.

He had arranged for some milk and biscuits to cheer her up once her knee had been cleaned and dressed.

She then insisted that he had to carry her around until her knee had fully recovered.

Something the elderly manservant was happy to comply with, in spite of his advancing years, until Vincent found out and put a stop to it.

Vincent smiled down at his youngest child, pleased that she had at least stopped crying and forgotten his reprimand. "He'll be fine darling he just had a little accident inside the vault."

Fortunately, it appeared that the young men were hidden from view when they carried Jasper out of the tomb, the dense foliage which surrounded the path masking them from the women as they continued their stroll.

Vincent was not attempting to conceal his part in Jasper's accident, but he was still pleased that Emily had not witnessed the aftermath.

Father James said his goodbyes and mounted his horse.

He looked back one last time and nodded to Vincent before he set off back to the church. The others watched him disappear behind a row of hedges before turning to make their way back to the hall.

Emily pulled on Margaret's arm, informing her that they needed to hurry to make sure that Jasper was alright.

Vincent linked arms with Corinne and Stella as they walked. He noticed the flowers still in his eldest daughter's hand, and he felt a twinge of guilt at not allowing her to place some on her mother's coffin.

Now that he thought about it, once he and Father James had replaced the wooden lid on his father's coffin, it would probably have been safe to allow the girls to lay their flowers and say a short prayer. After all, it was the marks on the inside of the coffin lid, not to mention the stake protruding from his father's chest, which would have distressed them.

In the semi-darkness, even with the torch lit, they would not be able to suspect that anything untoward had taken place.

It was his haste to see to Jasper, then set off for the church, which had been the main reasons Vincent had refused to allow entry, and he knew he would feel guilty for it until they were finally allowed inside to pay their respects.

He knew that little Emily was the only one who accepted his explanation without question. Damage caused by a few scavenging rodents would not be sufficient to prevent his daughter from offering a prayer for her mother.

Vincent hoped that once he had spoken to Father James' visitor that he would have the answers he craved. Then he would order the servants to replace the concrete top of the sepulchre and simply tell his wife and daughters, should they ask, that his father was not left in state due to the delay the journey had caused in them arriving at the hall.

For now, he just wanted to hear what the man back at the church had to say for himself.

Chapter Eleven

RALPH WATKINS LOOKED UP FROM HIS WORK AT THE sound of branches being trampled underfoot.

He waited to see if his son might finally emerge from the woods looking sheepish and full of apologies for leaving his father on his own all morning, while he had doubtless overslept in some girl's bed.

Ralph scoured the surrounding trees and brush, but there was no sign of Toby.

Something must have made the noise. "Toby be that you?" he called out. "Stop messin' about an' get over 'ere an' pull yer weight, yer lazy sod."

Still there was no sign of him.

It had not been the first time that his son had failed to arrive home after a night at the inn. Toby was a handsome lad, and very popular with the local girls, so if he had met someone last night after Ralph left it would not be surprising if after seeing her home, he was invited in to spend the night.

But Toby was never late for work. He knew how much his father relied upon his strength and agility, especially now that

Ralph was starting to feel the effects of old age catching up with him.

Even if he had raced home starving for breakfast after Ralph had left for the day, Toby would have caught up with him by now. The boy did not have a lazy bone in his body and was a credit to his old man for helping to keep a roof over their heads.

After a while, Ralph turned his attention back to the job at hand. It was clear that Toby was not hiding in the woods, and why should he be? He was not the type to play childish pranks, and he certainly had no cause to fear his father's wrath.

Ralph was not so old that he could not remember what it was like courting as a young man.

From the distance, he heard the sound of a horse approaching.

Ralph looked up once more. He animal was still not in sight, but he could tell from the sound of its hooves on the path that it was coming closer.

After a while, both horse and rider came around the bend into sight.

Ralph recognised Father James approaching and raised a hand in salutation.

The priest nodded toward Ralph but did not stop, instead he galloped past at speed, keeping his eyes on the road ahead.

It was very usual for Father James to ignore one of his parishioners. In fact, to his knowledge, this was the first time that Ralph ever remembered him not stopping to pass the time of day. He evidently had something pressing on his mind, or some urgent church business to take care of, but even so, Ralph still found his behaviour curious.

He would have at least liked the opportunity to ask the priest if he had seen his son that morning, but the horse was too far down the road now, and the noise of its hooves meant there was no point in trying to call after him.

Ralph rubbed his chin, thoughtfully.

He was perspiring heavily from his labours, but a sudden chill wind rushed through the trees and caused him to shiver. I left him with an eerie feeling he did not care for, but he shrugged it off and took one more glance of the surrounding area in case he could see Toby finally arriving for work.

The coast remained clear, so Ralph bent down and continued with the job at hand.

He considered making his way over to the Wild Boar when he broke for lunch, just to ask if anyone there knew where Toby might have gone last night. But the more he thought about it the less practical the idea sounded.

For one thing, he did not hold with drinking during the working day. He knew enough labourers who had lost their jobs as a result of it, and he did not intend to join their number.

Furthermore, the pub was far enough away from his work that by the time he reached there he would barely have time to ask about Toby before he would have to turn around and trudge back, let alone stop off for a drink.

He knew that if he was late back the new laird would understand if Ralph explained the situation to him. Not that the viscount was likely to ride past just at that moment, but Ralph knew that the head gamekeepers would be only too happy to report him if he was not seen at work during the afternoon, and he could do without the fuss of having to answer for himself.

Ralph decided that his questions could wait until after work, if Toby had not shown his face by then.

At that moment, Ralph remembered Toby telling him that he was planning to check his traps on the edge of the wood after leaving the tavern.

Now he was concerned. If Toby had gone out there and stumbled in the darkness, he might have knocked himself out, or worse still, set off one of his own traps with him as captive.

He could have screamed out till dawn with no one close enough to hear his cries.

Ralph knew exactly where Toby set his traps and the area was much closer than the pub, so he was confident he could make it there and back in good time.

He grabbed his bag with the sandwiches Enid had made for his lunch and set off for the far end of the woods.

The going was slower than he had anticipated. Thick undergrowth and loose foliage seemed to hamper his every step, and he was glad of his cane which prevented him from falling more than once.

The tall trees which loomed overhead converged on each other to block out most of the daylight, and Ralph could not help but wonder how well his son would have managed to navigate his way in the moonlight.

But then Toby had done just that on several occasions in the past without incident, so Ralph knew that he was probably worrying for nothing.

Still, if he did not check the area out then he knew he would never forgive himself if Toby was stranded up there, and neither would Enid. Toby was there only child and a gift from God as far as they were concerned. They had him quite late in life, long after Enid had given up any hope of ever bearing a child.

Because of her age, the doctor warned that she might experience complications with the birth. But on the day, Toby slipped out of his mother without assistance, and Enid even said that she felt no pain during the delivery.

Whether that was true, or Enid was simply overwhelmed with having given birth after trying unsuccessfully for so long, only she knew for sure.

Both she and her husband doted on their offspring, and thanked God every day for his gift of love.

Ralph could just make out the clearing up ahead where Toby laid his traps.

He pulled himself up the steep incline using his cane for support.

As he reached the top he could see no sign of his son, nor any evidence that he had been there recently.

Ralph waited while he caught his breath, then listened for any sound of Toby calling out, but there was none.

"Toby," Ralph called out, listening for the faintest hint of a response, no matter how far away. But still none came.

He called again, this time shouting as loud as his lungs would allow.

When there was still no response, Ralph moved forward and brushed aside some of the foliage to help uncover his son's traps. At least if they were empty, it should mean that Toby had been there last night after all.

To his surprise, the traps were still loaded, but the bait was missing from all of them.

Ralph tapped the side of one with his cane and it snapped shut upon contact.

If Toby had emptied his traps of their kill, it made no sense for him to reset them without fresh bait. Then again, if he had removed his kills, it made even less sense that he had not brought them straight home for his mother.

Ralph scratched his head.

Nothing made any sense.

A sudden breeze rustled through the trees and scattered the fallen leaves across the ground. From the corner of his eye, Ralph noticed something sicking out from behind the nearest tree.

He ventured closer to see what it was. Using his stick, Ralph moved the object to make it easier to see what it was.

A sudden chill ran through his body when he recognised Toby's cap.

Bending down, Ralph retrieved it and shook he loose leaves and mud from it. There was no mistaking it, Toby's mother had made it for him last Christmas, and since then he was never seen without it.

Strange now that he should have discarded it.

The more likely possibility was that he had dropped it, possibly as a result of a struggle with someone. There was no way so far as Ralph was concerned that his son would not have picked it back up if he were able.

So that led to him either being incapable of doing so or being prevented by someone else.

Toby was a big lad and more than capable of handling himself, so if someone had carried or dragged him off, they would have to be enormous. Or there was more than one of them.

Either way, Ralph needed to find out what was going on. It occurred to him that if Toby had lost his hat last night while he was checking his traps, then he could have been missing for fifteen hours, or more.

Was someone holding him?

Had he been abducted?

It did not make any sense. Toby was not the sort of person anyone would consider a potential abduction victim. For one thing, Ralph had no money to speak of so there would be no point in demanding a ransom.

Perhaps he tripped, staggered around for a bit, and fell.

"Toby," Ralph screamed out at the top of his lungs.

He waited patiently for his son to respond.

After a minute had passed, he tried again.

Only the sound of the wind ruffling the branches overhead, answered back.

Ralph began swishing his cane about through the under-growth, tossing leaves and loose branches about in every direc-tion. As he went, he called out to his son repeatedly, listening intently for any response, but none came.

Ralph continued to search until he had scoured that entire area of the woods.

Still there was no sign of Toby.

He knew that he should make his way back to the field, there were still several hours of the working day left, but he could not shake the feeling that something had happened to Toby. A part of him hoped that when he reached the field, he would find his son there, catching up on his lost morning, full of apologies.

But somehow, Ralph feared that would not be the case.

Removing his own cap, Ralph scratched his head and thought. His bag with his sandwiches in it was still lying across his shoulder, but he appeared to have lost his appetite.

Try as he might he could not rationalise the situation in his mind.

He knew that if he returned home that evening without their son, his wife would demand that he set off again to find him. As big as he was, Toby was still Enid's little boy, and always would be.

Ralph looked off in the direction of the tavern.

There was no way his son would be there at this time of the working day, so there was no use in heading that way and wasting more time.

Dejectedly, Ralph replaced his cap and set off back for the field they were meant to be working in. It did not do to be caught out leaving your area for too long, less you ended up being summoned by the groundskeeper.

He knew he would not be able to keep his mind on his work, but so long as he went through the motions, Ralph would keep his job. He could always make up an excuse for Toby's absence if it came to it.

Chapter Twelve

VINCENT PULLED UP OUTSIDE ST LUKE'S CHURCH AND tied off his horse.

There were dark clouds scudding across the leaden sky and he suspected that it would rain before too long. It occurred to him that he might have been better served if he had come by carriage, but it was too late now.

As inconvenient as it would be to be drenched on the way back to the hall, his business with the priest could not wait, and he wanted answers now.

He removed his hat and placed it under his arm as he strode up to the rectory door, slamming the knocker down against the wood three times.

After a moment, he could hear the sound of footsteps approaching from behind the door, and a moment later Father James opened it and beckoned him to enter.

He priest closed the door behind his visitor and shot home the metal bolt, the sound of it engaging with the casing echoed throughout the darkened hallway.

Father James led the way into the back of the property to the kitchen. As they entered the room, Vincent saw the sturdy figure of Mathew Hammond sitting at the far end of the long wooden table. He looked up when the men entered but did not move from his seat.

Vincent glared at the man whom he surmised must be responsible for his father's irreverent internment.

Sensing the viscount's animosity, Father James ushered him towards Mathew and introduced them to each other. At this point Mathew stood, scraping back his chair on the cold stone floor. He stood a fair head and shoulders above the newcomer and Vincent could feel himself lifting back his shoulders to accentuate his full height.

Mathew had very deep-set eyebrows which gave him an almost permanent *brooding* countenance. It did not dissipate even when he turned up the corners of his mouth in a half-smile as he was introduced to the viscount.

The two men shook hands then sat down opposite each other, with Father James between them. There was a large jug on the table from which the priest poured wine into three goblets. He slid one each over to his guests.

"Now then," Father James began. "We all know why we're here, and I thought it best to discuss the matter at hand without an audience. I'm sure you both agree." The priest raised his cup to his mouth and began to drink.

Mathew nodded his agreement.

"Regardless of whether we have an audience," replied Vincent, angrily, "let me warn you both that unless you have a convincing argument as to why you treated my father with such irreverence, I will not hesitate to take legal action."

Father James spluttered and choked, dribbling wine down his chin. He quickly wiped it away with the back of his hand. He turned to face Vincent, unable to disguise the uneasiness he felt at the viscount's threat.

Mathew, on the other hand, did not flinch as he took a deep swallow of his drink.

"Now, I'm sure once we explain the circumstances, they'll be no need for any of that," Father James offered.

Vincent turned on him. "Explain why you felt it necessary to deny my father his right to lie in state on his own land? Then to exacerbate the issue, while he is lying cold in his grave, to drive a wooden spike through his heart like a stuffed pig?"

Mathew slammed his goblet on the table.

The other two men both turned in his direction.

"Now, I know you don't know me," he began, "and there's no reason you should trust anything I say. But know this, I have been sent to this place as a representative of the church, and any action I feel fit to take has the church's blessing. Father James here will attest to that."

The priest turned back to Vincent and nodded.

"You have every right to take whatever action you see fit regarding your father's remains," Mathew continued, "but believe me when I say that the king himself condones the actions I take, although he prefers not to make the situation common knowledge."

"What situation?" Vincent demanded.

Mathew glanced over at Father James who lowered his head and nodded.

"I'm talking about the undead!" Mathew stated, looking directly into Vincent's eyes. "Bloodsuckers who roam the land draining the blood from their victims to enable them to stay alive, if you can call it living."

Vincent opened his mouth to speak, but no words came out.

Mathew's explanation was nothing short of incredulous.

"They do what?" Vincent demanded.

Mathew leaned in. "They drink the blood of their victims by biting them with their fangs, just like bats. And those who do not die, return as one of the undead themselves, and then they too need to find victims to replenish their blood supply, and so on it goes until we find them and put a stop to their bloodlust."

Father James placed a hand on Vincent's shoulder. "It's true my son, I have seen the evidence with my own eyes. These creatures are among us and without Mathew's able assistance our little community would be wiped out in a heartbeat."

Vincent was dumbstruck.

He turned from one man to the other, half expecting them to burst out laughing at his gullibility. But each kept a stern expression on their faces, as if they were in deepest earnest.

Vincent was no fool. He had travelled half the world, learned new cultures, traditions even suspicions, but he had never heard of these bloodsuckers Mathew referred to.

Were they trying to take him for a fool?

He did not know Mathew from Adam, regardless of who he claimed summoned him.

But he knew and trusted the father, so unless he had taken leave of his senses there must be some truth in what he was being told.

Still, the rationalist n him refused to allow him to accept their word.

Vincent stood up, almost knocking over his chair. "This is preposterous," he shouted. "Bloodsuckers turning people into the undead. What sheer nonsense! You'll have me believing in fairies and goblins next."

Mathew seemed nonplussed by Vincent's reaction. In fact, he had almost expected it. It was not uncommon, and he had witnessed others in authority take the same haughty position, until he had shown them the evidence.

Mathew refilled his goblet and took another drink.

Father James was far from calm and made no secret of the fact that he wanted to convince Vincent of his voracity before he sent orders for the militia. The church had been quite clear that it was down to him to quell any such action in order to keep the entire operation low-key until the danger had passed.

But Vincent was not just the local squire, he had also inherited his father's duties as magistrate, so he would not be an easy man to keep calm under the circumstances.

Father James stood up and walked around to retrieve Vincent's chair, standing it back up and pushing it in so the viscount could sit back down.

Vincent looked back saw the pained expression on the priest's face. It was almost as if he were desperate for the man to retake his seat. Perhaps, Vincent considered, he was scared of what action he might take if he stormed out of the house and made good his threat.

Vincent did not consider himself to be a vindictive man, and he surmised that there was more to the fantasy he was being asked to believe than met the eye. After all, until this moment he had always trusted Father James, and his own father had also held the priest in very high regard.

Even so, this story was nothing short of fantastic.

Vincent dropped back in his chair. He could hear Father James release an audible sigh of relief. The priest retook his own seat and offered his guest a top-up for his goblet which Vincent waved away as he had not touched his drink thus far.

From across the table Mathew rubbed his chin, thoughtfully, as if preparing what to say next. There was a part of him that had long since stopped caring about the opinions and feelings of the locals he encountered whenever he visited a new town. He was there to do a job, by order of both the king and he church, and if it were not for the discretion and secrecy he was commanded to observe, he would have gladly exposed the situation for all the world to see.

Most cases, including this latest one, were as a result of someone within the town inviting these creatures of the night into their community for their own gain. He was just left with the unenviable task of cleaning up the consequences of their stupidity.

That said, Mathew could still feel a modicum of empathy for

anyone who found themselves in Vincent's position. I was not his fault that his father had brought these creatures into his home and allowed them to run amok, decimating the surrounding area.

Mathew himself had once been in a similar position when his own father had sought out these devils to help rid him of a fatal blood disorder.

The act had ended in his father becoming one of the undead and attacking his mother right before the young Mathew's eyes. He watched in horror as his father sunk his fangs into his mother's neck, draining the life from her in less than a minute.

Driven by a combination of hatred and grief, Mathew had picked up a broomstick and impaled his father through the chest while his eyes were still closed, lost in ecstasy as he savoured his wife's blood on his lips.

Young as he was, Mathew was lucky to escape the noose. His father was greatly respected in their town, and no one was about to believe the rambling story of a young boy, out of his mind with guilt, about his father being a vampire.

Fortunately for him, the church stepped in and whisked Mathew away to be educated by the holy fathers who tutored him in the ways of becoming a vampire killer.

Since then, he had dedicated his life to defeating the undead.

But consistently, the hardest part of his job was having to deal with the disbelieving locals who it seemed went out of their way to disrupt his work, even though all he was trying to do was to save them and their communities from eternal damnation.

As far as he was concerned, it was the local priest's job to organise their flock so that Mathew was left free to complete his task. But when you had a situation such as this one, where the priest was obviously scared of what the local squire might do if he remained unconvinced, it made Mathew's task all the more frustrating.

The main problem now, as Mathew saw it, was that if they

could not convince the viscount of what was happening in his town, there was no way he would believe that it was actually his own father who brought this menace down on their heads.

Father James looked across at Mathew. The concern on the priest's face was evident and Mathew surmised that the bulk of the explaining would be down to him.

The problem would be in keeping the viscount in their company long enough to make him understand. He was clearly a non-believer, and they were always the hardest to convince unless you were prepared to show them conclusive proof that you were in earnest.

Well, thought Mathew, perhaps that time had arrived.

Chapter Thirteen

MATHEW LEANT HIS ELBOWS ON THE TABLE AND MADE a steeple with his fingers, resting his chin against the point. He glanced over at Father James and raised his eyebrows.

Vincent noticed the blood drain from the priest's face.

Here was obviously some form of unspoken communication between the two men which Vincent was not as yet privy to. It annoyed him that he was being kept in the dark, but at the same time he still felt in charge of the meeting. They were both desperate to convince him to be on their side, so if he felt he was not being trusted, all he had to do was stand up and leave. They could both make their excuses to the militia.

Father James' hand shook as he lifted his cup to his mouth.

Vincent stared at him while he drank, but the priest kept his eyes fixed on the space in front of him.

Finally, he had had enough. "Well, if one of you gentlemen does not explain to me exactly what is going on, I will have no option but to leave, now."

Mathew did not wait for Father James to respond. "You are quite right to demand an explanation your lordship, and unlike the good father here, I am able to view the circumstances with the cold eye of an outsider. So, I will tell you all there is to know, then you can decide what action you wish to take."

At last Vincent felt vindicated. He was not in the habit of being treated like a nosey brat who wanted to know what his elders were discussing. It seemed that Mathew at least had realised that he had been pushed to the end of his tether, and that his assertion to take legal action was no mere threat.

Relaxing, Vincent sat back in his chair and took a drink of wine. He did not wish to appear arrogant as a result of winning the argument, but he could not hide an inner sense of accomplishment.

"Pray continue," he said, looking at Mathew, "and please ensure that you leave no detail out."

"There is a remote village," Mathew began, "buried amongst the mountains of the eastern Carpathians, where the legend of these creatures first surfaced. The history of their origin has been told and retold over and over with very little being written down, so we cannot be exactly sure of the accuracy of the account. But what we do know is that the church has tried on many occasions to eradicate the problem by purging the village."

"Purging it," Vincent repeated curiously. "How exactly?"

"The church has launched many expeditions to the area over the years, priests, such as the good father here have accompanied men like me, and together we have hunted out every soul we could find and driven a stake through their hearts, before decapitating them and burning their remains."

"Vincent sat bolt upright. "What, children as well?" he asked, clearly shocked.

Mathew nodded, sombrely. "We do not act without good cause," he assured him. "No innocent soul ever set foot in that accursed place."

Vincent slumped back and took another drink to settle his nerves.

"Then," continued Mathew, "once the fires have died down,

the holy men conduct a ritual of special prayers over the land and dowse everything in holy water. We have literally left behind nothing more than a wasteland, yet still the evil grows and manages to resurface within a few short weeks."

"How?" demanded Vincent. "If you have killed every living soul in the entire village, where do the new ones come from?"

Mathew shrugged. "We don't know for sure. We have our suspicions, but nothing to confirm them one way or the other."

"What sort of suspicions?"

"Well, some believe that as soon as the villagers receive word of our arrival, they hide their leaders underground where they remain dormant until the coast is clear. Others claim that groups of these wretches are away from the area when we arrive, and that they merely return once we have left to repopulate the village."

"Away?" asked Vincent. "Away where?"

Mathew looked back at Father James. The priest had drained his cup whilst Mathew was explaining matters to Vincent, but now he knew he had to add his own weight to the argument, to help convince the viscount.

His voice trembled as he spoke. "What the church believes, and there's been evidence to substantiate this, is that knowledge of what these creatures can do has spread over the centuries, and now, those wealthy enough to afford it, summon them with the promise of untold wealth as well as multiple victims to satiate their cravings without interference from the law, in return for eternal life."

"Eternal life!" Vincent repeated. "Are you telling me these creatures have the power to bestow eternal life? That's incredulous."

"It's true my son," the priest assured him. "I have seen the results with my own eyes. Bodies rising from the grave days after they have been confirmed as dead. Their eyes no longer windows to their souls, but black, empty pits, devoid of all human emotion."

"We say 'eternal life'," Mathew interjected. "But what they become is the undead. *Nosferatu. Vampires who must feast on human blood for their very survival.*"

Vincent shook his head in disbelief. "But if these creatures rely on nothing but human blood for their existence, what need have they of wealth? Why travel across vast continents for the offer of money, when they clearly have no need of it?"

"You make a solid point," Mathew agreed, "and there you bring us to another belief. And that is that these creatures of the night are worshiped by a satanic cult, the members of which are spread throughout the known world, many we suspect are employed as high-ranking officials which makes their cover that much harder to expose."

"And you believe that they are the ones who arrange the transactions between these monsters and their wealthy recipients?"

"Exactly," Mathew confirmed. "Their greed is purely financial, though the church has yet to be able to link any of the proceeds directly to the men involved. They appear well versed in moving their finances in order to protect them, and their followers."

Vincent held his hands out in front of him to sop Mathew continuing.

He needed a moment to think.

This was an awful lot of information to take in in one go and his mind was racing as a result.

The three men sat in silence for a while.

Finally, Vincent asked. "If all this is true, what are these creatures doing here?"

Father James blushed and rubbed his shaking hands together. He knew the news should be delivered by him, rather than Mathew, but I did not make the task any easier to perform.

He shot a quick glance at Mathew, who nodded his agreement.

"You see my son," the priest began, "we have reason to believe that it was your father who summoned these creatures to our community. He had been very ill for quite a while, though I believe he kept it from most people, and towards the end he genuinely believed that the prospect of eternal life was far more likely to come via these bloodsuckers than by divine intervention."

Vincent slammed his hand on the table, causing his goblet to overturn, spilling red wine onto the wood. "My father! You dare to suggest that my father would have anything to do with these vile abominations?"

But he could tell at once from the expression on the priest's face that he, at least, believed it to be true.

Even so, Vincent felt the outrage of such a slander building up inside him, readying to explode at any moment.

Mathew appeared nonchalant with the situation. He had already decided to let the priest and viscount argue the point out between them, as he had done on numerous occasions when confronted by a similar situation.

He knew that as a stranger, his word would not be automatically believed, therefore it was always fortuitous to have a member of the clergy on hand, especially one who knew the local squire so well.

"Please calm down my son," Father James pleaded. "I know such information must be hard to take…"

"Hard to take!" Vincent shouted. "You come to me with these outrageous and unsubstantiated speculations, and just expect me to go along with them on your say so? After all my father did for this community, this is the way you intend to besmirch his good name?"

William pushed back his chair and rose from the table.

His sudden movement caused Vincent to staunch his attack.

For a brief moment, Vincent actually thought the man was going to charge at him, such was the look of annoyance on his face. But instead, Mathew turned and walked over to a table in the corner of the room, from which he carried a leather satchel back to his chair.

The three men sat in silence while Mathew rummaged through the leather case, from which he eventually produced a small stack of letters, bound by a leather strap.

He handed the hoard over to Father James, as if requesting approval before passing them onto the viscount.

The priest held onto the stack for a moment and looked to be saying a silent prayer over them before he reluctantly passed them over to Vincent.

Vincent took the letters and before undoing the strap, he immediately recognised his father's hand. He glanced up at the two men. Father James had his head bowed once more, whereas Mathew was helping himself to more wine.

Vincent undid the bundle and laid the letters out in front of him.

He spent the next several minutes perusing the contents, his brows furrowed in a combination of disbelief and anguish.

The letters from his father were all addressed to a firm of solicitors in London.

They were, as Mathew and the priest had suggested, propositions in which the deceased viscount offered huge sums of money in return for the recipient's undertaking that they would arrange for the passage of certain individuals-unnamed-from eastern Europe to Hasterley, via London. With the further agreement that once in the district, the viscount would guarantee these visitors exemption from prosecution for murder, in return for them guaranteeing him eternal life.

There were no copies of return correspondence from the solicitors. However, Vincent could piece together in his own mind what the responses might have contained by reading his father's follow-on letters.

When he was finished, Vincent let the last letter drop back onto the table as he buried his face in his hands.

He could not deny that the letters were genuine. He had known his own father's penmanship since he was a boy. But the mere thought that he could have been engaged in such a venture turned his stomach.

When he finally looked back up, both men were staring at him.

Father James' expression was full of remorse and pity, whereas Mathew simply nodded his head as if to confirm Vincent's worst fear.

Vincent took another drink for himself, his hands shaking as he raised the goblet to his mouth. A thousand questions swam before him, but his mind still refused to comprehend their most obvious answers.

Mathew finally broke the silence. "There's something I would like to show you your lordship, if you think you might be up to it."

Vincent frowned. Once again, he could see Father James shifting uncomfortably in his chair, his face etched with concern and trepidation.

"What is it?" asked Vincent dejectedly. "More evidence of my father's wrongdoing?"

"Not exactly," Mathew assured him, "but I think it will help to illustrate the plight which engulfs your community at present. But only if you feel you are up to it."

Vincent drained his cup and wiped his mouth with the back of his hand. "I am not a child who needs coaxing or, for that matter, protecting from the consequences of acts already beyond rectifying. So please, lead the way."

Chapter Fourteen

THE JOURNEY TO THE REMOTE COTTAGE ON THE outskirts of the church's land took no more than fifteen minutes. As the weather looked changeable it was decided all three men would travel in Father James' coach. Mathew took charge of the reins to allow the priest and Vincent a chance to discuss matters on a more personal level.

Before leaving, Father James had excused himself before returning minutes later with a small leather bag, which he now held firmly on his lap in the carriage.

As they arrived at the cottage the first specks of rain began to fall.

Mathew banged on the door with the side of his fist, and seconds later the door was opened by one of his team.

Once inside the cottage, the men all gathered around the large wooden table which dominated the main room. They all recognised Father James from the funeral of Mary Grant, but they eyed the viscount with the suspicion of outsiders in the company of a stranger.

Other than the priest, Mathew's men were used to staying in the shadows and associating with as few locals as possible.

Their work had taught them that it was best not to make unnecessary connections with people they may have to stake at some later date.

Mathew explained the reason behind bringing Vincent to their hideaway.

"The laird here needs to see for himself the face of this plague that has blighted his landscape," Mathew explained. "Once we have him on board, it will make our task here that much easier."

The men looked at each other while they considered their leader's words.

They knew full well that Mathew would never do anything that might jeopardise their mission, so if he believed Vincent could be an asset, then it was good enough for them.

Mathew acknowledged his team's approval of his actions.

"So where is it?" he asked.

"In the cellar," replied one of the men. "D'yer want us to bring it up?"

Mathew shook his head. "No, we'll come down, less chance of anyone hearing anything from outside."

Two of Mathew's team led the way downstairs, carrying candleholders to light the way and prevent anyone following from tripping over. The stairs creaked under the weight of each man, and those that followed waited for the first two to reach the bottom before attempting the descent.

Mathew went down next, followed by Vincent and then Father James who was still carrying his leather bag, with the rest of the men bringing up the rear with more light.

As he descended the wooden staircase, Vincent could hear something *hissing* and *spitting* from below. The sound mingled with that of rats scurrying to find protection from the approaching party. He felt a sudden chill run through him and was immediately glad for the company of the others. Focussing on each stair individually in the glow from Mathew's candle,

Vincent did not dare look up until he had reached the basement floor.

Once everyone reached the downstairs, Mathew's men carried their lights over to the far end of the cellar. Once they were in range, the glow from their candles illuminated a solitary figure, tied to a chair. The ropes which held the captive in place went around a thick wooden beam which extended to the ceiling, tethering both chair and prisoner to it.

As he lights drew nearer, Vincent could see that the person tethered was a woman.

He could not see her face as her head was down, and her thick mattered hair obscured any chance of recognition. She was dressed in white, her clothes tattered and torn as if she had been dragged through a hedgerow.

Her ankles were secured against the legs of the chair with stout ropes, which just about allowed her bare feet purchase against the dirt floor.

From beneath the straggly mop of hair, Vincent could hear once more the sound of *hissing* and *spitting* as the poor creature fought in vain against her bonds.

He heard a gasp of shock and surprise from behind and turned to see Father James holding a handkerchief against his mouth, as if to prevent him from choking. He glanced up a Vincent from behind his covering with apologetic eyes before turning away to cough and splutter. One of Mathew's team clapped the priest on the back several times with the flat of his hand, assuring him that he would be fine.

When Vincent turned back, the woman in the chair had raised her head so that now he could see her eyes through her hair. In the flickering light her orbs appeared to be pure black as she stared at him, ignoring the others around.

Vincent took an involuntary step back, as if afraid that the woman would suddenly spring forth from her confinement and leap across the floor at him.

If the others noticed his movement, they made no comment.

Just then, as if she had somehow managed to read his thoughts, the woman attempted to launch herself directly at Vincent, her entire body straining against her confinement.

Much to his relief, the ropes held.

Mathew's men moved, then relaxed when they realised her efforts were futile.

Vincent resisted the urge to move backwards this time. Instead, he stared down at the pitiful creature as she wrenched herself this way and that, desperate to free herself.

"What in God's name is this?" Vincent asked, evidently disgusted by the whole scenario.

"This is what we've come to your district to eliminate," Mathew informed him. "Here before you, you see one of the creatures your father invited to grant him eternal life." Mathew almost spat out the words, such was his contempt. "We captured this one when we first arrived and were hoping that it might act as bait to lure some of the others, but no luck thus far. It seems that they only care for themselves and are willing to sacrifice other members of their set so long as they get their fill."

The woman continued to grunt and strain in an effort to break free. It seemed to Vincent as if his appearance had suddenly given her a new thirst for freedom. Almost as if she knew that he was related to the man who summoned her here, and subsequently was the reason behind her capture.

The thought turned his stomach.

There was no way he was willing to believe that his father knowingly released such a curse on their town. He had obviously been lied to by someone for their own financial gain, and he was damned if he was going to stand by and allow their family name to be besmirched as a result of such treachery.

By hook or by crook, Vincent intended to get to the bottom of this debacle at all costs.

In the meantime, however, he would have to rely upon Mathew and his crew to help eradicate this menace before the area was overrun with creatures like the one before him.

"So, do we have your full support, your lordship?"

Mathew's question had an edge of sarcasm to it which Vincent did not appreciate. It almost sounded as if the man did not care what Vincent's answer was either way, as it was not going to have any bearing on how he and his men carried out their duty.

Vincent could feel his anger rise at the man's impertinence. Under normal circumstances he would have ordered him to be whipped for such insolence.

But these were no longer normal times, and the survival of his family and tenants had to take priority over Mathew's lack of respect.

Vincent nodded in answer to Mathew's question.

From behind, Father James now fully recovered from his earlier fit, moved in, and placed a comforting hand on Vincent's shoulder. "It's for the best my son," he assured him.

"So, it would seem," Vincent agreed.

He found himself transfixed by the woman's gaze. Even through her tangled locks her eyes managed to penetrate their way to his very soul.

Vincent shivered. "Why does she stare at me with such venom?" he asked rhetorically.

"Perhaps she knows you are related to the man who summoned her here to her fate," replied Mathew. "Who knows what goes on in their soulless minds besides their craving for fresh blood."

Vincent could not argue with the man's prognoses since he had had the very same thought himself, mere moments ago. Even so, it was still unsettling to hear it expressed by another.

"So then, what's to become of her?" Vincent asked, indicating with a nod of his head to the woman.

"Well now that you've seen the proof, and she's clearly not able to summon anymore of her kind here, she's served her purpose. Only one way to deal with her sort."

Mathew's words were spoken with a callous, unfeeling tone, it was as if he was speaking of a lump of meat, or a pile of stones rather than what was once, at least, a human being.

"Come on lads," Mathew continued, not bothering to wait for either Vincent or Father James to consent to his actions. "Let's get her on the slab."

As one, his men moved in, each man well versed in his task.

Those holding candles placed them strategically around the room so as to offer the most light. One of the men removed a rag from his pocket and forced it in the woman's mouth, taking care that she did not bite him while he worked. Once the rag was in place, another tied a rope around her head, securing the rag in place.

With the greatest care, four of the men untied the woman from her chair, while the other two gripped her by the arms to prevent her from flaying wildly once her binds were free.

Mathew stood over his men, his torch adding light to assist them in their task.

Once the woman was free, it took four of them to carry her over to a large stout wooden table at the other end of the room. Upon closer inspection, Vincent could see that the table was stained with dry blood, and the stench almost caused him to wretch.

He could only surmise that Mathew and his men had used it previously for a similar task, or that perhaps the cottage once belonged to a butcher who used the cellar as a cool place to store his carcases.

The woman bucked and kicked as she was carried over to the table.

Vincent turned to see how Father James was coping, half-expecting to see the clergyman turning away and retching to one side. But, to his surprise, the priest was casually preparing himself as if for mass.

His lips moved in silent prayer whilst he removed his apparel of office from his leather bag and kissed each garment before putting it on.

Having reached the able, the four men held the maniacal woman down, splaying her arms and legs with each of them taking charge of either a wrist or ankle.

The woman roared from behind her gag, her eyes wide in anger, threatening revenge.

Mathew appeared beside the bale holding a large wooden stake and a mallet.

Still uttering his prayers, Father James walked over to the table and took a small glass bottle from his tunic. He released the silver cap and shook the bottle over the woman.

Holy water splashed upon her, causing her to buck and twist as if she were being burned by acid.

Vincent looked on as Mathew placed the sharpened point of the stake on top of the woman's chest, holding it halfway down its shaft. He glanced over at Father James who continued with his prayers until his glass bottle was empty.

Then he looked at Mathew and nodded, solemnly.

Chapter Fifteen

ON THE JOURNEY BACK TO MANDRAKE HALL VINCENT could not clear his mind of the event he had witnessed back at the cottage.

After Mathew had staked the poor creature through the heart, he had then removed her head with an axe. Vincent could still hear the sound of it hitting the floor after rolling off the table. He and Father James had left the men to deal with the corpse while they travelled back to the church.

As the rain had subsided, Vincent declined the priest's offer of being driven home.

In truth, he hoped that his lone ride might help clear his mind of the vision of the woman's decapitation. Father James had assured him on their way back that the woman was no longer human, and thus, could not feel pain or suffering in the same way she would have before becoming a creature of the night.

But did he really know, or was he merely guessing?

How could one man know for sure what another was feeling, regardless of their circumstances?

Vincent had witnessed many hangings in his time, but he

could a least understand them. When a man committed a crime, which carried the penalty of execution, they knew what they were in for and were prepared to take the risk.

But there was something about seeing that poor wretch being held down, awaiting her execution, which did not seem right to him. Where was the justice? Regardless of whatever crime she was accused of, she did not have the benefit of a trial, or even a spell in the madhouse which may have seen her cured of whatever ailment possessed her mind.

The worst part was, as he stood there before her in that basement, watching her fight in desperation to launch herself at him, Vincent was only too glad to have the men deal with her. For there was a look in those dead eyes which froze the blood in his veins.

There was an argument of contradictions duelling it out in his mind.

Far worse was the fact that, according to Father James, there would be many more to despatch before their township could be deemed safe once more.

How many of those would Vincent have to witness?

At least he was not there when they desecrated his poor father's tomb. Vincent took little comfort in the fact that Father James and Mathew's men felt compelled to take the action they did. But if he were being honest, even just with himself, Vincent was glad that he was not present to see them do to his father what they did to the woman. For he knew that he would have been compelled to stop them, regardless of the circumstances.

As his horse cantered along the path, Vincent could see Ralph up ahead, toiling as usual. He made a point this time to stop for a moment and wish him well, in the hope that it might reset his mind to more normal and mundane matters before he reached home.

The last thing he wanted was for either his wife or daughters to see him like this.

"Hold Jessie, there's a good girl." Vincent pulled up his mount adjacent to where Ralph was working. "How are things with you today, Ralph?" he asked pleasantly. "And where's that no-good son of yours, sleeping off a hangover I'll be bound?"

Ralph walked over to him. Vincent could tell from the man's demeanour that something was lying heavily on his heart.

"What's wrong Ralph? Enid's well I trust?"

Ralph removed his cap before speaking. "Yes, your lordship, thank you fer askin'."

"So, what's up, you look like you've lost your last friend in the world?"

Ralph looked up, the pained expression on his face told a story all of its own.

"I'm sure it's nothing your lordship, it's just that Toby didn't come home last night, an' I've not seen him all day. You know what a good worker he is, 'e'd never slack off an' leave me to tend to all this on my own."

Vincent laughed. "He's probably me some young wench in the town and lost track of time. You see that he makes an honest woman of her before he makes you a grandfather."

Ralph attempted a smile, but it did not reach his eyes. "Yes, your lordship, I will that."

Vincent could feel the old man's unease, and although he was confident there was nothing to worry about, he knew that such a suggestion would be of little comfort to him.

Ralph was a long-term tenant and he deserved more.

Vincent gazed up at the sky. The rain clouds had passed but those left behind still had a menacing hue. "Tell you what, why don't you finish up for the day," suggested Vincent. "Take yourself off to the inn, you'll probably find Toby there still nestled in the arms of his new love."

Ralph bowed his head. "Oh, thank you, sir, if you're sure. I was going to go there at lunch to see if I could find 'im, but there wasn't enough 'im after I'd gone and checked the woods.

Thank you, sir." Ralph thought for a moment, then added, "But what if one of your gamekeepers sees me missing, I don't want them to dock my pay?"

"You leave them to me," Vincent assured him. "I'll make sure they know you have my permission."

Ralph continued to bow and thank Vincent as he moved back to collect his bag.

His kindness towards his worker had lifted his spirits somewhat, and Vincent now felt better armed to face his family.

If only he could keep the memory of the vampire's demise from his thoughts!

As he circled the grounds which led to Mandrake, Vincent saw one of his servants emerging from the hall to greet him.

He recognised the young man as Jonathan, and he handed him the reins after dismounting. The young man thanked his master and guided Jessie off towards the stables to have her rubbed down and fed.

As Vincent entered the hall, another servant took his coat, hat, and gloves from him, and informed him that his wife and daughters were awaiting his arrival in the main drawing room.

Vincent made his way to the room. He door was open, and as he approached, he could see his youngest daughter being comforted by Margaret. The little girl was sobbing uncontrollably, and Vincent immediately suspected that all was not well with Jasper.

Corrine and Stella were sitting opposite one another on matching couches, in front of the fire, and they both looked up when they heard Vincent arrive.

"Now what's all this?" Vincent asked cheerfully. "I've only been gone a couple of hours?"

Upon hearing her father's voice, Emily pulled away from her nanny and ran to him.

The little girl stopped short directly in front of him, almost as if to block his entrance to the room. Her cheeks were red from crying and from this distance, Vincent could see tiny droplets streaming down her face.

Bending down, he scooped Emily into his arms. "Oh, my goodness," he exclaimed, cheerfully, in an effort to lighten her mood. "You're turning into a right little lump these days."

Emily pouted, but at least his comment had the desired effect and she stopped sobbing for a moment.

"Now then, what are all these tears for? A father likes to see a cheery smile when he enters the house."

He tapped the end of Emily's nose with his finger, playfully.

"Jasper's not well," Emily spluttered, her breath coming in short, sharp bursts as if she were having trouble catching it in between talking.

Vincent turned slightly so that he could see over to where his wife and eldest daughter were sitting. "Did Doctor Harris call?" he asked, concerned.

Corrine left her seat and walked over to him.

She placed a tender hand on Emily's back before she spoke. "Yes, he came as you ordered." She tailed off without offering any further information.

It was clear to Vincent that she was reluctant to say too much for fear of upsetting Emily further. But if there was something seriously wrong with the old man, he needed to know the details, even if it upset his daughter.

"Well?" he asked. "What was his prognosis?"

Corrine raised her hand and began playing with Emily's hair in an effort to distract the little girl. "He's reacted badly to his fall." She continued, "For a man of his years it is not altogether surprising."

"I'll go up and see him now."

"The doctor gave him a draft to help him sleep. He said to try not to disturb him until it wears off. I asked one of the servants to stay with him, so he is not alone when he wakes."

Vincent nodded. "Good idea, thank you my dear. I'll go up there after dinner just to check on him."

"May I come with you, Papa?" Emily asked hopefully. "I promise I'll be very quiet."

Vincent smiled. "Perhaps, we'll see later, okay?"

Satisfied enough with his answer, Emily smiled and hugged him.

He handed her over to Corrine. "Now let's dry those eyes and have no more tears," he instructed.

Corrine carried the young girl back to her seat by the fire and sat her on her lap. She took out a handkerchief and began to gently daub her cheeks. After a moment, the young girl had cheered up considerably, and was ready to resume her tea party with her dolls.

Vincent asked one of his servants to bring him a glass of ale, his throat was parched from the journey. He considered running upstairs to see how Jasper was, but decided it would draw too much attention, and Emily would be begging him to come along.

So instead, he joined the others and drank his ale, desperately trying to keep his mind on the mundane and ordinary, rather than allowing it to switch back to that afternoon.

But try as he might, he could not eradicate the memory of that poor creature.

Chapter Sixteen

RALPH DETOURED BACK TO THE WOODS WHERE TOBY laid his traps, just in case his son had returned to the to see if there was anything there which he could bring home for supper.

Deep down, he knew it was a long shot, but in his mind the inn was his last chance of finding his son before returning home empty handed, and Ralph did not know what he was going to say to Enid if that ended up being the case.

She would probably demand that Ralph organise a hunt for Toby by gathering up all the locals from the area and sending them out to scour the countryside for him.

But Ralph could just imagine the ribbing he would receive asking for help to find his strapping six-foot son. If anyone could take care of themselves it was Toby, and that was known throughout the town.

As he feared, the area where Toby worked his traps looked just as he had left it when he searched the woods earlier that day. Disheartened, Ralph re-checked the traps for evidence that something had been caught and then removed, but there was no sign of them being disturbed.

The light was fading, and Ralph knew that it was pointless to start trudging through the undergrowth now, especially without any form of light to guide him. Even so, he could not help worrying that Toby might be somewhere nearby, lying unconscious after a fall, or as a result of being attacked by robbers.

He stood in place and scanned the surrounding area as well as he could in the dim light. Twice, he called out his son's name at the top of his voice, but the only response came from the wind whistling through the trees.

Reluctantly, Ralph turned back and made his way across the field to the inn. It was a journey he usually looked forward to at this time of day, but not on this occasion.

As he made his way down the slope towards the main path which led to the inn, he suddenly heard the sound of rustling coming from behind him.

He knew from experience that whatever made the sound was larger than any badger or squirrel, so he spun around, holding his stick up in front of him in an effort to warn off whoever it was, in case they meant him harm.

For a moment, he considered that it might be the same villains who had attacked his son, and he vowed to himself that he would beat them to within an inch of their lives if it meant extracting a confession from them.

But when he turned, the path was clear.

Ralph stood his ground, stick in hand, half expecting someone to pounce out of the shadows and try to take him down.

But there was nothing. No movement, no shadows, just the rustling of the branches overhead.

Finally, Ralph relaxed and turned back in the direction he had been travelling.

Just then, he could have sworn that he heard the sound of laughter, carried on the breeze. He spun back around, convinced this time that his foe had managed to somehow sneak up behind him.

As he turned, Ralph sliced his cane through the air in a wide arc, determined to make the first shot and take his enemy by surprise.

But yet again the path was clear.

By now Ralph's breathing was heavy and laboured and he could hear the sound of his blood thundering through his ears.

He felt foolish for being so jumpy. An old man scared by his own shadow.

And yet, he was sure he had heard that laughter.

Once again, he turned around and continued along the path towards the inn.

The light emanating from the Wild Boar was a comforting sight, and Ralph felt himself regaining his composure as he neared the entrance.

Inside there was the usual mixture of locals scattered around the various nooks and tables. Most turned when he entered, and those tha knew him nodded a welcome before returning to their conversation.

Ralph scoured the bar for any sign of Toby, but as he suspected, he was nowhere to be seen. Ralph felt his heart sink once more. He had no idea what he was going to tell Enid when he arrived home.

Frank Ross, the inn's owner, was serving behind the bar alongside his daughter Joan.

Toby had mentioned once before that he thought Joan had an eye for him, but Ralph had jokingly warned him off dating the innkeeper's daughter, especially as the Boar was the only one in the district. 'If you and her 'ave an argument, she'll ban us both out of spite' he had told him. But Toby took the warning in good heart.

As he approached the bar, Joan smiled. "Hello Ralph, no Toby tonight?"

Ralph shook his head, wearily. "Nah, I was hoping he might be in here already. I don't suppose you've seen him today?"

Joan shook her head. "Here, Dad," she called. "'Ave you seen Toby in here today?"

Frank was busy serving, but he looked up long enough to shake his head.

"Sorry Ralph," Joan apologised. "Why, 'ave you lost him?" she laughed.

Ralph gripped hold of the bar, tightly to prevent himself from reaching over and grabbing Joan by her apron. How dare she make a joke at such a time?

But then he considered that to most people, especially those who knew Toby and his reputation, his disappearance could only mean one thing. He was off somewhere with a girl, and his mind was on other things. It had been less than twenty-four hours since Ralph had last seen his son, and he knew that if he were to make an announcement here and now in the inn, asking for help to find him, he would be laughed out of the place.

"You stoppin' in for one, then?" asked Joan pleasantly.

Ralph had to admit that after the day he had been through, a pint of ale would be most welcome. The trouble was he felt too guilty to sit there drinking while his wife was at home, worrying.

Then he considered the possibility that Toby was there with her, now. Wasted after his night of passion, full of apologies and too ashamed to come out to meet his old dad for fear of reprisals. Big as he was, Ralph still had to remind him on occasion who was the parent.

Ralph wated as Joan poured out a pint.

His lips were dry and parched, and the sight of the dark liquid filling the tankard made his mouth water.

He decided that staying for just one would only add ten minutes onto his journey home. Enid would understand, in fact, she probably expected it of him. Plus, there was always the chance that while he was supping, Toby might appear. After all, he looked forward to his evening libation just as much as his father, not that he deserved it this night.

Ralph paid Joan and thanked her for his pint.

He took his drink over to an empty table towards one of the windows, so he could keep an eye out while he drank.

He savoured the first mouthful, letting the soothing liquid slide down his throat, and warm his belly. I certainly helped to ward off the night air, and Ralph still had a chill inside him from being caught in the rain that afternoon.

No one could begrudge him a single pint.

"No Toby, tonight?"

Lost in thought, Ralph turned to see Colin Sedgwick standing next to his table.

"Ah, no, not yet," replied Ralph. "Maybe later."

"Mind if I sit here, then?"

"No, please, sit yerself down."

Colin slid in opposite Ralph and held out his tankard for them to *clink*.

Outside the window the rain started beating down against the pane.

"Filthy night," observed Colin. "Not the sort of night to be out, especially with the way things are at the moment."

Ralph gazed at Colin over the rim of his cup. "You still stickin' to that story o' yours about young Mary Grant?"

Colin met his gaze, then shrugged. "I know what some around 'ere think of me, and frankly, I don't care," he informed him. "I'm a simple bloke, I live a simple life. But I knows what I saw." He glanced over his shoulder to check if anyone was listening. Satisfied that no one was, he turned back. "They paid me well to keep my mouth shut, but they didn't tell me what I was supposed to be keeping it shut about. If they 'ad, I'd 'ave told them to keep their money, priest an' all."

Ralph wiped froth from his mouth with the back of his hand.

He surveyed his drinking companion, suspiciously. They had

been friends for many years, and if he were being honest, Ralph had never known Colin to be the type to spin yarns.

What would be the point, anyway?

This tale of his only served to alienate him from the townsfolk, and he worked for most of them, so he was only risking his own livelihood by insisting that he was telling the truth.

Ralph leaned in. "I've never known you to have cause to tell me an untruth," he assured him. "So, just say fer the sake of argument that what you say 'appened, 'appened, why tell every Tom, Dick, and Harry about it? You must have known what some would say?"

Colin swallowed his ale. "I 'ad no intention of tellin' anyone about it," he confessed. "But then, after what I saw, I couldn't stop thinkin' about it. It was driving me mad. All day and all night, that was all that appeared whenever I shut me eyes."

"Why didn't you discuss it with the priest? After all, he was there too, so you knew he'd believe you."

Colin shook his head. "I jus' couldn't, that's all," he replied forlornly. "Don't you see, 'im being there made him part of the madness. I needed to tell someone who 'ad nothing to do with it an' see the belief in their eyes. Instead, everyone now thinks I'm some kind of village idiot. Well, they'll see soon enough."

"What d'yer mean by that? You're not planning on doing something stupid, are you?"

Colin took another drink before replying. "Nah, nothing like that." He leaned in a little closer, before continuing. "But you mark my words, I heard what some of them men were saying to each other while they were standing around the poor girl's grave. Something weird and unholy is going on around 'ere, and when it 'appens, everyone will see that I was telling the truth from the start. You'll see."

Ralph was desperate to leave for home, but he had to admit that Colin had piqued his interest. "When you say, 'weird an' unholy' what exactly do you mean?"

Colin sat back and shook his head. "I'm saying no more fer now, just you make sure you look to your own and keep 'em safe, that's all."

Ralph could hold back no longer. "I can't find my Toby," he admitted, bashfully. "I left him here last night before I went home, and I haven't seen 'im since."

Colin raised his eyebrows. "Aye, he spoke to me after you left."

Ralph's eyes opened wide. "Did yer see 'im leave with anyone. Like a stranger?"

Colin thought for a moment then shook his head. "Nah, 'e was alone, I'm sure of it."

Ralph could feel his heart thumping in his chest. "Are you sure? No one followed 'im outside, even a few minutes after he left?"

"I can't swear to it," Colin revealed. "I went back to me pint after 'e got up from the table. Sorry." He could see the look of desperation on his friend's face, and he felt bad for not being able to offer him some more comforting words.

Ralph sank back, dejected.

"P'raps 'e's reached home by now," he offered, hopefully. "He probably met some girl on the way 'ome an' lost track of time. He does 'ave himself a reputation like that."

Ralph looked back up.

There was no denying what everyone else was thinking.

He had had the same thoughts earlier in the day.

"You'd best get off home," advised Colin. "'e's probably waitin' there for you now, full of apologies."

Ralph could feel Toby's hat sticking out of his pocket.

He wiped away a tear and finished his drink, before standing up. "Aye, yer probably right," he agreed. "I'll be seeing yer."

Chapter Seventeen

Ralph left the Wild Boar with an uneasy feeling in his gut. Having spoken to Colin he was now more concerned than ever that something untoward might have happened to Toby, even though his friend had done his best to allay his concerns.

If Colin was right, and there was something sinister taking place in Hasterley, there was no reason to suspect that Toby had become involved. But the fact that he had not been seen since leaving the inn last night had to be more than just a coincidence.

Toby was no fool, but he certainly had an eye for the girls, and they reciprocated. He remembered back in the summer Toby mentioning that he quite fancied young Mary Grant. At the time, Ralph had just rolled his eyes and slapped him on the back, reminding his son that he fancied anything female that walked past.

But now with the poor girl dead, and Colin insisting that she had somehow come back to life at her funeral, Ralph could not help but wonder if Toby would have been fooled by her if she had risen from her grave and approached him on his way home from the inn.

Of course, taking everything Colin described into account, the poor girl could not have come back to life after being decapitated. But what if the same fate had befallen some other girl, and she had not been dealt with as Mary had?

What if she had been laid to rest by her parents who were unaware that their daughter had been inflicted with the same plague as Mary Grant?

Could a young girl manage to free herself from the confines of her coffin, and dig her way out through six feet of earth?

What if she had help?

What if there were more of them hiding in the woods, waiting for night to fall so that they could resurrect others of their kind?

Could Toby have been unfortunate enough to encounter such a creature?

Ralph shivered at the thought. He knew that he was allowing his mind to run away with him, and he chastised himself for it. Colin's words were starting to send his imagination into overdrive and that was not helping the situation.

Ralph had always prided himself on being a level-headed individual, and he was way too long in the tooth now to be losing himself in fantasy and fairy tales.

If here was still no sign of Toby by tomorrow-heaven forbid-he would go and see Father James himself and demand some answers. If anyone knew anything about the alleged strange goings on with people rising from the dead, it would be him.

Just then, he heard the echo of strange laughter emanating from the trees to his left.

Ralph spun round, his stick once more crafted as a weapon, ready to defend himself.

He waited, his breathing laboured in anticipation, but once again there was no sign of whomever it was making the sound.

He listened, intently. Annoyed by the fact that the breeze had suddenly picked up, and the wind rustling through the trees was masking all other sounds.

He fancied he recognised the laughter as being the same as that he had heard earlier just before entering the Wild Boar.

Was it his imagination playing tricks on him, or was there really someone lurking in the woods, waiting for a chance to jump out and attack him?

Then again if that was the case, had they really stayed outside in the cold while he was in the inn, just for the chance to rob a penniless old man on his way home? It did not make sense.

Ralph's eyes darted from side to side, sill half-expecting to see someone emerge from the trees when they saw their chance. But in the darkness, it was impossible for him to distinguish anything resembling another human being.

A quick rustling from his left made Ralph spin around, his sick raised in anticipation, ready to strike.

But nothing moved. At least nothing substantial enough to cause him concern.

He surmised it was probably just a rodent on its nightly quest for food.

After a while, Ralph lowered his stick and resumed his walk home, keeping his ears peeled for anything which sounded out of place.

When he finally reached home and opened the door to his cottage, Enid came rushing round the corner from the kitchen, her face beaming. But when she saw that it was only her husband, her smile vanished.

Ralph did not take exception. He shared his wife's disap-pointment and anxiety.

He went over to her and put his arms around her, hugging her tightly.

"I was so sure it was him," Enid admitted, her voice choked

with emotion.

"I know, darling," Ralph replied comfortingly. "I've searched everywhere I can think of, I don't know what else to do."

Enid's tears flowed freely as she buried her face in his chest.

Ralph could not help but feel inadequate for not being able to do more to reassure his wife that Toby would return safe and sound. But he knew there was no point in giving her false hope, so if needs be he decided then and there that after his dinner he would go back out and scour the entire area for him, even if it took him all night.

He could not bear to see his wife so desolate.

Enid pulled away and dried her tears. "Come on, your dinner's ready, I'll keep some back for Toby."

"And 'e better have a good excuse when he arrives," Ralph said, trying his best to sound positive.

Ralph set another log on the fire and warmed himself in front of it.

He had to admit, even if it was only to himself, that the night cold had set in his bones, and he was not looking forward to venturing out again to search for Toby. But he knew when the time came, he would tell Enid that he was just fine, and too full of dinner for sleep, so a good long walk would be just what he needed.

He only hoped that he would not have an argument on his hands. His wife could be a feisty woman when she had a mind to, and he had lost many an argument over the years because of it.

Enid carried in a large bowl full of soup and set it down on the table.

Ralph took his place and cut them both some bread.

As he buttered his slice, the door of the cottage flew open.

Enid screamed and dropped the ladle she was using to stir the soup onto the floor.

Ralph stood up, knocking back his chair.

They could both see a large silhouette blocking the open doorway.

As Ralph reached for his stick, Toby entered the cottage.

It took a moment for either of his parents to realise that it was him. There was something different about him, though at that precise moment, neither of them could tell exactly what it was.

Toby's frame was illuminated by the flickering firelight.

"Hello, Mum, hello, Dad, am I in time for dinner?" Toby rubbed his hands together as if to ward off the night chill. As he stepped further into the room, both his parents could see his face more clearly.

His eyes were wide open as if he was staring a something glorious, and his mouth was stretched back across his teeth in a rictus grin.

Even so, Enid ran to him and threw her arms around him, hugging him furiously.

Ralph was a little more hesitant as a feeling of uneasiness swept over him which he could not explain.

"Where the devil 'ave you bin lad? Your mother an' I 'ave been frantic with worry."

Toby was not reciprocating Enid's gesture, instead he kept his arms dangling down by his side, clenching, and unclenching his fists.

"Sorry," he replied, casually, his facial expression still unchanged as of frozen in place. "I met a couple of friends on my way home last night and time just sort of got away from me."

"Never mind," sobbed Enid. "You're back now, that's all that matters. Oh, I've been praying all night and day for your safe return, and here you are."

"Here I am," Toby repeated, a mocking edge to his tone.

"What friends?" Ralph asked, perplexed.

"Eh."

"I said, what friends did you meet last night?"

"Oh, no one you'd know, Dad."

"Never mind all that now," Enid broke in. "Sit yourself down, the soup's ready, and I've made mutton pie with leeks and carrots, your favourite. Shut the door Ralph before we lose all the heat."

Ralph went to comply with his Enid's wishes, but he could not ignore the feeling that there was something uncanny about his son which was causing him great unease.

Enid untangled herself from her son and returned to the table, busying herself setting out the cutlery for their dinner before disappearing back into the kitchen.

As Ralph reached the door to close it, he felt a hand clamp down on his shoulder from behind. He turned to see Toby staring directly at him, although it almost appeared as if his son was somehow looking through him.

For the first time in his life, Ralph was physically afraid of his son.

"Don't shut the door, Dad," said Toby.

Ralph tried to hold his stare but found himself looking away. "Why not, it's freezing out there, you heard what your mother said."

He felt odd having to explain himself to his own boy, but just at that moment Ralph felt as if he was standing before a stranger. It was his penetrating gaze which unnerved Ralph the most and he found himself having to resist the urge to grab his son by the shoulders to try and shake it out of him.

Ignoring Toby's instruction, Ralph turned back to close the door.

It was then that he noticed a small group of people standing on his front doorstep.

The shock made Ralph stop dead in his tracks. He opened his mouth as if to speak, but no words came out.

The group standing outside all seemed to share the same

frozen grin as his son, and their eyes, like his, were wide open and unblinking. Ralph could feel the blood freezing inside him as he stared, transfixed by the figures. He looked quickly from one to the next and back again. It was almost as if he were afraid to stare for too long at any one individual in case they somehow managed to hypnotise him.

Turning back to face his son, Toby's maniacal grin was still spread across his face, wider than ever now.

"You don't mind my friends joining us, do you, Dad?" Toby enquired.

"What?"

"They're my friends I was telling you about. I promised them a hot meal if they followed me home."

"What's all this?" Enid asked, emerging from the kitchen with their main meal.

Ralph looked past his son towards his wife. Suddenly, he felt an overwhelming urge to run to her and throw his arms around her for protection.

Before he had a chance to move several of the strangers rushed in past him, one of them grabbing him by the collar and yanking him backwards until he lost his balance.

Ralph's back slammed against the hard floor, knocking the wind out of him.

Unable to move or regain his breath, Ralph closed his eyes in pain as two of the strangers dragged him outside into the cold night air.

In the distance he could hear Enid screaming, but he was helpless to assist.

Before he could move, one of the strangers, a young woman who looked even younger than Toby, ripped open his shirt and sunk her teeth into his neck, whilst her comrade ripped off one of his trouser legs and bit deep into his exposed thigh.

He could hear his son's guttural laughter as he closed his eyes for the last time.

Chapter Eighteen

VINCENT WAS STIRRED FROM HIS SLEEP BY THE SOUND of a gentle knocking on his bedroom door. Bleary-eyed he threw back the covers, making sure his movement did not disturb Corinne, and swung his legs over the edge of the bed before making his way towards the bedroom door.

Much to his annoyance, there followed a louder, more insistent knock, before he managed to reach the handle. Vincent resisted the temptation to call out to whomever was causing the racket for fear that he might disturb his wife, so instead he merely took a longer stride so that he would reach the door sooner.

Turning the handle, Vincent flung open the door, only to find one of his younger servants standing outside, looking almost petrified for having disturbed his master.

"I beg your pardon, your lordship," the young man began, bowing his head and reaching for a cap which he did not realise immediately that he was not wearing.

Vincent placed his index finger over his own mouth. "Ssshh!" he demanded, indicating towards his left.

The young servant realised the relevance of the signal and mouthed an apology.

"What's the matter?" asked Vincent, keeping his voice down to a whisper.

"I'm sorry sir, but it's Jasper," the servant explained, straining to keep his own voice down now that he had been warned. "He's awake now, and he's calling for you. I tried telling him he needed to wait until the morning, but he's instant that he sees you now. He even threatened to leave his bed to come to you. I had to force him back under the covers before he collapsed under his own weight."

Vincent held up his hand as if to announce that he understood, and the servant could stop talking. "Okay, go back to him and tell him I'll be there, directly."

The young man nodded, and turned away, scuttling back down the corridor.

Vincent crept back inside his bedroom and pulled on his slippers and dressing gown.

Once in the corridor he pulled the door gently behind him until he heard the lock *click* into place.

He stood there for a moment, suddenly realising that without the benefit of the lit candles by his bed, he was in almost total darkness. Vincent cursed himself for not telling the young servant to leave his lantern with him. There were several at either end of the landing perched on end tables, but he did not wish to start fumbling with flints in the darkness.

The only ones left lit overnight were those downstairs by the main door, but he knew that there was no use in stumbling down the stairs just to fetch one. That would be asking for trouble.

It made more sense just to try and acclimatise his eyes to the gloom and make the best of it.

Cautiously, Vincent felt his way along the corridor using the banister for guidance.

Once he reached the bottom of the stairs at the end of the landing, he stretched out his hands so that he could feel each step before trusting his weight on it.

As he reached the halfway mark, Vincent heard the sound of laughter echoing up from somewhere below.

He stopped in his tracks to listen.

At first, all was quiet. Then he heard it again.

A young girl's laughter. Not Stella's, he was convinced of that. For one thing there was no fathomable reason for her to be about at such an ungodly hour.

It was doubtless one of the servants up to mischief. He would make a point of speaking with Mrs Bales in the morning. She would find the culprit and deal with them accordingly.

In the pitch darkness Vincent could not deny that he found the laughter unnerving. But he put that down to the fact that he was unable at that moment to identify the culprit and admonish them.

He heard the laughter once more, but this time it sounded further away as if the instigator had moved further down to another floor.

Vincent waited on the stair a moment longer. Then, convinced that whoever it was had now ceased their merriment he returned his concentration to the matter at hand.

He managed to navigate the rest of the way without incident, and upon reaching the top Vincent made his way along the upper landing towards Jasper's room. As a senior servant, Jasper did not have to share a room like most of the rest of the staff, with the exception of Mrs Bales, the head housekeeper.

As he neared Jasper's room, he could hear the old man arguing with the young servant, demanding that he be allowed to dress before entertaining the Viscount.

Vincent knocked and entered without being invited.

Sure enough, the young man was desperately trying to keep Jasper in his bed, fighting with him over the covers.

When Jasper saw Vincent, he immediately began apologising for his appearance. He tried once more to free himself of the other servant's grasp so that he could at least climb out of bed and stand in his master's presence, but Vincent moved closer and reassured the old retainer that under the circumstances it was best that he remained in bed.

Reluctantly, the old man agreed and finally stopped struggling.

In the light of the lantern's candle which burned brightly on the table next to Jasper's bed, Vincent could see the look of excruciation etched on the old man's face. He appeared to have aged ten years since his accident in the sepulchre that morning.

Vincent felt a sudden tug of guilt at his heart for the old man as he could not deny that he was to blame for his fall. Still, Doctor Harris was the best in the area and Vincent swore he would pay whatever the cost, without complaint, to see his servant well again.

Vincent perched himself on the edge of the bed. "Now then, Jasper, tell me what's so important it could not wait until morning? You need to rest in order to recover."

The old man's eyes darted from Vincent to the servant, then back again.

"Tell Carl to wait outside," Jasper said, almost pleading. "What I have to tell you is not for his ears."

Vincent was perplexed by the old man's request, but in order not to distress him further he turned and asked the young man to wait outside.

Once Carl was out of earshot and had closed the door behind him, Jasper tried to force himself into a sitting position, but his frail arm could not support his weight and he fell back on the mattress.

Vincent moved in, realising what the servant was trying to accomplish, and gave him his own arm for support until he was propped up against the headboard.

"Thank you, my lord," said Jasper, gasping for breath, the mere effort of raising himself up even with assistance had, it seemed, proved too great for him.

"It's okay," Vincent assured him. "Now, tell me what's so urgent."

Jasper still glanced around the room as if to check they were alone before he began to speak. It appeared as if he were afraid that someone might be lurking in the shadows waiting to eavesdrop on their conversation.

Finally, he spoke. "Your lordship knows how loyal I was to your dear father. In all my years here, I never betrayed his confidence, nor would I yours, you do believe me?"

As he spoke, Jasper's whole body began to shake as if he were about to suffer a seizure. Vincent placed his hand on the man's arm to try and calm him down.

Jasper's eyes were wide and alert, still checking the corners of the room while he spoke.

"Jasper, please calm down," begged Vincent, "or I'll have to send for young Emily, and she will be very cross with you for becoming overexcited."

Although he had made the threat jokingly, Jasper reached out and grabbed Vincent by the wrist, squeezing it as tightly as his weak muscles would allow. "No!" he cried. "No one else must hear what I have to say. Only you, only you."

Though taken aback by the old man's reaction, Vincent did his best to assure him that whatever he said would be in confidence.

Jasper seemed to relax slightly, comforted by his master's promise.

He cleared his throat before continuing his tale. "Towards the end, your father began to lose faith in his religion. Although he had always been a devout Christian all his life, he confided in me that he feared there would be no paradise waiting for him when he closed his eyes for the last time."

Vincent was shocked to hear his words. His father had been a great supporter of the church, and he had never once heard him express doubt the hereafter.

Even so, Jasper had no reason to lie.

"He became so obsessed with his own mortality," Jasper continued, "that in the end he sent to London for academics who were the top of their field in researching alternative religions and cults. He paid them a small fortune to come here and discuss their findings with him. Barely a day went by without some new professor arriving to see him. Then one morning, this man appeared." Jasper shivered at the memory. "I did not like the look of him. He had deep set eyes of the blackest hue and a stern harsh face which looked as if it had never attempted a smile. One of the housemaids screamed and dropped a set of breakfast cutlery when she accidently bumped into him. I did not have the heart to chastise her for her clumsiness, for he had a countenance that exuded pure evil, and even my blood ran cold upon sight of him.

"I presented him to your father, and they stayed locked in the main drawing room for hours. I was told not to disturb them, so I told the rest of the household to do likewise. Finally, when your father opened the door, he informed me that he was to accompany this man back to London.

"He was gone for weeks. I wasn't sure how long to leave matters before writing to you, I was so concerned for your father's safety. None of us trusted that man. Then, when his lordship finally returned, he took me to one side and informed me that as a result of a programme of treatment he had embarked on, he needed to undergo certain procedures which would be organised and conducted by a foreign medical team, and that for the treatment to be a success he would have to adhere to certain eccentricities of theirs, the manner of which no one but myself would be privy to.

"I agreed to help in any way I could, naturally. Though at the time I had no idea of the abhorrent nature of the practices his experts were planning on exercising."

Jasper started coughing and spluttering in his haste to formulate his words. It was as if he somehow knew that his time was short, and he needed to tell Vincent everything before he expired.

Vincent poured Jasper a glass of water from the jug by his bedside. He kept hold of the glass as he gently tipped it towards the old man's lips.

Having drunk a sufficient amount to whet his whistle, Vincent helped Jasper sit up a little further, and propped another pillow behind him for comfort.

Jasper thanked him before continuing. "Your father made me employ builders and stone masons from another county so that no one locally could ever know of his plans. They erected a chapel and several stone altars in the alcoves of the catacombs according to your father's wishes, and when they were completed, we received a delivery one night of wooden coffins, filled with earth. It was truly bizarre, but your father appeared delighted by their appearance, so I never felt it my place to question him.

"Soon after, that evil-looking individual returned to survey the work for himself. He seemed satisfied, and your father had three large chests full to the brim with gold coins placed in his carriage. The man opened one in front of me to inspect its contents, but even the sight of all those riches did not bring the merest hint of a smile to his lips.

"Days later, he returned. This time he brought six hooded figures with him. It was in the small hours of the morning, and your father and I led them down to the catacombs and the purpose-built chapel. I never saw the faces of any of the new arrivals, but from the way they moved I surmised that three of them were women.

"Earlier that day, at your father's behest, I had placed candles all around the alter which had been built in the centre of the chapel. Once lit, the area looked as if it had been bathes in sunlight as opposed to being so far underground as was the case. Your father bid me to stay while the evil-looking man performed a ceremony of sorts which included the addition of some black candles he produced from his leather bag, as well as a silver chalice and a large crucifix which he placed upside down in the middle of the altar.

"I watched in horror as the ceremony continued, and at one point the man produced a huge dagger from inside his cloak. He was chanting something in Latin, and though I am no expert, I could understand certain words and one of those was 'sacrifice'. I felt sure that I was about to be hoisted above and carried over to that stone slab where he would plunge that dagger deep into my heart. I cannot describe to you the fear I felt at that moment, but then, to my relief, the man lifted his own sleeve and using the dagger, sliced deep into his own flesh. He held his arm over the chalice while his blood poured into it. The process seemed to take forever, and I even grew fearful for his own health at the amount of blood he was losing.

"But worse was still to come. Once the chalice was full, he held it up and recited another chant, then he began passing it to each of the six hooded figures in turn, and they all drank from it. Then, he handed it to your father, and he too drank deeply, emptying the chalice."

Vincent pulled back. He could not believe what he was hearing.

Though he had no reason to doubt the words of the elderly retainer, in his mind he could not rationalise the thought of his own father taking part in such a monstrous spectacle.

He could feel his heart humping deep within his chest, and his breathing became laboured. Vincent stood up and walked over to the window, opening it to allow him to breath in some fresh air, and help clear his mind.

As he gazed out onto the grounds which surrounded Mandrake Hall Vincent noticed the willowy figure of a woman, dressed in white, disappear into the trees.

Chapter Nineteen

VINCENT STRAINED TO MAKE OUT WHAT HE WAS seeing. He held a candle close to the pane, but his reflection made his view of the outside less substantial, so he moved it back and cupped his hands against the glass to stare outside.

The woman had all but vanished, masked from sight by the overlapping trees. There was the faintest glimpse of her white garments which appeared momentarily between the branches which was all the proof Vincent had that he had not imagined the figure in the first place.

Vincent wished he had someone else in the room to summon and be his witness. There was no point in asking Jasper to climb out of bed, the poor old man seemed to barely have the strength to speak right now.

There was the other young servant outside the room, but before Vincent decided to call him, the woman had all but disappeared into the woods.

What angered Vincent the most was that she appeared, from his vantage point, to have emerged from the hall, or at least, the road which ran alongside it. Quite what a young girl was doing parading herself in nothing more than a skimpy gown at such a time in the morning was a mystery to him. But then he remembered the laughter he had heard on his way to Jasper's room. Girlish laughter which echoed up the stairs from down below.

Could the figure he witnessed be one of his own servants?

If so, what on earth did she think she was doing acting in such a way?

Had she forgotten her position, or had she been stealing wine from the cellar, taking advantage of Jasper's incapacity?

Either way, he would get to the bottom of it by the morning, and that young lady would find herself without a position by breakfast.

Hearing Jasper splutter, Vincent refilled his glass and brought it over to him, holding it in place while the old man took another drink.

So far, the old retainer's story had seemed like nothing more than pure fantasy.

Stone altars being erected to house coffins filled with earth, blood sacrifices as part of some pagan ritual, it all sounded like total nonsense to Vincent.

But then he considered what Father James had shown him.

Could there possibly be any connection between what Jasper had witnessed and the spate of attacks in the vicinity Mathew was describing.

A sudden feeling of oppression and horror came over him.

Could his father's invitation to those who performed the ritual actually be the catalyst for the deaths of so many of his townspeople!

Vincent could feel his blood turn to ice at the very thought.

He turned back to Jasper. The old man was propped up against his pillows and looked a little stronger in the face after his last drink of water.

As much as Vincent hated to press the man for information, he concluded that Jasper might be the only living soul for miles around who knew exactly what had led to Vincent's father's demise.

Vincent sat back on the edge of the bed. "Jasper," he said, solemnly, "I know you have more to say about these goings on. Please say you have the strength to continue or else I will come back tomorrow."

Jasper sprang forward and grabbed Vincent's arm, gripping it as tightly as he was able in his present condition. "No, master, you must hear all now. I fear my time might be short and I promised your dear father I would tell you everything when you arrived."

Vincent patted the old man's hand. In truth, he was relieved that Jasper felt strong enough to continue with his tale as Vincent was not a patient man and there was far too much going on, even in his own house, which he was unaware of.

He smiled, reassuringly at the old man. "I won't go anywhere you just tell me all you know in your own good time."

Jasper appeared to visibly relax at his master's words. "After the ceremony with the blood, I couldn't believe my eyes. The hooded group the man had brought with him all climbed into one of the coffins which had been laid out, and closed he lids over them. I could tell from his expression that their actions even took your father by surprise, but he looked to be taking his cue from the evil-looking man who had carried out the ritual.

"Once all the coffins had their lids secured, the man in charge led your father and me out of the catacombs, distinguishing all the lights as we left. He told your father in no uncertain terms that no one else should be granted access back there until he gave the order.

"We were told that the six individuals in the coffins were drained after their long journey, and that they needed to rest undisturbed to regain their strength. Once they were fully rejuvenated, the man told your father that his transformation would begin. The end result being that he would be granted eternal life. It all sounded like complete nonsense to me your lordship, but your father was so excited by the prospect that I dared not mention my concerns."

Vincent assured the old man that he understood his reticence with his father, and that no one could blame him for it.

"After that," continued Jasper, "your father made regular visits to the catacombs for his 'transformation' as the evil-looking man called it. After his third visit, the man departed for good, and I never saw him again. I had hoped that with him out of the way, your father might eventually lose interest in the others and send them back from wherever they had come from. But instead, he grew worse. His visits became more frequent, and I began to notice he had developed a most ghastly pallor. He soon found himself unable to go outside in bright sunlight, even to the extent of not being able to perform some of his legal duties, and you know how seriously he took those.

"Eventually, I took courage and questioned his actions. Up until that moment, he had not invited me back to the catacombs to witness whatever operations were taking place, but on the next occasion he did. As reticent as I was, I naturally agreed to accompany him, hoping in earnest that I might be able to persuade him not to continue with whatever treatment he was receiving once I had witnessed it.

"The ritual was a sight I can never unsee. Once we were in the catacomb your father ordered me to light the lanterns, bathing the place in a yellowish glow. He ordered me to help him undress until he had on no more than his under trousers. I watched in horror as he lay down on the stone altar and the lids of the coffins began to rise. The six occupants climbed out, and upon seeing me, their eyes opened wide in excitement and hunger, and if it were not for your father's timely intervention, I feel sure that I would not be here today to tell the tale.

"As it was, he commanded them to leave me be and attend to him instead. I remember desperately trying to control my breathing after the initial rush of fear at seeing those creatures preparing to lunge at me. As I watched, they surrounded the altar where your father lay. Two of them lifted your father's legs, hen sunk their fangs into his ankles. Your father did not seem to flinch or cry out, which in itself made me question if their treatment had actually made him resistant to pain. In the same instant, two of them raised his arms and bit into his wrists, while another chewed at his stomach, and the last one at his neck.

"For what seemed an eternity, they feasted on him. I could hear the awful sucking noises they made while they drank away his life's blood, but still your father appeared impervious to what must have been an intolerable experience."

Jasper seemed to be visibly shaking as he continued the tale, so Vincent moved in and squeezed his wrist to reassure him.

The old man calmed down and took another deep breath before continuing.

"When they were finally finished with their unholy feast, they all pulled back and raised their heads. I could see the remnants of your father's blood streaming down their faces as they used their fingers to sweep the red overspill back into their mouths. It turned my stomach, but I knew I had to stay as I suspected after such an ordeal, your father would need my help to redress and leave that accursed place.

"One by one, those creatures disappeared through an archway in the catacomb. I knew that your father had ordered the builders to create an exit tunnel which led out to the woods, so I suspected that was where they were heading. To do what, I could only imagine at the time, but now, I think I know.

"As I suspected, I had to virtually carry your father out of that place, he was so weak from the loss of blood. I tried many times after that to dissuade him from returning, but he was adamant, and after each visit he grew visibly weaker and paler. I was sure that he was being taken for a fool, but he would hear none of it. Then suddenly, one day, he did appear stronger and more vibrant than I had seen him in many a long month. He still had difficulty going outside in bright sunlight, but otherwise he more closely resembled his portrait commissioned when he was in his early twenties.

"He began going out on long rides after dinner, often not returning until the early hours. He told me not to bother waiting up for him, but I felt it my duty to do so, even though I kept to the shadows in case he needed assistance. His visits to the catacombs became less necessary which was a blessing, but by stealthily following him one night, I discovered that he was liaising with the six figures from the coffins and taking them with him on his long nocturnal rides.

"As his strength grew, so did his temper, to the extent that he refused to be seen by any of the servants save for me. Then one night, just after I had watched him return from his nightly jaunt, I was about to retire when I heard a scream. It only lasted a second, but I know what I heard. I came running out of my room to try and discover the source of the cry, and to my horror I saw your father carrying what looked like a large roll of carpet down the stairs. The object was draped over his arms, and I remember thinking at the time how much fitter and stronger he had become as a result of his 'procedures'.

"I did not dare follow, and as it appeared no one else in the house had stirred, I returned to my bed. The next morning, we discovered one of the housemaids had disappeared. We searched everywhere, but to no avail. She was a new girl, and to be honest, a bit flighty, so we naturally assumed that she had run off with some young man from the town. But I could not get that image of your father on the stairs, out of my mind."

"What! You think he was carrying the body of this young girl?" demanded Vincent, his brows furrowed. "For what conceivable purpose, pray?"

Chapter Twenty

JASPER SEEMED PHYSICALLY TAKEN ABACK BY HIS master's outburst. The colour drained from his cheeks leaving him looking pale and ashen. He held up a trembling hand. "Forgive me your Lordship, I forgot my place for a moment."

Vincent, realising the affect he had had on the old man, took a deep breath through pursed lips. Although he could not deny his outrage at the man's words, he also realised that Jasper was doing his best to relay a very sordid tale as openly and honestly as he knew how.

"It's alright, Jasper," Vincent assured him. "You must forgive me for my sudden outburst. I realise how difficult it must be for you to say these things to me and I promise to keep my temper in check, so do not be afraid to fill in every detail."

Vincent was relieved to see the old man relax at his words.

Jasper thanked his master and asked for another sip of water before continuing.

Once the old man had settled back, he carried on with his tale.

"Naturally, I had no proof that your dear father was carrying anything other than a rolled-up carpet down the stairs, but it occurred to me that he would have no reason to do so. If he wanted something moved, he only had to instruct one of the servants, as always."

Vincent nodded. "Yes, I understand that. But if, by some strange quirk of fate, he was carrying the girl's body in that carpet, where do you suppose he was taking it to?"

Jasper looked shocked by Vincent's question. "Why, down to the catacombs to give to those monsters in the coffins, where else?"

Now, it was Vincent's turn to look shocked. "Do you mean to tell me that the catacombs you speak of are here in the house?"

Jasper nodded. "I apologise you Lordship, but I thought you knew."

Vincent stood up and walked a couple of paces across the room, before stopping and turning back. For a moment he kept his gaze fixed firmly on the floor in front of him.

Jasper could see that his master was both dumbfounded and disturbed by his latest revelation, and he blamed himself for not making the position clearer from the beginning.

Vincent looked up at his old servant. "Jasper, I've known this house my entire life. I've explored every nook and cranny it has to offer. How is it then you are now telling me that there is an entire area which I know nothing about?"

The old man shook his head, solemnly. "Your father every intention of showing you I have no doubt. But once those creatures had been placed in situ, I believe he was waiting until he no longer needed their intervention and could send them back to that evil monster who brought them here in the first place. Alas, something happened during one of his rituals with them and he suffered a fateful reaction. He barely managed to crawl his way out of the catacombs and summon help, before being carried to his room. Doctor Harris did all he could for him, I'm quite sure, but your dear father passed away before morning."

"And those accursed creatures?" demanded Vincent. "What of them?"

Jasper swallowed and glanced downwards. "I'm afraid to say that they are still down there, your Lordship."

"What!" Vincent ran back over to his servant and grabbed him by the arm. Realising at once that he had taken too strong a hold, he released his grip and sat back on the bed. "Are you telling me that the vile creatures who killed my father are still residing under the protection of this house?"

Jasper nodded, slowly.

Vincent could feel his face flushing red in anger.

He knew that the fault did not lie with his servant, he was a good and loyal individual who was doubtless waiting for the right moment to tell him about the horrors of the catacombs.

Bu now that he had been made aware of them, he knew that he must act, and do so without delay.

Vincent rose from the bed and pulled back the covers, holding out his hand. "Come Jasper, you must show me these catacombs at once. At the very least I will dispel these wretches who caused my father's death and send the out into the night without protection from me or my father's good name."

Jasper reached out, his hands trembling. "No, please your Lordship, you must understand these are very dangerous creatures, and there are six of them. You must not go there alone."

Vincent smiled. "I don't care if there are sixty of them, they won't argue against some good old British steel. I'll show you their true colours."

Jasper looked horrified by his master's suggestion, but Vincent either did not notice, or shoes to ignore his concerns. Walking over to a chair by the window, Vincent grabbed his servant's long coat and house shoes and carried them back over to the bed.

"Now you get yourself dressed," he instructed, "while I fetch my sword. I'll not spend another night asleep in this house while those creatures remain under my roof."

Jasper lunged forward and grabbed Vincent's arm. "No, master no, I beg you. You cannot face these abominations alone, I have seen what they are capable of, you must understand, they are not human!"

Vincent stared down at him, in shock.

He realised that the old man was simply concerned for his welfare, he had always been proudly protective of him, as he had of his father. But, as a mere servant, he could not be expected to appreciate the onerous responsibility Vincent carried on his shoulders as the new Viscount. It was a responsibility which Vincent took extremely seriously and included the protection of all his tenants, as well as his own household.

Vincent smiled to reassure the old man. "You're becoming overwrought Jasper, please try and calm down, I have the matter well in hand."

"But your Lordship…" The old servant protested.

"Now, now, there's nothing to distress yourself over. Human or otherwise, I'll know how to deal with these creatures, and if necessary, I can have the Militia here in next to no time. Colonel Drake will vanquish them in no time."

Jasper seemed to visibly relax a little. "Yes, yes please your Lordship, let us wait for the Colonel and his men to arrive before venturing down to the catacombs. Such a show of force may well scare these creatures away, forever."

Vincent smiled. "Quite so. However, I wish to face them first myself, if for no other reason than I can inform the Colonel exactly what he is up against. So, you get yourself ready and lead the way. I'm intrigued to see how we gain access to these secret tunnels which have been kept from me for so long."

Having been lulled into a false sense of security, Jasper suddenly realised that his master had no intention of summoning the Militia before entering the lair of those evil monsters who had killed his master.

It was too much for the old man to contemplate that he might lose two masters in such a short space of time, for he knew in his heart that, regardless of how adept the new Viscount was with a blade, he would still be no match for the six beasts who slumbered in their coffins, beneath the hall.

Jasper made to protest once more, but Vincent had already made his way to the bedroom door and was instructing Carl to assist the old man in dressing, while he fetched his sword.

The old servant knew that to offer any further argument would be useless.

Vincent was every bit the son of his late father.

Stubborn, pigheaded, irascible at the best of times, especially when challenged.

But still, Jasper felt it was his duty to protect his master, regardless of the circumstances, even if he was determined to thrust himself into danger.

With Carl's help, Jasper pulled on his coat and shoes, and instructed the young servant to help him down the stairs.

"Shouldn't we wait for the master?" Carl asked nervously.

"No, he knows where to meet us, it'll take me long enough to get there, even with your assistance. Now bring the lantern with you and take my arm."

Reluctantly, the young servant helped jasper t of the door and across the landing towards the stairs. Together they negotiated each step, one at a time, until they reached the ground floor.

There was still no sound of Vincent approaching from above, which Jasper was grateful for as he knew he only had one chance to save his master from being attacked by the creatures in the catacombs, and he intended to make full use of the time.

Even if it meant his own demise, Jasper was more than willing to take the risk.

If he could somehow warn them of his master's intention, perhaps they would leap at the chance to flee before being discovered. After all, any kind of head start on the Militia would be an advantage, even those as disturbed in the mind as these vile individuals must realise the benefit of that.

Jasper ordered Carl to assist him to the wine cellar.

He could tell that the young man was deeply concerned that he was ignoring his master's direct instructions, so Jasper assured him that he would take full responsibility if there should be any repercussions.

This seemed to calm the young man down, slightly, and they continued their journey in silence.

Once they reached the wine cellar, there was not enough room for them to take the stairs side-by-side, so to prevent an accident Jasper instructed Carl to lead the way holding the lantern to illuminate the staircase so that the old man could see where he was putting his feet.

When they reached the cellar floor, Jasper held onto the railing for a moment to catch his breath. Once he was confident that he could carry on alone, he asked Carl for the lamp and instructed him to go back upstairs and await the Viscount.

"Ask his Lordship to wait upstairs for me, I will call up when I am ready."

Nervously, Carl agreed, and left the old man in the cellar as he returned to the ground floor.

Once he was alone, Jasper made his way across the cellar passed the rows of wine racks towards the structure which housed the oak barrels of ale at the far corner.

Jasper shivered as he reached his destination, and he was not sure if it was as a result of the cold air, or the fact that he was truly nervous to venture any further on his own. He knew only too well what waited for him behind the secret panel in the wall, and without his old master there for protection Jasper was in no doubt that his life may well be in terrible danger. For even though he came with a warning which any normal human being might appreciate, the creatures who dwelt below the cellar were anything but human, and if they decided to kill him before fleeing from his master, Jasper knew he would have no chance of persuading them otherwise.

But then he considered the possibility that the creatures may not take flight when he informed them of the Viscount's intentions. What if they decided they were too powerful to fear such a man, even armed as he would be?

What if they not only turned on Jasper, but also his master?

Two generations of the Goddard family, murdered on his watch.

The mere thought turned his blood to ice.

"Jasper!" He could hear his master calling his name from above. Evidently his instructions to Carl had been ignored, and Vincent was determined to face his prey head-on, without delay.

Jasper turned back to face the staircase as the sound of footsteps echoed down to where he stood.

What was he to do now?

If he opened the secret panel, his master would doubtless follow him into the catacombs. There would be no time to close the entrance before he reached the cellar floor.

But what then? If Vincent followed him in, the beasts inside might easily overpower him and take his life without giving it a second thought. No amount of pleading by the old servant would dissuade them if they so elected to act.

"Jasper!" His master's voice grew louder as he descended the stairs.

Jasper could see the light from his master's lamp casting its glow on the staircase.

Unable to decide what to do, Jasper suddenly felt a tightening in his chest. He grabbed for his arm as a tingling sensation ran through it, causing his left hand to go numb. His lamp fell from his grasp the glass phial smashing on the ground, as the old man sank to his knees on the hard stone floor.

By the time Vincent reached him, Jasper was already dead!

Chapter Twenty-One

CEDRIC STOBART HAD BEEN THE HEAD groundskeeper for Mandrake Hall since his father passed away ten years earlier. Like his father, he prided himself on earning his keep, and ensuring that all those under him did likewise.

His life ran like clockwork, and he believed that everything else in life should be arranged in a similar manner. His wife Hetty knew and understood the importance of Cedric's regime and did all she could as a dutiful wife to ensure that no domestic obstacles ever managed to intrude on her husband's schedule.

Cedric rose as 5:00am every morning, including at the weekend. His breakfast was on the table by no later than 5:30am, otherwise he had been known to leave for work without it. During the winter months, the workers were given the privilege of starting work later than during the summer. Neither the present Viscount, nor his father before him expected their people to work in the dark. However, Cedric still liked to be on site by 6:00am regardless, so that he could watch the workers arrive when their time was due.

He had several acres to cover each day, and if for some inexplicable reason he ever fell behind, he would happily forego his lunch to ensure that he covered all his ground before going home for supper.

This morning was no exception. Cedric had been informed by Vincent the previous evening that he had allowed Ralph to finish early so that he might look for his son, who had mysteriously gone missing. But that did not give cause for the two of them to be late this morning. Cedric took out his prized pocket watch which had originally been presented to his late father by the then Viscount. By his reckoning the men were already over fifteen minutes late, and there was still no sign of either of them coming up the hill.

If there was one thing Cedric could not abide, it was someone taking advantage of another's good nature. Ralph may well have had a good reason to knock off early the day before, but there was no way he was still looking for Toby over twelve hours later.

No. The pair of them had probably me up last night in the pub and were both sleeping off a hangover, confident in the knowledge that the Viscount would never know.

Well, not on Cedric's watch, that was for sure.

There were still several fields to check on that morning, but Cedric decided that this matter required his immediate attention. He would go to Ralph's cottage and catch the lazy so-and-so's still asleep, or too groggy to make their way out to do an honest day's work and drag them both before the Viscount to explain themselves.

Cedric had no personal grudge against either man, but duty was duty and he felt he would be failing in his if he did not deal with the situation decisively.

Ralph and his son could plead and beg all they liked, but they knew there was no excuse to show such disrespect towards their lord and master, especially when he had been so lenient with them only the day before. By rights, they should have both been stopped pay for their lack of work yesterday, and that would certainly have been the case if it was left up to Cedric.

But such a decision was the Viscount's to make, and his alone. Cedric for his part would just present the facts when he caught up with the two men.

Shaking his head in disgust, Cedric set off across the woods towards the cottage where Ralph and his family resided.

It was a dull morning. The sun had barely managed to pierce the cloud cover, and it appeared as if yesterday's rain had more to offer.

The wind seemed stronger than the day before, and Cedric had to hold his cap in place as he walked, or else risk losing it. The ground through the woods was still soft and slippery underfoot from the soaking it had received, and on more than one occasion Cedric found himself having to reach out and grab a tree or bush to prevent himself from slipping over.

At last Cedric could see Ralph's cottage come into view.

He noticed that there was no smoke trailing from the chimney, which seemed odd at that time of day. The closer he came the more concerned he grew that something was not right.

Beside the lack of smoke, Cedric also saw that the front door had been left open, and as he drew level with the cottage, he also noticed the general disarray of furniture inside the kitchen. The table and chairs had all been knocked over and left askew across the floor.

Upon closer examination, Cedric noticed that there was also a mixture of broken plates, cups and assorted cutlery strewn throughout the kitchen.

Realising that not all was as it should be, Cedric felt a gurgle of unease in his belly which made him want to take flight and run for help.

But as a man of position, he knew that he would become a figure of fun if it later transpired that something as everyday as a loose pig had managed to sneak in and cause such mayhem, and that he had been too afraid to investigate further before raising the alarm.

Cedric knew that Ralph had a small holding with some livestock, so it was perfectly plausible as an explanation.

He waited outside the main door for a few moments, hoping to hear or see some evidence that nothing untoward had taken place. He listened intently for the sound of the Watkins clan returning to their home after securing the pen that had unleashed the wild hog. The men full of apologies for being late for work, and Enid offering to make him breakfast to help subdue his fervour for reporting her husband and son to the Viscount.

But there came no such sound.

All he could hear was the sound of the wind rushing through the branches behind him, whispering as if to warn him not to venture any further.

Stealing himself, Cedric slowly entered the abode, calling out to Ralph as he crossed the threshold. He waited just inside the door, but no answer came.

Staring down at the carnage of upturned furniture and broken crockery, Cedric considered his option of running for help, once more. But reaching out he steadied himself against the door jamb and collected his wits, deciding this was no time to be found wanting.

His duty came with certain responsibilities, whether they were officially part of his job description or self-imposed, and he knew that this present situation called for fortitude.

He called out once more before moving forward, but as he expected, there was still no response. Using his cane Cedric moved aside any debris in his path as he made his way through the kitchen towards the first bedroom.

The door was closed, so he reached out with the end of his cane and pushed against the wood. Slowly, the door creaked open revealing a stout wooden bed to one end of the room. On either side of the bed stood a small wooden chest, and as neither had been disturbed Cedric surmised that whatever had caused the upheaval in the kitchen had not spread throughout the rest of the cottage.

He heaved a small sigh of relief. His escaped pig theory began to grow in plausibility.

Smiling to himself, Cedric pushed open the door a little further and stepped inside.

As the entire room was revealed to him, Cedric caught sight of Ralph and his wife in the far corner, suspended upside down from the ceiling by a rope, their arms dangling, fingertips almost touching the floor.

Both their faces were turned towards him, each a mask of pure horror.

From the ghastly pallor of their cheeks, they both appeared to have been drained of every ounce of blood save for what appeared to be a small pool of dried blood staining the floorboards beneath each body.

The limp forms swayed gently from side to side. Their movement was almost imperceptible to the naked eye, as if Cedric's opening of the door had somehow caused a draft sufficient for the task at hand, although he knew this could not be so.

Frozen to the spot, Cedric was unable to move. Desperate as he was to turn and flee the awful scene, his legs refused to obey his brain's command for flight.

Cedric swallowed hard, forcing back a scream which had surreptitiously worked its way up to his throat, desperate for escape. No matter how hard he tried, he was unable to tear his gaze away from the tortured faces of Ralph and his wife.

Suddenly, a noise coming from another room brought him out of his reverie.

There was someone else in the cottage with him!

Cedric listened strained to hear if the noise had merely been his imagination. Under the present circumstances no one could possibly blame him for hearing things which were not there.

Using his stick to balance himself, Cedric managed to take a few tentative steps backwards, his gaze unable to leave the grotesque similes which had once belonged to the farmer and his wife.

He was grateful when he had moved back sufficiently so that the open door obscured the two bodies languishing on their ropes like some macabre puppet show.

Once he was clear of the bedroom, Cedric concentrated on the direction the other sound had emanated from. He fancied I came from his left, and sure enough, there was another door there tucked into an alcove. Cedric guessed it might be Toby's room. Was the poor man lying in there, another helpless victim of whatever had attacked his parents?

The urge to flee was still as strong as ever, but something deep inside him argued that Toby might be holding on to life by a thread at this very moment, and Cedric could be the only one close enough to offer him some much-needed care.

If he chose to leave now, without investigating further, Cedric knew that speculation and rumour would follow him for the rest of his days if it transpired that he could have saved Toby if he only acted in time.

Summoning up what little courage he had left, Cedric held up his cane as a weapon, taking a tight grip on the handle. If anything ran at him when he entered Toby's room, he intended to be in a position where he could-at the very least-defend himself, or at best slay whatever vile creature had attacked Toby's parents.

Cedric crept slowly across the floor, once more trying desperately not to make too much noise while negotiating the broken bric-a-brac in his path.

As he reached the door, Cedric leaned his ear against the

wood, straining to listen for any clue as to what to expect when he ventured inside.

At first, there was nothing. No sound of movement of any kind.

Then he heard it. Low at first, barely audible through the wooden door. Cedric had to strain to make sure that it was not just his imagination playing tricks on him.

Then I grew louder!

Just loud enough to ensure that Cedric knew he was not imagining it.

Laughter.

But not the cheerful sound of someone enjoying themselves or responding to a good joke or a witty play. No, this was low guttural sound, more a growl than a laugh, but underneath there was something mocking in the tone.

Cedric pulled back. His reserve to venture further had finally abandoned him. Let them say what they liked, after what he had witnessed in the next room no man could be expected to investigate further without back-up.

"Are you not coming in, Gamekeeper?"

Cedric felt his blood turn to ice.

Something in that room knew that it was him outside, and no they were taunting him to face them.

"We're all waiting for you. All you have to do is push the door open and you'll have us all to yourself."

Finally, his legs took over, and Cedric found himself backing out of the cottage. He almost lost his balance twice, tripping over upended furniture, but he managed to stay upright as he continued in his quest.

He kept his eyes fixed firmly on the closed door for fear something horrible and inhuman might realise he was making good his escape and fly out of the room after him.

From behind the door, the raucous laughter grew louder and

the words more threatening. "We know where you live, Game-keeper. We'll be seeing you soon enough."

At the front door, Cedric finally turned round, half-expecting to see some ogre waiting for him. But to his relief the way appeared clear.

Without turning back, Cedric ran for all he was worth.

Chapter Twenty-Two

CEDRIC RAN ALL THE WAY BACK TO THE HALL, ONLY stopping to catch his breath when he felt he could no longer continue without passing out. He could not help but notice the curious looks from the farmers he passed along the way, some of whom had never seen the Groundkeeper in such a panic before.

When he arrived at the hall, Cedric could tell almost immediately that something was awry. The servant who opened the door to him had a very sombre look for such a young man, and as he was led into the study to await the Viscount, Cedric was sure that he could hear crying echoing through the parlour.

Cedric warmed himself by the fire while he waited for his master to appear. Although still somewhat flushed from his exertion, there was still a chill in his bones from the early-morning air as well as a shiver deep inside him as a result of the sight which had greeted him at the cottage, which he hoped the comfort of the fire's warmth would help to eradicate.

He spun around as the door opened and Vincent strode into the room.

Cedric lifted back his shoulders and bowed respectfully, but his master hardly seemed to notice the gesture of deference as he took his seat behind the large oak table in front of the window.

Vincent signalled to the chair opposite him, and Cedric sat down.

"What seems to be the trouble?" Vincent asked in a matter-of-fact tone.

Cedric could tell at once that the Viscount had not slept well the previous night. Here were heavy bags under each eye, and his cheeks seemed to have lost their usual cheery hue.

"I am very sorry to trouble you, your Lordship," Cedric began slowly, turning in his seat to check that the door to the study had closed, properly. "I've just been to Ralph Watkins' cottage as he and Toby were not at their post as usual this morning, and..." Cedric could feel the blood draining from his own face as he remembered the sight of the farmer and his wife's corpses dangling from the ceiling.

He placed a handover his mouth as if to prevent himself from vomiting.

"Speak up, man," insisted Vincent, clearly in no mood for theatrics that morning.

Cedric cleared his throat and held up a hand in apology. "There's no easy way to relay this to your Lordship," he continued, nervously. "But when I reached the cottage, I could see straight away that things were not as they should be. Furniture was upturned and kitchen items were strewn across the floor. There was no sign of Ralph or his wife, so I began a search of the property, and when I ventured into their bedroom, I saw them...Hanging upside down from the ceiling, their bodies white as a sheet."

Vincent, who until this point had his mind clearly on other things, suddenly sat up in his chair, frowning. "What?" he demanded.

Cedric nodded, apprehensively. "Yes sir, it was exactly as I say. Their dead bodies were strung upside down, and it looked as if every drop of blood had been drained from them."

Vincent shot up from his chair, scaping it back on the stone floor.

Cedric did, likewise, feeling awkward to be sitting in his master's presence when he himself was upstanding.

"Did you see any sign of their son, Toby?" Vincent asked.

Cedric blushed and shook his head. He decided not to tell Vincent about the strange laughter he had heard coming from Toby's room. He was still too ashamed of the fact that he had not bothered to investigate further at the time.

The two men stood there in silence.

Cedric could tell that Vincent was thinking, and he did not dare disturb his train of thought.

Finally, Vincent spoke again. "Cedric, I need you to do something for me, but you must carry out my instructions to the letter, do you understand?"

Cedric nodded, respectably.

"I need you to go to the presbytery right away, take a horse from the stables, tell the lads I gave you permission. Ride straight there, do no stop for anything. Tell Father James what you witnessed at Ralph's cottage, and then escort him and his associates back there, and wait for me."

"You are not coming your Lordship?" Cedric was pleased that he was no being asked to return to the cottage alone, but even so, he would much prefer it if Vincent were the one to explain to the priest what was waiting for them at the farmer's cottage.

What if the priest did not believe him, and refused to follow him?

Would Cedric have to travel back there alone to await the Viscount?

"No," replied Vincent, "not right away, we lost one of our servants during the night, the doctor has only just left. I've sent for someone to transport his body so that it can be made presentable for his funeral."

"I am very sorry to hear that," Cedric expressed, sincerely.

"Thank you. I'm afraid my youngest daughter has taken the death particularly to heart. She was very fond of the old man. I want to stay long enough to ensure that my servants carry his body out with the proper dignity it deserves, whilst trying to keep my daughter from seeing him."

"I understand your Lordship," confirmed Cedric. Still secretly wishing that his master would accompany him to tell Father James.

As if hearing his prayer, Vincent grabbed up a quill and a piece of paper and began scribbling something. After a moment, he sealed with paper with wax and the imprint of his ring, before handing it to Cedric.

"Take this with you and hand it directly to Father James, no one else, understand?"

Cedric took the roll of paper gratefully and shoved it deep within his inside pocket.

Whatever the Viscount had decided to write on the paper, Cedric felt sure that it would make his explanation of what he had seen that morning easier for the priest to digest, without the need of endless questions.

Cedric turned to leave. As he reached the study door, Vincent called out to him.

"Make sure you tell no one other than Father James any of this. I am swearing you to secrecy!"

Cedric nodded his understanding and left.

Vincent waited behind in the study for several minutes after his Groundkeeper had gone. This was the last thing he needed on top of everything else that had happened.

Since finding Jasper's body down in the cellar, Vincent had checked every nook and cranny in order to discover the entrance to the catacombs the old man had spoken of, but his search was to no avail.

He cursed himself for not realising just how ill the old servant had been. He should have insisted that Jasper describe the way to the entrance to him while he was still recuperating in bed. That way he would have the knowledge he so desperately required, and the old man might still be alive.

Now it seemed he would have to deal with the murders of Ralph and his wife, as well as explain to Father James what he had discovered from Jasper. If those creatures were still down there, using his home as their refuge, then it made perfect sense that they were also responsible for the demise of the farmer and his wife.

As Vincent left the study, he saw four of his servants carrying the Jasper's corpse from the cellar. They had wrapped him in several thick blankets as instructed, and they stopped in their tracks upon seeing their master.

Vincent looked over the poor man's coverings to ensure that they had completed the job properly, then once he was satisfied, he nodded for them to continue.

The men carried their dead colleague with great solemnity out through the back pantry towards the tradesmen's entrance. It was not meant as an act of disrespect, but merely to avoid little Emily witnessing their task.

When the house stirred, Vincent had explained what had happened to Corrine, leaving out the part concerning the potential hiding place of the creatures beneath the hall. He merely told his wife that Jasper had stirred during the night and insisted upon speaking to him.

Vincent claimed that the old man had grown unnecessarily concerned about an inconsistency in a recent delivery of port and insisted that he venture down to the cellar to show it to him.

Vincent lied to his wife that he tried to stop the old man, but that Jasper insisted, so reluctantly Vincent agreed to accompany him, but the strain was obviously too much for the old man, especially after his fall the previous day.

They decided between them that it was best to tell the girls straight away, a task that was made even more expedient by Emily's insistence upon waking that she be allowed to go and comfort the old man, as she had been denied the task the previous day.

So it was that Vincent and Corrine took both girls as well as Nanny Lawson into the living room to explain the tragedy.

Upon first hearing the news, Emily refused to believe it, and tried to break free from the room to go and see for herself. Vincent blocked her path and on haunches did his best to convince his youngest daughter of her friend's demise.

Eventually, when she could see from her father's eyes that he was in fact telling her the truth and not playing some cruel game with her, the little girl ran into her nanny's arms and began to sob uncontrollably.

She had been like that for the rest of the morning, even refusing breakfast.

Stella too was clearly upset by the death of the old man but being so much older she was able to keep her emotions far more intact. Both she and Corrine tried on multiple occasions to coax Emily to take comfort in their arms so as to allow Nanny Lawson the chance to eat breakfast, but little Emily was having none of it.

Now that Vincent had seen the removal of his old retainer for himself, he ventured back into the living room.

As he entered the living room, Vincent was pleasantly surprised to see that his youngest daughter had, at last, stopped crying. It was only when Corrine placed her index finger over her lips that he realised the reason for it was because she had fallen asleep in her nanny's arms.

Vincent tiptoed over and smiled down at Nanny Lawson

whose magic touch had once again done the trick when no other remedy worked.

Leaning down, he gently stroked Emily's hair.

He could see from the strained expression on the nanny's face that his daughter had fallen asleep on her at an odd angle, leaning most of her weight on the nanny's arm. He appreciated that, given the present circumstances, the poor woman was doubtless afraid to try and retract her arm from underneath the girl for fear of stirring her from her crying-induced slumber.

As carefully as he was able, Vincent bent down and managed to slip an arm underneath Emily's back. He then placed his other one under her knees and lifted her gently off Margaret, just long enough for the grateful nanny to slide off the couch.

Vincent then placed his youngest daughter's sleeping form gently back on the sofa allowing her head to rest on the edge of the nearest cushion.

The girl stirred, and moaned, softly, before turning over and pulling her knees up towards her chest.

Everyone held their breath for a moment until they were sure that the little girl had resumed her sleep.

Margaret stood over the little girl, rubbing the numbness out of her arm.

"You'd better go to the kitchen and have Mrs Bales fix you some breakfast," Vincent whispered. "Corrine and Stella can look after her in the meantime."

The nanny thanked him and left the room, ensuring that she opened and closed the door as quietly as possible.

Vincent walked over to Corrine and bend down to whisper in her ear. "I need to go out for a little while," he informed her. "Trouble with one of the farmers. I'll try not to be long."

Corrine looked concerned. "Can't someone else deal with it?" she enquired. "I know Emily will be comforted by your presence when she wakes."

Vincent smiled. "If there was any other way I would leave it, but it requires my immediate attention. I'll try to clear things up as soon as I can," he assured her.

He kissed Corrine on the forehead and placed a comforting hand on Stella's head before leaving.

If there was any way he could avoid the next part of his day, Vincent would have grabbed it. But he knew his presence was necessary, and with what he now knew concerning the visitors in his cellar, he had to speak to Father James and his helpers as soon as possible.

He would have time later to fully mourn the loss of his retainer with his daughter once the present tragedy had been sorted out.

Chapter Twenty-Three

CEDRIC WAS INDEED GRATEFUL FOR THE LOAN OF A horse to make his journey. The aftereffects of his earlier run to the hall were still coursing through his body. Although it was far too early in the day by his normal standards, Cedric wished now that he had asked Vincent for a small shot of something to steady his nerves after his ordeal.

The stable lad had given him an odd sideways glance when he requested the loan of a horse but relented when Cedric assured him that the request came from the Viscount. Whilst saddling the mount the young man explained that the previous Viscount had always been very reluctant to loan one of his own horses to anyone, save for close personal friends and family.

The ride to the presbytery took no time at all on the swift horse, and upon reading the note that Vincent had sent to him, Father James quickly gathered up Mathew and his team and they all followed Cedric to Ralph's cottage.

Cedric hated to admit it, even to himself, but he felt immensely grateful to the Viscount for instructing him to fetch the priest and his crew before returning to the cottage. Had

Vincent have ordered him to go back there alone to await their arrival, Cedric was not sure how he would have responded.

The mere thought of being in such close proximity to that place so soon after what he had found there, sent shivers through his body, even now.

As it was, he managed to gallop with his head held high and his chest puffed out, with Mathew and his men at his heels.

When they arrived at the cottage, they saw Vincent's horse tethered to the nearest tree. The Viscount himself was nowhere to be seen, so Cedric surmised he had already ventured into the property to see things for himself.

Cedric remembered the eerie voice which spoke to him from behind the second bedroom door. What could he possibly say in his defence if Vincent had ventured in and discovered whoever, or whatever, lurked behind the door and confronted them?

He could always maintain that he had heard no such voice when he was there.

Whether or not he would be believed, was another matter. But he could not bear the shame of everyone thinking that he had been too scared to enter the room.

Furthermore, what if whatever it was had taken the Viscount by surprise?

Was his carcass to be discovered suspended from the ceiling, drained of blood like those of Ralph and his wife?

Desperate as he was to show his bravado, Cedric could not stop his hands shaking as he tied up his horse, so he turned his back to the others to cover his lack of fortitude.

Determined to be seen as one who is control, Cedric led the way to the door, and called to the others to 'take care' as they ventured in after him.

Much to his relief, Mathew shouted back that he and his men would enter first as they were armed.

Once inside, Cedric saw that the general disarray of the place had remained untouched. He released a pent-up breath when the Viscount emerged from Ralph's bedroom, his face ashen and his hands shaking.

When he saw the others, Vincent held up his hand. "Prepare yourselves, gentlemen," he warned. "It is not a pretty sight that greets you in there."

Without speaking, Mathew and his men entered the bedroom, leaving the priest, Vincent, and Cedric in the main room.

Vincent straightened an upturned chair and slumped down on it, taking in a deep breath.

Father James, obviously prepared for such an occurrence, removed a flask from his inner pocket and handed it to him. Vincent received it gratefully and took a long swallow before handing it back.

The three men all looked up when Mathew re-entered the room.

He looked directly at Father James and shook his head, slowly.

The priest nodded his understanding and made his way into the bedroom to perform the last rites over the bodies. He waited inside the door as Mathew's men cut the ropes and slowly lowered the farmer and his wife back down to earth.

For the moment, they placed the corpses on the bed to allow them some dignity.

As father James began to recite the prayers of the dead, the men all bowed their heads in solemn respect for the ritual.

Outside the room, Cedric watched uncomfortably as Mathew discovered the second bedroom that he had refused to enter earlier that morning.

Certainly, there was no evidence of anyone lying in wait inside it at present. No terrifying voice beckoning them to enter. But even so, Cedric could not help but experience the fear of trepidation that was building up inside him.

Mathew clearly had no fear when it came to such an investigation and strode towards the closed door without hesitation.

Cedric decided to accompany him, but at the last moment, Cedric's nerves took over, but he still felt compelled to speak. "Shouldn't you wait until the rest of your men are ready before entering in there?" he offered helpfully.

Mathew stopped at the door and turned back. "They'll be a while," he answered. "How about you covering my back, just in case?"

Before Cedric had a chance to answer, Vincent shot up to his feet. "We both will," he announced, drawing his sword, and holding it in readiness.

Mathew took out his own blade and, leading the way, he opened the door and let it swing inwards.

From their vantage point, the room appeared to be empty.

As all three men ventured inside, Cedric let loose a huge sigh of relief from behind the other two, hoping that it escaped their attention.

The room held a bed, a wardrobe, and a small night table with drawers. There were thick drapes on the windows which obscured the sunlight giving the room a faint, dull glow.

The three men waited for a couple of minutes without moving.

Cedric suspected it was so that Mathew could listen intently for any signs of movement from within the room.

There appeared to be none, so Mathew walked over to the bed. He turned back to the two men behind him and placed his index finger across his lips, indicating that Vincent and Cedric should stay quiet.

Dropping to his knees, Mathew dropped forward onto his forearms and swept his blade under the bed in a large arc. When there was still no sign of movement, He ripped off the covers which partially obscured his view and made another search of the space underneath.

Once he was satisfied that the coast was clear, he stood back up, but still kept his blade at hand.

Cautiously, he strode over to the wardrobe. Once there, he indicated for the other two men to take up positions on either side, so as to block the path of anyone who might be hiding inside, thus preventing them from fleeing.

It was now that Cedric could feel his legs starting to buckle.

It occurred to him that the owner of the voice he had heard earlier may not have skedaddled as he had first presumed. In which case the obvious place for them to be hiding would be in the large wardrobe.

He did not wish to question the wisdom of Mathew's plan to check under the bed first, but it seemed to him that someone lying in wait, waiting to pounce on them, would find he task pretty awkward stuck on their belly under a bed. For one thing they would hardly be able to lunge out from a prone position.

But standing in a wardrobe, weapon in hand, now that was quite a different matter.

Cedric considered his position. Mathew had stationed himself directly in the line of fire should an assailant launch themselves from within. If they somehow managed to slip passed him, Vincent was the next in line, his sword drawn in anticipation.

Which just left Cedric with his walking cane as his only line of defence.

What worried him most at this stage was the prospect of him trying to fend off an attacker who had already managed to defeat two skilled and experienced armed men, with nothing more than a shaft of polished wood.

He decided the brass handle was going to be his best chance, so he slipped his hand down the shaft so that he could hold it more like a club.

He saw Mathew nod towards them, and Vincent replied straight away in like manner.

Cedric held tightly onto his cane as Mathew yanked open the door.

Nothing happened. Mathew glanced inside and began moving aside clothes and spare bedding with his blade. Now that the wardrobe door was open it was obvious to Cedric tha there was not as much hiding room inside as he first suspected.

Either way, it was a relief that the owner of that maniacal laughter had obviously fled the scene.

Vincent too heaved a sigh of relief at the sight of the vacant wardrobe, which made Cedric feel he was not alone in his concerns for safety.

The Viscount glanced around the room as if ensuring that there were no more unchecked corners in which an intruder might hide.

Once satisfied, he announced, "We could do with more light in here."

As the closes to the window, Cedric strode over and grabbed the thick material of the curtains and pulled them to one side to let in the daylight.

As he moved the cloth, the twisted, grinning face of Toby stared right back at him!

Before he even had the chance to scream out, Toby launched himself forward, sending Cedric crashing back onto the floor. As he hit the solid wood, Cedric felt the wind being knocked from him, and before he was able to attempt a breath, Toby was upon him, pinning his arms by his side and leaning over his face, his wide frenetic eyes baring down on him.

Cedric managed to turn his head slightly to one side as a droplet of saliva slipped through Toby's exposed teeth, splashing against his neck.

From a sideways glance, Cedric could just make out the elongated pointed teeth which protruded from underneath his assailant's upper lip.

Toby appeared totally oblivious to the fact that there were

two other armed men also in the room, such was his focus on his prey. Opening his mouth as wide as possible, Toby released his fangs and lowered his head ready to sink them into Cedric's exposed neck.

From behind, Mathew grabbed Toby by his collar and dragged him off the helpless Cedric, throwing his backwards against the side of the wardrobe.

As big and strong as he was, the impact of Mathew's attack seemed to have little effect on Toby who, although taken by surprise, appeared to be completely unhurt by his collision with his wardrobe.

Instead, the farmer's boy merely smiled up at Mathew as he regained his feet.

Vincent took advantage in the moment and pulled Cedric free, helping him up once they were a safe distance away.

Mathew and Toby rounded off at each other. Although he was armed and as such the one with an advantage, Toby seemed unconcerned by the long blade in Mathew's fist.

In the blink of an eye, Toby launched himself a Mathew and managed to knock the big man clean off his feet, sending him tumbling over the bed. As he fell his knife flew out of his grasp and landed with a *clunk* on the floor on the other side of the room.

Toby released a guttural growl which sounded as if it belonged more to a rabid animal than a man. But looking at his former employee, Vincent could not help but wonder if this creature before him was in fact still human.

Seeing Mathew's predicament, Vincent raised his sword until it stood level with Toby's chest. "That's enough!" he demanded. "Stay where you are."

Toby leaned his head slightly to one side, like a dog trying to understand its master's command.

Mathew lifted himself half onto the side of the bed, evidently still feeling the aftereffects of his fall. "Don't," he cried out, looking at Vincent. "Call the others."

In spite of the weapon aimed at his chest, Toby began to advance on Vincent. His eyes eager and bright as if he were about to tuck into a succulent steak.

Vincent took a step back, unable to fathom how someone could not be afraid of a sword held a such close quarters. It was almost as if Toby was challenging him to strike.

"Help, help, someone please help us." It was Cedric who called out, realising the enormity of their situation. If Mathew was no match for Toby, and Vincent's sword did not intimidate him, what chance would Cedric have once the other two had been vanquished.

The sound of footfalls echoed from the next room as the rest of Mathew's crew responded to Cedric's cry.

The sound seemed to resonate with Toby who glanced up in the direction of the open doorway for a moment, before returning his gaze to Vincent. He hissed loudly at his former master, baring both rows of teeth, then turned on the spot and leaped towards the closed window, crashing through the glass and wooden frame, landing outside on the wooden decking.

As Mathew's team bundled through the door of the bedroom, Vincent saw Toby racing towards the woods, his head bowed and his hands covering his face as if he could not bear for sunlight to touch it.

Chapter Twenty-Four

AS MATHEW, VINCENT AND CEDRIC RECOVERED FROM their ordeal, Mathew's men ran out into the woods, looking for Toby.

Father James stayed back as well to administer what help he could to the victims of Toby's rage. He helped Mathew ono the bed so that he could catch his breath, having had it knocked out of him as a result of his fall.

Vincent assisted Cedric to a chair. The groundskeeper was still visibly shaken from his encounter with Toby, and by now he had lost all pretence of projecting a brave front.

The viscount offered the trembling man a snort from his flask, which he accepted gratefully. Cedric took a long swig before handing it back to his master. After which, the groundskeeper began coughing and spluttering from the burning liquid. He held up a hand to ensure Vincent that he was alright, having seen the sudden look of concern on his face.

Vincent offered his flask around the room, and Mathew also took a long slug, but unlike Cedric he was used to the taste of strong liquor, so there was no such reaction from him once he had swallowed.

Father James refused, politely.

Vincent drained what was left in his flask before replacing it inside his jacket pocket.

Of the four men present, neither the viscount nor his staff member had ever experienced anything the lie of what they had witnessed in that room, minutes earlier. As the shock and realisation of what they had seen set in, Father James could tell that he would have more questions to answer before the morning was over.

Sure enough, almost as if he had heard his thoughts expressed out loud, Vincent glanced over at the priest. "What in name of the almighty was that?" he asked, nodding towards the broken window Toby had thrown himself through, moments before.

Father James shook his head, wearily. "Alas your lordship," he replied solemnly, "that is what becomes of someone who has been infected by his horrendous curse which has come upon us."

Vincent did his best to absorb the response, but his mind was reeling. "Are you telling me that everyone infected acts in such a manner?"

This time Mathew answered. "Aye, that's so. Once bitten they develop the strength of ten men, an' their thirst for human blood becomes almost insatiable. They're no longer livin' so they don't care what 'appens to them in their quest for sustenance."

"Sustenance! You mean they are craving human blood as if it were food and drink for them? What is all this nonsense?" It was Cedric who interrupted just as his master was about to speak. But for once, he did not seem aware of his transgression. He made to stand but, his legs gave way beneath him before he could even reach halfway.

Vincent helped him back down and patted his shoulder. "Calm yourself, Cedric, it's over for now."

Cedric turned and gave a weak smile. He was clearly still a wreck and Vincent wished that he had not finished off his flask before offering it to his employee for another shot.

Mathew did not seem the slightest bit deterred by Cedric's outburst. "It's better he knows what to expect, ow that he's witnessed it fer himself," he continued, looking at Vincent. "There's no point trying to keep this quiet anymore, there's too many of 'em getting' infected too fast. We need to form a brute squad to go out an' deal with 'em all."

The moment he spoke, Vincent could see a scowl of disapproval descend over Father

James. The priest rubbed his hand over his face and swallowed, hard. It was clear to Vincent that he wanted to speak but was evidently having trouble formulating his words.

"I suspect Father James does not totally agree with your recommendation," offered

Vincent, indicating towards the troubled cleric.

Mathew turned to look at him, clearly baffled by the viscount's comment.

But upon seeing the priest's expression, he knew right away that Vincent had called it correctly. "You can't be serious?" Mathew asked, raising his voice louder than he intended. "After all that's gone on here so far, and now with the disease spreading, an' more people discovering the truth," he pointed towards Cedric, "you must agree to inform the archdiocese that we need more support."

Father James signalled for Mathew to calm down. He knew how passionate the man was concerning his work, but screaming the odds in front of Vincent, and especially someone who had, until now, not been in their confidence, still seemed to him completely unnecessary.

"I will write to the archbishop directly," the priest assured him. "But you know full well that I cannot authorise any change to the present arrangement without receiving word from his first."

Mathew shrugged and grunted to himself. He knew that what Father James said was true, and it was in neither of their interests to go against the rule. Even so, he hoped that the priest would properly emphasize the immediacy of the situation and not try to sugar-coat it as he had been known to do in the past.

This infection was not just going to slip away on its own.

During his career Mathew had had come across several priests who seemed unwilling, or incapable, to accept the situation which had descended upon their congregation, regardless of the letter from the archbishop Mathew brought with him by way of introduction.

But that attitude usually turned once the priest had witnessed one of the un-dead coming back to life, for themselves. Then they suddenly grew grateful for having Mathew and his crew in their province to protect them and rid them of these terrible creatures, and suddenly, nothing was too much trouble.

The four men sat in silence for a while, awaiting the return of Mathew's crew.

For his part, Mathew had wished he had managed to chase after them, but Toby's attack had taken him by surprise and left him gasping for breath. Not a situation he could afford to allow to repeat itself. If it had not been for the timely intervention of his men, Mathew knew that he might well have succumbed to Toby's onslaught.

He made a mental note to keep his wits about him and never to be taken by surprise like that again.

After a while, Father James spoke up. "I'll have to send word to Colin Sedgwick to come and collect the bodies from the next room. The ladies from my parish will take every care in washing and dressing hem. I suggest we hold the funeral as soon as reasonably possible." He looked over to Mathew. "Do you think they will need dealing with when we bury them? They seem perfectly fine to me."

Mathew sighed. "I agree, I think they're out of danger now, but you know only too well we owe it to the rest of the community not to take any chances."

Father James nodded, dejectedly. "I suppose you're right."

"I'm afraid Sedgwick is probably still engaged in the task I gave him this morning," Vincent informed the priest. "I'm afraid we had a death at Mandrake last night, and I called him to collect the body to prepare for his funeral."

Mathew suddenly looked concerned. "Another death," he called out, rising from the bed. "What, like those lying in there?" He thumbed over his shoulder towards the bedroom where the bodies of Ralph and his wife now lay on their bed, having been cut down by Mathew's lads, and covered over at the priest's insistence.

Vincent rolled his eyes. "Calm down man," he instructed. "My elderly manservant passed away in his sleep. Here was nothing dramatic about it. I was with him when he passed."

Mathew eyed Vincent, suspiciously. What reason he might have for trying to protect his employee, Mathew could not fathom, but he had come across such an odd occurrence in the past, so he did not believe in taking chances.

"We'll still have to inspect him before burying him," he informed Vincent.

"You can inspect him at your leisure," Vincent replied, "but he was a loyal and faithful servant for many years in my household, so you will not desecrate his remains in any way, shape, or form. I trust I make myself clear?"

Mathew did not look at all convinced and opened his mouth to respond but was cut off by Father James who held up his hand and indicated for Mathew to calm down.

"As a precaution, it will be best if we inspect your manservant's remains, just to be sure," the priest said, keeping his voice calm so as not to antagonise the situation. "But I am confident from what you are telling us that it will only be a matter of formality."

This appeared to have the desired effect on both Vincent and Mathew, as both men seemed to visibly relax.

Just then, they heard the sound of Mathew's crew arriving back at the cottage.

As the first of the men entered the bedroom he glanced at Mathew and shook his head.

"No sign at all?" asked Mathew, looking at each man as they walked in.

"Nothing," admitted the man in the lead. "It was as if the damn thing vanished amongst the trees."

The others looked as disappointed as their colleague by the revelation.

"Well, you must get back out there and look some more," Cedric cried, excitedly, jumping up from his chair before Vincent could calm him down. "We can't have someone like that roaming the countryside, we'll all get murdered in our beds."

The four crew members exchanged glances and grinned, broadly.

"If yer think it's that easy," offered Mathew, "yer welcome to go out and look for yerself. Don't let us stand in your way."

Cedric's cheeks turned puce with rage. Striding across the room he planted himself in front of Mathew. "Now see here," he shouted, pointing an aggressive finger down at his target. "You chaps are supposed to be the experts here, so just you get out and do the job you're paid for."

Mathew slowly rose to his feet, standing head and shoulders above Cedric.

Without realising it, the games keeper took an unsteady step back, the anger in him dissipating as quickly as it had risen.

Father James stood up with his back to Mathew and put his hand on Cedric's shoulder. "I realise this is all very new and naturally frightening for you, it was for me when I first received news about Mathew and his team arriving. But allow me to assure you that there's no one alive more experienced at dealing with this abomination than these five men here. We would all do well to listen to their instructions and heed their advice."

Cedric glanced from the priest towards Mathew.

The big man still had a menacing look on his face which he was not trying to hide.

Cedric gulped. "My apologies," he muttered. "I didn't mean any disrespect."

His apology had the desired effect, and Mathew nodded his acceptance.

"So, what's the plan as thing stands?" asked Vincent.

"Well, first and foremost we need to arrange for Mr Sedgwick to collect the two bodies from next door," answered Father James, "then we must arrange their burial as soon as possible. We will of course carry out our procedure upon them in private as there are no living relatives that we know of."

Vincent moved forward and clapped his hand on Cedric's shoulder, making the nervy man jump, slightly. "Will you do me the favour of riding out and bringing Sedgwick back here to collect the bodies? Stay with him until he has unloaded them for washing and shrouding."

Cedric turned his face ashen. "But my lord, what if when we return that thing is waiting here for us?"

"I'll leave two of my men here until you get back," promised Mathew. "You'll be fine."

Cedric visibly relaxed and thanked Mathew for his consideration.

As Cedric set off on his task, Mathew gathered his men together to arrange who was to stay behind.

Seizing the moment, Vincent asked Father James for a quiet word, out of earshot from the others.

Chapter Twenty-Five

FATHER JAMES FOLLOWED VINCENT OUTSIDE THE cottage so that they could speak in private. The priest could tell from the expression on the viscount's face that he had something concerning him on his mind, and he suspected it had something to do with that morning's events.

Being the local laird Father James appreciated that Vincent felt responsible for the welfare of his flock, much in the same way that he himself did.

However, there was no way he could have anticipated the information he was about to receive.

Vincent waited for Cedric to gallop away before he began to speak. "There's something important I need to tell you," he began earnestly, "but for now at least I want you to give me your word as a man of God that you will not disclose anything I say until I give you the okay."

Father James looked at him, unable to disguise the concern on his own face.

As a priest he had been privy to many confessions which had remained between him and God. But they were not in the confessional now and Father James felt obliged to remind

Vincent of that fact. "My son, are you sure this is the proper way of discussing such a mater? Perhaps we should reconvene at the church where I can hear your confession in private?"

Vincent shook his head. "It's nothing like that," he informed him. "But I have to tell someone now because I am in need of guidance."

Still perplexed, Father James nodded his understanding.

"Before Jasper died, he told me a story which I find hard to believe, yet I cannot dispel it under the present circumstances. He told me that my father, scared by the prospect of his own mortality, had invited someone over from abroad who claimed to have discovered a way of extending human life indefinitely."

"My son!" the priest exclaimed, clearly shocked by what he was hearing. "Only the good lord can prolong life or shorten it as he sees fit. It is not for mere mortals such as us to…"

"I realise that," said Vincent, cutting him off in mid flow, "but from the sound of it my father had grown desperate due to his failing health. Anyway, that's not the point. This 'Healer' for want of a better word, brought with him six disciples who were all given shelter by my father somewhere beneath Mandrake. Jasper said he saw them operate on my poor father by sinking their teeth into him and draining his blood."

Now Father James suddenly realised what Vincent was trying to tell him. His eyes widened in shock and terror as he slapped his hand over his mouth, afraid for a moment that he might call out and bring Mathew and his crew running.

Vincent held up his hand. "I know, I know," he assured him. "I was naturally taken aback when I first heard the tale. But the truth is that Jasper was adamant, and I've no reason to believe him capable of any untruth. He had always been loyal to my father, and I could see in his eyes how much it pained him to tell the story, even to me."

The priest held out a shaky hand. "But if what you are saying is true, then…" This time he broke off on his own, his mind reeling at the new information. He had never been told how the infection arrived in their corner of the world, or indeed who might be responsible for unleashing it on them.

The old viscount was the last person he would have suspected.

Vincent waited for the for a moment to allow the information to fully set in before continuing. "Anyway, the reason I needed to speak to you is because Jasper never had a chance to show me where these creatures are hiding out before he died."

Father James frowned. "But didn't you just say that they were concealed somewhere under Mandrake Hall?"

"Yes, but according to Jasper, my father arranged for a secret room to be built in the catacombs beneath the cellar, and poor Jasper passed away before he had a chance to show me how to gain access to it."

Father James was still perplexed. "If you know the entrance is somewhere under your cellar, then surely it will not take long to locate it?"

"I've been trying to find it all morning," explained Vincent. "I've checked behind each barrel and pushed against every wall, nothing gives any indication as to where it might be."

"Then we need help," the priest reasoned. "I'll call Mathew and his men and together we can all search until we find it."

Vincent winced at the suggestion. "I know that would be the most obvious suggestion, but the fact is I really don't want my family to know what's going on. They've only just arrived at Mandrake and so to send them away on some pretext would seem highly suspicious. Not to mention the loss of Jasper has hit my youngest girl extremely hard, she was very fond of the old man, so I cannot in all good conscious send her away before his funeral. She would be desolate."

"But you do realise that to leave them in situ with those… things under the house, puts them directly in the path of mortal danger? What if they escaped and ran amok killing everyone in the house, what then?"

"I know, I have thought about little else all morning, but from what Jasper told me my father arranged for an escape route to be built leading to the outside of the hall so that they could come and go without disturbing the household. Therefore, I was thinking that perhaps we could set some sort of trap in the grounds to catch them when they emerge. That way my household would remain unaware of my father's involvement in all his, and we can deal with those devils discreetly."

Father James scratched his head. He understood Vincent's reasoning behind the suggestion, and for that he could not blame him. It was only natural that he would wish to protect his father's good name and reputation, regardless of whether or not he deserved such consideration considering the circumstances.

Although the priest's knowledge of these creatures was fairly minimal, Mathew had already explained to him that during the daylight hours they were considerably weaker than at night, which made the option of seeking them out sooner rather than later far more attractive.

However, if as Vincent claimed he had no idea how to reach them through the cellar, it made perfect sense to try and trap them when they emerged for their nightly scavenge.

He hated the fact that Vincent had trusted him with such information alone.

The priest knew that wiser counsel needed to be sought before such a decision was made. But if the viscount insisted on secrecy it put Father James in a very awkward situation.

"We must confer with Mathew," he insisted. "He knows far more about these creature's habits than anyone else in the vicinity, if not in the entire country. He's been trained for such events by the church, his entire life. We cannot launch an expedition to capture them without his input, you must see that?"

Vincent thought for a moment. The priest's words made

perfect sense, even if he was loathed to admit it. "Can I at least rely on their discretion not to reveal to the world how these things came to be?"

"They will have to make a full report to the archbishop, but I see no reason why anyone else outside the church needs to know," the priest assured him.

"Can you guarantee that?"

Father James shook his head, solemnly. "No, I cannot guarantee it, but what I can do is write to the archbishop myself and request that it be so. He will, I'm sure, take my recommendation into account before any further decisions are made. It is in no one's interest to publicise these events and cause mass panic."

The priest's words brought Vincent some comfort at least. It made perfect sense that the church would not want to advertise the fact that such a menace existed unbound. At least, not until they had complete control of the situation, and who knew how many more of these monsters lurked in the shadows of towns and cities throughout the country, if not, the world.

Vincent bit his lower lip and thought, then he put his hand on Father James' shoulder and looked him directly in the eyes. "Alright, I agree with what you're saying in principle, so here's what I suggest by way of a compromise. Say nothing for today and I will continue to try and locate the secret entrance to the catacombs. You arrange Jasper's funeral for tomorrow, that way if needs be I can get my family away the day after. Once the funeral is over, we can discuss what the next step should be, agreed?"

Father James listened but could not disguise his unease. "That still leaves these creatures tonight to venture out and spread their disease. You don't expect them to remain dormant just because you have not found their lair?"

"No, but I need time, just a little. Surely you can afford me this one small courtesy out of respect for my father and our position."

Just then, they heard the sound of Mathew and two of his men exiting the bedroom they had been talking in.

Vincent shot Father James a wide-eyed glance as if trying to compel him to accept the conditions he had laid down, without question.

He could see that the priest was still reluctant, but before turning to greet Mathew, Father James offered Vincent an almost imperceptible nod of his head.

Unaware of what had been taking place while he was inside the cottage, Mathew made his report to Father James. "I'm leaving Tom and Ned here to wait for the two men with the cart to arrive. I think it's best that we despatch these two bodies without delay, just in case."

Father James turned back towards Vincent, but he had already turned his back on him and was striding towards his horse.

The priest watched him mount his steed and nod towards the men before galloping off, back towards the hall.

It was obvious that Vincent desired no more to be discussed on the matter, and now that he had left, Father James felt reluctant to betray his wishes, even though he could not disguise the unease he felt with the status quo.

He turned back to Mathew. "What do you think our next step should be?" he asked, innocently.

"Can you think of anywhere that Toby might be hiding out?" Mathew asked. "Until we track 'im down no one is safe."

Father James blushed. "I've only ever known him to live here with his parents. I can't think of anywhere else he might consider a sanctuary, certainly not in his present state."

Mathew nodded. "He'll probably try and lie low somewhere until it turns dark, so it'll be better all round if we can catch him while he is at his weakest."

"He seemed pretty strong in there," Father James noted, indicating towards the cottage.

"True," Mathew agreed, "but during daytime is our best chance to subdue him, so while Ned and Tom wait 'ere, Stuart, Gregory and I will carry on the search. You travel back with the lads after the bodies have been collected. I don't want you being left alone, not while this lunatic is on the loose."

Father James thanked him for his concern. In truth he was glad of the suggestion. He knew that he would be no match for Toby if he should see him travelling along the road alone, daylight or not.

Chapter Twenty-Six

COLIN SEDGWICK CRACKED HIS WHIP ABOVE THE HEAD of his horse to hurry it along. He had only just delivered poor Jasper's body to the church hall for the ladies to prepare him for burial when Cedric arrived on horseback summoning him to Ralph's cottage.

Although he should have been glad of the work, since the incident in the graveyard with Mary Grant's corpse, he had grown wary of transporting dead bodies and wished he could afford to turn the work down.

At least with Jasper he knew that the old man had passed away due to natural causes, but from what Cedric had told him en route, there was nothing natural about the way Ralph and his wife had expired.

Worse still was the story the groundkeeper had relayed about Ralph's son Toby, and how he was most likely the murderer of his own parents. Cedric's description of the farmhand and the way he had attacked him back at the cottage, reminded Colin of the savage display the young Grant girl had displayed after rising from her coffin to attack Father James' men as they were about to bury her.

He remembered telling Toby about it in the pub only a couple of days earlier, and now here he was attending to Toby's parents after such a violent death.

Just like Cedric, Colin had been reluctant to go to the cottage for fear that Toby-or what had become of him-might be waiting to launch another attack. But Colin assured him that there would be a least two stout men from the priest's entourage waiting to receive them and assist them with the loading of the two bodies.

Even so, Cedric did not wish to take any chances of Toby rushing at them from out of the woods, so he kept his horse's pace brisk all the way to the cottage.

Both men heaved an audible sigh of relief when they came around the final bend and saw Father James and Tom and Ned waiting for them.

The four men loaded the tow corpses onto the cart, and Colin covered the with a large sheet, weighing it down at all four corners.

Once the task was complete, Father James thanked the men and asked Colin to take the bodies back to the church hall for burial preparation.

"As there is no next of kin," the priest began, "well, except for their son," he continued, his cheeks flushed, "I will have to arrange their burial with the church council when we next meet."

"Father," Tom broke in, "under the circumstances I think Mathew will want them to be taken care of today. We can't really afford to waste any time, just in case."

Father James knew that the man was right. Under such unusual circumstances proper procedure would have to take a back seat. He was sure that once the details were revealed the church council would agree to covering the charge of the funeral, he just did not like to take such matters for granted.

As it was, if the council did raise any objections Father James was sure that he could rely on the viscount moral, and possibly financial, support.

"Yes, you are quite correct," he agreed. "Colin, please alert the ladies at the church hall to expedite matters concerning Ralph and Enid. Jasper is to be buried tomorrow at the viscount's request, so, if necessary, they can complete his preparations later on today, and focus on these two good people as a priority."

Colin nodded his understanding.

"Will you return with us Cedric?"

"No thank you father, I've left the viscount's horse back at Colin's yard, so I'll return with him to fetch it."

With that, Colin and Cedric climbed back on board the cart and headed back towards the church hall.

"Did Mathew inform you gentlemen that he wished you to remain with me for the time being?" he asked Tom and Ned.

They both nodded. "Yes, Father," replied Ned. "'e told us 'e didn't want you left alone while that mad creature is on the loose. We won't let 'im anywhere near you, you can count on that."

Father James felt a flood of relief wash over him. Although his faith was strong and he knew that once within his own church the only protection he needed was that supplied by God himself, he had to admit he felt better in the knowledge that the two men would remain there with him. At least until Toby had been caught.

His knowledge of the six other creatures hiding out somewhere at Mandrake Hall did little to ease his nerves, but he took comfort in the fact that if they did venture out after dark that night, he would have the additional protection of Mathew and his other two men to look forward to.

On their journey back to the church, Father James wrestled with his decision to keep the viscount's secret to himself for the time being. There were so many permutations as to what might happen if he was unable to track them down during the daytime. Even then, judging by the strength and stamina which Toby displayed earlier, the priest could not help but worry that the viscount would be no match for six of them, alone.

It made far more sense to him for all of them to converge on the hall and start the search together. If Mathew and his crew could locate and despatch the six creatures who had killed Vincent's father, then the vast majority of the contamination which gripped the countryside would be eliminated.

He cursed himself for not standing up to the viscount and insisting that they tell Mathew all and let him decide what the best course of action would be.

Now that Mathew's men had been split up it could take hours before he returned to the presbytery, and by then it would be too late to launch a thorough search of Mandrake Hall, with or without Vincent's permission.

For one thing, there would be the burials of Ralph and his wife to attend to, which would require all of Mathew's team in situ. After which, it would be too late to attend to the hall. Especially as the creatures might already be on the prowl by then.

It was going to make for a very tentative afternoon, but the priest knew that all he could do was wait and pray that Vincent discovered the creature's lair and managed to either dispose of them or get word to Mathew so that his team could assist with the task.

Either way, it was going to be a long day.

———

When Vincent reached Mandrake Hall, he was disappointed to hear that his youngest daughter had been returned to bed on the suggestion of Nanny Margaret because throughout the morning she refused to eat a thing and had not stopped crying.

Vincent's first instinct was to run upstairs and see if he could not cajole the young girl into rejoining the rest of the family, but Corinne convinced him that Emily needed time to adjust to the shock of Jasper's demise and suggested that the extra sleep might help.

"You have a bigger fish to fry, Papa," Stella chimed in.

For a moment, Vincent was taken by shock. How could his daughter possibly know of his intention to search the cellars to try and find the catacombs?

He looked at her, perplexed.

"Emily is very cross with you for not allowing her to see Jasper last night," she explained. "She is of the belief that had she managed to spend some time with him, he would not have died because she would not have permitted it."

Vincent relaxed, visibly, hopping that his initial anxiety had somehow gone unnoticed. "I can see I will have a lot of making up to do later this evening," he confessed.

"I'm sure she will come round soon enough," offered Corinne. "Especially when she comes down and finds you here with your arms open wide."

"Ah, yes, speaking of which, I have a little business to attend to and I cannot be disturbed whilst I conduct it. It should hope-fully not take too long, but if Emily surfaces before I do, assure her that I will be along soon."

"You'll join us for luncheon though?" Corinne asked. "I'm hoping little Emily will be awake for that. Poor thing hasn't had a bite all morning."

Vincent smiled. "I can't guarantee it at this precise moment, it really depends on how much progress I make by then, still, the sooner I start the more chance that I'll finish in good time."

"Oh, Vincent," Corinne protested.

He held up his hand as if to prevent any further discussion. "I know, I know, but needs must, and this is vital work I need to complete. I'll be as quick as I can," he promised.

Closing the door behind him, Vincent summoned Clive to his study. As the oldest servant, now that poor Jasper had died, Vincent had him in mind to take over his position.

It was true that he did not know him as well as he had done Jasper, but he had been with the family for many years now, and to his knowledge his father had never had any cause to reprimand him.

There was a knock at the door and Vincent ushered Clive in.

Once they were in private, Vincent addressed the servant directly. "Clive, I know you've been with the family for many years now, how long as it been?"

"Twelve, your lordship."

"Good, and in that time, I trust you have always found your work here to be satisfactory?"

"Oh, very much so sir."

"Right. Well, there's no point in beating about the bush. With the loss of poor Jasper last night, I'm going to need a new senior butler, someone I can trust and rely upon to uphold the family name and keep all our skeletons locked away. How do you feel about taking on the added responsibility?"

"I'd be delighted your lordship," Clive seemed genuinely touched by the offer. "It would be a great honour to continue in poor Jasper's footprints."

"Good man. You have no qualms at all?"

"None that I can imagine, sir."

"Excellent," replied Vincent, unable to keep the relief out of his tone. "Well then, circumstances have forced my hand somewhat, and I am going to have to trust you with some information which cannot go any further, do you understand?"

Clive rose from his chair. "You can trust me, your lordship," Clive assured him.

"Well, let's hope you feel the same way after I've told you what I need you to do for me. But make no mistake," Vincent emphasised, "if anything I tell you leaves this room, I'll have you out of my house within the hour, without a reference."

Vincent could see the horror displayed on the servant's face. He suspected that, eager as he was to accept his new position, the man's mind was probably reeling now with thoughts of what he had signed up to.

Reluctant as he was to divulge the full enormity of the situation to his manservant, Vincent was acutely aware of how few his options were. Clive seemed to all intents and purposes to be a loyal and faithful retainer, and the viscount could not deny that he was too unnerved by everything that was happening to undertake the search for the catacombs alone.

In hindsight, he wished that he had asked Mathew for the loan of one of his men. But to do so would be to reveal the full extent of his family's involvement in this awful business, and that was something Vincent was not prepared to allow.

Not yet anyway.

"Sit down, Hobson," he said, indicating towards the chair Clive had just risen from. "Let me explain the situation as it stands, and hopefully you will not regret your decision."

Chapter Twenty-Seven

THE SEARCH FOR TOBY WATKINS HAD PROVED fruitless. Mathew and his men returned to the presbytery just as dusk was settling in to help with the preparations for Ralph and Enid's funeral.

Other than a short stop off at the Wild Boar for lunch, the three men had searched the woods relentlessly, looking inside every outbuilding, barn and deserted shed they came across.

Mathew knew that Toby could not be the only bloodsucker in the vicinity. For one thing, someone must have turned him, and from what he had learnt about the farmworker the incident must have only taken place in the last day, or so.

Therefore, it stood to reason that he was being hidden by another vampire, or possibly even a nest of them. Usually in such circumstances Mathew and his crew were quick to suss out the creature's lair, as someone in town was always suspected by the locals, usually with good reason. But here no one specific stood out from the crowd, and even the local gossips seemed reluctant to point the finger.

Mathew had heard about the riots caused as a result of the first killings, and the fact that there had been several mob executions without proper proof, so much so that the militia were called in to quell the uprising, so it stood to reason that the locals now might still be reluctant to start pointing the finger again.

To that end, Mathew could not blame them.

The ladies who worked for Father James had done their work diligently, and both Ralph and Enid had been washed and shrouded for their burial.

As rumour of their demise spread throughout the town, several locals had expressed a wish to attend heir funeral, which Father James had promised would take place before it grew too dark. So, it was agreed that Mathew and his men would complete their rituals over the bodies before taking the for burial, rather than wait for them to rise as the undead as in the case of young Mary Grant.

Ideally, it was always best to leave such actions until the coffin was about to be lowered into the ground, because somehow the undead instinctively knew that that signalled their time to rise. The only problem then was the risk of onlookers and mourners witnessing the staking and decapitation, and that in itself led to word being spread all over town by first light. Closely followed by mass panic setting in.

That was something that everyone from the archbishop down wanted to avoid at all costs.

Mathew and his men, along with Father James, gathered in the church hall where the bodies had been left in state.

The worst part for Father James at this juncture was that without waiting to see if the bodies might come back to life before being buried, there was no way of knowing if they actually were potential vampires or were indeed just dead bodies. This meant allowing Mathew's men to stake and decapitate two possibly innocent Christians who deserved the dignity of a proper funeral.

But, as much as he hated to admit it, Father James knew that there was no sense in running the risk, and if they did and the corpses suddenly rose from their graves in front of the congregation they would lose trust in his capabilities, possibly forever.

It was getting late, and Colin Sedgwick had his cart waiting outside to transport the bodies to their final resting place.

Still inside, away from prying eyes, Mathew and his men set about staking the two bodies, while Father James spoke solemn prayers for the departed over them.

Once the stakes had been hammered through far enough to allow the coffin lid to close properly, the men set about removing the heads form the corpses with practiced blows from their axes.

Once the deed was complete, Father James turned to Mathew, his face red with anger and frustration. Mathew shrugged. "We have to be careful Father, you know that. Such desecration will do them no harm in the eyes of the almighty."

Father James turned back without answering and watched as the men replaced the coffin lids and hammered them into place.

The journey to the graveyard took no longer than ten minutes, with Father James leading the way on foot, followed closely by Colin with the two coffins on his cart, and Mathew and his crew carrying their shovels in order to dig the graves.

There was a reasonably sized group of mourners gathered at the entrance to the graveyard, and Father James welcomed them and thanked them for coming out so late at night. So far, no one had complained to him about the lateness of the hour, but even so the priest had already decided to keep the service short so that the townsfolk could still arrive home at a decent time.

After all, he had already repeated many of the prayers for the dying he usually saved for the graveyard back at the church hall while Mathew and his team worked.

The night wind whipped through the trees as Father James read from his book, causing most of those gathered to shiver involuntarily under their overcoats.

As he spoke, the priest could not help but stare unblinking at the two coffins, almost as if he half expected the corpses within to burst out through the wooden lids and point an accusatory finger at him for his part in such sacrilege.

But still he managed to keep his voice still and calm, so as not to alert anyone around him of his apprehension.

Once he was done, he stood back with the others while Mathew and his men made short work of digging the grave. They had decided with Father James' agreement to dig one large whole and bury the married couple side-by-side in the ground.

By the time the last of the earth had been replaced to fill in the hole, most of the mourners had departed.

Father James had already given Colin permission to leave immediately after the coffins had been unloaded from his cart, so now only the pries and Mathew and his men remained.

They stood there in unspoken silence for a while, almost if afraid to evacuate the area for fear that the old couple might still rise up as the undead, even after being staked and decapitated, to wreak havoc on the community.

It was Mathew who eventually spoke up and suggested that they leave.

————

Just like the search for Toby, Vincent, and Clive's search of the cellar for the entrance to the catacombs had proved fruitless.

Having explained the situation to Clive earlier in the day, Vincent had been pleasantly surprised to find that his faith in his new senior retainer was well placed. Clive had heard rumours concerning the murders which taken place locally, and he confided in Vincent that he had witnessed both Jasper and Mrs Baines chastising some of the younger members of staff for discussing such matters when they ought to be working.

Clive admitted that, although Jasper would never break a

confidence, he had suspected that something odd was going on when the previous viscount arranged for all the building work to take place, without offering the job to local talent who had proved themselves worthy in the past.

The two men worked on throughout the morning and into the afternoon.

Together they scoured every inch of the wine cellar until it seemed as if between them, they had pressed and pulled every brick in their quest to find the secret panel which would reveal the entrance to the catacombs.

By evening they were both frustrated and exhausted.

Vincent dismissed Clive from his duties for the rest of the day and went upstairs to bathe and dress for dinner.

When he arrived downstairs, he was pleased to see that Emily was with everyone else in the drawing room, awaiting his presence. He had been afraid after that morning's incident that the little girl would still be tearful and refusing to eat. But from her appearance it was obvious that she had washed, dressed, and appeared far more cheerful than earlier.

"Good evening, ladies," Vincent announced as he walked over to the fire.

Before he reached his target, Emily slid off the sofa and ran into his arms. Vincent swept her up and gave her a big hug, clearly overjoyed that Stella's earlier threat had no basis.

Or so he thought.

"I am very upset with you, Papa," Emily announced, looking at him, sternly.

Vincent kissed her nose, making her wrinkle her face. "I know my darling, your sister informed me this morning, and I am very sorry for causing you such distress. I hope you appreciate that I didn't mean to upset you?"

Emily considered the apology. "I know," she said finally, "but if you'd only have allowed me to see Jasper last night, he might have felt better."

Vincent smiled. "I know he would have appreciated a visit from you, but you see, he was very tired, and he told me he was afraid that what ailed him might be infectious, and that he would never forgive himself if he passed it onto you."

Emily mulled over her father's explanation, and it seemed to make sense.

"Will he be buried in the crypt alongside grandpapa?"

"No, my love, that's for family only. Otherwise, by the time I die there'll be no room left for me, and they'll have to dump me somewhere in the grounds."

Emily threw her arms back around his neck. "No, Papa, you mustn't say such things. You're going to live forever, just like Mama, Stella, and Nanny."

Vincent winked at his wife over Emily's shoulder. "Alas my angel, we all have to go sometime. But with God's grace, not for a very long time yet."

"Have the arrangements been made for Jasper's funeral?" asked Corinne, feeling as if it was safe to broach the subject in front of Emily since the little girl had already mentioned the crypt.

"Yes," Vincent answered. "Father James is arranging everything for tomorrow."

Emily pulled back. "Will I be allowed to say goodbye, Papa?" she asked, concerned.

"Of course, you will," Vincent assured her. "We'll all be there together to say our goodbyes."

Emily smiled and gave her father another tight hug.

After a moment, Vincent lowered her back to the floor. "Right then, you little monkey, allow your poor papa to have a drink before we go into diner. He's exhausted."

"Did you manage to finish that business you were talking about earlier, Papa?" asked Stella, welcoming her younger sister back onto the sofa.

Vincent continued pouring himself a large measure of

whiskey while he answered, glad that he could keep his face turned away. "Most of it, I still have some more to attend to, but that will have to wait for the moment."

"You work far too hard, Vincent," observed Corinne. "We've barely seen you all day."

Vincent turned back and raised his glass. "I promise I'll try and make more time for you all, my dear. You'll be sick of the sight of me soon."

He shot back the tumblerful in one go, feeling the hot, stinging liquid course down his throat. As much as he needed it, Vincent was used to taking his whiskey with a threat of water, so he had to control himself to stop a fit of coughing.

As lovely as it was to be with his family for the evening, at the back of his mind he was afraid of what he was going to tell Father James in the morning.

Since he had failed to locate the catacomb there was every chance that he would not be able to prevent the priest from revealing all to Mathew, and he knew that they would demand entry to make a search for themselves.

If that happened, he would have to allow them in. Under the circumstances, the law would be on their side, regardless of his position. There was too much at stake.

Without realising it, Vincent poured himself another large glass of whiskey.

He did not notice the concerned glance from Corinne as he threw it back.

Chapter Twenty-Eight

VERA CUNNINGS ROLLED THE LAST OF THE EMPTY wooden barrels along the ground, placing it with the others ready for collection. She had worked at the Wild Boar ever since her sister Maggie had missed her footing on the ladder in their father's barn and broken her ankle.

Their family needed her wages desperately, so Vera was persuaded by her father to take over her elder sister's responsibilities until she was well enough to go back to work. Otherwise, he was afraid-quite justifiably-that Adam Spool the landlord would give the job to someone else, and Maggie would be out of work.

Vera hated the job for the most part. She was a farm-girl at heart and enjoyed working outside, even in the most inclement of weather. Even tilling the soil, something which Maggie hated, brought the younger sister an immense feeling of pride and accomplishment.

Her passions included taking care of the animals they reared, even though she knew that most would eventually be led to slaughter.

Animals were far easier to relate to than people, so far as

Vera was concerned. They never cared how she looked or whether she had bathed or washed her hair that day, and they never sneered or made snide comments behind her back, like so many townsfolk did.

Unlike her sibling, Vera had not been blessed with good looks or a desirable body. She was extremely fit from all the manual labour she undertook on the farm, but she took after her father who was large-boned and muscular, whereas Maggie was the spitting image of their mother, tiny and petite in looks and mannerisms.

Added to which, Maggie had a perkiness and a sauciness about her which Vera neither possessed nor understood. In her mind her sister had too many personalities which she seemed to switch depending on the company she was in.

Such traits did hold her in good stead as a barmaid, no doubt. For one thing she was forever being chatted-up by the punters and being bought drinks, but such behaviour often led to her being chastised by their parents, neither of which wanted a daughter with that kind of reputation.

For her part, Maggie did not seem to care, or at least claimed that she was not overly concerned by their parent's admonishments.

But Vera suspected that her elder sibling merely hid behind her blasé front.

It was Vera that was first on the scene when Maggie fell from the stable loft, and when she arrived having heard her sister's cries, she caught Toby Watkins there, hurriedly trying to re-fasten his breeches while negotiating the ladder's rungs on his way down to the fallen Maggie.

Even in her agony, Maggie pleaded with her sibling not to tell their parents what she had seen. Tony was hastily ushered out of the barn to escape over the back field before their father arrived, because Maggie knew that no innocent explanation would ever be believed.

As it was, Vera appeared more concerned for her sister's welfare, rather than her reputation, and she promised Maggie that her secret would remain safe with her.

For now, at least.

Despite the fact that Maggie had all the men in town running after her, whilst they never gave Vera so much as a sideways glance, Vera made out as if the situation never bothered her.

But now that she had been handed such an exquisite bargaining tool, she would keep it to herself, until she needed it.

With the last of the barrels in situ, Vera leaned against one of them and took in the night air. It had been a hard slog of a shift, with the inn far busier than usual. She heard from one of the regulars that there had been a funeral nearby, which accounted for the extra drinkers coming in so late. She was shocked when she heard who the funeral was for and was surprised that Toby had not come in for a comforting drink after the ceremony.

Still, she suspected that he may have been too upset for the busy inn and perhaps needed to have some time to himself.

The night was crisp and clear, without a cloud to obscure the moonlight.

Vera gazed up at the stars shimmering above her and wistfully remembered her time on the farm, watching the horizon as dusk began to settle. It was one of the things she missed the most being stuck behind the bar. She always seemed to be either changing barrels or serving customers when the sun began to wane.

She was counting the days when Maggie could take back her job and leave her to rejoin their father on the farm.

As she was about to return to the pub to collect her belongings for the journey home, Vera heard something moving about behind the inn. It sounded too large to be cat or a dog, so she tensed, ready to run back inside if whatever showed itself turned out to be unwelcome.

She waited a moment, but there was no further sound.

Vera stared off into the darkness from where the noise had originated, squinting to try and ascertain movement among the shadows.

"Hello darling."

Vera spun round, taken aback by the sudden shock of hearing a voice so close behind her when she had been unaware of anyone else being in the yard.

Such was the speed of her reaction that Vera lost her balance and primed herself for a fall she could do nothing to prevent.

But at the last second Toby managed to grab her around the waist and support her, keeping her upright.

Vera was not sure whether to be glad or annoyed by his presence. True he had just saved her from might have been a painful accident, but on the other hand if he had not crept up behind her and scared her in the first place, her accident would not have been imminent.

Toby held onto her even after she had regained her composure.

His arms were strong and comforting as he pressed her against his hard body.

Although she hated to admit it to herself, Vera found his forwardness quite exhilarating. After all, this was the first time she had been held by a man in such a manner.

"Get orf," she cried, feeling as though her modesty demanded it.

"Oh, come on now, you don't mean that," Toby sneered, keeping his grip on her torso. "I only want a little cuddle."

Vera was confused. She was wise enough to know that some men would do anything to gain a woman's affections, especially if there was a chance of it ending in a physical coupling. But he was her sister's bloke, and until this minute had never given her so much as a kind word or second glance.

Vera stopped struggling, but still kept both hands on his chest, ready to push him away. Their faces were mere inches apart and she could smell the fetid odour which emanated from his mouth.

Even so, she tried not to pull a face as she stared into his eyes.

Although Toby had a broad smile across his lips, it did not appear to reach his eyes which were wide and staring with more than just lust behind them.

"I was sorry to hear of your parents," Vera offered in an attempt to normalize the situation. "'ow come you didn't come in after the funeral with the others?"

Toby shrugged his huge shoulders, his leering smile never wavering. "Dunno, just fancied a walk on me own. But I don't want to be alone anymore, d'you fancy coming with me fer a stroll?"

Vera considered the odd request, but under the circumstances she supposed that Toby might be feeling out of sorts on such a day, which perhaps explained his strange behaviour.

"At this hour?" Vera asked, perplexed.

"Why not, it's a lovely night."

Vera shivered as a chill wind cut through, rustling the trees opposite where they were standing. "It's getting' cold, an' I've got to get home or me dad will go mad."

Toby laughed, but again Vera was unsettled by the fact that his eyes did not seem to reflect his humour. "That's easy," he replied. "You've got me to keep you warm, an' we can walk back to your place together. We'll be there in no time."

Vera considered the prospect. "What if Maggie catches us?" she suggested.

"Who cares. It's about time she knew she 'ad competition. She's 'ad it too easy all these years if yer ask me, leading blokes on then turning her back on 'em. Besides, I've always fancied you more than 'er."

Vera was still locked in his embrace, and although she did not believe what she was hearing she did begin to wonder if

Toby might be revealing his true feelings as a result of feeling vulnerable with the loss of his parents.

Against her better judgement, she closed her eyes and leaned in to kiss him.

Their mouths met, lips mashing against each other. Vera let her hands slip down Toby's body so that she could wrap them around him and pull him closer.

She could feel his protuberance pushing against her pelvis, and suddenly she decided to throw all caution to the wind. He definitely wanted her and whether it was just for now, or for ever, she found she did not care.

Vera grabbed his buttocks with both hands and pulled him against her, opening her legs wider as if to prove to him that he was welcome, and wanted.

She moaned loudly as Toby moved his mouth away from hers and kissed a trail across her cheek towards her ear. Once there, he nibbled gently on her lobe before moving down further towards her exposed neck.

Still clutched in his tight embrace Vera was unable to pull back as his fangs pieced the side of her neck.

She attempted a scream, but the sound was lost in the wind as she felt herself drift away as feelings of pleasurable desire cascaded over her, warming her to her very core as if she had just stepped into a soothing bath.

Vera felt her legs begin to buckle beneath her, but Toby still managed to hold her upright without strain.

She felt the darkness sweep across her consciousness as she fought to prolong the pleasure of his touch.

Chapter Twenty-Nine

EMILY STIRRED FROM HER SLEEP. SHE BLINKED TWICE as the shadows cast in the room from the one candle left burning on the mantlepiece came into focus.

She had always had a profound fear of the dark and what might be lurking in the shadows, so her initial reaction was to pull the covers over her head and wait for sleep to reclaim her.

Emily had been plagued with nightmares for as long as she could remember. They did not intrude on her every night, but often enough so that Nanny Lawson had continued to stay in her bedroom with her to keep an eye on her and be on hand should such night terrors descend.

This was a practice which, during her career, Nanny had ceased when her charge reached the age of five, and initially, she had done so with Emily. But when the nightmares returned with such alarming frequency it was agreed with the viscount that she would continue to remain in Emily's room until it was deemed appropriate for her to stop.

Emily turned her head to one side and located the sturdy chair which Nanny Lawson used each night as a bed and was comforted by the shadow of the woman slumped in it with her needlepoint in her lap where she had dropped it when she had dozed off.

The little girl turned her head to the right and took comfort in the slither of moonlight which shafted in through the slit in the closed curtains.

I was then that she heard it.

Albeit it faint and somewhat far away she could definitely hear the sound of someone singing. It was the most beautiful voice she had ever heard, and it took her a moment to fathom where it was coming from.

At first, she suspected that it was one of the maids preparing the house for the family.

But then, upon reflection, she reasoned that that could not be the case. For one thing if the moon was still visible through her window, it was far too early for anyone to be awake. For another, the staff knew better than to make any noise while the family still slept. She had heard her dear friend Jasper berating one of the servants for just such a folly.

As she listened, the singing grew louder and clearer.

It was definitely a woman singing. The tune was unfamiliar to Emily, but it was so sweet and melodious that she felt herself drawn to it, like a moth to a flame.

She sat up in bed, no longer perturbed by the nightmare which had caused her to wake initially. The singing came from her right, which meant it must be someone from outside her window.

Her curiosity was too overwhelming to ignore, so Emily swept back her covers and tiptoed over to the window. She held back the curtains just far enough to allow her to see outside, without letting in too much light. The last thing she wanted was for Nanny Lawson to wake up and find her out of bed.

As she held her hands up to the glass for a better view Emily could see the figure of a young woman standing on the grounds in front of the house. She was dressed in what appeared to be a flowing white gown, and she had long dark hair, much like her own.

The woman was looking up at her window, and Emily was in no doubt that her song was meant for her ears.

Emily was transfixed for a moment, both by the woman's obvious beauty as well as by her harmonious song.

Feeling an immediate connection to the woman, Emily waved, shyly.

The woman immediately waved back and blew her a kiss, which made the young girl giggle.

The woman in white continued to sing to her, her voice, clear and soft, seemed to actually be penetrating the glass of the window to ensure that Emily could hear every word.

As the little girl looked on, the woman began to beckon to her.

Feeling as if she were already breaking too many rules, Emily shook her head, sadly.

In response, the woman as if somehow understanding Emily's reluctance to be naughty as well as feeling her deep longing to join her on the lawn, tilted her head slightly to one side and held out her arms as if offering the girl a hug.

A wave of warmth and comfort suddenly washed over Emily causing her to close her eyes as she became lost in the woman's comforting embrace.

When she opened her eyes once more, the woman beckoned to her again.

There was a power in the woman's command which made Emily feel as if she dared not ignore it. Such was the pull to be swept up in those loving arms that she no longer cared about her nanny's rules, or who else she might upset by venturing outside in the middle of the night.

Emily felt herself nodding her compliance and the woman smiled up at her and held out her arms once more.

Moving back from the window, Emily located her slippers

and dressing gown and slipped them both on. Cautiously she made her way towards the bedroom door, taking care to avoid the floorboards she knew from experience *squeaked* when she trod on them.

As she came up against her nanny's chair, she could hear the gently sound of the woman's snoring. She was obviously lost to sleep, but Emily was aware that the woman had assured her on numerous occasions that she would wake at the merest of sounds.

It was odd then that she had not been roused by the woman's singing. But Emily surmised that if her song had been sung especially for her, then perhaps no one else in the house could hear it.

Satisfied by her rationalisation, Emily focussed on opening the door without disturbing her sitter. Creeping passed Margaret's chair she turned her small frame around in a full circle so that she could concentrate on the job at hand without risking making any inadvertent sounds.

Opening the door just wide enough to allow her small frame to exit, Emily slipped out into the hall, closing the door behind her.

She stood still for a moment allowing her vision to adjust to the gloom before she made her way along the corridor to the top of the stairs. She negotiated her way down one stair at a time, making sure that she kept a tight hold of the banister at all times. The soft sole of her slippers padded her footsteps perfectly, so that even she could barely hear them as she descended.

The main front door had been bolted as usual, but Emily managed to gain access to the top lock by standing on an occasional chair which she carried over from the waiting area outside the parlour.

She took one last look behind her as she stepped out into the cold night air, just to ensure that no one had followed her down.

Standing on the main stoop, Emily cold see the woman who had beckoned to her, only now she had moved further away from the house and was standing closer to the row of trees which surrounded the grounds.

Emily felt a sudden flush of trepidation sweep over her, and her initial response was to turn and flee back inside. But as the thought came to her, almost as if she knew what the girl was thinking, the woman held out her hand in a gesture similar to the one her sister made to her whenever she wished her to stay close while they were out walking.

The familiarity of the movement had the desired effect, and Emily lost all sense of conflict and apprehension as she walked down the steps to the gravel drive and crossed it towards the lawn.

Once she was on grass, she no longer feared that her progress could be heard by anyone from inside. There was still a vague chance that someone might be glancing out of a window on his side of the house, but she was already far enough out of reach to be concerned about being caught.

If she were seen and reported to her father, then that was a problem to be dealt with tomorrow. For now, all that concerned Emily was reaching the beautiful woman with gorgeous singing voice who was waiting for her at the edge of the woods.

As she moved closer, Emily could see the woman close-up, and she was indeed the most attractive woman she had ever seen. Her hair was of a jet-black, and lustrous, with flowing locks cascading over her shoulders. Her skin radiated in the moon-light, accentuating her high cheek bones, and her eyes were of the most vivid deep blue, and radiated a feeling of longing tinged with a faraway sorrow which, Emily truly believed, could only be eradicated if she were to comply with their every wish.

As she moved to within reach of the woman, she bent down on her haunches and held out her arms to the little girl. The smile on her lips, just as with her eyes, showed a faint hint of sadness as if she were afraid that the little girl might reject her advances.

But there was no doubt in Emily's mind. Feeling obliged to reciprocate Emily ran into the woman's arms and wrapped her own around her neck, squeezing tightly.

The woman swept her up and planted a loving kiss on the little girl's cheek.

With their faces in such close proximity, Emily suddenly realised who this beautiful woman was. Although for a moment, she was almost too afraid to ask.

With a deep breath, filled with anticipation, Emily asked, "Are you my real mama?"

The woman smiled. "Yes, my darling, I am."

"Have you come back to me?"

The woman nodded. "Yes, I've been waiting for you for so long. I've been so cold out here alone. But now I've got you in my arms, I am as warm and snug as if we were standing in front of a fire."

Emily thought for a moment. Her seven-year-old brain fighting desperately to make sense of what was happening.

Why had her father told her that her mother had died?

Why had she waited so long before revealing herself to Emily?

How could her father marry someone else while her mother was still alive?

Again, as if somehow being able to read the little girl's thoughts, the woman smiled and answered her. "I know you must have a million questions swimming around in that pretty little head of yours," she began, "and I promise you that I will answer as many of them as time allows. But we must be quick, if your papa sees us together, he will not be pleased. You must trust your mama and come with me to a secret place I know where you can ask me all the questions you want. What do you say?"

Emily did not have to consider the prospect. She beamed up at the woman and nodded her head, eagerly.

The woman planted a kiss on the end of her nose, which made Emily chuckle.

Turing, the woman carried the little girl into the woods.

Chapter Thirty

MAGGIE WOKE WITH A START. THERE WAS SOMEONE IN the room with her!

She sat up and rubbed her eyes to clear the sleep so that she could better focus on the shadows around her. She was still in somewhat unfamiliar territory. Due to her accident in the barn, she was still unable to climb the stairs to the room she and her sister Vera had shared since childhood, so their father had set up a temporary bed for her in what had, until recently, been the storeroom.

The room had one tiny window right at the top of the farthest wall which barely let in enough light to see by. But, as her mother kept reminding her, it was her own fault for being so clumsy in the first place.

Maggie suspected that her mother did not believe her story about catching her boot heel on the rung of the ladder as the only reason for her accident. Knowing her daughter as she did, Sybil Cunnings was deeply suspicious that there was more to the tale than her eldest daughter would ever admit to.

There had to be a man involved.

Sybil and her husband's biggest fear for a long time would be that Maggie would announce one day that she was pregnant. Knowing Maggie, it would not be a joyous occasion with a wedding being planned in good time to hide the upcoming birth from the prying eyes of the local gossips. No, in her case it would probably mean her poor father having to track down the man involved and marching him down to the church with a shotgun to his head.

It was that same suspicion that Sybil eyed her daughter whenever she complained about the pain in her ankle, and the fact that she missed her job in the pub.

Fortunately for her, her father was far more forgiving, or at least easier to convince.

He was genuinely more concerned for his daughter's welfare, and his main concern, once she had been settled in her new room, was how long his daughter Vera would need to be away from the farm.

Maggie felt far more guilty for the extra work her father had to undertake due to her clumsiness than she was about her mother's suspicions that her daughter had loose morals.

Since being moved into the old storeroom, Maggie had found it difficult to sleep. The familiar surroundings of her own bedroom had been a great comfort to her over the years and had always felt lie somewhere she could escape to when things did not go her way.

Regardless of what her mother, and her sister come to that, thought about her morals, Maggie had had her heart broken more than once. Men who had promised her the earth if only she would submit to their carnal lusts, and who acted as if they had never met her the next time their paths crossed.

Such men were beneath contempt, but Maggie seemed incapable of falling for their honey words and wandering hands. The worst part for her was that having been used in such a way, she had no one to confide in and take comfort from. Most of her friends had either married or moved away, and those who were still in the vicinity no longer trusted her because of her reputation, and would no doubt take delight in her pain.

There was no point in talking to her mother about it, for she knew that all she would receive was a harsh lecture about what happened to girls with no moral fibre. Even Vera was no help. On occasion, when Maggie had attempted to reach out to her for support having suffered a recent rejection, all she would hear in return was her sister emulating their mother with harsh words and sharp dismissal.

Therefore, burying her head in her pillow or focussing on the familiar surroundings of her childhood bedroom until she fell asleep had become an act of great comfort to her.

Now that she had been relocated to the cold, stark and unfamiliar environment of the storeroom, it felt to Maggie as if she had lost a close friend whom she could no longer rely on to see her through the dark, stormy nights.

Naturally, she knew that the move was only a temporary one, but even so, she felt the loss greatly. She had even considered asking Vera if she would move in with her, just for the familial comfort of hearing her sister's breathings whenever she woke up during the night.

But knowing Vera, her request would be laughed at. After all, she was doubtless enjoying her time alone in their room without having to listen to Maggie's constant wining about lost love and heartache.

Maggie focussed on the doorway at the far end of the storeroom to see if she could ascertain in the dimness if it was open or closed. She knew that her father had closed it before retiring, so if it was open then someone had definitely entered the room.

Maggie held her breath for a moment so that she could concentrate on any sounds an intruder might make. She had no idea of the time, but she knew that her parents always left the front door unbolted to allow Vera access after she shift at the pub, as they used to do for her when she worked there.

Therefore, if Vera had not arrived home by now, it was plausible that someone could have easily gained entrance to the cottage without too much trouble.

The thought suddenly made her feel totally vulnerable.

Both her parents were deep sleepers, so if she needed to attract their attention Maggie knew that she would have to scream her lungs out in order to be heard.

She looked around her but there was nothing at hand which she could use as a weapon should the need arise.

Without protection and being alone on the lower level of the cottage, Maggie felt completely isolated from any form of help. She had to fight the instinct to bury herself under the covers and hope that whatever may be lurking in the shadows just went away without disturbing her.

But she knew that if someone had broken in there was no way they would just up and leave without being challenged.

Turning back, she tried to focus on the door once more. From her bed it still appeared to be closed, but in the darkness, it was impossible for her to tell for sure.

She had asked for a candle to be left alight on her bedside table when she had first been moved into the storeroom, but her mother would not hear of it, stating that it was a waste of money which they could not spare. In truth, Maggie felt that it was just another example of her mother punishing her for lying to them about the exact circumstances surrounding her accident.

Maggie was sure that she could talk her father around to the idea of supplying her with a nightlight, but she knew full well that he would be in trouble with her mother if he blatantly went against her wishes, so she decided to save him the aggravation by not putting him in such an awkward situation, to begin with.

That, alas, did not help her in her present situation.

If she knew for a fact that someone had broken in, Maggie would have no hesitation in screaming for help. It would, after all, be her only option as she was in no fit sate to deal with an intruder in her present state.

However, she also knew that if she woke her parents up unnecessarily, neither one would be too sympathetic with her plight, and as her mother often reminded her, she was not too old for 'a damn good hiding'.

Right at this moment, the prospect of a beating seemed almost insignificant compared to the fact that, if there were someone in her room, she might be in danger of suffering something much worse.

Even so, Maggie wanted to be sure, or at least fairly sure, before raising the alarm.

But still she could not be sure whether or not she had heard someone moving around her room, or she had merely dreamt it.

The light offered by the tiny window did nothing to allay her fears. In fact, she surmised that unless the intruder was at least seven feet tall, there was no way in which she could discern his presence using the shaft from the window alone.

"Hello, sister mine."

Maggie spun round. Somehow Vera had appeared right beside her without making a sound. In the same instant Maggie was both relieved to discover that it was only her and irritated by the amount of stress she had caused her by not announcing herself upon first entering the room.

"Bloody hell Vera," Maggie exclaimed, holding her head in her hands. "You scared the living daylights out of me. What were you playing at?"

"I just wanted to see how you were doing, that's all. No need to get all het up about it."

Maggie looked at her. "No need? I nearly had a heart seizure. I thought that someone had broken in. I was this close to shouting out to Dad." Maggie held her index finger and thumb close together to elucidate her point.

"You're too nervy for your own good," Vera responded

sarcastically. "Besides, Mum and Dad wouldn't have heard you anyway. Not now."

Maggie furrowed her brow. "What do you mean, not now?"

Vera laughed. "Never mind, I'll tell you later."

Although their faces were close enough so that Maggie could be sure that it was her sister she was speaking to even in such poor light, there was something odd and unfamiliar about her voice, which gave her cause for concern.

"I've brought someone to see you," Vera announced casually.

The words brought Maggie out of her reverie. "What, who?" She suddenly felt completely vulnerable in her night dress with only a flimsy cover to hide her modesty.

"Someone wo waned to check on how you're feeling. Isn't that lovely?"

Maggie turned around and scanned the room, or what little of it she could make out. There was still no obvious sign of anyone else being in there with them. That said, she did not see or hear her sister creeping up on her when she arrived, so that was no infallible indication that they were alone.

Perplexed by not being able to make out another figure in the gloom, Maggie turned back to Vera. "What are you talking about?" she demanded. "There's no one else in here with us. Stop playing silly games, it's too late for such shenanigans." She could feel the role as elder, and in theory, wiser sister kicking in. Maggie had no idea what Vera was up to, but whatever childish prank she was about, it was time for it to stop.

"Hello darling, I was worried about you."

Maggie shot her head around so fast she felt a *click* in her neck.

On the other side of her bed, where no one had been seconds before, stood Toby Watkins, beaming down at her.

Instinctively, Maggie brought her knees together made sure her body was covered.

She may well have had a quick fumble with him in their

barn, but if he thought this was a good opportunity to carry on their session, he had another thing coming.

Maggie turned back to face her grinning sister. "What the hell were you thinking bringing him in here, are you totally insane? Mother and father would have a fit if they found him here after dark. Get him out, Vera, for God's sake, before they wake up."

This time both Vera and Toby laughed together.

Maggie was puzzled. Her sister's behaviour was not normal by any means. Vera had always been the sensible one, too sensible by half as far as she was concerned. Bringing Toby into their home in the middle of the night seemed completely out of character to Maggie.

Plus, which, there was something odd about her sister which Maggie could not quite put her finger on. The way she was speaking, the constant giggling, her wide staring eyes, none of this smacked of the girl Maggie had grown up with.

Then it occurred to her. Vera had been working her shifts at the pub.

So, this was what her sister looked like drunk.

Vera had never had a taste for alcohol. Even a Christmas she used to turn her nose up at whatever drink their father bought to welcome in the season.

Obviously working behind the bar, she had formed a taste for it, and once she had a couple down her Maggie guessed it did not take much for Toby o sweet-talk her into this little adventure.

Maggie had no wish to drop Vera in hot water. Although they were pole opposites in almost every way, she was still her sister after all.

Maggie looked back at her. "For the love of all that is holy, get him out of here before Mum and Dad hear you. We'll both get it in the neck if he's discovered here, and you know it."

This time both Vera and Toby laughed out loud as if neither cared who might hear them.

Maggie could not understand her sister's attitude. It was almost as if she wanted to be caught and hang the consequences. Well, so far as Maggie was concerned, she had been warned. If she did not care about being caught then so be it, Maggie would not share any of the blame.

"That does it," she said reproachfully. "If Mum and Dad come down, I'm telling them his was all your doing, and don't you come crying to me later when Dad takes his belt to you." She turned back to Toby. "And the same goes for you. My dad will skin your hide for daring to come into my room uninvited, just you see."

Toby grinned and leaned in closer.

Maggie instinctively pulled back as far as she could.

There was something weirdly menacing about the way he was looking at her, and his breath smelled of something foul, a bit like rotting meat. Maggie could not believe that she had fancied him in the first place, but if he had any designs on stealing a kiss right now, he really had another thing coming.

"But you see," he replied, smirking "I was invited in."

Maggie wrinkled her nose at the stench of his breath from such close proximity.

"I invited him in," Vera confirmed. "And you can forget about Mum and Dad interfering, Toby's friends have already taken care of them," she laughed.

"What!" Maggie switched from one to the other. Nothing either of them was saying made any sense to her, and she just wanted them both gone.

"Come sweet sister, a little goodnight kiss." Vera moved in closer, her mouth less than an inch from Maggie's neck.

"Me too," added Toby, his fetid breath hot on her ear as he too lowered himself towards her.

Maggie felt as if she was about to throw up. She hoisted

herself up to a full sitting position, determined to escape both intruders even if it meant damaging her ankle further.

Before she had a chance, Toby and Vera both grabbed hold of her and flung her back down onto the bed. In one swift move they sank their fangs deep into her exposed throat.

Chapter Thirty-One

THE MORNING WAS DULL AND OVERCAST, threatening rain. It seemed a fitting accompaniment for the sombre mood of a funeral.

Vincent had sent a rider out early that day to enquire from Father James at what time he intended to conduct Jasper's service. It seemed odd to him as he relayed his instructions that he could not remember Jasper's last name.

All servants at Mandrake were addressed by their surnames, but ever since Emily had insisted on learning Jasper's Christian name, everyone else had just followed suit, and from that moment on he was simply known as Jasper.

Everyone, especially after the previous day, had expected the little girl to be inconsolable at the prospect of saying goodbye to her departed friend. In fact, Corinne had even suggested to Vincent that perhaps it would be less traumatising for Emily if she did not attend the service.

But Vincent believed that his youngest daughter was old enough to appreciate the concept of death, and as such it might do her good to accept that her friend would not be coming back.

To everyone's surprise, Emily seemed quite cheerful at

breakfast, and her appetite had certainly improved since the previous day. She sat at the breakfast table, chatting away aimlessly about anything and everything, even making plans for that afternoon when everyone suspected she would simply wish to stay in her room and mourn her departed friend.

The little girl happily skipped along the path holding Stella's hand to pick some flowers to place on Jasper's grave, seemingly unaffected by the prospect of attending her old friend's burial.

Vincent had given the staff permission to attend the funeral, and he laid on carriages to convey them to and from the service.

There were many tears shed during the service, but curiously none from Emily, who stood solemnly, head bowed in prayer, clutching her flowers until the moment she was allowed to sprinkle them on Jasper's coffin.

It was Corinne, Nanny Lawson, and Stella who appeared most concerned by Emily's lack of emotion, and they all passed concerned glances between themselves, unable to disguise their unease.

As the funeral progressed, Vincent's attention moved to the conversation he was due to have with Father James after the ceremony, where he would have to admit to the priest that he had been unsuccessful in his endeavour to locate the secret entrance to the catacombs beneath his house.

He knew deep down that regardless of what Father James agreed to, Mathew and his troop would insist on searching for themselves as a result of his failure to locate the creatures.

As the time drew nearer Vincent could feel the trepidation of such a venture encroach on his mood.

He knew that he still had every right to forbid them entry to Mandrake, and there was no law in the land to which could force his hand. However, even to him, a search by the only men in the town capable of defeating the underground dwellers seemed more beneficial than his original suggestion of merely allowing Mathew and his team to lie in wait in the grounds until the creatures emerged.

Furthermore, the situation at hand was of a delicate and extremely unusual nature, and if he refused to acquiesce to the search, he genuinely feared the potential consequences. After all, if there were creatures dwelling below grounds what was to stop them creeping throughout the house during the night, possibly even harming his wife or children.

He could always place a guard in the wine cellar. Vincent had already taken Hobson into his confidence, so her knew the man was trustworthy and would carry out the duty without question. But whether such an arrangement would satisfy Father James and Mathew was another matter.

Added to which, what if the creatures appeared during the night, how would Hobson be able to raise the alarm before they set upon him? According to Mathew, these creatures had immense strength and agility, and even if he were armed Vincent feared that Hobson would be no match for them.

There seemed to be no way out.

As much as he hated lying to Corinne and the girls, Vincent knew that he would have to come up with some elaborate excuse as to why there were strange men scouring the wine cellar, unless he could somehow sneak them in without anyone noticing.

As the ceremony drew to a close, Vincent ushered his family back to their carriage, telling them that he would be along later as he needed to speak to Father James.

"We can wait here for you, my love," offered Corinne, "then we can all ride back together."

Vincent smiled. "No thank you, that won't be necessary. My business with the priest may take longer than anticipated. You all go back to Mandrake and have something warm to ward off the day's chill. I'll be along presently."

"Thank Father James for such a lovely service, Papa," said Emily, still oddly unmoved by the ceremony.

"Of course, I will, my angel," Vincent assured her. "Now off you go, and I'll see you later."

Vincent waited as the carriage disappeared around the first bend.

The servants who had attended their colleague's funeral filed past, hurrying to reach their respective carriages, thanking him as they did so for allowing them to attend.

As there was no cause to suspect poor Jasper might have risen from his coffin, Mathew's men all stood back behind the mourners, while the gravediggers Father James usually employed for the task set about their work, filling in the old man's grave.

Vincent removed several coins from his pocket and handed them to the nearest member of the team. "Here, you gentlemen have a drink on me for poor old Jasper," he said, cheerily.

The men all thanked him and continued with their labour.

Vincent rode back with Father James to the presbytery, while Mathew and his crew rode in a separate carriage.

Vincent was glad of the privacy so that he could speak to the priest alone before involving the other men.

"How did you get on with your search?" asked Father James, his expression belying the fact that he suspected that Vincent had been unsuccessful.

Vincent shook his head. "It was useless, Father. I and one of my most trusted servants searched all afternoon. We virtually pulled the damn place apart, but to no avail."

The priest nodded his head, slowly. "I've been thinking my son," he began. "Could it be possible that old Jasper was mistaken in what he told you?"

Vincent frowned. "How do you mean?" he enquired.

The priest shrugged. "I just wondered if poor old Jasper might have imagined the scenario regarding the ceremony taking place beneath the hall, as well as your father's involvement in it."

Vincent could not believe what he was hearing. "What, you think the old man was delusional? He certainly seemed convinced when he was warning me."

"Not delusional as such, I'm sure he witnessed some form of ceremony, I just wonder if it actually took place somewhere else, and at the moment he relayed the details to you his mind somehow mixed the details up. It would explain why you cannot find the entrance."

"Father, I would love that to be true. But even I must concede that there has to be an element of truth in what Jasper told me. He certainly had no reason to besmirch my father's good name. He was a loyal and faithful servant."

The priest held up his hand. "I understand my son, all I was suggesting was that perhaps the old man became confused after his fall and mixed up the location of the resting place for these vermin."

"But where else could it be?" Vincent asked, perplexed.

Father James scratched his head, moving his hat back until it looked as if it were about to fall off. "Well, I was thinking perhaps a priest-hole with the entrance hidden behind a wall somewhere else in the house. It may well lead to the catacombs beneath the wine cellar, but it does not automatically follow that the entrance has to be down there, too."

Vincent considered the priest's suggestion for a moment. Then said, "So you believe that when Jasper went down into the cellar to find the entrance, he was actually in the wrong part of the house?"

Father James nodded.

"Well, that would certainly explain why I wasn't able to locate the entrance. If only we could get hold of the builders whom my father employed to complete the building works. If anyone knows for sure where the entrance is, it would be them."

"There are no records of the transaction?"

Vincent shook his head. "No, it appears my father purposely destroyed any such information."

Father James nodded. "The problem now of course is how do we go about locating this lair. We can hardly start knocking down walls at the hall?"

Vincent looked up at him. "I'm sure Mathew and his crew would have no qualms about such an action if given free rein. I suspect he would see the hall razed to the ground in an effort to locate his prey."

"You mustn't judge Mathew too harshly my son, he has been brought up by the church with the sole purpose of tracking down and destroying this abomination, during the course of which he has saved many lives, and seen many friends trans-formed into one of the undead. Friends whom he has subse-quently had to put to death himself, just to free their immortal souls."

Vincent nodded his agreement. "I suppose so. But, if we tell him where we think these monsters are hiding, can you guar-antee that he will not take his men charging into the hall, axes at the ready to batter down the walls?"

"It is certainly a quandary," Father James agreed. "Perhaps when we reconvene at the presbytery, we can decide on a solu-tion that works for all of us. In the meantime, I think it would be best to keep what we know between us and pray that we reach a viable solution before there are any more victims amongst our congregation."

Chapter Thirty-Two

CEDRIC CROSSED THE FIELD WHICH SURROUNDED HIS home and made his way towards the first farm he intended to visit that day. After all the excitement of the previous day he was conscious of the fact that he did not manage to check on the vast majority of the viscount's holdings, and even though he knew it would not be held against him, personally he felt that he had not given full value for his wages, so he intended on completing a full round today.

After the business with Toby Watkins, or what had once been Toby Watkins, Cedric had barely slept a wink all night. Although he knew his master was relying on his discretion regarding the entire incident, Cedric felt compelled to tell his wife Hetty everything.

There was no point in keeping anything from her, she knew at once when he arrived home that something had upset him, and she was not the kind of woman to leave the matter if she suspected that whatever it was would continue to play on her husband's mind throughout the evening.

To give her her full due, Cedric knew that she was not the type to gossip. So, anything he told her would remain private.

Even so, he felt awkward about breaking a confidence of his master, so once he realised that he had no choice other than to give in, he emphasised to Hetty the importance of keeping the details to herself.

Like most of the village, she had already heard rumours concerning the recent deaths and disappearances. But her eyes spread wide as she listened to the events of her husband's day.

That night, while Hetty prepared their dinner, Cedric reinforced their front door, as well as all the windows in their cottage.

Hetty made his favourite, rabbit stew that evening, and it was not lost on her when Cedric barely touched a bite. Even a cup of strong ale did not seem to help him relax, and by the time they retired for the night, Hetty knew her husband would find it nigh-on impossible to sleep.

They never had any children, but it was not for the want of trying. After a while they both just accepted the situation and decided to make the best of it.

Hetty was not in the mood for lovemaking that night, but when she saw how restless Cedric was, she decided to help him to relax by relieving him with her hand. At first, Cedric moaned that he too was not in the mood, but Hetty persisted, knowing that he could not resist her touch indefinitely.

As it was, it still did nothing to aid his sleep, but as far as she was concerned, Hetty had done her duty, so she managed to turn over and drift off with a clear conscience.

Cedric skirted the fence which encased some of the livestock on the Cunning's farm. Usually, by this time of the morning, Ted Cunnings could be seen attending to his animals, with young Vera close at hand. Cedric was aware that the Cunning's youngest daughter had been forced to step in to cover her elder sister's job at the local inn, but even so, she would often help her father on the farm before her shift began.

Therefore, it was strange that Cedric could not see either of them from his vantage point. He waited for a couple of minutes while he filled his pipe, just in case either the father or daughter were hidden from view inside one of the sheds on the property.

But when, after ten minutes, neither of them emerged, Cedric felt duty-bound to go and check that all was as it should be.

He climbed the fence and crossed the field, keeping an eye out for any stray cows who might suddenly see him as an intruder. He knew that a least one of Cunning's herd was in calf, so he knew better than to antagonise them by announcing his presence.

Once he reached the nearest shed, Cedric stuck his head in to see if anyone was there.

To his surprise, the pigs which they kept were still penned in, and by the way they were behaving it seemed to Cedric as if they had not been fed yet that morning.

Confused, but still not overly concerned, Cedric moved on. The cottage was closer now than either of the other outbuildings, so he decided to try there first, expecting to see the family still sat around the breakfast table.

To his surprise, the door to the cottage was wide open.

Cedric was immediately struck by an uncomfortable sensation of déjà vu.

The business at the Watkin's place yesterday was still vividly clear in his mind, and he had to fight a sudden overwhelming feeling to run.

Looking around him once more, Cedric stepped up to the threshold and listened for some indication that all was as it should be.

But there was nothing, the cottage looked abandoned.

At least, he reasoned, the downstairs furniture had not been thrown asunder as it had in the Watkin's cottage, so that at least should be a good sign.

Cedric's overpowering urge was to flee. But he knew deep

down that if it had not been for yesterday, he would be intent on investigating what was going on here.

Finally, Cedric called out, loud enough so that anyone inside, even if they were upstairs, would be able to hear him. He listened intently as his voice echoed up the stairs without response.

There was an annoying little voice in his head screaming at him to get away from the cottage before it was too late. But Cedric knew that when he made his report to Vincent, one of the first questions asked would be 'did you search the cottage for any signs of life?'

Cedric knew he could not leave his task half-done. The thought of standing in front of the viscount and those men who worked with Father James, and admitting he was too afraid to so much as enter the door of the cottage, was more than he could stomach.

He called out again just in case there was a genuine reason why he had not been heard the first time.

Still no reply.

Stealing himself, his walking club in hand ready to be used as a weapon, Cedric took a step inside. As he gazed around him, everything looked in its place. All the plates and cutlery were lines up on the sideboard at the far end of the room, the chairs around the dining table had all been pushed in, even the coats and shoes belonging to the occupants were placed smartly by the front door, as if waiting for their owners to come down and slip them on.

Cedric's initial fear eased a little, but not enough for him to barge in unannounced and brazenly start throwing open doors.

But deep down he knew that was exactly what he must do in order to make a full sweep before his report.

Cedric moved into the middle of the room, keeping his ears pinned back for any sound of movement.

Still nothing.

Cautiously, he checked the downstairs rooms, the kitchen, the larder, the storeroom, but there was no evidence of anything untoward.

Cedric knew from previous visits that all the bedrooms were on the upper floor, but all he could think of was the sight of Ralph and his wife strung up the previous morning with all the blood drained from their corpses.

Holding his club firmly, Cedric placed a foot on the first step and hoisted himself up.

The stair *creaked* under his weight, which caused him to freeze to the spot.

He stood there a moment, desperately fighting that annoying voice in his head which was still telling him to run before it was too late. But he surmised that if his calling out had not managed to rouse any of the inhabitants from their beds, there was little chance that a creaky stair was going to do the trick.

Even so, Cedric saw no harm in calling up again.

Taking a deep breath, he shouted up the stairs, warning of his pending arrival.

Nothing!

Then he heard it!

Movement from upstairs.

Cedric paused and strained to listen. Perhaps there was a completely innocent reason as to why there seemed to be no sign of life on the farm.

What if Ted had taken the girls into town for something, and Sybil was upstairs tidying up, lost in her work and therefore unable to hear him calling?

It was perfectly plausible.

Cedric chided himself for allowing his imagination to run wild. He knew full well that it was as a result of yesterday. Had this same situation have occurred last week, he would have thought no more of it.

Imbued with a new-found confidence Cedric opened his mouth to shout up, again.

But just as he did, a shadow appeared at the top of the stairs. There was a window behind whoever it was, and although the day was not the brightest, there was still enough light pouring in through it to prevent him from making out who was there.

Cedric shielded his eyes with his hand, keeping a firm grip on his stick with the other.

"Hello," he called up, "who's there?"

As quickly as it had appeared, the shadow vanished from sight.

Were his eyes playing tricks on him due to his lack of sleep the previous night?

There had definitely been a figure there a moment ago.

"Hello."

No answer.

"It's Cedric Stobart. Ted, are you there?"

Still no reply.

Cedric raised a tentative leg and placed his foot on the next step. He saw that his entire body had started to shake, uncontrollably, and he reached out for the wall beside him to steady himself.

"Ted. Stop playing silly beggars and get yerself down 'ere now!"

Somehow, Cedric did not expect any reply to his call. By now he knew that something was amiss. He could not just blame the events of the previous day for his suspicions, this was all far too coincidental.

Cautiously, keeping his hand pressed firmly against the wall for balance, he took a step backwards. Then he heard movement coming from above, once more. But this time it was not the singular sound of someone moving around on their own. Now it sounded more like several pairs of feet shuffling along the floor, hastily trying to make their way towards the top of the stairs.

Forgetting for a moment that he was still one step up, Cedric turned to flee. Missing the bottom stair completely he was unable to prevent himself from falling head long towards the floor.

He cried out as his trusty staff flew from his grasp. He heard it *clatter* against a distant chair as he held up both arms in front of his face to break his fall.

As Cedric hit the hard floor his elbows and knees took the brunt of the fall. The impact knocked the breath from his body, but at least his quick thinking prevented his head making contact with the stone.

He lay there for a moment, desperately trying to regain his composure.

From behind, Cedric could hear the sound of feet descending the stairs, the *creaks* from the old wood announcing their advance.

There were voices, but they sounded far away, much too far to be coming from those approaching him from behind. Some were soft, sweet, almost melodic as if trying to enchant him, or lull him into a false sense of security. But they were interrupted by harsh, guttural cackling, infused with evil intent.

Cedric fought to take in a decent breath. He pushed against the floor, the pain in his elbows as a result of his fall, crying for him to take it easy, but he knew this might be his one and only chance to make good his escape, and he could not afford to wase it.

Whatever was behind him continued to advance, their pace unrelenting.

With a mighty effort born of fear and panic, Cedric managed to regain his feet.

Without turning around to see what stalked him, he ran for the open doorway convinced that he would be pounced upon before he managed to reach the outside.

The voices behind him grew in volume and urgency, a sudden realisation that their prey was about to make good its escape.

Cedric could hear them now, much more clearly. They were calling to him, urging him to stay. Offering him delights beyond his imagination if he would just turn back.

In his haste to leave, Cedric tripped over the front stoop, but this time he managed to duck his head beneath his arm and roll over onto the soft mud outside.

The force behind his fall propelled him forward, allowing him to regain his feet like a gymnast emerging from a spin.

Still refusing to look back, Cedric took flight, running for all he was worth, ignoring the pain in his knees from his earlier tumble inside the cottage. His only goal now was to find the viscount and raise the alarm. He no longer cared what anyone thought of him for not venturing upstairs to make a proper investigation. This was a job for Father James' men to deal with. After all, they were trained for this kind of thing, he was not.

Cedric leapt over the fence in one jump. His landing sent shudders up his weakened legs, but he ignored them, his fear powering his flight.

At the end of the lane, he stood at the crossroads. To his right was Mandrake Hall, a good few miles away and no picnic for a man in his present condition.

If he carried straight on, Cedric knew that he would reach the presbytery far sooner.

He remembered that it had been Jasper's funeral that morning, but he surmised that Father James should have returned home by now, and even if he had not, Cedric somehow knew that he would be far safer in the closed confines of a holy abode than alone on the open road.

Besides, at least some of the priest's henchmen were bound to be there, and they would know what to do.

His decision made Cedric headed for the presbytery.

Although he was now far enough away from the cottage to feel safe, he was still unable to force himself to look back.

Chapter Thirty-Three

VINCENT, FATHER JAMES, MATHEW, AND HIS CREW ALL sat around the large dining table at the presbytery finishing their meal. Mrs Oakes, the church housekeeper began collecting their plates for washing.

Father James had convinced Vincent to stay for some refreshment after they arrived back from the funeral, suggesting that with full stomachs they might be able to better decide how to proceed with informing Mathew of their suspicions, regarding the coffins in the catacombs at Mandrake Hall.

"Thank you, Mrs Oakes," said Father James. "That really was an excellent meal, and most welcome."

The middle-aged housekeeper nodded and continued collecting up the empty plates.

Mrs Oakes was, in the priest's opinion, an indispensable addition to his flock. A widow who had lost her husband far too young, she never considered remarrying and had confessed to Father James on numerous occasions that her love for her departed husband was sill as strong as the day they married.

A devout Christian, Mrs Oakes seemed to take great pleasure in her duties, which were both onerous and plentiful. Regardless of the task Father James set her, the woman never complained, even if it was not something strictly within her remit as housekeeper.

Beside keeping the presbytery spotless, she also cooked all the priest's meals, washed his clothes, replenished the flowers in the church, took charge of cleaning and shrouding corpses for burial, and when occasions dictated, such as now, she looked after the priest's guests by making up their beds and pandering to their needs.

Above all else, the woman was the very soul of discretion. Father James knew that if he were to say anything in front of her, no matter what the substance of the conversation, it remained as sacrosanct as if spoken in the confessional.

Even so, regardless of how many times Father James assured others of the woman's discretion, some were still suspicious and preferred to discuss their business in private.

As was the case with Vincent, who waited patiently for Mrs Oakes to finish her duties in the dining room before discussing his concerns regarding Mandrake Hall.

"Gentlemen," he began, clearing his throat, "Father James and I have something to tell you which we feel might shed some much-needed light on our present situation."

Mathew and his men exchanged anxious glances.

Father James felt a sudden rush of relief that Vincent had decided to share his thoughts after all. He had been feeling the weight of the burden of keeping the information from Mathew since Vincent had first spoke to him, and although he could very easily understand the viscount's apprehension at revealing what he knew, the situation was fast growing out of their control and needed the expert opinion of a professional in this matter.

Vincent could feel the burning stares of the men around the table as he took another drink of wine to give him courage.

"As you know, my servant Jasper was buried this morning. Well, before he died, he told me a tale to which I can hardly give credence, save for the fact that we find ourselves in such a position as we have."

Mathew leaned in a little further to listen.

Vincent felt immediately threatened by the big man's intimidating movement, but he managed to keep his resolve intact.

"According to Jasper, my late father, may God rest his soul, took it upon himself to invite a stranger to our shores who claimed to possess the knowledge of how to extend a man's life beyond that of medical intervention. This man, in turn, brought with him, according to Jasper, six cohorts all of whom took up residence somewhere within my house."

Vincent could tell from their exchanged glances that Mathew and his men suspected where this story would lead.

Their excitement was almost palpable, and Vincent began to wish that he had not started his revelation without first securing their absolute assurance that they would not act in haste once he had finished.

The thought of the men crashing into his home, scaring his wife and daughters and upsetting his staff while they tore the place apart looking for the secret entrance to the catacombs, suddenly felt dangerously real to him.

But he knew that it was too late to turn back now.

Doubtless sensing the viscount's obvious discomfort, Father James felt that he needed to say something in support of his squire. "Gentlemen, you must understand that all of this is mainly supposition. Without Jasper here to confirm or deny the rumour the viscount can only relay what he was told by a dying man with his last breath. Other than God, who knows what passes through the memory of one of his flock with the angels beckoning them away."

Though Vincent appreciated the sentiment, he knew that Mathew had heard too much already to be dissuaded from his present line of thought.

Vincent nodded his thanks to the priest before continuing.

"These six, whatever they are, performed rituals which included…" Vincent gagged, and held a cloth to his mouth to prevent himself from losing his meal. He took another drink to calm his nerves. "Which included extracting my father's blood and drinking it."

Mathew shot to his feet sending his chair cascading back across the floor.

He pointed an accusing finger directly at Vincent. "The undead dwell at your house, and only now do you tell us?"

"Please, gentlemen, calm down," Father James held up his hands to try and quell the situation before I grew out of hand.

Vincent felt his temple grow hot. "I know nothing of the sort," he retorted, his voice booming with anger and frustration. "All I know for sure is what Jasper told me, but I've no way of knowing if it was true, or merely the delusional ramblings of an old man."

"'e must know more," interjected Ned, standing beside his leader. "These rich folk only know 'ow to protect themselves, not botherin' about us ordinary folk."

"We need to burn the place to the ground," suggested Tom.

"Aye," agreed Ned, "then we'll see them creatures face their comeuppance. It's the only way to be sure."

Vincent rose to his feet, instantly reaching for his sword before remembering he had not worn one to the funeral. "No one is burning my ancestral home to the ground," he barked. "And it will be over my dead body gentlemen that any of you will so much as step foot over the threshold without my say so."

"You have no authority over my orders," Mathew replied, menacingly. "My orders come from God." He wagged his finger at the ceiling.

Father James could see how the situation was almost past the point of no return.

He too jumped to his feet. "Gentlemen, gentlemen," he yelled, making sure his voice could be heard above the others.

"This kind of knee-jerk reaction was the very reason the viscount and I held off on giving you this information until we could make some formal enquiries to ascertain if there was any truth to them."

Mathew now turned on the priest. "You knew of this, and you said nothing?"

Father James took in a deep breath before answering. He was desperate not to become part of the problem. "The viscount informed me yesterday, just after Jasper passed away, and like him, I was perplexed as to whether such a story could have any truth in it. Since them, the squire and his servants have virtually torn Mandrake Hall apart searching for this alleged secret entrance to where the aforementioned rituals took place, but without success."

Mathew chewed his bottom lip contemplating what would be for the best. Ned's supposition that they should burn the house down was no more than a hot-headed reaction, which carried no merit.

But if there were such creatures still dwelling inside Mandrake Hall, the quicker they exposed and disposed of them, the better. No one could possibly disagree with that assumption, not even the viscount.

"So, this servant Jasper never actually told you where to find these creatures?"

Vincent felt his temper easing off. "Jasper told me that they took place in a specially built catacombs somewhere below the house. He tried to show me where, but he only reached as fa as the wine cellar before collapsing and dying. Since then, my servants and I have scoured every inch of that cellar, looking for the secret entrance. We've moved every barrel, pushed and shoved against every stone in the wall, hammered on every flag-stone, but nothing reveals the entrance to the secret chamber."

Mathew thought, scratching his unshaven face with the tip of his dagger.

Finally, he said. "So, what if me and my men were to discreetly, without scaring your family, search the place ourselves? I can assure you there'll be no attempts made to burn the hall down, no matter what we find." He turned his head towards Tom and Ned to hit home the nail, then he turned back to Vincent. "I'm sure you must agree that something needs to be done before the entire district falls under the spell of these creatures, your loved ones included."

Vincent mulled over the suggestion. If he were being honest with himself, he already knew that having failed to locate the secret entrance, more decisive action needed to be implemented.

The problem was that he could not envisage Mathew's team searching the house without raising an alarm. What was he supposed to tell Corinne and the girls?

Furthermore, here were the servants to consider.

Whereas he could expect loyalty from the vast majority of them there was still the chance that someone would let something slip in a drunken moment, then what?

There would be rumour and speculation abound, and before long he would need to call in the militia to defend his home from his own subjects.

No, if Mathew and his crew were going to search the hall then they would have to concoct an elaborate story for such an operation to pass by without raising concern.

"Well?" asked Mathew, growing impatient. "What say you?"

Vincent turned to Father James for guidance.

The priest sat back down, indicating for Mathew and Vincent to do likewise. There was a hostility in the air which made him very uncomfortable, and he was determined that everyone should calm down before any decision was made.

As it was, he could not see any viable alternative to Mathew's decision.

He turned back to Vincent and nodded his head.

The action was not wasted on Mathew's team. "Well, what are we waitin' fer?" demanded Tom, ready to rise.

Mathew grabbed his arm and kept him in his seat.

"We need to formulate a plan of action," Father James interjected. "We cannot just go barging into the hall mob-handed, otherwise it will cause distress to the viscount's young family, not to mention speculation amongst the staff."

"Just tell 'em to mind their own business," suggested Tom. "The result of doing nought could be much worse."

Vincent looked up in despair. "It's not that easy!" he tried to explain, exasperated by the fact that Mathew allowed his men to but in whenever they felt the urge. This conversation would have been far more proactive if they had insisted that only Mathew attend from his side, but I was too late now.

"Squire's right," Mathew interjected, holding up his hand to quell any argument from his men. "There's no point going in chargin' when we don't even know where the entrance is. That said, it would be wise to try and find it during the daylight hours when their powers are diminished. Come nighttime, their strength and ability rise tenfold, and if there's six of them and only four of us, perhaps we should send for reinforcements before we rush in."

"There's not just those six we need to concern ourselves with," added Father James. "What about young Toby Watkins, he's still out there somewhere beyond the reach of God?"

"Not to mention any others he may have infected by now," added Vincent.

"'ere, I hope you're not blaming us fer not catching 'im yesterday." Gregory sat up straight in his chair, his eyes slanted, his cheeks flushed. "It were not our fault 'e got away, we searched all day fer 'im."

"No one is blaming you for your efforts," Vincent assured him. "I was simply making a statement of fact. We have no way of knowing exactly how many of these creatures we're dealing with."

Just then, there was an urgent, loud banging on the presbytery door.

The men could hear the shuffling feet of Mrs Oakes outside the room, making her way to answer it.

They listened, intently, then heard the catch being lifted and an excited voice demanding to speak to Father James.

The next second Cedric burst into the room in front of a very flustered-looking housekeeper.

Sensing the urgency with which Cedric had barged in without waiting to be announced, Father James thanked Mrs Oakes and the woman smiled weakly before returning to her duties.

"What's the matter, man?" asked Vincent, sharing the priest's concern.

Cedric heaved and wheezed, unable to fully catch his breath having run all the way there. "It's Ted...Cunnings...place...you have to come...now." He began jabbing his finger behind him as if he were being followed. "I think...same as...with Ralph and his wife...oh my God." With that, the man collapsed to the floor, desperate to try and catch his breath.

Chapter Thirty-Four

THE MEN RACED TO THE CUNNINGS' FARM IN TWO
carriages. Mathew took the reins for his with his men in the
back, while Vincent led the way with Father James in the church
wagon.

Having relayed his tale to the best of his ability, a very
shaken Cedric was given wine to fortify him and help to calm
his shattered nerves. Even then it was decided that he was far
too distraught to be of any use back at the farm, so he was left
in the capable hands of Mrs Oakes while the others left in the
two carriages.

Father James, his eyes closed, recited prayers for the protection of them all on their latest quest. Vincent looked over at the
priest and saw that his hands were trembling, as he held them
together.

Regardless of the situation, Vincent could not help feeling a
modicum of relief that the arrival of Cedric had managed to
swerve the conversation away from Mathew's insistence that he
and his men storm Mandrake to search for the catacombs.

Vincent knew in his heart that such action was a natural

conclusion after his confession, but still he found himself unable to contemplate telling his wife and children of their situation.

His initial idea to just take them on holiday would in itself raise questions as they had only just returned to the hall for him to take up his new position as viscount. But the alternative of admitting what he knew, and the details concerning the involvement of his late father seemed intolerable to him.

As much as he believed that Jasper was in earnest when he relayed his story, Vincent could not help but wonder if the old man had not mixed up his facts, due to his condition at the time.

What if the catacombs existed, but were not even in the hall?

He would be putting his entire household through unimaginable distress for nothing.

In the back of his mind Vincent felt that Mathew, and especially his overeager team, would not accept being unable to locate the catacombs a Mandrake, and then they would allow their obsession to take over their reason, which may result in who knew what.

After all, they had the church's warrant to carry our all such investigations as they saw fit in order to track down and extinguish these creatures of darkness. Would that include them demanding to interrogate Vincent's staff, using violence if they believed they were not being told the truth?

Where would it end?

How safe would Vincent's own family be in the hands of such ruffians?

If, as he had suggested back at the presbytery, Mathew sent for more reinforcements, Vincent had a vision of his house swarming with interrogators suspecting everyone, including himself, and demanding answers that none of them had to offer.

Vincent still remembered learning of the witch trials from the last century, and the extreme measures the witchfinders employed in their efforts to force those accused to confess.

Those men too carried out their duties because they had the backing of the church.

Such overzealous practices were not above being utilised now by anyone, no matter how misguided, who felt that they were working for God, and thus immune from prosecution and damnation.

In Vincent's mind he could almost hear the dulcet tone emanating from Father James' mouth, telling him that 'it was for the best, my son' while a group of thugs dragged his wife towards the nearest tree to string her up because they believed she was one of these creatures of the night.

A sudden jolt of the carriage after one of its wheels rode over a loose branch in the road forced Vincent to shake such thoughts from his mind. For now, they had others matters to attend to, and as such needed to focus all their attention on them.

He heard Father James say 'Amen' as he finished his prayers.

"Amen," Vincent repeated, holding the reins in his left hand as he made the sign of the cross. He could see how visibly shaken the priest was at the anticipation of encountering a similar incident as the day before.

He could not help but feel sorry for the poor man. A humble priest who, until now, had taken delight in administering to the modest congregation in their relatively small corner of the world, now thrust into a battle for their immortal souls. Even with the assistance of Mathew and his band, the toll of the oper-ation was etched across the holy man's brow.

"Perhaps it would be better father, when we reach the cottage, if you stayed in the carriage and leave whatever awaits us inside to Mathew and his gang? There's no need for you to confront the danger head-on."

Father James turned to Vincent, and smiled, weakly. "You are very kind my son, but what is the point of my telling our congregation each week that they must have faith in our Lord and that he will protect them, if at the first sign of trouble I turn tail and run?"

"No one would ever question your faith, Father," Vincent assured him.

"I would, and then how could I ever face God when my time comes, knowing that when my faith should have been at its strongest, I was left wanting? No, my son, I will put my trust in the almighty and face whatever lies ahead."

Vincent knew there was no point arguing with the priest, and for his part, he could fully appreciate his stand. He was obviously a lot braver than he looked.

Around the next bend in the road, the Cunnings' farm came into sight.

Vincent steered the horses around to the main field which led directly to the cottage.

Both carriages drew up outside the building, and before Vincent had a chance to help Father James down, Mathew's team had already raced into the cottage, pistols in hand.

Mathew had loaned Vincent a sword and a pistol from his stash back at the presbytery. Father James had rejected such an offer, preferring his crucifix and bible for protection. Some of Mathew's men sniggered disrespectfully at the priest's words, but they soon retracted their insolence when Mathew reminded them that crucifixes were a formidable weapon against the undead, and able to subdue them more effectively than a musket ball.

Mathew stood by the carriage while Father James climbed down. "Perhaps you'd better wait out 'ere," he suggested. "It sounds like from what Cedric told us there might be more than one of them inside, waiting."

The priest smiled, shaking his head.

"I've already suggested that," offered Vincent. "But the good father insists on entering with us."

Mathew nodded his understanding. In truth he already knew

the priest's views, so his decision did not surprise him. "Okay then," he continued. "Try and stay close by me."

The three men entered the cottage. Mathew took the lead carrying a dark leather bag, followed by Vincent with Father James bringing up the rear.

Once inside they could hear Mathew's men searching the downstairs rooms, checking in cupboards and under the makeshift bed Ted had set up for Maggie. After Toby jumping out at Cedric from behind a curtain yesterday, they did not wish to leave any stone unturned.

The rooms were small and quite tight, so Ned and Stuart took one, while Tom and Gregory took the other.

Mathew noticed that unlike the previous day none of the downstairs furniture was in disarray. It just appeared as if the family had stepped out for a while.

Vincent scanned the room for any indication that there might be something out of place. It was then his eye landed on a walking cane which he recognised as belonging to Cedric. He picked it up and hefted it in his hands.

"Something interesting?" asked Mathew.

Vincent nodded. "Unless I'm mistaken, this belongs to Cedric. He must have dropped it in his panic to flee."

"Keep it at hand," suggested Mathew. "It might come in handy as a stake, later."

The other four men emerged from the downstairs rooms. Mathew turned to them, and they all shook their heads to indicate they had not found anything.

Mathew opened his bag and removed several wooden stakes with their ends filed down to points and handed one to each of his team. He placed one inside his own belt, before closing the bag placing it on the nearest table.

He signalled to his men, and one by one they began to climb the stairs to the upper rooms. Tom led the way, followed closely by Stuart and Ned, with Gregory hot on their heels. Each man had one hand on their pistols as they climbed.

Mathew followed on behind his men, leaving Vincent had Father James to pick up the rear.

As Tom neared the top step, a stair creaked under his weight. He paused and turned back, an expression of annoyance on his face. It was too late now, the damage was done, so Mathew indicated for him to continue on his way.

The men behind tried to avoid placing their weight on the exact spot which had caused the sound, but the entire step seemed to be unwilling to assist them in their task.

Gregory waited until Ned had cleared the top step before stretching to avoid the last one altogether, even though it was probably already too late. If there was someone waiting upstairs, they would already have heard his colleagues thanks to the *squeaky* board.

Once on the landing, the men were confronted by three closed doors.

Between them, they signalled their next move. Tom and Stuart took the room nearest to them on the left, while Ned and Gregory did likewise with the room on the right.

Mathew reached the top just in time to see his men disappear into their chosen rooms. He held up his hand to halt Vincent and the priest behind him, removing his pistol from his belt in anticipation of what was to come.

Seconds later, Ned emerged from the room he and Gregory had entered. His face was flushed, and his eyes wide. He wiped his arm across his face to clear away he perspiration before signalling to Mathew to follow him back into the room.

Mathew turned back and indicated for Vincent and Father James to follow him as he walked along the landing and entered the bedroom.

As he suspected, the bodies of Ted and Sybil Cunnings had been strung up, upside down, just like those of Ralph and Enid

Watkins. Their pale corpses hung limply suspended by rope from the beams above their bed.

It was obvious to all in attendance that both had been drained of every ounce of blood.

"Oh, my good lord!" Father James slapped his hand across his mouth, having spoken out without realising.

Mathew turned back, unable to disguise his exasperation.

He placed his index finger over his lips to reaffirm his instructions to both the priest and to Vincent. Then he signalled for them to stay put while he moved past them back onto the landing.

As he left the room, his other two men emerged from the room opposite. Stuart, upon seeing his leader, shook his head, solemnly.

Mathew indicated towards the room at the end of the corridor, and both Stuart and Tom walked towards it, their pistols drawn.

Suddenly, there was a crash of glass. It took the men a moment to realise that it had come from the last room. With no time to lose, Stuart moved in and twisted the handle, but the door was locked from the inside.

Taking a step back, he launched himself at the door, shattering the wood around the lock as his full weigh crashed through.

Closely followed by Tom and Mathew, the men ran over to the broken window at the far end of the room. They peered outside, but there was no one to be seen below.

Chapter Thirty-Five

AS THE THREE MEN GAZED OUT OVER THE FIELD below, searching for any sign of movement which might indicate where they prey had landed, they suddenly heard the sound of running footsteps above them.

Instinctively, the three men looked up and saw Toby Watkins and Vera Cunnings looking down at them from the ceiling.

In an instant, both Toby and Vera fell to the ground, perfectly landing on their haunches, before standing to their full height, cutting Mathew and his men off from leaving via the door.

Tom moved forward, his pistol raised ready to fire, but before he managed to let off a shot, Toby moved in and swiped the gun from his hand, sending it *clattering* across the floor.

Toby's arm shot forward and grabbed Tom by the throat, lifting him off the ground as if he weighed next to nothing.

Mathew and Stuart both raised their pistols, but Toby began to swing Tom in front of them like some bizarre life-size marionette, making it impossible for either of them to take a clear shot without risking the chance of hitting their friend.

Both Toby and Vera had maniacal grins plastered across their faces, and Vera began to cackle insanely, clearly amused by her colleague's antics.

Frustrated by their lack of options, Mathew turned to Stuart and shouted, "Charge!"

Together the two men ran at Toby, spreading their arms to ensure that at least one of them would be able to grab their colleague en route.

But Toby was too quick for either of them. He danced to one side just as the two men were about to make contact, and still managed to keep his stranglehold on Tom.

Both men ended up face-to-face with the grinning Vera before they had a chance to pull up. In an instant, she managed to grab each of them by their collars and slam them into each other, cracking their heads together.

Releasing her grip, both men staggered back. Stuart caught his leg on the foot of the bed, and fell backwards, landing on the floor in front of Toby.

Mathew managed to keep upright and let off a shot from his pistol.

Although the angle was far from perfect, his bullet rammed home into Vera's left shoulder. She let out a scream which filled the room and grabbed the place where the shot had entered.

If she were in pain, the moment passed almost immediately as she turned her attention back towards Mathew.

With his only shot spent, Mathew cast his weapon aside on the bed and made a grab for the wooden stake in his belt. But before he had a chance to raise it sufficiently to strike, Vera launched herself at him, sending him reeling back onto the floor, with her full weight pressed on top of him.

Stradling his torso, Vera held both his arms down by the wrists.

No matter how hard he tried to fight her off, she was impossible to move, and she knew it. Lowering her face towards his,

Mathew gagged as Vera's stinking fetid breath assailed his nose and mouth.

Behind him, Mathew was aware of Stuart climbing to his feet after his fall, but his attention was focussed on Toby, trying to force him to release their friend.

Vera opened her mouth wider, barring her razor-sharp fangs.

Her dead eyes almost seemed to glint with excitement and anticipation as she surveyed her catch. A tiny droplet of saliva dripped off the end of her tongue and splashed on Mathew's chin. Instinctively he turned his head to one side, repulsed by a combination of the stench of her breath, and the spittle on his chin.

It suddenly occurred to him that by moving to one side he was in fact exposing his neck to the hungry vampire, so he snapped his head back to face front just as she was about to sink her jaws into him.

Vexed by his movement, Vera let out another howl of frustration, and squeezed her thighs even tighter around his middle, knocking the air from him, making it almost impossible for him to take in a breath.

From somewhere behind there came a loud retort.

Having his view blocked by Vera, Mathew was unable to see what was going on, but the noise clearly sounded like gunfire to him.

Sure enough, he heard Toby let out a roar of anger, and he heard the sound of a body dropping to the floor. Mathew hoped that Tom had finally been released without any permanent damage being inflicted on him by the farmhand.

The sudden sound of flint hitting steel forced Vera to turn back to see what all the commotion was. As she turned, Vincent moved in and took a swing at her with Cedric's stick. The ball on the end made contact with the side of her face, cracking the bones in her cheek.

For a split-second Vera released Mathew's arms as she tended to her wounds.

Once again, she appeared to be more angry than actually hurt, but her reaction gave Mathew the freedom he desired to act. Slipping his stake out of his belt, he shoved it forward forcing the point into the hole his bullet had made earlier, in the woman's shoulder.

This strike seemed to have a more beneficial effect than his bullet, and Vera lifted back her head and screamed so loudly it felt to those present as if the entire cottage would crumble under the sound.

Ned charged in out of nowhere and managed to knock Vera off his leader. The two of them tumbled over a couple of times, until Ned crashed against a wardrobe which was off to one side.

For a moment Vera lay beside him, the momentum of their fall had caused her arms to envelope his body and they resembled a pair of lovers waking up post-coitus.

Mathew, finally free of his restrains, lifted himself of the ground, helped to his feet by Vincent. "Thanks," offered Mathew. "I said that might come in handy."

Between them, Mathew saw that Tom, Stuart and Gregory had Toby cornered.

Each man held out a stake before him, and Mathew could see that Toby was holding his right arm, which he suspected might be where one of his team had shot the vampire.

Gregory had discarded his weapon on the bed, which suggested to Mathew that he was the one who must have fired at Toby when he entered the room.

This only left, by his account, Stuart and Ned with loaded pistols, and right now, Ned did not appear in any state to use his, crushed up against the wardrobe by Vera.

Mathew considered reloading his gun, but with the time it took he could not envisage the vampires standing around waiting for him to complete the task before attacking again.

At least Stuart had his gun aimed directly at Toby's chest, which seemed to have the desired effect of keeping him at bay. Mathew noticed that Tom and Gregory both had their stakes at the ready, so were clearly waiting for the perfect chance to strike.

Hearing a loud *hiss* from behind, Mathew spun round to see Vera regaining her feet.

As she stood up, she clutched the protruding stake and ripped it out of her chest.

Fortunately, she appeared to have forgotten about the prone body of Ned, lying next to her, unable to defend himself. Instead, she seemed to have all her hatred focussed on Mathew, which he did not mind as it distracted her from Ned.

Without seeming to take any precise aim, Vera threw the wooden stake a Mathew. It flew end over end towards his head and at the last minute he was just able to deflect it with his arm.

Mathew began to circle around to Vera's right, keeping his eyes locked on hers. She still conveyed a malevolent hunger in her stare which made him feel slightly uneasy, but he knew that in the storm of battle fear was not an option.

To his surprise, Vincent moved in next to him, his club still in his hand. "What should we do?" the viscount asked, his voice trembling.

"I'll edge to her right, you do the same to her left," instructed Mathew. "We just need to distract her enough to either pull Ned free or reach Tom's pistol which I think might be behind him on the floor."

"Then what?"

"We hit the bitch with everything we have and hope for the best."

Vincent suspected that there might have been a tinge of gallows humour in Mathew's reply, but under the circumstances he allowed it to pass. This was not the first time he and his men had been in such a position, so whatever it took to keep them going was okay with him.

Mathew and Vincent edged their way slowly around the menacing figure of Vera.

She seemed totally aware of what they were planning, whether it was as a result of her hearing their plans or sensing them by using her newfound telepathy. Either way, she stood her ground, legs bent, ready to pounce, arms outstretched as offering them some gruesome hug.

They all heard a groaning and looked down to see Ned coming back around.

Vera spun her head back and forth between the encroaching men and the fallen combatant. He still appeared dazed and only half awake, but Mathew hoped that he might soon be conscious enough to act on the situation.

As if reading his leader's mind, Ned grabbed his gun from his belt and began to lift it towards Vera. Seeing the movement from the corner of her eye, or possibly just sensing it, Vera lifted her right foot and slammed it down hard on Ned's wrist, pinning it to the floor.Ned cried out and immediately dropped his weapon.

Without warning, Vincent leapt forward and swung Cedric's cane in a huge arc, catching Vera squarely on the side of her head.

The blow was not enough to knock her over, but she staggered sideways, holding her head, and releasing Ned's wrist in the process.

From behind them they all heard a further report as someone fired another bullet.

Mathew hoped it was Stuart, whom he surmised was the last of his men with a loaded gun to hand, and that he had managed to hit his target.

Turning his attention back to the matter at hand, Mathew

charged at Vera, catching her off-balance and sending her careering across the floor towards the open window.

Grabbing his chance, Mathew picked up Ned's gun, and in doing so he saw Tom's lying behind his fallen comrade. With a loaded pistol in each hand, Mathew stood up and turned to face Vera.

In his peripheral view, Mathew saw Tom, Stuart and Gregory charge Toby who was backed into a corner, nursing his wound.

Vera too had seen Toby's predicament and made as if to run to his aid, but Mathew cut her off with a wave of his pistol, so that she too was cornered.

Vincent managed to edge behind Mathew to reach Ned, and gabbing him by the arm, pulled him away to relative safety.

Vera, furious at having lost her prey, moved forward towards Mathew, but the sight of both guns being pointed at her face, caused her to rethink her move.

At that moment, Mathew heard a cry coming from his right, he turned his head and saw Toby striking out at his men, wind-milling his arms frantically. Tom caught a hard right on his jaw and fell backwards, leaving only Stuart and Gregory to try and subdue Toby.

But within the flash of an eye, Toby took full advantage of the situation and grabbed Gregory, wo was closest to him, and hoisted him above his shoulders, before throwing him at Stuart as if he weighed no more than a sack of potatoes.

Stuart tried to grab his friend in mid-air, but the force with which Gregory had been thrown sent both men tumbling backwards.

Mathew aimed one of his pistols and pulled the trigger, hitting Toby in his arm. The bullet seemed to have little or no effect as the vampire turned his fury towards Mathew.

Sensing her moment, Vera launched herself at Mathew, grabbing him around the neck and pushing his head to one side to allow her a good bite of his neck.

Suddenly, from behind, a crucifix was thrust against the forehead of the female vampire. The wooden cross burnt deep into her forehead, causing smoke to rise as she screamed for her life.

She released her hold on Mathew, but Father James managed to keep the cross in place, pushing it further into her skin as he recited a prayer to God, begging for help with his task.

Vera fell to the ground with Father James beside her.

She screamed as if her entire body was on fire, but Father James kept the crucifix in place as he gazed into her malevolent eyes, knowing that this might be his one chance to subdue the vampire enough to allow one of the men to strike home the final blow.

As if to answer his prayer, Mathew appeared beside him and thrust a stake deep into Vera's heart. He forced it home with all his weight behind it until she eventually stopped screaming and her body jerked on the floor like a slice of bacon left in a frying pan.

The effort had taken a toll on Father James, and once he was sure that Vera was dead, he fell backwards on the floor, clutching the crucifix to his heart.

Toby released an enormous cry of rage and took a step towards Mathew who was still on his knees beside Vera's corpse.

Before Mathew had a chance to reach for his other pistol, his men leapt at Toby and knocked him off balance, using their combined bodyweight to pin him down.

Seeing his chance, Vincent grabbed a stake from the floor which one of the men had dropped earlier and leapt into the air, yelling to warn the men to move aside. Following Mathew's example, Vincent aimed the point of the stake directly at Toby's heart, using his momentum to drive it home.

Once the stake was in, Tom moved Vincent aside and used his hammer to smash it in until he could feel the end hitting the floor, under Toby's writhing body.

They all stood back and watched as the vampire twitched and turned, scrabbling about on the floor as it desperately tried to no avail to remove the stake from its chest.

Eventually, Toby stopped moving and just lay there, crumpled on the floor with the wooden stake protruding from his torso.

Chapter Thirty-Six

Once the men had all recaptured their composure, Mathew remembered the sound of footsteps on the roof which they had heard earlier when they first entered the room.

It was obvious to him that someone must have broken out through the bedroom window and somehow managed to escape onto the roof before he and his men arrived.

Vincent stayed back with Father James who was still shaken from his encounter with Vera, while Mathew and his men made a thorough search of the farm. They found a ladder in one of the outhouses and used it to gain access to the roof, but there was no sign of anyone ever being up there.

They searched every barn and shed across the entire property, but once again they came up empty. Whoever it was who Mathew heard running across the roof had obviously made good their escape.

Worse still, none of them had actually seen the escapee so they had no idea who they might be hunting.

Frustrated at their lack of success, Mathew and his team returned to the cottage.

Once they had checked on Father James, Mathew's men began loading the bodies on their cart. Even though they were confident that both Vera and Toby were dead, as a precaution they hacked off their heads before moving their bodies.

Ted and Sybil Cunnings, though clearly victims, would still have to undergo the same process before burying, but it was decided as a mark of respect that their ceremony could wait until after they had been cleaned and dressed for burial.

Mathew sat at the table with Vincent and Father James. Vincent managed to find a bottle of wine in the larder and had poured the priest a cup full to help steady his nerves and palpitations. Although his hands were still shaking, Father James assured them both that he was feeling much better, and they had no need to worry.

Vincent insisted that he send for Doctor Harris, but Father James grew quite insistent that he did not want any fuss, so reluctantly the viscount acquiesced to his wishes.

Mathew held his hand up to refuse Vincent's offer of a drink. He needed something stronger after their exertions, so decided to wait until they arrived back at the presbytery to enjoy some of the priest's fine brandy.

"I take it you had no luck in locating your prey?" Vincent asked.

"Nah, whoever it was they must be long gone," replied Mathew. "Not to worry, we'll track 'em down soon enough. Whoever they were, they won't be able to stay hidden for long. These creatures need to feed."

Father James cleared his throat. "The Cunnings had another daughter, young Margaret. I haven't seen her at church for a while, I believe she recently had an accident which left her temporarily incapacitated."

"If that were 'er she seemed pretty flight of foot running across the roof," noted Mathew. "But if she's the only one missing, she sounds like a safe bet."

"Another family wiped out by this awful plague we must do all we can to stop it before anyone else is hurt." Father James was clearly distraught and when he had finished speaking, he began to cough into his hankey.

Vincent poured him some more wine, which the priest accepted gratefully once he was able to drink.

Vincent glanced over at Mathew. Father James' supposition was clearly not lost on the man, and he even suspected that the priest might have been indirectly referring to him when he spoke.

"You'll be wanting to search the hall as soon as possible I take it?"

To his surprise, Mathew shook his head. "Not now, we have too much to do with these corpses once we get them back to the church. Plus, it'll be dusk soon and our time will be better spent searching the woods and the surrounding area for these things. If what you say turns out to be true, and there are some of them living under your cellar, then chances are they'll emerge soon for their night feed so we might be able to deal with them before they have a chance to return."

Vincent could not disguise his relief. It would be far easier to explain away a search during the daylight hours, and he might even be able to arrange a trip to keep his family away until it was all over.

Either way, he was feeling far too drained to have to deal with it all tonight.

"We'll need to arrange the funerals for tomorrow," Father James observed.

"That would be best," agreed Mathew. "We don't want to take any chances."

Father James planted his elbows on the table and dropped his face into his hands, rubbing his temples. "All these killings," he said solemnly.

"Don't you worry yourself father, they'll be over soon enough, just you leave it to us," Mathew assured him.

Once the cart was loaded, Mathew and his men made one final search of the cottage, just to ensure that they had not missed any secreted hiding places where another creature might be lurking.

Once they were finished, they all left for the presbytery.

As Mathew had noted, the sun was already on the wane and the sky had lost much of its light. Tom and Gregory travelled back with Vincent and Father James as the other cart carried the four corpses.

No one spoke on the way back, each man lost with his own thoughts.

Vincent could feel a headache creeping on. He was still unable to fathom his father's involvement in their latest predicament, much less the fact that he had actually been the instigator.

Had the late viscount have suspected what a terrible toll on his community his actions would have had, Vincent felt sure that his father would never have embarked on such a journey to begin with.

Now it was down to him to ensure the safety of his town and he vowed to himself not to rest until this plague had been vanquished.

Once they arrived back at the presbytery Mathew and his men set about laying out the corpses for their pre-burial bathing. As Ted and Sybil Cunnings had been victims rather than perpetrators, Vincent now understood that part of the ritual would involve them being staked and decapitated. The thought turned his stomach, but he knew that such a precaution was far safer than risking the alternative scenario.

Ted had been a good and loyal tenant so to have to sit back and see him and his wife be treated in such a manner just chipped away at the guilt he already felt for their loss.

Cedric at least, seemed to have regained some of his composure thanks to the care and attention of Mrs Oakes. Even so, the ashen pallor of his skin along with the faint faraway look in his eyes, told Vincent that the man had not fully recovered his senses, and who could blame him.

The shock of the last two days had certainly taken their toll on the poor man, and when he rose from his chair to accept a ride home from Vincent, his entire demeanour seemed to be that of a man who had aged greatly during the last few hours.

On the way to his cottage Vincent informed Cedric of their findings at the Cunnings' farm, presuming that the man would be curious to know of where his initial warning had led. But, not surprisingly, he only received the odd nod or one-word answer from his gamekeeper as they rode along, and Vincent feared that the man might require more than just a hot meal and a good night's rest to see him right again.

Vincent pulled over across the path from Cedric's cottage, but the gamekeeper did not appear to realise that he was home. Instead, he just sat in his seat, his head hanging low with his chin against his chest, and the rest of his body slumped against the backrest.

Vincent slapped him on his back. "Come on man, you're home now, Hetty will be wondering what kept you."

Cedric looked up as if suddenly realising that he was being spoken to. "Oh, I'm sorry your lordship, I was away with the fairies."

Vincent laughed. "Worse places to be right now, eh?"

Cedric attempted a smile, but it fell short.

"Tell you what," said Vincent, "why don't you take tomorrow off, spend the day with your lovely wife. Go for a walk in the sunshine if we get any. Try and take your mind off the circumstances of the last few days. What do you say?"

The offer seemed to snap Cedric out of his reverie. "Oh, there's really no need for that your lordship, I've barely done any work at all for the last couple of days, I should feel as if I've let you down if I miss another whole day."

"Nonsense," insisted Vincent. "I insist, and I'll brook no discussion on the matter."

Cedric, realising that it would be churlish to refuse such a kind offer, nodded his acceptance. "Thank you, your lordship, I must admit, my nerves are feeling a little shattered at this moment."

"Go on, off to your wife, let her look after you, you've earned it."

Cedric climbed down from the carriage and waved Vincent off.

His feeling of guilt still outweighed his joy at the prospect of a day off work, but he was sure that his wife would appreciate it, nonetheless. She was always telling him that he worked too hard and that he needed more rest than his duties allowed.

Cedric walked over to his cottage. The glow from the firelight flickering through the small window next to the front door warmed him inside. He had no doubt that Hetty would have a hot stew in the pan, and he could really use it.

He opened the door and called out to her.

"I'm in here my love," Hetty called back, her voice echoing through the stone building.

It was a rare occasion when she was not at the door to greet him, but Cedric thought no more of it and took his seat at the table. The aroma of his wife's stew assailed his nostrils and made his stomach growl.

After a moment, he heard his wife emerging from their bedroom, the soft fall of her footsteps padded on the hard floor, as she made her way towards him.

"I've got some good news," Cedric said, not bothering to turn around. "His lordship has given me the day off tomorrow on account of all that's been going on. It's a bad business Hetty, there ain't no use in denying it. Will the stew be long?"

He felt his wife's arms circling him from behind. She planted a tender kiss on the side of his neck, followed by another, and another until her mouth was level with his earlobe, which she then proceeded to gently suck at.

Cedric squirmed in his seat.

This was not his usual welcome, but he was very grateful for it.

He wondered if his wife was feeling guilty because she had not been receptive to him the previous night. Using her hand on him had been more than adequate compensation as far as he was concerned, but if she was captured by the mood this evening, he was happy to oblige. If nothing else, it might help to ease his nerves from the last couple of days.

He moaned softly as Hetty slid her hands inside his shirt and began stroking the thick matted hair of his chest.

She slipped her tongue inside his ear and lapped at it, making circular patterns with the tip.

Cedric could feel himself growing harder by the second, all thoughts of a hot meal had now taken second place to his wife's advances.

She led him by the hand to their bedroom. Cedric noticed she was already wearing her bedgown, which she had left unbuttoned at the top so that it showed off her creamy-white shoulders.

Once inside the bedroom, Cedric shed his clothes while Hetty lay back on the bed, her legs bent as she slipped her hand between them enticing Cedric to make short work of his task.

As soon as he was on top of her, Hetty grabbed hold of him and guided him inside her. She let out a loud moan of pleasure as he began to thrust himself deeper inside her moist cleft.

Lost in his passion, Cedric barely registered what his wife was saying.

"Young Maggie came round to see me today," Hetty breathed. "I never realised what a buxom young thing she's grown into. No wonder all the boys in town are obsessed with her."

"Mmmnn," was the best Cedric could manage by way of response.

He could feel his seed already starting to rise. Hetty dug her nails into his back, dragging them across his flesh from tailbone to shoulders.

"We spent a lovely afternoon together," Hetty continued. "She has the most amazing body."

Cedric had his eyes closed and his mouth clamped on one of Hetty's breasts when the enormity of what she was telling him registered.

Even so, he was too far gone to pull back now.

Hetty placed a hand on the nape of his neck and began stroking his hair with her nails.

The other hand she slipped down between her legs until she located her husband's sack. Once there, she started to fondle it gently between her fingers. It was a trick her mother had told her of on the day of her wedding, just in case Cedric was unable to become fully aroused that night, due to too much celebration.

It was a trick which had held her in good stead ever since to save her husband's embarrassment if he could not perform.

Now she used it as a means of distraction.

Cedric groaned with pleasure as he continued to thrust himself inside his wife.

When he finally exploded, Hetty grabbed him by the hair and pulled his head to one side before sinking her fangs into the soft tissue which covered his carotid artery.

Even as she drank his life's blood, Cedric continued to enjoy the last few spurts from his throbbing member as he sank into a deep state of unconsciousness.

Chapter Thirty-Seven

Vincent arrived back at Mandrake Hall physically and mentally exhausted.

Jonathan, one of his younger servants, was waiting as instructed to greet him on the path. Vincent instructed him to go to the stables and ask one of the boys there to take the carriage back to the presbytery.

Hobson was waiting for him inside the main door.

"How's everything?" Vincent asked, while his servant helped him with his coat.

"The ladies have been very concerned about you, your lordship. They missed you at tea and have insisted that supper is not served before you arrived home."

Vincent smiled. "Well, you can tell cook to give me five minutes to change, then I'll be down."

Vincent went straight upstairs to his bedroom to change for dinner without stopping first to see his wife and daughters in the parlour. His headache seemed to be growing worse by the minute and he hoped that a stiff drink before supper would do the trick.

Failing that, he would send for Dr Harris in the morning to

supply him with a draught of some sort. He knew the reason behind his malady was doubtless due to the stress he was under as a result of the latest killings.

Both Ralph Watkins and Ted Cunnings had been good tenants of long standing, and they deserved a better ending than they received.

His guilt from the knowledge that his father may have been the instigator of their demise did nothing to alleviate his anguish, and he feared that there would be many more victims to account for before this ordeal was over.

Over the last few days Vincent had begun to care less about his reputation and standing than he did about the potential loss of life among his people. He had been initially pleased that Mathew had forgone a search of the hall this evening, but the more he thought about it the more he knew that he was merely putting off the inevitable.

If word broke out in town that he was harbouring the creatures responsible for the killings he feared there might be a riot with his own tenants turning against him. How would he protect his family against hordes of angry townsfolk brandishing torches and pitchforks, threatening to tear the hall down in their quest to root out the culprits?

Even if he were to send word to Colonel Drake to bring back the militia, Vincent could not be sure if, once he knew the facts, the colonel might not view him as the protagonist and side with the town.

He almost wished that Jasper had not taken him into his confidence regarding his late father's involvement. At least then he could concentrate of ridding his district of this menace without the added pressure of knowing how it had come about in the first place.

But he knew deep down that to ignore the facts and pretend to be nothing more than an interested party would be the coward's way of behaving, and he would rather face death than dishonour.

Once he was dressed, Vincent joined the others in the parlour.

When he opened the door, he saw immediately the look of relief on his wife and eldest daughter's faces. Emily appeared too involved with her doll in front of the fire, and Nanny Lawson had actually dozed off in one of the armchairs.

He kissed Corinne and the girls and poured himself a large drink, waving aside the servant who stood by to provide such a service. His head was pounding, but Vincent managed to smile and deflect any concern his family expressed for his absence since the funeral that morning.

"How's the little one been since you arrived back?" he asked Corinne when they had a moment alone.

Corinne smiled. "Remarkably jubilant," she replied, "considering the circumstances."

Vincent raised his eyebrows. "Really? You do surprise me. I thought she'd be in floods of tears all day. Mind you, she did seem oddly cheerful at the funeral. I dare say she'll deal with things in her own way."

"She managed a long sleep this afternoon after luncheon," Corinne informed him. "So that may have helped. She was looking a little peaky beforehand, but the nap seems to have done her the power of good."

"Unlike Nanny," Vincent observed, indicating towards the woman who was still asleep.

"I know," Corinne agreed. "She has been quite light-headed all afternoon. I did ask her if she was okay and she said that she was, but I'm glad you've noticed too. Perhaps an early night might do the trick."

Stella shook her old nanny awake on her way to the dining room. Margaret sat up abruptly, and straight away she could feel the room around spinning. She held herself upright by holding onto the armchair with both hands while apologising for having fallen asleep.

"Are you feeling alright, Nanny?" asked Vincent, jokingly. "You appear to be away with the fairies."

Margaret apologised once more. "I don't know what's wrong with me," she replied. "I had a little nap while Emily was asleep, had the strangest dream."

"Well, you must tell us all about it over supper," Vincent insisted.

Margaret blushed. "Oh, I'm afraid it's not fit for the table, maybe after."

They went in to dine and to his dismay Vincent realised that his stiff aperitif had done nothing to alleviate his headache.

During the meal, Emily chatted away animatedly, apparently oblivious as to whether or not anyone else was listening. Corinne could tell that her husband was not his usual self, and she suspected it had something to do with whatever business he had conducted with Father James after Jasper's funeral.

Had they been dining alone, she would have enquired as to what was troubling him, but in company, she did not wish to upset the girls, especially little Emily.

Corinne was relieved that the little girl had not reacted in the way everyone thought she would during the funeral. It was a little odd, but considering how close she had been to Jasper, it was almost as if he had merely left on holiday instead of dying.

Stella had tried to take her younger sister's mind off the situation on the way back from the service by coaxing her to name all the different types of trees they passed on their way home, and although Emily played along, it felt as if she were doing so more to accommodate her sister, than because she enjoyed the game; or needed the distraction.

Halfway through their meal Emily began talking about what she believed happened to people after they die.

Everyone else paused for a moment, fearing that the little

girl was finally about to reminisce about her friend, and end up in tears.

But instead, she carried on her conversation quite matter-of-factly until she looked up and asked her stepmother. "What do you think, Corinne?"

It being the first time anyone at the table had heard Emily call her stepmother by her Christian name there was a stunned silence as they all exchanged glances.

Finally, Stella spoke up. "Why are you addressing Mama by her Christian name Emily, it's not polite?"

"Because she's not my mama, or yours Stella."

Vincent dropped his cutlery. "What is all this nonsense young lady?" he demanded. "You will apologise to your mama this instant."

Emily looked perplexed. "I'm very sorry if I caused any offence Corrine, I can assure you that it was not my intention."

"You will address your mama in the correct manner, this instant!" Vincent could feel his temper rising. On top of his headache, this was the last thing he needed.

Emily laid down her fork and knife, pushing them together although there was still half a plateful in front of her. "I have already apologised to Corinne and explained that I meant no offence, Papa. But I do not feel it necessary for you to raise your voice in that manner, I am merely stating a fact, nothing more."

"Emily," whispered Stella, sharply. She could tell from his expression that her father was close to boiling point.

Emily glanced over at her sister. "You know that I am speaking the truth, Stella, and no one should ever be chastised for doing that."

The young girl's manner seemed to have lost its innocent childlike wonder which everyone had been used to, and instead taken on a more defiant, even brusque edge, which Stella could tell her father-above all-did not appreciate.

"That's enough!" Vincent shouted, slamming his hand on

the table. The force of his action caused everything near him to vibrate, including his wine glass which actually fell over, spilling the crimson liquid across the table.

One of the waiting staff standing nearby rushed over to mop up the spill, but Vincent waved him away as he was blocking his view of his youngest daughter.

Corinne could tell that her husband had had enough, and before he opened his mouth to speak, she cut him off. "The child's obviously distraught and exhausted after the day's events," she offered comfortingly. "Perhaps desert and then bed, what do you think?"

But Vincent was not in a forgiving mood.

He turned to Corinne. "Either she apologises this instant for her discourtesy, or she will have to suffer the consequences." Vincent looked over at Emily. "Do I make myself abundantly clear young lady?"

"Yes, Papa," Emily replied, but with no visible concept of her present position.

"Well," continued Vincent. "I'm waiting."

Emily shrugged her little shoulders, nonchalantly, and gave her father her sweetest smile.

Vincent's cheeks flushed red, and he threw his napkin down on the table.

He turned his anger towards Nanny Lawson. "Is this how you tutor my daughter?" he demanded. "To show such disrespect to her mama?"

Margaret opened her mouth to speak, but closed it again without uttering a word, deciding that it would not be worth her while to defend herself at that moment.

"Papa, please," Stella interjected, feeling an overwhelming duty to defend her nanny from such accusations.

"And I'll tolerate no backchat from you either, young lady," Vincent retorted, feeling as if his head were about to explode.

He turned his attention back to Nanny Lawson. "Nanny, you will take Emily straight to bed, without desert."

"But, darling," Corinne objected, "cook has made her favourite lemon cake for dessert. Emily's been looking forward to it all day."

"Well, she should have thought of that before being so disrespectful." Vincent managed to keep his temper in check, not wishing to upset his wife any further.

Not waiting to be told twice, Nanny Lawson wiped her moth with her napkin and rose from the table. She walked over to Emily and stood next to the girl, hoping that she would not cause a scene and exacerbate matters further.

Unconcerned, Emily pushed back her chair and walked over to her father.

Vincent stared straight ahead as if unwilling to acknowledge her.

Sighing, Emily stepped on the lower rut of his chair and lifted herself up so that she could kiss him on the cheek. "Goodnight, Papa," she said sweetly.

She then walked over to her stepmother who leaned in for her goodnight kiss without encouragement. "Goodnight my little one," she offered, smiling.

"Goodnight Corinne," said Emily.

"That does it!" Vincent exploded. "I think before lights out Nanny Lawson, young Emily here could benefit from six harsh strokes with the hairbrush, what say you?"

Margaret looked at him with sheer horror on her face.

"Papa," Stella cut in, "you know full well that Nanny Lawson has never laid a hand on either of us. You cannot ask her to do so now!"

Vincent waved his index finger at his eldest daughter. "Do not tell me how to manage my household staff, young lady. Either Nanny Lawson carries out my wishes, or she can find another appointment, come the morning!"

Margaret choked back tears as she cleared her throat.

She knew that the viscount was in earnest, and that to cross him now would definitely mean the end of her employment with the family.

Even so, he had gone too far this time, and everyone around the able knew it, even if they were too afraid to give it utterance.

But the thought of leaving Stella and Emily behind was more than she could take.

Margaret had grown to love both of them as if they were her own. She had happily exchanged any chance of romance she might have had to raise them after their mother had passed away, and to treat her with such callous disregard now felt as if she were being stabbed in the stomach.

The silence was broken by the sound of Stella sliding back her chair.

"And where might you be going?" demanded Vincent.

"With your permission, Papa, I am going to administer the discipline you so crave." She walked over to Corinne and kissed her on the cheek. "Goodnight, Mama," she whispered. "Please don't be upset with Emily, she's not herself today."

Corinne kissed her back. "I know, my darling, thank you."

Stella walked over and kissed her father. "Goodnight, Papa, see you in the morning."

Emily, still unperplexed by the situation, held out her hand to Stella as she neared her chair. Stella took it and led her younger sister upstairs.

Chapter Thirty-Eight

ONCE THEY REACHED THEIR LANDING, STELLA TOLD Nanny Lawson to go to her own room for a change. The nanny had been half-asleep for most of the afternoon, and with the added stress of being ordered to punish Emily, she looked as if she were about to pass out.

Margaret had not slept in her own room for ages, her priority was to be on hand should Emily have a nightmare. A responsibility she took extremely seriously.

"But what if Emily should wake up in the night and find no one there?" she asked, startled. "She cannot be all alone, not with everything else that has gone on lately."

Stella looked down at her younger sister and sighed. She knew that not only could Nanny Lawson not bring herself to discipline little Emily herself, but she would also hate to have to stand by and watch such an act take place.

"You don't need to concern yourself for tonight," Stella assured her. "I'll stay with Emily."

Emily, upon hearing her sister's resolution, skipped on the spot, still holding tightly onto Stella's hand.

Reluctantly, although secretly relieved at being excused,

MARK L'ESTRANGE

Margaret kissed both girls' goodnight, and gave Stella's arm a gentle squeeze of gratitude before making her way along the corridor to her own room.

Stella walked Emily to her bedroom door and opened it. "Right then you," she said. "I'm going to change, and when I return, I want you in your nightshirt, understand?"

Emily looked up, a big beam of excitement on her face, and nodded.

"Do you need me to come in and check for monsters first?"

Emily laughed as if the idea seemed ridiculous to her, although it was a ritual which she had insisted that Nanny Lawson carry out every night, up to and including last night.

"No thank you, I'll be fine," Emily assured her.

Stella watched her little sister enter her room and close the door. She knew that the servants would have already lit the fire and left a candle in the room for added light, so she made her way to her own room to change for bed.

She hoped that their father might appear before it was too late and retract his edict that Emily needed to be punished. It was not a task that Stella was looking forward to, although Emily herself appeared strangely unconcerned by the prospect.

Stella supposed that her younger sister might be of the opinion that it was all a big joke, although seeing their father in such a rage should have left her in no doubt that he was in earnest.

Her only hope now was that he had calmed down and that Corinne had persuaded him to come upstairs and relinquish Stella from her onerous task.

Stella purposely took her time undressing and brushing her hair, leaving her father plenty of time to appear. But after a while she realised that it was not going to happen, which left her little choice.

Stella took the candle from her room and made her way back to Emily's bedroom.

As instructed, the young girl had put on her nightgown, and was patiently sitting at her dressing table, waiting for her sister's arrival.

Stella looked back over her shoulder once more, just in case she could hear their father's footsteps on the stairs, but there came no such sound.

Just then, she heard someone at the far end of the corridor, and her heart leapt.

They were too far away to be seen from such a distance, so she waited as they made their way towards her. As they did not carry a candle, she had to wait until they were within the glow from her own before she recognised them.

To her disappointment, it turned out to be one of the servants.

The young man, whom she believed was called Jonathan, although she could not remember his surname, held her gaze for the merest of seconds before glancing down at the floor.

"Good evening...Lady Stella," he mumbled, half under his breath. "I'm sorry if I startled you, I was just checking that all the fires had been lit."

"It's quite alright," Stella assured him. "I thought it might be my father coming up to wish us goodnight."

The young man kept his head bowed and cleared his throat before replying. "I believe your father is still at supper, I left him and your mother in the dining room before I came up."

His was not good news, but Stella tried not to let it reflect in her tone. "Not to worry, goodnight."

"Oh, goodnight, your ladyship."

Jonathan waited for Stella to go into Emily's room and close the door behind her before he continued on his way.

Once inside, Stella carried her candle over and placed it on the shelf above Emily's dressing table. "Now then," she said, sternly. "What's going on with you this evening? Why were you so rude to Mama, she did nothing to deserve it?"

Emily gazed at her sister's reflection in the mirror. "I did not intend to be rude. I did explain that to Papa, but he didn't seem to care."

"But why did you refuse to address her by her proper title?"

Emily turned on her stool. "But she isn't our mama, and you know that. She is our stepmother, and it doesn't mean that I love her any the less."

Stella could feel her own anger rising. "But why suddenly refuse to call her Mama? You were calling her that right up until las night, what's changed all of a sudden?"

Emily smiled. "Because I saw our real mama last night, and she is still alive and wants us to go and live with her."

The news took Stella completely off guard.

She could feel her face flush. "What are you talking about," she demanded. "Where did you see our mama?"

Emily indicated over her shoulder, towards the window. "Out there, on the lawn," she replied, her face the picture of innocence as if she were merely relaying a fact of no import or significance. "She called to me in the night, and when I looked out of my window, I saw her near the trees, beckoning me to join her."

Stella sighed, deeply. "You had a dream, nothing more. All this fuss over a silly dream."

"I didn't," Emily retorted, defiantly. "She was there, and we spoke together for ages. She said that next time I was to bring you, too, but if you're going to be horrid about it, I might just go alone, and tell her you didn't want to come!"

Stella could tell that there was no use in arguing with her sister. Emily had obviously made up her mind that her dream was real, and nothing Stella could say was going to change that.

"All right then, have it your way," Stella said in exasperation.

"You don't believe me, do you?" Emily demanded.

"It doesn't matter what I believe, does it? It's what's rattling around in your little head that's causing all this unpleasantness." Stella crouched down next to her. "Look, no matter what you saw, or think you saw, the fact is that you've really upset Papa. Why don't we go downstairs now, before it's too late, and you give Mama a great big hug and apologise for upsetting her."

"But she's not our mama," Emily argued.

Stella could see that she was not going to win the argument at any cost.

Emily had made her mind up, and that was an end to things.

She did not even seem bothered in the slightest that she had upset Corinne, or their father, nor that the fact that she had placed Stella in such an awkward position.

Stella dropped her head forward and glanced down. "Where are your slippers, young lady," she asked.

Emily looked down as if she had not realised that they were not on her feet. "I must have forgotten to put them on," she replied. "Not to worry, I'll be in bed soon."

"You'll catch your death on the cold floor first," Stella warned her. She stood up and walked over to Emily's bed. Finding the footwear under it, she picked them up and carried the over to her sister.

As she was about to place them on Emily's feet, Stella noticed that the soles of both slippers were caked with dirt.

She glanced up at Emily. "How on earth did you manage this?" she asked, confused.

Slippers were for the bedroom only, and the floor was swept daily.

Emily shrugged. "I don't know, it must have been when I went outside last night."

Stella stared at her young sister for a moment, then looked back down at the soiled underside of her slippers. There was no denying that a walk on the grass outside would have left the footwear in such a condition. But it still made no sense to her.

How on earth could Emily leave the house alone?

Surely, Nanny Lawson would have woken up if Emily tried to leave the room in the middle of the night?

Had she been sleepwalking?

It was the only explanation that made any sense.

Emily must have had a nightmare, and sleepwalked downstairs, somehow finding her way outside in the grounds.

If only she could convince the little girl of the truth. But she had obviously made up her mind that the evens she had dreamt of were real, and nothing anyone said was going to change that.

Stella gently took her sister's ankles and helper her on with her slippers.

Then she stood behind her and began brushing her hair for her.

Emily appeared to have calmed down and was humming to herself while her sister gently swept the bristles down her silken locks.

Stella purposely took her time, as she had done so with her own hair, hoping against hope that their father would appear at the door with a reprieve.

But deep down she knew that the time for such an act of kindness had passed.

Once she had finished brushing Emily's hair, Stella turned the brush over and slapped the wooden side against her palm. The shock from the pain made her jump. She had only used a minimal amount of force and yet the result stung far more than she had imagined it would.

Stella shook her hand to clear the pain. "You do realise that I'm supposed to spank you with this on your bare bottom if you don't go down at once and apologise."

Emily turned back. "I've already done so. Mama did warn me that Papa would not take the news well now that he had a new wife. I expect that is why he is acing so outraged."

"Very well," sighed Stella, exhausted by the whole situation, but mainly her sister's reluctance to make an apology. "Don't say you hadn't been warned."

She walked over to the bed and sat down on the edge, the brush beside her.

Stella indicated with her index finger for Emily to follow, which she did.

Stella situated her sister on her right-hand side, before lifting her up and pulling her across her knees. She lifted over the girl's nightdress, exposing her milky-white cheeks in the glow from the fire.

She held her sister in place with her left hand, and retrieved the brush with her right, gripping it firmly by the handle.

Stella paused. "This is all of your own doing, Emily," she warned. "There's no one else to blame but yourself."

Emily lay there in her prone position and did not offer an answer.

Taking a deep breath, Stella slapped the back of the hairbrush down hard on Emily's left cheek. He little girl squealed upon impact and began to wriggle as if to make good her escape.

Realising her plan of action, Stella tightened her grip with her left arm around her sister's waist, and aimed another sharp slap, this time on her other cheek.

Again, Emily cried out, and wriggled, although now her movement was far more restricted by her sister's tight grip.

Stella released the next four spanks one after the other, alternating which of her sister's cheeks received the swat.

Once the six were completed, Stella could hear her little sister snuffling with her head still down, facing the floor. The chances were that she did not want her big sister to see her cry. A final defiance against her punishment to prove o her father that she was right to stick by her guns.

Stella lifted Emily off her and placed her on her bed. The soft cotton sheets which covered the mattress should have been cool and soothing for the girl's saw bottom, but even so, she allowed a little *squeal* to escape her lips when her bare bottom made contact with them.

Stella retuned the brush to the dressing able and walked back over to Emily.

The little girl looked up at her sister pouting, with her bottom lip protruding beyond what must have felt comfortable, so Stella knew that it was more for affect than anything else.

Stella pulled back the sheets and coaxed Emily into bed, removing her slippers first and placing them under the bed.

Once she was settled, Stella slipped in beside her sister and placed a tender arm around the little girl shoulders.

At first, Emily refused to respond. But after a moment, she slid across so that her head lay on Stella's shoulder. Then she snuggled in even further until her mouth was mere inches away from her sister's pale white neck.

Eventually, they both fell asleep.

Chapter Thirty-Nine

ADAM SPOOL CARRIED THE EMPTY BARRELS OUT FROM the Boar's Inn and stacked them in the yard for collection. It had been a very long and hard night working on his own without any assistance form his so-called barmaid, Vera.

Inside, he was kicking himself for being such an easy touch.

He had only given Maggie Cunnings a job because deep-down he hoped to one day marry the girl.

Since his wife had passed away the previous year, Adam had ignored the more obvious advances from some of the local widows and spinsters who doubtless saw him as a good catch. He and his wife had not had a perfect marriage by any means. His late father had bullied him into proposing to her because her father and he had been in business together.

The truth was he never fancied her with her sour expression and spiteful nature.

Their love life had been more-or-less non-existent because she claimed to not enjoy their infrequent unions, and claimed she only allowed him near her once a month because it was her duty as his wife.

In truth, he had grown to lose any pleasure he had once

taken from the event due to her lack of enthusiasm, until finally they stopped attempting the ac altogether.

Once she died however, Adam made himself a promise that if he ever married again, it would at least be out of lust, if not love. In his mind he had a lot of catching up to do and he intended to have his share before he was too old to enjoy it.

When Maggie came along asking for a job, Adam saw his chance.

True, she had a bit of a reputation amongst some of the young lads in town, but that just meant that she was willing to offer herself up without complaint, which was just what he was after.

The fact that she was young enough to be his daughter was of no matter to him. Many men in the town were married to girls far younger than themselves, and at least he had a successful business which afforded him a modicum of respectability amongst his fellow men.

That in itself he knew would be enough to convince Ted Cunnings that he was good enough for his daughter. Added to which, once she was married and out of reach of all the young men thereabout, it would give her an edge of respectability which right now, she sorely needed.

Adam had treated Maggie with nothing but kindness since she came to work for him, then she had to go and have an accident, resulting in her not being able to make it into work, let alone stand behind the bar and help with the barrels at night.

He had agreed to take Vera on as a temporary replacement because in his mind it kept the link between him and Ted Cunnings intact. Also, it meant that once she was able to move around again, Maggie would come back to work, and he could carry on wooing her.

Now, not only was Maggie laid up, but Vera had failed to show up for work. This was the gratitude he was shown for giving the ugly mare a job and allowing her time away from the drudgery of having to work on the farm, spending her days up to her armpits in mud and muck.

Well, no one made a fool out of him. If Vera did not show up tomorrow with a damn-good excuse as to why she had let him down today, he would sack her on the spot. Then, he would march down to Cunnings' farm and demand-not ask-for his daughter's hand in marriage as soon as she was able to move around again.

If Cunnings refused, then Adam would sack Maggie as well, leaving them without the extra income and no prospect of her managing to find another position nearby. He would make sure that he spread the rumour that she was lazy and unreliable, which would put paid to anyone else willing to take a chance on her.

Adam placed the last barrel in line, then sat down to take in the evening air.

He was fast becoming too old to manage on his own like this, there was no point in denying it. His back had seen much better days, and his knees were not far behind.

As he stared up at the stars, he noticed something from the corner of his eye, moving amongst the shadows in the wood opposite. Adam focussed his attention on the area in question, straining to make out any actual forms amongst the trees and bushes.

After a moment, he convinced himself that it was merely the wind billowing against the shrubbery causing his mind to see movement where there was none.

He chided himself for being spooked.

"Hello boss," said a sultry voice behind him.

Adam spun round so quickly that he almost lost his balance on the barrel.

Maggie laughed, softly. "Steady on there," she whispered. "I don't want you doing yerself a mischief now, do I?"

Adam was shocked to see his employee up and about. Only

the day before he had been assured by Vera that her sister would be laid up for at least another couple of weeks.

"What are you doing here?" he asked, trying to regain his composure.

Maggie moved in a little closer. She was still mainly in shadow, but close enough that Adam could make out her full silhouette.

"That's no way to welcome your favourite barmaid," Maggie purred. Her voice sounded a little deeper than usual, and there was an underlying edge of seduction in the way she was speaking which Adam had to confess he found extremely intoxicating.

Adam cleared his throat. "Well, you took me by surprise, that's all," he replied apologetically. "I thought you were still laid up on yer back. At least, that's what Vera told me yesterday. An' speaking of which, where was she tonight? She let me right down not turning up for work. You can tell her from me she'll not see a penny for tonight."

Maggie took another step towards him. Now she was close enough so that her facial features were revealed by the moonlight.

There was something different about her which Adam could not place his finger on.

It was not just her face which seemed to radiate as if lit from beneath, but her entire demeanour. She seemed to have taken on an altogether new persona, one which Adam heartily approved of.

If he had ever had any doubts about asking her father for her hand, they were now a distant memory.

Maggie reached out and placed a hand on his chest.

Adam took in an involuntary breath.

"I can feel your heart beating," Maggie informed him. "It's really fast. Is something exciting you?"

Adam was suddenly struck dumb.

Was she coming onto him? It certainly seemed so to him.

Perhaps she was worried that because of her sister she might have lost her position.

If so, Adam realised that he could play that to his advantage. Keep her guessing until she was willing to give him the right inducement to convince him to let her stay.

Maggie moved in closer.

Adam could feel the tips of her shoes touching the ends of his.

They were close enough to kiss.

Behind him, Adam could hear the faint rustle of something in the woods, but his attention was focussed on Maggie, so nothing else mattered.

Adam looked deeply into her eyes.

He could feel himself growing hard as Maggie slowly ran her hand up and down his torso, stopping at his belly and loitering there for a moment, teasing him, before starting back up to his chest.

He closed his eyes and felt her breath on his neck.

"Now!"

The scream came from somewhere off in the darkness.

Reluctantly, Adam opened his eyes to see Maggie running away from him with two men giving chase.

"What the…" Adam turned around, hearing what appeared to be scuffling behind.

There he saw Mathew and two of his men, desperately holding onto two men, using all their strength in an attempt to subdue them.

One of the men they were wrestling with fell to the floor, taking Ned down with him.

The man kicked and bucked, desperate to throw Ned off, but he held on for all he was worth, keeping his arm across the man's neck in an effort to turn his face away from him.

Mathew pulled a wooden stake from his belt and lunged at

the man that Tom was holding around the waist, trapping his arms by his side.

The sharpened end pierced the man's chest, and Mathew drove it home with all his might, knocking the man to the floor as Tom moved aside and went to help his colleague.

Adam heard the man on the floor scream in agony as Mathew used his full weight to drive the stake home. He felt as he should do something, but he had no idea what. He knew that Mathew and his men were here at Father James' invitation, so he suspected that whatever they were doing it was also at his behest.

Even so, he was not prepared for the sight which was unfolding in front of him.

Suddenly there was screaming and shouting coming from behind the pub.

Adam turned back and saw two more of Mathew's men dragging Maggie towards him. Each man had hold of one of her arms, and she was kicking and writhing wildly in a desperate attempt to escape their clutches as they dragged her closer to him.

Adam held out his arm as the men approached. "Hey, what the hell is going on here?" he demanded, determined to block their path until he received a reasonable answer.

From behind he heard another cry, and he spun around just in time to see Mathew nail the other man which Ned and Tom were holding with a stake through the heart, just as he had with the first one.

Before he could look back, Stuart and Gregory dragged the screaming Maggie passed him, towards Mathew.

"Now wait just a minute," Adam cried out, feeling totally out of depth in the presence of these five huge men, but still determined that he would be heard before they harmed his future wife.

Stuart and Gregory stopped once they were in front of their leader.

Maggie, seemingly oblivious to the fact that she was totally outnumbered, continued to writhe and scream, demanding to be released whilst threatening the men with damnation if they refused.

Mathew grabbed Maggie's chin and held it firmly, forcing her jaws apart. He gazed inside her mouth, revealing her elongated upper canines to the rest of his men.

"Come here," he ordered, looking at Adam. "Come and see what fate awaited you if we hadn't 'ave been on hand."

Perplexed, Adam did as he was instructed. When he was in front of Maggie, Mathew turned her head towards him, still clutching her chin, and showed him her fangs.

Adam pulled back, covering his mouth with his hand to prevent him from crying out.

"That's what was waiting for you seconds before we struck. Are yer satisfied now?"

Adam nodded his head and took several steps back.

"Now, go back inside and leave this mess to us," Mathew ordered. "And don't tell no one what you've seen 'ere tonight, or you'll 'ave the militia on yer doorstep to answer to."

Without responding, Adam turned and ran back into his pub, slamming the door behind him and bolting it before stopping to draw breath.

He could hear Maggie still ranting and raving outside, her scream piercing the night, but he no longer cared what happened to her. She was clearly no longer the girl he had lusted after for so long, and as far as he was concerned Mathew and his men could all have their way with her if they wanted. Just so long as they kept her away from him.

Adam clapped his hands over his ears to block out the sound of Maggie's screeching, but it did not good. He could still hear her cries, some of which were aimed at him, begging him to save her while pleading her innocence.

But Adam knew what he had just witnessed, and he shuddered as he contemplated the outcome had Mathew and his team not intervened in the nick of time.

He dragged himself over to the bar and poured himself a large shot of brandy, downing it in one swallow.

Chapter Forty

ONCE AGAIN EMILY AWOKE WITH THE SOUND OF sweet singing in her ears.

She stretched out her little arms and yawned, ensuring that she did not hit Stella who was fast asleep beside her.

Sliding out from under the covers, Emily crept over to the window and glanced out. As she expected, she saw her mother waiting for her in the middle of the lawn. She waved down to her and was about to make her way back outside as she had done the previous night, when her mother spoke to her telepathically, giving her an alternative suggestion.

Emily enthusiastically nodded her understanding, and slipped out of the bedroom, closing the door silently behind her.

As instructed, Emily made her way downstairs, holding on tightly to the banister so as not to risk tripping in her haste to meet with her mother once more.

She crept silently into her father's study and retrieved the key to the cellar from where her mother had told her it would be. She lit a candle from the dying embers of the fire to give her some light to help her negotiate the darkened stairs which led down to the cellar and made her way back outside and across the hallway to the wooden door.

The key was stiff and awkward to turn once she managed to slide it into the lock, so Emily placed her candle on the floor, far enough away so as not to risk her nightgown catching fire, but still close enough for her to benefit from the light it afforded.

Using both hands, she finally managed to slot the bolt back.

Once inside the doorway Emily shut the door behind her. The glow from her candle cast eerie shadows all around her, and suddenly Emily's excitement was tempered with a touch of fear. She took a step back and her frame leant against the solid wood. For an instant she reflected on the practicality of her little adventure and without thinking she plonked herself down on the top step to consider her options.

Having forgotten about the spanking she had received earlier that night, her bottom, clad only in her nightshirt, felt as if it were on fire when she placed her weight on the step.

Yelping, Emily shot back up, rubbing her saw behind with one hand whilst clinging onto the candle with her other.

It was then that she heard her mother's voice calling to her through the stone walls which surrounded the cellar. The comforting sound made her forget both her fear and discomfort, and Emily began taking the steps one at a time, leaning out against the wall for balance.

In her haste to go to her mother, Emily had left her bedroom without her slippers, so she placed each foot down tentatively, just in case there might be a loose nail or wooden splinter waiting to greet her.

Once she reached the bottom, the dust and muck on the cellar floor ground itself into her soles with each step. But her mother's call egged her on as she made her way over to the place which held the secret entrance to the catacombs.

As instructed, Emily pressed each brick in the wall in the combination she was given. The second she released pressure on the fourth one, she heard the sound of stone grinding against stone as the wall nearest to her began to separate and move apart.

Emily's heart began to race as the figure of her mother appeared between at the opening she had just created. Emily put down her candle and raced into her arms, hugging her tightly.

At first, Emily did not notice the man and woman emerging from the entrance, but as she pulled away from her mother's embrace, they both loomed over her.

Unlike her mother, their expressions did not exude kindness and love, but malevolence and horror. Their eyes, wide and vacuous, seemed to slice through into her very soul. The cruel smiles which spread across their lips revealing their elongated fangs, only worked to enhance their evil intent.

With a wave of her hand, Emily's mother seemed to wake them from their terrifying reverie. Both of them stood back, reluctantly, their eyes belying their desire to rush the little girl and take what they believed was rightfully theirs.

Instead, they waited while Emily's mother spoke to her through her mind.

Emily listened, intently. She had followed her mother's orders from the previous night, and she informed her that Nanny Lawson was already subdued from the blood she had sucked out of her veins during her afternoon nap.

Without having to speak, Emily informed her mother which room belonged to her nanny and confessed that she had not been able to resist telling everyone at dinner that she knew that Corinne was no longer her mama.

Her mother chastised her for revealing their secret, so Emily told her of the punishment she had received as a result, which seemed to do the trick and once again her mother took her in her arms and hugged her.

Whilst they embraced, Emily was aware that the man and

women who had emerged from the secret panel along with her mother had both moved past them towards the stairs.

They made no sound as they crossed the cellar floor, and almost seemed to drift rather than walk as they made their ascent upstairs to the ground floor.

Emily was suddenly afraid that they were going to hurt her sister for carrying out her father's demands that she be punished. But her mother assured her that that would not be the case.

Taking her by the hand, her mother led her through the opening to show her the catacombs where she and her other vampires lived.

Emily left her candle behind, burning on the floor.

Somehow, she was no longer afraid of the dark.

———

Stella woke from a deep sleep, during which she had dreamed of being carried away by some mysterious kidnapper out of the house and deep into the woods.

Once outside, she had flown through the air as if suspended on wires, somehow managing to avoid crashing into any and all objects which loomed up before her.

Even in the darkness, Stella was strangely able to see as clearly as if it were day, and her ears were filled with the sweetest music she had ever heard, sung as if a lullaby by someone watching over her.

At some point, she had been placed on a gigantic pillow, as soft as a cloud, and there she lay while Emily insisted on helping her on with a cloak to ward off the night air.

In her haste, Emily had managed to prick Stella's skin with the broach which held the cloak together, but in her dream the pain only lasted a moment and Emily insisted on kissing the place where she had accidently pricked her sister, better.

Stella sat up in bed and stretched out her arms. She had slept throughout the night and yet she still felt sleepy, which was very unusual for her. She looked over and saw the crumpled form of Emily still fast asleep, her messed-up hair covering her face, and her knees pulled up to her chest.

Stella decided to allow her little sister a few more minutes of slumber. She was still feeling guilty for the punishment she had been forced to mete out at the behest of their father the previous night.

She knew that Emily had been very rude to their mother but given the fact that she had attended the funeral of her old friend Jasper only that morning, Stella believed that their father could have settled for the telling-off he had given her over dinner.

Stella swung her legs out of bed and fished on the floor with her bare feet to find her slippers. Once on, she pulled on her dressing gown and made her way over to the window.

It was a crisp autumn day, without a cloud in the sky, and as she stood there, she could feel the warmth of the sun through the glass.

Just then, she saw her father walk into view. He seemed to be dressed for riding and was making his way down the path towards the stable. It seemed particularly early for him to be setting off, but Stella supposed that he must have some important business to attend to, so she thought no more about it.

Once her father had moved out of sight, Stella walked over to the dressing table to brush her hair. Though not nearly in the state of her younger sister's it was still fairly dishevelled after her night's sleep.

Stella sat in front of the mirror and picked up a brush. As she was about to begin the task at hand, she suddenly noticed something odd on her neck. Moving her hair to one side and leaning in for a closer inspection, Stella noticed two tiny pinpricks on the side of her neck.

Frowning, she tied off her hair to keep it out of the way and picked up a hand mirror, holding it directly in front of the marks and angling it to give her a clearer view.

She touched the marks with her other hand and felt two miniscule heads where her blood had presumably congealed.

Inspecting her fingers, she saw that no blood had come away, meaning that the wounds, wherever they had come from, must have had sufficient time to dry, completely.

Her thoughts returned to her strange dream and Emily's attempts to fasten a clasp on her cloak. Was it merely a coincidence that she now bore evidence of the event actually taking place?

But that was impossible. There was no such cloak in the bedroom, and even if there were, why should Emily be trying to attach it to Stella in the middle of the night.

It made no sense to her whatsoever.

Far more plausible was the notion that her little sister had spent a restless night and somehow managed to scratch her on the neck without realising it.

Shaking her mind of the situation Stella continued brushing her hair. The marks were tiny and with her hair down she could easily hide them and avoid any awkward questions.

Stella was halfway through her task when she heard a high-pitched scream echoing from down the hall.

She turned towards the direction from which the scream had come, just in time to hear another one, equally as loud and terrifying.

Stella turned on her see if he cries had disturbed Emily, but to her relief the little girl merely stirred in her sleep and turned over.

Stella crept across the floor and out of the room, closing the door firmly behind her to try and mask any further outburst which might follow.

Once in the hallway, Stella could see a couple of the servants gathered at the far end of the corridor. One of the younger maids was clearly in some distress and was being comforted by one of the others.

As Stella moved closer, Corinne appeared from the other direction, demanding to know what all the commotion was about.

Hobson, their new senior manservant, suddenly emerged from within Nanny Lawson's bedroom. His appearance caused Corinne to stop dead in her tracks, clearly taken aback by the sight of a male servant exiting the bedroom of a female member of the family.

Corinne released a pent-up breath. "Would you please explain to me the meaning of this, Mr Hobson?" she said, as calmly as the situation allowed. Regardless of the circumstances, Corinne was first, and foremost a lady, and so not one to raise her voice, even amongst her own staff.

"My apologies your ladyship," Hobson replied, bowing his head. "I am afraid that young Jessie here was delivering Miss Lawson's hot water and clean towels, when she entered the room and discovered that the lady had passed away during the night."

As he explained the situation the young maid let out another wail of tears, while the older maid tried desperately to hush her.

Without waiting to hear anymore, Corinne rushed into the nanny's bedroom, closely followed by Stella. They were both met by the sight of the old nanny with her head draped over the side of the bed and her eyes wide open.

The bowl in which the maid had carried in the water was lying in pieces scattered around the floor.

Stella closed her eyes and turned away in shock.

Corinne, seeing the reaction of her stepdaughter, ushered her out of the room and closed the door behind them.

Once back out in the corridor, Corinne managed to regain her composure almost immediately. "Hobson, I would like you to send for the Doctor immediately please and see to it that no one enters this room until he arrives."

"Yes, your ladyship," Hobson assured her.

"And please take this poor young girl downstairs and have someone make her a strong cup of tea. She is excused of her duties for the rest of the day."

Hobson assured her once more that her instructions would be carried out, before escorting the maids towards the stairs.

Stella, still clearly in shock, still had her hands pressed against her mouth as if to prevent a scream from escaping.

Corinne moved forward and put her arms around the girl, holding her tightly.

After a while, she asked. "Where is Emily?"

Stella looked up. "She's still asleep, though heaven knows how she managed to remain so during his commotion."

Corinne nodded. "That is for the best under the circumstances, the poor angel has had enough upset to last her a lifetime, and now this on top of it all."

"I saw father heading towards the stables earlier," mentioned Stella. "I suppose it's too late to call him back now."

"Perhaps whoever Hobson sends for the Doctor will pass him on the road and tell him. To be honest, I am more concerned of Emily finding out. She cannot afford to lose two people so close to her in such a short space of time."

"I'll keep her amused this morning," Stella assured her. "We can have breakfast in the kitchen, she'll like that. Cook always makes a fuss over her. At least then she will not be able to see the Doctor come and go."

Corinne rubbed the girl's arm. "That's a splendid idea. What would I do without you? I'll go downstairs and make sure that no one mentions what has happened in front of her."

"I wish father were here."

Corinne smiled, wryly. "Me too, my darling, me too."

Chapter Forty-One

VINCENT PURPOSELY SET OUT EARLY THAT MORNING so that he could see Cedric. He knew his gamekeeper too well to imagine that he would take a day off work, even at his master's insistence, but the poor man had suffered so much over the last couple of days that Vincent wanted to ensure that he stayed home with Hetty and relaxed.

The problem was that once he left the house, it would be that much harder to convince him to return home, so Vincent decided to intervene before his employee had a chance to leave.

After seeing Cedric, Vincent intended to go to the presbytery to speak again with Father James and Mathew concerning their search for the creatures he suspected dwelled beneath his home.

As much as Vincent wanted to protect his family from the potential truth of what might be happening right under their roof, his ultimate goal had to be the welfare of the people of his town. Too many had died already: Mary Grant, Ralph, Enid and Toby Watkins, Ted and Sybil Cunnings, plus their eldest daughter Vera. Even Jasper had been a victim of this curse, albeit indirectly, as the shock of seeing his own father's corpse had caused the old retainer to fall. A fall which ultimately led to the old man's demise.

It was all too much, and the situation was not going to rectify itself. How many more townsfolk had to perish before Vincent took charge and dealt with the situation head-on?

He had already decided that Mathew needed a free rein. He was by far their best chance they had for survival and Vincent had resolved to assist him in any way he felt necessary. After all, if the church had put their faith in him who was Vincent to discern otherwise?

As he approached Cedric's cottage Vincent was struck by the fact that there was no smoke coming from their chimney. Perhaps Cedric had taken him at his word and he and his wife were enjoying the freedom of a rare lie-in, after all?

If that appeared to be the case, Vincent was not going to disturb them. He would merely listen in at their front door and if there were no sounds of anyone moving around, he would leave them to their peace and move on.

Vincent pulled up at the side of the cottage and tied off his horse. He walked around to the front and peered in at the first window. There was no evidence of life inside from what he could see, so he decided to leave Cedric and Hetty in peace.

As he turned to leave, a sudden breeze crossed the field in front of the house and Vincent heard the unmistakable sound of a door swinging on rusty hinges.

Presuming that either Cedric or Hetty had seen him outside and had opened the door to greet him, Vincent turned back to greet them. But there was no one there.

Puzzled, Vincent retraced his steps and noticed the front door stood ajar.

He waited for a moment, half expecting one of them to appear in the opening, but after a moment Vincent realised that no one was coming.

Suspecting an innocent explanation, Vincent rapped against

the wood with his cane and waited. After a couple of minutes there was still no sound of any movement from inside, so he pushed the door slightly and allowed it to swing open.

Inside the cottage everything appeared to be normal, but there was still no sign of the occupants. Calling out, Vincent crossed the threshold and stood just inside the door.

He waited for a response, straining to hear any sounds of movement, but after another minute he decided that the situation required investigation.

Vincent took a deep breath to ward off his initial feelings of trepidation.

He wished that he had Mathew and his gang with him for protection. Their experience in such matters far outweighed his own, but he knew that he could not justify leaving the scene to go and fetch them without making a full investigation of the cottage first.

Vincent called out again, louder this time to ensure that anyone inside would hear him, regardless of their task. His voice echoed back at him. The modest cottage suddenly took on an eerie atmosphere of fear and dread, and Vincent's mind raced back to the previous day at the Cunnings' farm, only then he had not been alone.

Vincent released the catch on the handle of his cane and withdrew the blade from the wooden sheath. There was no doubt I his mind that something was amiss, and he thought it best to be prepared for the worst.

Slowly he began to make his way through the cottage.

As with the front parlour there were no initial signs of foul play, but he could not ignore the overall feeling of menace which pervaded the atmosphere.

Having checked every room for signs of life and finding none, Vincent decided that he would make a further, more thorough search of the property. Something was definitely wrong he could feel it in his gut, and he knew that if he left the task half-done the guilt would weigh heavily on him until he returned.

This time Vincent searched inside cupboards and under the couple's bed for any sign of something untoward having taken place. His guilt at feeling like an unwanted intruder was over-powered by his desire to discover the truth of what had happened to his gamekeeper and his wife.

At the back of his mind grew the seed of a nagging doubt that Cedric and Hetty had decided to take advantage of a rare day off and set off early on a trip outside town. The mere fact that they had forgotten to lock their front door was neither here nor there.

If that did turn out to be the case, then Vincent would be only too happy to apologise for his intrusion. Although as the landowner he had every right to enter one of his properties at will, his father had taught him that respect for one's tenants was all important, and not something to betray without good reason.

Having searched the cottage thoroughly, Vincent found himself back in the kitchen.

There was nowhere to hide in the small room with the possible exception of the larder, which barely looked large enough to house a hanging pig.

Even so, it was the last place to look before he left, so Vincent opened the wooden door and dropped his sword. The weapon clattered on the stone floor, shattering the silence, and as he stumbled backwards Vincent almost tripped over the nearest chair.

There in the larder, his body suspended upside down, hung the naked body of his faithful gamekeeper. Cedric had not been a particularly tall man, but within the confines of the larder the bottom half of his corpse lay crumpled in a heap on the floor.

As Vincent took in the gruesome spectacle, he noticed that Cedric's head had lolled to one side, facing in his direction. His eyes were open and seemed to him to reflect the horror of the last thing he saw before death.

It was obvious to Vincent what had taken place. The corpse was almost pure white, and it was clear to him that every drop of blood had been drained from it.

Questions began to bombard Vincent's mind: Who had done this? Where was Hetty? If she too were a victim of the same perpetrator, why was her corpse not dangling beside her husband's?

As he slowly began to regain his composure, Vincent was confident that there was nowhere left within the cottage for anyone to hide. Even so, he scrabbled on the floor to retrieve his sword, feeling instantly more secure once he held it in his hand.

As much as he hated to leave his loyal servant in such a state, Vincent reminded himself that Cedric was now beyond embarrassment and the priority now was to inform Mathew and Father James of his demise. They would doubtless wish to perform one of their ceremonies on him before burial, and from experience Vincent knew that it must be so.

There was nothing to be gained by taking unnecessary chances.

Avoiding the gaze from Cedric's dead eyes, Vincent used the end of his sword to push the larder door shut.

As he galloped on to the presbytery Vincent could not erase the sight of Cedric's dead eyes from his mind. The thought that the perpetrator might be one of the creatures hiding out below his cellar made him feel physically sick to his stomach. He cursed himself now for not allowing Mathew and his men to search the hall earlier. Just because he had failed to locate the secret location, did not mean that they would have similar success.

For him though, the worst part was knowing that his father had, albeit unknowingly, been the cause of this monstrous phenomena which he had now inherited.

Upon arrival at the presbytery Vincent wasted no time in telling Father James and Mathew of what he had discovered at his gamekeeper's cottage.

Father James buried his head in his hands for a moment in silent prayer.

After a moment, he lifted his head and spoke. "Mathew and his men had quite an eventful night themselves," he informed Vincent. "They managed to capture three of the beasts, including the Cunnings' youngest daughter, Maggie."

Vincent looked visibly shocked. "So, she must have been the one that gave us the slip yesterday, the one who ran across the roof while we were dealing with Toby and her sister?"

Father James shrugged. "We can only presume so. The good news is that they managed to intervene and save poor Adam Spool's life just as Maggie was poised to strike."

"So, who were the other two men?"

The priest shook his head. "I didn't recognise them, but they certainly weren't from around here."

"Do you think that they might be part of the group hiding under the hall?" asked Vincent, hopefully.

"They certainly could be," Mathew shot in. "And if they are, that now makes three we've taken care of that the father 'ere doesn't recognise."

"Three?" asked Vincent, curiously.

"Remember when you first came to see me?" the priest reminded him. "They had just captured that poor creature in the woods. The young girl they despatched in front of you."

Vincent nodded. That incident had slipped his mind. "So that means there is a chance that there are no more than three of these creatures dwelling beneath my home, if there were only six to begin with, as Jasper maintained."

"Unless they've turned others and take them there," offered Mathew. "Either way, the quicker we locate their lair the better for all concerned."

Father James glanced over towards Vincent. He was well aware that the viscount still held reservations concerning such an intrusion at Mandrake Hall. Especially with his entire family in situ.

Much to his surprise, Vincent responded with. "I agree. We've waisted far too much time already. Once we've eradicated the cause of the problem it should be that much easier to round up any stragglers who have been changed along the way."

For the first time Vincent appeared to be in agreement with the rest of them.

Mathew and his men had already made the necessary arrangements concerning Maggie and the two vampires from the previous night, and their corpses were ready for burial.

Mathew suggested that he and his men return to the gamekeeper's cottage to retrieve his body and bring it back for preparation. Once that was done, it might hopefully leave enough daylight to make a search of the hall, but only time would tell.

Vincent decided to ride back the cottage with Mathew and his men, as it was on the way back to the hall. He still was not sure what excuse he was going to give his wife and daughters concerning the impending search in the cellar, but right at that moment the circumstances did not seem to warrant too much concern.

They would accept whatever he told them, as would the servants.

The most important thing was to keep these deaths and the details thereof, away from Mandrake Hall.

Vincent offered to re-enter the cottage with Mathew and his team once they arrived, but Mathew assured him his time would be better placed preparing his household for their upcoming intrusion.

Having left them to it. Vincent carried on at a gentle canter towards his home.

After a short time, he came across Colin Sedgwick's cart on the road.

Vincent pulled up beside hm. "Morning Colin, what brings you out this way on such a fine day?"

Colin's expression immediately dropped. He stooped his head and began mumbling something incoherent which Vincent could barely hear.

"Speak up man, I can't hear you." Vincent was starting to lose his temper with the man.

Finally, Colin cleared his throat and turned his head up so that he could look into Vincent's eyes. "I thought you'd already know your lordship," he muttered. "I've been summoned to your home by Doctor Harris, apparently one of your staff died during the night. He just wants me to take the corpse over to the priest."

The revelation sent a cold shiver through Vincent, causing him to shiver involuntarily.

A death, during the night, while he was asleep. It was all too much to contemplate.

"Did the doctor say how the victim died?" he demanded.

Colin doffed his cap and apologised for not having any of the information which the viscount sought.

Exasperated, Vincent did not wait to thank the man, but just stirred up his steed and raced back to Mandrake Hall.

Chapter Forty-Two

Vincent raced back to Mandrake not bothering to wait for Colin Sedgwick. He was curious to find out which of his servants had passed away, and more importantly, how.

Naturally, he feared the worst.

Had the creatures which dwelt under his property made their way out and randomly chosen one of his staff to feed on?

Father James had convinced him that of the original six-supposing that Jasper had his facts correct-there were only three left. But that was still more than enough to be afraid of. It only took one to spread carnage, and once one person was *changed,* they in turn could easily spread their poison amongst the rest of the community.

For the first time since his whole nightmare started, Vincent wished that Mathew and his team would make haste in arriving at the hall. He intended to ensure that all his guns were loaded and kept close at hand from now on. His family's protection would be his sole purpose until the last vampire was lying dead in the ground with a stake through its heart.

Vincent arrived at the hall just as Doctor Harris was descending the steps to the drive.

When he saw Vincent approach, he stopped and waited for him to pull up.

Vincent dismounted and passed the reins to a waiting servant.

He pulled the doctor off to one side. "Who was it this time?" he asked, anxiously.

"I'm afraid it was the girls' nanny," Doctor Harris revealed.

"What?"

"Yes, I know. She seemed in rude health when I saw her the other day, but you can never tell for sure."

"What was it?" asked Vincent, suspecting the worst.

The doctor shook his head, thoughtfully. "She appears to have passed away during the night. No obvious signs of violence on her body except for two sets of pin pricks on either side of her neck. Probably made by a broach pin or something similar."

Vincent shuddered. It was as he had feared. "Anything else?"

The doctor scratched his head. "Well, looking at the corpse I was struck by how pale the skin was. It looked almost as if all the blood had been drained from it. Curious thing. It reminded me of young Mary Grant when they called me in to see her."

"Nanny Lawson was never one for the sun, she always made a point of remaining in the shade and carrying a parasol," offered Vincent. It was not much of a theory, but he did not want the doctor to raise the alarm, unnecessarily. If Margaret had been taken by a vampire, then he would have Father James and Mathew deal with it.

"I've sent for Colin Sedgwick he should be here any time now."

"I know," replied Vincent. "I passed him on my way in."

"If you like, I could have him bring the body back to my surgery for a closer inspection?"

"No, no thank you doctor, that won't be necessary. I'll arrange for him to take her to the presbytery so Father James can make all the necessary arrangements for her funeral."

Doctor Harris nodded. "Very well. Would you like me to leave you a couple of sleeping powders for your daughters? I can show you how much to give each of them so that they can have a decent night's sleep. You can't be sure how something like his might affect them."

"That's very kind, but I think they'll be fine. Lord knows they've been through the mill recently."

The pair of them saw Sedgwick's cart turning the bend for the hall.

The doctor made his farewell and boarded his carriage.

Vincent raced up the stairs and into the hall. His main concern for the moment was how Stella, and especially little Emily were coping with their latest loss.

He could feel the guilt weighing heavily in his chest for sending Emily up to bed with no desert the previous evening. Not to mention his insistence that she be physically repri-manded for her behaviour. There was no denying that she was being uncharacteristically rude to her mother, but with the funeral that day, and now with the loss of Nanny Lawson, he knew that Emily would doubtless be inconsolable.

He wanted nothing more than to sweep her up in his arms and assure her that everything would be alright.

Hobson greeted him just inside the door. "I take it your lord-ship is away of the tragedy which took place during the night?" the butler asked as he helped Vincent out of his overcoat.

"Yes, thank you Hobson, how are my daughters coping?"

"Lady Stella has kept Lady Emily amused in the kitchens. The Viscountess asked us not to make Lady Emily aware of her nanny's passing."

"I see. Very well. Sedgwick is just pulling up in his cart around the back, could you arrange for Nanny Lawson's remains to be taken out to him?"

"Of course, your lordship."

"And where might I find my wife?"

"She has just been served tea in the drawing room, sir."

"Thank you, Hobson, carry on."

Vincent made his way to the drawing room. There he found Corinne just as Hobson had said he would. She looked exhausted, and Vincent went over to her and hugged her.

"Hobson's brought me up to speed," he began. "How are you?"

"I'm fine," Corinne assured him. "That tea did the trick. Did Hobson inform you that we haven't told Emily yet?"

Vincent nodded. "He said Stella was keeping her amused."

"She's been wonderful. I'm dreading how Emily will react when she finds out, but now you're here I'm feeling a lot more confident."

"I'm having her body taken out via the back stairs, Hobson's arranged it, I've got a Sedgwick waiting to take her body to Father James to prepare her for burial."

Corinne nodded. "Who'd have thought we needed his services again so soon. Did you see the Doctor before he left?"

Vincent nodded.

"Did he tell you what he thought the cause was? He seemed a little vague when I asked him, but I wasn't sure if that was because he felt the answer might not be fit for my ears."

Vincent kissed her on the forehead. "No, he wasn't a hundred percent sure. He suspects natural causes. After all, she wasn't a young woman."

Corinne accepted his explanation without question, although she too had noticed the paleness of the woman's skin when she first went into her bedroom.

"So, what are we going to do about Emily?" Corinne asked, concerned. "We cannot keep the truth from her indefinitely."

"No, you're right," Vincent agreed, moving over to the pull cord by the door.

A moment later one of their servant's appeared.

"Could you ask Lady Stella to bring Lady Emily to us?" Vincent asked. "And perhaps we'd better have some more tea, and milk and biscuits."

The servant bowed and disappeared.

"Keep them here for me, I won't be a moment." With that, Vincent left the drawing room and made his across the hall to his study. Once there, he unlocked the drawer in his desk which housed the key to his gun cabinet.

He took each gun out in turn to check that it was fully loaded, and those that were not he made sure he replenished from the spares he kept in the cabinet drawer.

Once he was satisfied, he re-locked the cabinet and placed the key inside his waistcoat pocket in case he needed it in an emergency.

Returning to the drawing room, he found Stella and Emily had already joined Corinne. The fresh tea had been served, and the old tray removed.

As he opened the door, to his surprise Emily ran into his arms, and hugged him.

Vincent looked over his youngest daughter a Corinne and Stella, an expression of quizzical curiosity on his face.

He had certainly not expected such a welcome after the previous evening.

They all sat down to tea, Emily to her milk and biscuits.

"Don't eat too many of those," warned Stella. "You'll explode after the breakfast cook prepared for you."

"Did you have a scrumptious breakfast my darling?" asked Corinne.

Emily nodded, enthusiastically. "Yes, thank you, Mama. It was delicious."

Emily's use of the word 'mama' was not lost on the others.

Corinne looked up at Vincent and smiled, obviously relieved that the status quo had been resumed, at least for the moment.

Vincent surmised that Stella had spoken to her little sister during the night, and probably this morning, eventually managing to make her see the error of her ways.

The four of them drank and chatted amicably, until Emily suddenly looked around her and piped up. "Where's Nanny Lawson? I haven't seen her his morning."

Vincent glanced at the others before placing his cup and saucer back on the tray.

He stretched out his arm towards Emily. "Come and sit with your papa a moment, poppet." Emily put down her milk and skipped over to him, clearly oblivious to the news she was about to receive.

Vincent sat her up on his knee as he gently explained to her about Margaret's demise.

The little girl did not speak throughout his explanation, but nor did she cry or try to run away. It was as if she were being told what they were having for supper.

Once he was finished, Vincent held his daughter close to him as if awaiting tears which never came. Perhaps, he wondered, Emily was just cried out after Jasper, and too exhausted to start again.

Even so, her reaction was decidedly underwhelming.

After a while of no response, Vincent kissed her on the top of her head and suggested she go and finish her milk before it went cold, which the little girl did.

Now that Father James and Mathew had another corpse to deal with as well as Cedric's, Vincent thought it highly improbable that they would have time before dark to return and search the cellar.

He was in a quandary as to what to do.

He and Hobson had already searched the area without success, so there seemed little to be gained from wasting another afternoon on the same task.

Perhaps with his loaded guns by his side, Vincent thought that he could just lay in wait in the cellar and catch the buggers if they tried to slip out during the night.

That would give him a modicum of comfort, but even then, he would feel safer with a least a couple of Mathew's men at hand, tooled up just in case of action.

Either way, now that the Emily situation seemed to have rectified itself far easier and quicker than he had anticipated, Vincent wondered if it might be profitable for him to return to the presbytery to see if he could be of any use there.

Even if it meant sorting out the coffins for burial, if it meant freeing Mathew's team in time for them to return to search Mandrake before darkness, then it was time well spent.

He could not just sit around the hall all day pretending to all and sundry that everything was as it should be.

Clearing his throat, Vincent spoke softly. "I forgot to mention that I have some men due to take a look at the foundations. They won't have to disturb you, they'll probably be working in the cellar for the most part, so just in case they arrive before I come back, just tell the servants to send them down to the cellar to get started. Hobson will know what to show them."

Corinne turned in her seat. "You're leaving us again, so soon. Can't you spend the day with us together?"

Vincent walked over to her and took her hand, holding it in both of hers.

He lifted it up and kissed her wedding ring. "I know my darling, and I'm truly sorry, but I must speak to Father James concerning Nanny's funeral arrangements, plus it appears that one of my gamekeepers has also passed away during the night, so I do have business to attend to."

From the expression on both Corinne's and Stella's faces, he could see that they wished it were not so, but they understood as Viscount and local justice of the peace, Vincent's many tasks were onerous and could crop up at any time.

Therefore, when the time came, they all kissed him goodbye, with Emily offering another hug.

Chapter Forty-Three

EMILY WAITED FOR HER FATHER TO LEAVE continuing to play with her doll as if she did not have a care in the world. She had done as her mother had told her the previous night by feigning ignorance concerning Margaret's demise. The only thing she had not managed was a fresh batch of tears when receiving the news from her father, but that was a minor detail.

Although pretending not to hear, Emily had listened carefully to her father explaining about the men who were coming to inspect the cellar.

When her mother had shown her the secret place she and others rested during the day, she had been very specific about Emily not disturbing them unless it was an emergency. Well as far as she was concerned, having a group of strange men poking around in the cellar certainly constituted an emergency.

What if they accidently discovered the secret entrance to the catacombs?

Worse still, what if that was the real reason that they were there in the first place?

Emily knew that she had to act for her mother's sake. In truth, she did not much care for the other two friends her mother kept company with. Emily felt decidedly uneasy in their presence, especially the way their eyes seemed to bore into her. Even after they had fed on Nanny Lawson, they still made her feel as if she might be their next victim.

Her mother had fed on her while the others were upstairs. She explained to Emily that because of her condition she needed to feed nightly, but she did not take too much, just enough to make it through until the next night.

Not that Emily minded. She would have been happy to give up her entire blood supply if it made her mother happy. But she had explained to the little girl that soon she would not need her blood anymore, and that once she had taken enough, Emily would become like her and that they would then go out at night together and have great adventures to make up for all their lost time.

For now, Emily knew that she had to concoct some form of subterfuge to allow her time to warn her mother of the impending arrival of the men. She knew that her options were limited. She could not just walk off without telling Corinne and Stella what she was up to, otherwise they would insist on an explanation.

Everyone always seemed to want to know where she was and what she was doing, which had become very tiring most recently.

Still, she knew that she had to play the game for now.

Propping one of her dolls up in the corner, Emily rose and announced that she was just popping upstairs to fetch a companion doll from her bedroom.

Corinne and Stella exchanged a worried glance. They did not want Emily to stumble across the men carrying Margaret's body down the back stairs, just in case she decided to use them instead of the main flight.

Such amusements often occurred to children, and it did not seem worth the risk.

"I need to fetch a clean handkerchief from my room," announced Stella. "Would you like me to collect your doll for you?"

Emily looked at her quizzically. "You don't know which one I want," she said.

Stella smiled. "You could always tell me."

Emily shook her head. "It's okay, it'll be easier if I go. I won't be long."

Just then Corinne stood up, barring the little girl's path.

She smiled down at Emily. "Could I ask both of you to wait here for a moment? I just want to check on something before I forget."

The excuse did not seem particularly plausible, even to a seven-year-old. But Emily's mother had explained to her last night that she had to make a point of being good and not causing a fuss to ensure that no one suspected anything untoward was taking place.

Irritating though it was, Emily smiled up at Corinne and walked back to her doll.

Corinne winked at Stella before leaving the room.

It suddenly occurred to Emily that once Corinne returned, Stella would still wish to escort her upstairs which would make things slightly awkward for Emily to disappear for a while. Then she remembered her own handkerchief which was fresh and unused.

She took it out from her sleeve and handed it over to Stella. "Here you are," she said, sweetly. "Save you going upstairs."

Stella accepted the offer gratefully. "But what about you?"

Emily shrugged. "I can always choose another one when I pick up my doll."

After a few moments Corinne re-entered the room, a little out of breath.

"Everything okay?" asked Stella.

"Oh yes, everything is fine," Corinne assured her. She had

bumped into Hobson by the stairs, and he assured her that Margaret's body was already on its way to the presbytery.

Although Emily had been quite subdued by the revelation of the loss of her nanny, here was nothing to be gained by allowing her to see the dead woman's corpse being removed from the house. So, disaster avoided.

Emily, still watching the room and sensing a new lack of tension between the grown-ups, waited for Corinne to sit down and return to her sewing before announcing that-if no one had any objections-she would like to retrieve her other doll.

Once outside the drawing room, Emily made a sideways movement towards her father's study. She knew that he did not appreciate anyone going in there without his say so, but time was not on her side as he could return with his men at any time.

Emily lit a candle from the fireplace and grabbed the keys to the cellar.

No one saw her cross the floor to the cellar, and she managed the key easier this time than she had the previous night.

There was no time for fear or trepidation, speed was of the essence.

Emily quickly located the first stone to push and completed the sequence to open the secret chamber in seconds.

Once the entrance was ajar, Emily paused for a moment. She had a sudden feeling in the pit of her stomach that the other two friends of her mother might be up and about and waiting to greet her. If her mother was still asleep in her coffin, Emily knew that she would have no chance of escape before the other two leapt on her and ravaged her frail body.

She shook the thought clear. Her priority had to be to warn her mother.

Taking a deep breath, Emily ventured into the catacomb, keeping her candle out in front of her o light her way. She remembered the sequence of passages from last night, although to be fair she had been a little *woozy* after her mum had fed off her.

Determined to complete her task, Emily strode on, double-checking each turning before she took it.

Finally, she found herself in the main chamber where the six coffins sat on their concrete plinths. She knew exactly which one her mother rested in. She had shown her the previous night.

Emily crept passed two of the other coffins until she reached her destination.

She placed the candle on the stone plinth and gently pushed at the lid of the coffin in an effort to dislodge it. Emily was only just about tall enough to see over the coffin, but that did not make removing he heavy wooden lid any easier.

Grabbing the lip of the lid with both hands, Emily heaved for all she was worth.

A sudden sound of wood scraping from behind her in the darkness, caught her attention, and Emily stopped what she was doing to turn around.

Even with the glow from her candle the size of the catacomb made it impossible for her to discern anything moving in the shadows.

But she had definitely heard *something*!

Nervously, Emily returned to the task at hand. She shoved at the wooden lid with all she had, but it still would not even give her an inch.

There was another echo of wood being scraped against something somewhere off in the distance, but still close enough that little Emily could hear every sound.

Out of sheer desperation Emily began to knock as hard as she could against the solid wood side of her mother's coffin.

There were footsteps being dragged across the floor, and she knew that someone was approaching her from behind, but she was too frightened to turn around to see who it was.

In truth, she suspected that she knew exactly who was

closing in on her, and they were cutting off her escape back to the entrance, so she only had one chance of survival.

To her relief, the lid of her mother's coffin began to rise, and seconds later Emily watched as her mother's elongated fingers peeped over the top of the side of the coffin, followed by her head and shoulders.

The look on the woman's face caused Emily to take a step back.

It was definitely her mother, but instead of the usual smile she wore her face was twisted into a mask of pure evil. She sat up in her coffin and glared down at Emily who was now so scared she took another couple of steps backwards, only stopping when the back of her legs bumped into someone standing directly behind her.

She wanted to scream, but her throat was too dry.

This was not the welcome she had expected by any stretch.

Emily waited patiently while her mother climbed out of her coffin and swung her elegant legs to the floor. All the time her eyes remained fixed and unforgiving on the little girl, and Emily inadvertently clenched her bottom cheeks together in anticipation of another spanking.

"Why have you disturbed our vital slumber?" her mother demanded, moving in close enough so that Emily felt trapped between her and whoever was standing behind her.

Emily looked up. For the first time since they had met, Emily felt a tinge of doubt that she was actually in the presence of her mother. Mothers were meant to be kind and sweet, and never grow cross with their little girls.

"I...I heard Papa announcing that some men are coming to search in the cellars," Emily muttered. "I was afraid they might be trying to locate the secret entrance, so I thought I'd better warn you, just in case...I'm sorry, did I do wrong?"

Her mother's rigid expression of anger evaporated almost at once, and she held her arms out for Emily to embrace her.

Emily ran to her and buried her face in her gown. She could hear her mother speaking to her comrades in a language she did not understand, but which her mother had promised to teach her in time.

Once she had finished speaking, the other two vampires scuttled away and disappeared around a nearby corner.

Emily's mother pulled her daughter's head back so that she could look into the little girl's eyes. "You did very well," she assured her, gently touching her cheek with the side of her finger. "You may have just saved my life my precious little one."

She bent down and kissed the top of Emily's head.

"I was so afraid you'd be cross with me," Emily replied, relieved. "I know you said not to disturb you unless it was an emergency, but I thought that this qualified."

"Indeed, it did little one. I am immensely proud of you for having the initiative to act I he way you have. But now you must go back up before they miss you. No good can be gained from arousing their suspicions as to where you have been."

Emily nodded her understanding.

Then she asked. "Can't I please go with you, Mama?"

Her mother shook her head. "Not just yet, but soon, I promise."

Reluctantly, Emily stayed for one more hug before collecting her candle and making her way out of the catacombs.

She hit the stones in order to secure the entrance and made her way back up the stairs.

Peering through the cellar door, she was glad to see that there was no one milling about hallway. So as stealthily as she was able, she locked the cellar door and tiptoed back to her father's study to replace the key.

For a moment she wondered if she should hide it, thereby preventing the men, when they arrived, from accessing the cellar. I would certainly give her mother more time to relocate herself, and her colleagues.

But she knew that there was bound to be a spare set somewhere else in the house, and it would not take her father long to locate them. Plus, he would also be suspicious as to where the original set disappeared to, which in turn might result in awkward questions being asked.

Therefore, Emily left them in situ and returned to the drawing room.

Both Corinne and Stella looked up when she arrived.

"Where's your doll?" asked Corinne, smiling warmly.

"Oh," replied Emily, suddenly remembering the reason behind her rouse. "After all that, I couldn't decide which one to bring. Silly of me."

The two women thought nothing of it and just returned to their books.

Chapter Forty-Four

WHEN VINCENT ARRIVED BACK AT THE PRESBYTERY, he found a hive of activity awaiting him. With the latest arrivals of Cedric and Nanny Lawson, they now had a grand total of nine corpses awaiting burial.

Although all but the latest additions had been prepared by Mathew and his men, Father James informed Vincent that the local carpenter who supplied the coffins was struggling to keep up with the orders and was beginning to question the sudden increase in volume.

Not wishing to arouse suspicion, Father James had claimed that a sudden turn in the weather was to blame, but deep down her felt it likely that they would have to let the man in on their secret and swear him to silence.

Vincent assured the priest that if it came to it, he himself would speak to the man and pay for silence. In such circumstances he knew that money always talked.

"One of Mathew's men had the idea that we could dig a mass grave and place all the vampires, along with those who had no living relatives, in together," Father James confided.

"But I must confess, it doesn't sit well with me. Even if a person has no one to grieve for them, they should still be afforded the dignity of a Christian burial. Regardless of what they became at the end, they were once good, honest, God-fearing people."

Vincent nodded. Although he could see the validity of expediting the process, especially in light of the sudden influx in cases, he knew he would never forgive himself if he agreed to deny his own people the most fundamental of Christian rights.

But that did nothing to help with his situation. He wanted those vampires found and dealt with as quickly as possible. Now that they had begun to infiltrate his household, he feared it would not be long before one of them found its way into his wife, or daughters' bedrooms.

He could not live with himself if anything happened to one of them.

Especially as he knew the secret of where the danger lay.

Vincent and Father James both looked up as the catch on the side door *clanked* open and Mathew entered the room. He acknowledged Vincent and slumped down in a chair opposite him.

"How is it all going?" asked the priest.

"My men have done their duty by your two servants from this morning," he replied, looking a Vincent. "They're wrapping the corpses now, but we desperately need those coffins, Father. The bodies are starting to stack up in the cottage."

Just then Mrs Oakes entered the room, carrying a jug of wine and plate of cakes.

Father James thanked her, as Mathew grabbed the jug and poured out three cups of wine, downing in his one go, before re-filling his cup.

Once the housekeeper had shut the door behind her, Father James said. "I know Mathew, I know, but we've only the one carpenter in town and he works alone. If I try and rush him too much, he'll start asking awkward questions."

Mathew downed half his cup, before asking. "Have you thought any more about Ned's suggestion? We can start digging as soon as the boys finish swaddlin' the last corpse. It'll certainly help to move things along. At this rate me and the boys'll 'ave no room to sleep, and the smell'll not get any better, neither."

Father James winced. "I have already explained the theory to his lordship, but like me, he too believes in everyone deserving a proper Christian burial."

"Well, 'e don't 'ave to share 'is home with a bunch of corpses, do 'e?"

Vincent smiled. In spite of the man's arrogance, he still had admire his practicality.

The situation they found themselves in was unique to say the least, and as such perhaps there was a need to forgo some of the more civilised proprieties they were all used to.

Such a plan would indeed speed things up, and time was not on their side.

Vincent could feel his anxiety rising at the prospect of another night with the vampires free to roam his ancestral home.

"Perhaps, Father," Vincent began, "we might consider burying the bodies without coffins."

Father James turned to him, sloshing his wine down in his chin in his haste.

He wiped the overspill away with his tunic sleeve.

"Before you say anything," Vincent continued, holding up his hand. "All those poor souls that had to be buried in mass graves during the plague were still Christians, but circumstances dictated that such actions were necessary."

"Yes, but, I mean, we cannot compare half a dozen corpses to the thousands at that time. Plus, which, there was the risk of spreading the disease if steps weren't taken to eradicate it. Once Mathew and his men have staked and beheaded our victims, they are no longer a danger to any living soul."

"I appreciate that father, but I'm not saying we just dump the bodies unceremoniously in the ground one on top of the other," offered Vincent.

"That's exactly what I was suggesting," added Mathew, bemused.

"I know," Vincent assured him, "and I appreciate your reasons behind it, possibly more than you could know. But what I'm suggesting is that rather than waste time waiting for the coffins which could take days, or even weeks, we bury each body, respectfully, in their own grave, just not in coffins. You would naturally still perform a proper Christian service over their graves."

Father James mulled over the proposal. There was certainly nothing specific in the Christian ritual which demanded a coffin be used. I had just become common practice as a way of keeping the worms and maggots away for longer to give the dead a little more dignity once they were in the ground.

But, in principle, he could see no reason why a coffin had to be used.

"Well, I suppose under the circumstances..." The priest trailed off.

"We'd better get started then," Mathew jumped in, knocking back the last of his wine. "If you want us to dig nine separate graves, an' then fill 'em back in, it's gonna take the rest of the day, and then some."

This news was not what Vincent wanted to hear. Although he had argued for the process to take place, he had hoped that it would still leave plenty of time for Mathew and his men to make a search of Mandrake.

Now he knew that was no longer feasible.

"What if we find you more help?" suggested Vincent. "That would speed things up."

Mathew's brow furrowed. "Who do you 'ave in mind?" he asked. "We can't ask any old Tom or Dick. No unless you want the world and 'is wife to know your business."

Vincent turned to Father James. "What about the two gravediggers you had before Mathew and his men arrived. Do you think they would be willing for a few extra crowns?"

Father James shook his head. "I fear not, my son. After what they witnessed at the burial of young Mary Grant, they confessed to me that they no longer wished to be involved in any such similar burial. They only agreed to act for Jasper because they knew the old man, and I assured them that they had nothing to fear from his corpse."

"But these corpses have all been dealt with by Mathew, can't you convince them that they have nothing to concern them, unduly?"

Father James sighed. "I can but try, but I fear it will be a waste of time. Like I said, they only agreed to work on Jasper's because they knew him personally."

"But you will try," urged Vincent. "Tell them I will double their usual fee."

"I'll send word now," Father James agreed.

Vincent followed Mathew back to the cottage where his men were completing the preparations for Cedric and Nanny Lawson.

Mathew explained the situation to his men, who all seemed to be of a like mind concerning the burials, no doubt, Vincent assumed, because it meant that they would not have to spend the night with a bunch of corpses under their roof.

By the time they had finished with the last body, Father James appeared to inform Vincent that he had not been successful in his task to persuade his usual gravediggers to take part in the afternoons exercise.

Vincent was furious at the news, but he was sure that the priest had done his best.

He considered riding back to the hall to enlist the help of some of his younger servants. He was sure that he could buy their silence for a little extra money and the threat of their positions being on the line if they ever revealed the details of what they were being asked to perform.

But that would take time. Time which he knew cold be better spent if he himself helped out with the labour. Added to which, deep down he still preferred the idea of the fewer of his staff knowing the truth, the better.

When this living hell was all over, Vincent firmly believed that he and his family could return to their normal lives, with no fear of any stigma attached.

Mathew and his men all enjoyed a good chuckle when Vincent suggested that he help with the graves. But once he removed his jacket and rolled up his sleeves, they saw that he meant business. Even though he was not used to physical labour, Vincent was still young enough and fit enough to be more help than hindrance.

At first, Vincent insisted that they leave Margaret's body untouched. He could not envisage burying her without a proper funeral that the family could all attend.

But as the day wore on, he grew more complacent about the act, especially as Father James was conducting a full burial service for each corpse, treating each one with equal reverence.

In the end, as the sunlight was fading and the men were close to exhaustion, he relented and insisted on digging the old nanny's grave himself.

They all stood around the final grave with their heads bowed as Father James repeated the solemn words for the dead to rise once more in God's glory and ascend into heaven.

Drained from their labours, the men all slouched back to the presbytery where Mrs Oaks had prepared hot stew, fresh bread, and a custard pudding. As they all sat down to devour their well-earned meal, Vincent excused himself insisting that he must return to Mandrake to keep a watchful eye over his family.

In between mouthfuls of stew, Mathew asked him what he intended to do in order to safeguard his loved ones. Vincent explained that he had loaded all his guns and that if needs be, he intended to keep a vigil, positioning himself outside he cellar door just in case any of the bloodsuckers ventured out during the night.

Now that they had proved themselves arrogant enough to look for sustenance within the household, he was determined that Nanny Lawson would be their last victim from under his roof.

Mathew washed down his stew with a large cup of wine and released an enormous belch, apologising to Father James for his manners. "How about this," he began. "You go home an' 'ave yer supper with yer family, then later tonight, after your family 'ave gone to bed, me and the lads will come to the hall to keep vigil for yer? There's five of us so we can take it in turns to keep watch, an' if there are only three of these devils left, we'll outnumber them an' see them off. What d'yer say?"

Vincent did not attempt to hide his gratitude. After the full day the men had had, I seemed like too much to ask for their protection, so Mathew volunteering seemed like a prayer answered.

Vincent walked around the table and shook Mathew's hand, then clapped the other men on the shoulder, thanking them repeatedly for their gesture, and insisting that he would pay them handsomely for their protection.

They agreed that Mathew and his team would arrive at the hall by eleven that night, allowing Vincent time to ensure that the rest of his family were all tucked up in bed.

Most of his staff would have retired by then, so Vincent intended to take Hobson into his confidence insofar as telling him that the men were coming, though not the actual purpose of their visit. He knew that he could rely on the man to see to it that the rest of the staff would already be in their rooms by the time the men arrived.

Chapter Forty-Five

VINCENT ARRIVED BACK AT MANDRAKE COMPLETELY
spent. His whole body ached from the manual labour he had
engaged in that afternoon, and his clothes certainly showed the
evidence of his endeavour.

He saw the shock in Hobson's eyes when he opened the door
to him, the butler unable to hide his initial surprise. "Did you
have an accident your lordship?" Hobson asked, concerned by
his master's appearance.

"Nothing to worry about," replied Vincent. "If you could
draw me a hot bath before dinner."

After helping him off with his outer coat, Hobson ran on
ahead up the stairs to do as his master commanded.

Vincent considered entering the drawing room to see
everyone before going up, but then decided that the explanation
for his condition would take too long, and too much out of him
as he would have to lie about why he was so dirty and dishevelled. So instead, he followed his butler up the stairs to clean
himself up.

As much as he wished to relax in his bath and allow the hot
water to soothe the aches and pains from his joints, Vincent

knew that supper would soon be ready and that everyone else would be waiting, so he just spent long enough to clean himself off before dressing.

"Oh, Papa, there you are, we were getting worried," exclaimed Emily as he walked in through the door.

Vincent smiled. "I know my loves, my apologies. Business took longer than I'd anticipated. He walked over and kissed Corinne, apologising again in her ear, before walking over to his daughters and hugging them both.

He ordered himself a large whiskey and slumped down in an armchair by the fire, the warmth made him feel as if he was still in his bath and he eased back as it penetrated his tired limbs.

He was dreading his youngest daughter asking when they would hold Margaret's funeral. Being an inquisitive child, she was bound to bring it up before the night was through, so Vincent decided that he would lie to them all and just say he needed to make the arrangements with Father James.

As much as he hated the deception, he was afraid that there was no easy way to break the news of what he and the other men had done that afternoon, and he suspected that such a revelation might be more than little Emily could cope with.

Tonight, more so than usual, he needed his loved ones to go to bed without fuss or suspicion. Therefore, he intended to announce the arrival of the 'builders' later that evening, whilst obviously keeping the real reason for them being there from the rest of the family.

Fortunately for him, Emily was in one of her chattiest moods a supper, even to the point of chastising her father for devouring his soup so quickly.

Properly rebuked, Vincent apologised for his manners, much to the amusement of the others. He could not deny his hunger, but as with the fire warming him from without, the soup and wine was doing a fine trick from within.

"So, what were you doing all day, Papa?" asked Emily curiously.

"Ah, well, I was talking to those men I mentioned earlier, the ones who need to come over to check the foundations. I've arranged for them to come over later tonight."

"Tonight!" asked Corinne, stopping her spoon midway towards her mouth.

Vincent had expected such a response, so he was ready for it and pretended as if the matter was nothing out of the ordinary. "Yes, apparently, they need to see the foundations at night first before inspecting them during the day. Something to do with the building having cooled down after a day with the sun shining on it. Not that we've had too much of that lately."

"How late will they be staying?" enquired Corinne. "Should I arrange accommodation for them?"

Vincent laughed. "Good heavens no, we don't want them moving in, they're here to work not enjoy themselves. They shouldn't stay too late. Once they're done, I'll leave one of the servants to let them out."

Just then one of the servants arrived carrying a silver tray with a cover concealing what was underneath.

Vincent used the distraction to his advantage.

"Ah, he main course, lovely. I could eat a horse."

Again, everyone joined in with laughing at his comment.

He was glad that the moment had passed and quickly switched the subject by asking the ladies how they had spent their day.

———

The rest of supper passed without incident. Vincent was surprised that Emily did not ask about Nanny Lawson's funeral, but by the same token he was relieved that she had not.

Due to Margaret's demise, Stella volunteered to sleep with

Emily again, just so that someone was there in case she had a nightmare. Emily readily agreed, even though she insisted that nightmares were for children and that she was now too old to suffer from such maladies.

Everyone else, including Corinne, retired by ten thirty, which suited him perfectly.

After supper Vincent had arranged for Hobson to set up some chairs and torches in the cellar for Mathew and his men, along with some cold-meat sandwiches and wine to keep them company during their long vigil.

As he stood on the veranda awaiting their arrival, Vincent could feel his eyes closing.

He had to admire the men for their steadfastness, not to mention stamina, in agreeing to keep watch over his family while he slept. Vincent could not deny the relief he felt knowing that they would be there throughout the small hours.

He assuaged any guilt he felt at not being part of the watch by deciding to give each man a guinea for their troubles in the morning.

With any luck, he hoped that by then they might have caught the last three vampires and put an end to the torment that had plagued his town since his return to his ancestral home.

In truth, he felt relieved that no one had started pointing the finger in his direction by linking his return with so many recent deaths.

He knew that anyone with such ideas would naturally thin twice before voicing such an opinion against their lord and magistrate. That said, Vincent had heard of the mob riots which had taken place just before his return to Mandrake. It proved that when men suspected something, with enough ale in their belly's, they were capable of anything, even murder.

In the distance Vincent heard the rumble of carriage wheels along the path.

He heaved a sigh of relief when it came into view.

Once Mathew and his men had unloaded all their paraphernalia, Vincent led them inside and down to the cellar. En route, he showed Mathew where the front door key was housed just in case any of them needed to exit the house during the night.

Vincent was impressed by the sheer volume of sords, guns and stakes the men had with them. More than enough to deal with three vampires, and then some. He was going to suggest that he left them some of his firearms but seeing their plethora he decided that it was unnecessary.

"I thought that Father James might accompany you to say a prayer over the corpses should you catch any tonight."

Mathew grinned. "'e wanted to, but he was exhausted, poor man. I convinced him a decent night's rest would be more beneficial, especially if he has more services to conduct tomorrow, dependin' on 'ow things go tonight."

"I wish I could direct you to their lair," said Vincent, "but all I know is what my old servant told me. The entrance is somewhere down here, but as to where." He shrugged his shoulders.

"Not to worry," Mathew assured him. "If they're down 'ere and they try anything tonight, my men'll get 'em."

"And let's hope that will be an end of it all," said Vincent resignedly.

"Aye, let's hope that's the case," agreed Mathew.

"Is there anything else you think you might need?"

Mathew shook his head. "Nah, these sandwiches look fine, an' thanks for the wine."

"Not at all," Vincent assured him. "Now if you need me for anything during the night, just walk up to the first-floor landing, and my room is the first on your right."

Mathew thanked him and told him they would only disturb him to tell him all the vampires were dead. Otherwise, he could sleep in peace.

"There's a much greater chance of that now I know you and your men are here," Vincent assured him.

Having left the men in the cellar, Vincent went upstairs. Before he entered his bedroom, he walked along the corridor and gently opened the door of Emily's bedroom.

Peering inside, he saw both his daughters snuggled up together, sleeping peacefully.

Vincent smiled to himself and went back outside.

Passing Corinne's door, he had a sudden urge to go in. What with one thing and another, they had not had a chance to be together since returning to Mandrake.

Even with everything else going on, Vincent could feel himself stirring at the thought of making love to his wife.

He placed his hand on the door handle, then stopped himself.

In his mind he imagined them both in the midst of passion suddenly being disturbed by Mathew and his men running up the stairs, eager to announce their triumph over the vampires.

Reluctantly, he left the handle unturned and continued on to his own room.

Chapter Forty-Six

EMILY OPENED HER EYES. SHE COULD HEAR HER mother calling to her from outside.

Gently, she extracted herself from underneath Stella's protective arm, and slid out from under the covers. She crept over to the window and pulled back the curtains.

Her mother smiled up at her from the lawn.

She wanted Emily to let her inside the house.

Emily understood immediately, they did not need to exchange actual words to understand each other.

Excited by the prospect of seeing her again, Emily left the room and stealthily made her way down the stairs to the front door. As with the last time, Emily removed the front door key and turned it in the lock as quietly as she could.

Her mother was already standing directly outside the door when she opened it, her beautiful countenance beaming down at the little girl.

Emily stepped back to let her in, then closed the door behind her.

Once inside, Emily rushed to her mother and buried herself

in her white gown. Her mother hugged her back and stroked her tousled hair.

After a while, Emily released her hold and stepped back, looking up at her mother and smiling. She was curious to know why her mother had risked coming into the house, knowing that there were men only a few short feet away looking for her and her companions.

Her mother assured her that all would be fine. She said she had to come because she needed to feed, and of course, she wanted to see her little girl again.

Upon hearing this, Emily immediately pulled down her nightdress, exposing the right side of her neck. Her mother explained that she could not take any more from her so soon after the last time, but that she would follow her upstairs and take some from Stella and Corinne.

Emily was disappointed at the news and allowed her bottom lip to protrude in order to display her displeasure.

Her mother hugged her again and assured her that she would always be her number one source of nourishment but explained that it was important that she also feed from Stella to prepare her for when they would all be together, once more.

Corinne, on the other hand, she needed to keep on board in helping to persuade her father to allow Emily to go with her when the time came, and it would be far easier to convince her to help once she had taken some of her blood.

Emily frowned. She could not see why her mother needed anyone else to be with them. But she conceded that she would miss her big sister, so finally accepted the plan as being necessary.

Emily led her mother up the stairs by the hand to Corinne's door.

Her mother turned the handle so softly that Emily did not even hear the bolt slip out of the lock.

Corinne was fast asleep, lying on her left side, facing them as they entered the room.

Almost as if floating on air, Emily watched as her mother drifted over to the side of the bed, and in the blink of an eye she was feeding directly from Corinne's neck.

Corinne, though still fast asleep, began to moan softly as the vampire sucked at her exposed neck.

When she was finished, she turned and summoned Emily to join her.

The little girl did as she was told and even though she had to climb on the bed to reach Corinne's neck, the sleeping woman did not stir.

Emily inserted her fangs into the holes already made by her mother, and drank, deeply. As her teeth were a little closer together, she made a slightly deeper impression in Corinne's neck the more she sucked.

Eventually, her mother tapped her on the shoulder, signalling for her to stop.

Emily smiled up at her mother, proud of her own effort as she licked away the smeared blood as if it were sugar from her desert.

Next, they slipped into Emily's room where Stella had not stirred since her sister had left. Just as before, her mother drank first, then lifted Emily onto the bed to take her turn.

As with Corinne, Stella moaned and sighed in her sleep as her blood was being drained, but not once did her eyes so much as flutter open.

Fully satiated, Emily's mother told her that she needed to go now before anyone else in the household stirred and revealed their secret.

Emily hugged her tightly, not wanting her to leave so soon, but her mother promised her that she would return the following night, and perhaps then they would be able to spend more time together.

She explained to the little girl that while those men were hiding out in the cellar it was too risky for her to outstay her welcome. If one of them should venture upstairs out of curiosity, there was every chance that she would be discovered, and then she might be prevented from visiting Emily ever again.

The mere thought made Emily hug her mother even tighter.

Like a doting parent, the vampire swept Emily up in her arms and carried her around the bed to her ow side. Once there, she tucked the little girl under the covers and kissed her gently on the forehead.

Emily was still determined to try and convince her mother to stay a little longer, but before she had a chance to say anything her mother began singing to her whilst gently stroking her cheek.

Within seconds Emily fell fast asleep.

————

Father James sat up in bed with a jolt.

What was that noise? He wondered, rubbing the sleep from his eyes.

He was sure he had heard something, but then, as so often was the case, his mind played tricks on him while he was asleep, and he thought he could hear something when there was, in fact, nothing there.

There was a familiar dull ache in the pit of his stomach, and he knew all too well the reason behind it.

That second bowl of stew last night was definitely a mistake. Not to mention all the wine he had consumed. But he had been so exhausted after conducting all those funerals that his body cried out for sustenance, and the wine was merely to compliment Mrs Oakes' cooking.

That was a lie he often told himself when he had overindulged.

Gluttony was still a sign, regardless of how he dressed it up, and he knew that at his age he should really be dining on a more modest plate, especially at night.

Having guests, such as they were, was another reason he used to excuse himself from overindulging. But he knew that his sin would find him out and waking halfway through the night with indigestion was a penance he must accept with God's grace.

He sat up in bed and contemplated reading from his bible for a while. The candle by his bedside had almost burned down to the bottom, but there was still enough light to read from, and anyway, he doubted he could stay awake for much longer than a couple of verses before drifting back off.

Resigned to his fate, Father James sat up in bed and reached over for his reading glasses. He perched them on the end of his nose and picked up his bible.

Just then, he heard something.

Scratching.

There was no mistaking it this time.

As quickly as it had started, it seemed to stop. Father James looked off into the distance and tried to concentrate to hear if the noise repeated itself.

After a moment, the sound resumed.

He considered that it might be rats under the floorboards, scurrying around on their nightly hunt for food. But the longer he listened the more convinced he became that the sound was emanating from somewhere outside the presbytery, rather than below it.

He allowed the noise to continue for several more seconds before he decided it warranted investigation.

Replacing his bible and glasses on his night table, Father James swung his legs out of bed and stood up. His head began to swim and before he knew it, he had landed back down on his mattress with a *thump*.

Doctor Harris had warned him about sudden movements, and this was the proof.

He waited a moment for his head to clear, then reached over and slipped on his dressing gown and finally, his slippers.

This time he purposely stood up more slowly, allowing his body plenty of time to absorb the shock.

Once he was sure that his dizzy spell had passed, Father James picked up his candle and walked out of his bedroom. Once in the main parlour he listened out again for the scratching noise which had roused his attention.

There it was again, louder this time and definitely coming from somewhere within the presbytery.

Using his candle to light his way, he walked across the parlour, passed the kitchen and over to the main dining area. He stood there for a moment, his heart beating in his ears.

There it was once more. This time he was sure that it was coming from outside, but from his advantage point he could tell that it was directly outside the main door.

He walked towards the door, and sure enough he could hear someone scratching against the wood from outside.

"Hello. Is anyone there?" he asked timidly.

"Father. Father James. Please help me."

It was a familiar sounding female voice but just for the moment he could not be totally sure who it belonged to.

Whoever it was, they seemed to know his name, so presumably they belonged to his congregation and were safe to let in.

Regardless of the hour, Father James was well known for receiving members of his flock at all hours if they had something urgent that they wished to discuss or confess to, which was-more often than not-the case. He often reminded them during Sunday service that he was there as God's representative in their most needy hour, and as such he was happy to make himself available to minister to them whenever the need arose.

His was clearly one of those occasions.

A lady, clearly in distress, needed his attention and he was happy to oblige.

"Just a moment," he called out, reaching for the key which hung on the nail beside the door.

Twisting it in the lock, he could feel his fatigue seeping away as the chance to help a parishioner in need rejuvenated his spirit. After the last couple of days witnessing untold horrors, he was more than ready for a return to his more normal duties, and a soul in need of comfort or guidance, regardless of the lateness of the hour, was exactly what he craved.

Father James pulled the door open and found a rather bedraggled Hetty Stobart standing outside, shivering in the night air. Her torn and muddy clothes made it look as if she had been dragged along behind a horse, and her hair appeared to be unkept and matted with twigs and leaves, rather like she had slept under a bush.

Father James could not disguise his initial shock at seeing the woman who was usually so well turned out at Sunday service, looking in such array, and Hetty must have read the expression on his face.

"I'm sorry to present myself to you in this way father. I've been away to visit some cousins in the next town, and our cart lost a wheel on the way home. We've just returned home and found the place empty with the door off the latch looking as if someone has been riffling through our things. There's no sign of my Cedric, and I'm really worried Father. I'm sorry but I didn't know who else to turn to. Do you know where he is?"

Father James groaned, inwardly. This poor woman obviously had no idea what had taken place in her absence, and here she was, asking him for a rational explanation when one did not exist.

His first port of call had to be to take her inside and make her warm.

He stood back from the door. "Come on in my child," he ushered. "You look half-frozen and in need of a warm drink."

Hetty crossed the threshold and from the shadows behind her emerged another couple, looking equally as desperate for warmth and a hot drink.

He priest frowned and turned to Hetty.

Noticing his concern, Hetty explained. "These are my cousins that I told you about, they came back with me to visit. I was so glad of their company when I found our home in such disarray. May they come in?"

"Of course, of course," he turned back to the couple, "the lord's house is always open to weary travellers, please come in."

The couple moved past him so quickly that Father James did not manage to see their faces in the light from his candle.

Once inside, he closed the door behind them.

"Now then," he continued, locking the door. "I'm willing to bet that you could all do with something comforting to drink, and are any of you hungry? I'm sure that we have some stew and bread left over from supper."

"We're starving father," confirmed Hetty.

Father James knew that she should not waste time in letting the poor woman know about her husband. But, under the circumstances, he felt that no harm could come if he fed them all first. Harsh news was always better received on a full stomach, and a few cups of wine might even help to soften the blow, albeit temporarily.

"Now then, if you'll all follow me, I think I can manage some good food and something fortifying to drink."

"That's very kind of you, Father," replied Hetty, "but there's no need for you to prepare anything. You already have everything we need."

Father James stopped in his tracks.

Hetty's words made no sense to him, and he could not help

but notice that her voice had changed, giving it a guttural undertone.

He turned to look at her.

The figure that glared back at him with ravenous eyes and protruding fangs no longer resembled the shivering woman who stood outside his door moments before.

Her hideous features forced the priest to stumble backwards, catching his heel on an uneven paving stone. His candle went flying from his hand as he fell backwards, removing the only source of light which afforded him any comfort.

He landed with a jolt on the hard stone floor, the impact of the blow forcing the breath from his frail body.

Before he could regain his composure all three vampires set upon him.

Chapter Forty-Seven

THE NIGHT WENT BY UNEVENTFULLY FOR MATHEW and his men. As usual they enjoyed each other's company as well as the wine and food Vincent had left out for them.

They had all taken it in turns to doze while their colleagues kept watch, but under the circumstances most were too wired to relax enough to actually fall asleep. Therefore, by the morning most of them were completely exhausted.

Once the night had passed, Tom ventured out to see if the sun had risen.

When he returned to the others to confirm that it was so, they packed up their belongings and left the cellar.

Once outside, Mathew instructed his men to make their way back to their cottage in the grounds of the church. Now that all the corpses had been removed, they could relax and catch on some more sleep.

Mathew informed them that he would make it back alone as he wanted to discuss the way forward with Vincent when he woke up. He warned his men that it would mean another overnight vigil that night, so he suggested that they rest as much as they could for now.

Mathew watched the cart carrying his men away turn the corner out of sight. He decided he would remain outside to wait for Vincent, mainly because he did not wish to unduly concern his wife and daughters, but also because it was a fine bright morning and he had always enjoyed this time of day.

Eventually, Vincent emerged from the hall and came over to meet him.

"My servant saw you loitering out here," Vincent began. "Why did you not wait for me inside?"

"I didn't want to risk upsetting your family, seeing a strange man 'anging about in their 'ome might have sent them into a panic."

Vincent had not considered that. "That was very considerate of you, thank you. "Where are the rest of your men?"

"I sent them back to the cottage to get some sleep. I've got an idea about 'ow we should plan tonight's vigil."

"How do you mean?" asked Vincent, curious to hear what Mathew had to say.

"Well as none of 'em showed themselves last night, it's obvious that they some'ow knew we were lying in wait fer 'em. So, what I reckon is they must 'ave snuck out by some other way."

"You don't think they might have just laid low rather than risk getting caught?"

Mathew looked at him. "These creatures need to feed. You must understand, their lust fer blood is not a thing of choice, they 'ave to 'ave it to survive." He gazed around the grounds for where he stood. "Somewhere out there is a new victim we've yet to find." He turned back to face Vincent. "All we know fer sure is that it's not one of yours."

A sudden thought struck Vincent.

Having been summoned by Hobson he had rushed straight down to see Mathew, without first checking if the rest of his family were okay.

"I need to go in, quickly," he revealed. "You've just made me think, I have to check on the rest of my family."

"If they didn't get passed us, here's no other way they could 'ave got into the hall, unless someone inside let 'em in," Mathew reminded him.

The thought made Vincent pause in his tracks.

Was it possible that one of his servants could be some sort of willing disciple for the vampires? Could such an individual have somehow perpetrated his staff, left in situ by the individual his late father first summoned to the house to arrange the installation of these vile creatures?

Was that individual even now preparing their breakfast, arranging a bath for his wife or one of his daughters?

He remembered that strange female laugh he had heard on the stairs the night he went to attend to Jasper. In all the confusion since then, he had taken no further steps in ascertaining who that person might be.

He had been determined at the time to speak to Mrs Bales the head housekeeper to ask her to make enquiries as to whom it was. But that was days ago now, so no one was going to admit it.

Was that simply one of the younger servants breaking heir curfew and venturing out to meet their lover, or was it a spy in his own household, setting off to release the vampires from through their outside escape hatch?

His head began to spin.

Just when he thought he had the situation sown up, a new spanner was thrown in the works.

Vincent turned back to Mathew. "Will you stay for breakfast?" he asked solemnly. "The girls need only know that you are a builder checking the foundations, and afterwards we can scan the grounds together to see if we can find the escape route of these accursed creatures."

Mathew scratched his chin through the wiry bristles of his

beard. "Well, only if yer sure. I don't mind eating with the servants if yer prefer."

"Nonsense, we'll set a place at the table. First, I just need to pop up and see that my wife and daughters are all okay."

Thankfully, Corinne and the girls were fine. Vincent explained to Corinne about them having a guest for breakfast. He could tell from the curious expression on her face that could not make out the reason behind the gesture. Tradesmen were not usually welcomed at table, but she suspected that Vincent had his own reasons so left I at that.

"You're looking a little tired my love," he mentioned, having kissed her good morning. "Did you not sleep well?"

Corinne nodded. "Yes, I slept throughout the night, but I did have some odd dreams."

"Perhaps an afternoon nap?" he suggested.

"Good idea, I might join Emily when she has hers."

Corinne had noticed the slight bruising on her neck when she bathed, and although she had no explanation for how it came to be there, she decided it was not worth mentioning to her husband. He clearly had enough on his plate right now.

When Vincent knocked on Emily's door, she called back that he must not enter because Stella was helping her on with her dress.

Vincent excused himself, smiling. His youngest daughter was evidently growing up faster than he wished. Still, the important thing was that she sounded happy.

Vincent felt a sudden stab of guilt that he had not informed her that they would not be able to attend Margaret's funeral, but he pushed it to one side so that he could focus on the task at hand. He was glad that Mathew had agreed to search for the vampires' escape route with him. He clearly had far more experience at dealing with such things.

The question was, what would they do if they found it?

Even during daylight Vincent would have preferred that

there were more than just two of them against at least three of those creatures. He had seen firsthand how strong and agile they were and could not forget how it took seven of them, including Father James, to subdue Toby and Vera that day.

He decided that he would leave their strategy to Mathew.

Thanks to Emily, breakfast was as entertaining as usual. Unlike her elder sister and mother, she was not able to hide her astonishment at the sight of the big man waiting for them when they entered the breakfast room.

As always, she was full of questions and mischievous comments, it being an advent for them to have someone new join them at breakfast.

"How did you manage to grow so big?" she asked innocently. "Do they feed you special food?"

"Emily!" Stella objected, giving her sister a stern look. "That's not the sort of question a young lady asks a guest."

Mathew just laughed. "That's okay your ladyship," he assured her, wiping his mouth on a napkin having just finished his third helping of sausage and bacon.

He leaned forward and looked at Emily. "If you promise to keep it a secret between us, I'll tell you," he replied, winking.

Emily was agog. Her eyes wide with childlike wonder as she nodded, eagerly.

"Well," he began, his expression stern and sincere. "Sometimes, when I'm really hungry, I find myself a little girl who asks too many questions and I gobble her up. Yum-yum."

For a moment Emily looked as if she were about to hide under the table. Then her childlike mind realised that she was being fooled with and that everyone else was in on the joke. She planted her hands on her hips in exasperation while the rest of the table joined in with the laughter.

"Don't worry your ladyship," Mathew assured her. "I only ever eat naughty girls, and your papa assures me that you are always good."

Emily blushed as she glanced over at Vincent, who wagged a mocking finger at her.

After breakfast, Vincent and Mathew began their search.

They began with a complete perimeter of the hall as Mathew believed the escape route would be more than likely a tunnel leading straight up from the catacombs and exiting as close to the hall as possible.

After almost two hours their search had proved fruitless.

"What if there's some sort of release mechanism that is only accessible from inside the catacombs?" Vincent surmised.

Mathew thought for a moment before answering. "Well, that'd explain 'ow they get out, but 'ow do they get back in? They won't leave the exit open until they return, it could be hours an' anyone might find it in the meantime."

It made perfect sense, but Vincent was starting to clutch at straws in his desperation.

He knew that he could rely on Mathew and his crew to keep watch in his cellar, but if they could not find the vampires' other exit, they may never use the one which led into the cellar again.

A hundred men could be standing guard in the cellar and the vampires would still be able to escape for their nightly bloodlust.

"What other options are there?" Vincent asked, stopping to catch his breath.

Mathew looked over at the trees which surrounded the grounds. "There's always a chance that they dug a tunnel under the ground which comes out somewhere in them woods. It'd give them more cover to 'elp 'em come an' go whenever they wanted."

Vincent scoured the tree-lined surrounds. "What chance have we to locate and escape hatch out there? If I called in the entire militia, we could be at it all year and still come up empty."

Mathew nodded. "You're right, sure enough, we'd 'ave to

rely on luck more than judgement, an' even then there'd be no guarantee."

"So, what do you suggest?"

In the distance they heard the sound of hooves galloping towards them.

They waited for a moment, then saw Ned rounding the corner on one of the horses they used to pull the carriage.

He pulled up beside them. "You need to come back to the priest's house," he said to Mathew, not bothering to dismount.

"What's up?" asked his boss, shielding his eyes from the sun.

"It's the priest, 'e's dead."

"What!" shouted Vincent, clearly taken aback by the announcement.

"We'd finished our breakfast and were just going to try and get some sleep, when the old dear what looks after the priest came thudding on the door, screaming that the priest was dead. We went round there an' sure enough, they've drained 'im dry."

Chapter Forty-Eight

THE NEWS OF FATHER JAMES' DEMISE THROUGH everything into disarray. Vincent asked Ned to ride down to the stables and ask one of the lads there to bring up two fresh horses for Mathew and himself.

He rushed back inside the hall and informed Corinne that he had to go back into town to see the priest on some parish business. Although she did not know the priest very well, he suspected that the news of his death might come as a shock to her, and he did not wish to upset her.

Even though she insisted that she had enjoyed a good night's sleep to Vincent she still appeared peaky and a little washed out.

Typically, Emily overheard his conversation and ran out to ask if it had anything to do with her nanny's funeral.

Caught off-guard, Vincent almost let it slip that Nanny Margaret was already six feet under, but he managed to stop himself in the nick of time and informed Emily that the funeral was one of the topics he needed to speak to Father James about.

He knew it was just a lie upon a lie but being cornered like that Vincent felt that he had no other option, without causing his daughter distress, and right now he was happy that she seemed so bubbly and happy, despite her nanny's recent death.

By the time he left the hall again the stable lad had arrived with the two horses he had ordered. Mathew had already chosen one for himself and climbed aboard.

He three men raced back to the presbytery and arrived to find a desolate Mrs Oakes being comforted by Gregory. When she saw Vincent arrive, the poor woman threw herself at him, burying her face in his chest and sobbing uncontrollably.

Her reaction took Vincent a little by surprise as he had only met the woman on a couple of occasions. But he soon realised that it was his office more than his person that she was clinging to.

"Oh, your lordship," she sobbed, "who would do such a wicked thing to a man of the cloth? What kind of monster is out there slaughtering at will? Is it the Devil himself, or just one of his minions?" She turned back towards Mathew and his men. "You were supposed to protect him, where were you all last night, off carousing with some local girls?"

Vincent did the best he could to comfort the woman, but he was lost for words that might bring her any succour. When he looked up, he noticed that Mathew, Ned, and Gregory all had their heads bowed as if in shame. But as Vincent knew, they had no reason to reproach themselves. They had been watching over his family at his insistence and none of them, including Vincent himself believed for a moment that Father James would be in any direct danger.

It was obvious to him that the vampires had used their secret escape tunnel to evade capture, and with Mathew and his men all housed in the cellar, they were free to run riot and attack whomever they chose, at will.

This was as much his fault as anyone else's, and he could feel the guilt weighing down on him like a lump of rock in his chest.

Finally, Vincent managed to manoeuvre the woman into a chair.

His tunic was soaked with her tears, but still she was not finished. Her grief appeared to be inconsolable, and she continued to sob into her apron while rocking herself back and forth.

"Is there any brandy in this place?" Vincent asked the men.

Mathew nodded and walked off towards the pantry, returning moment later with half a bottle and several cups. He poured them all a measure, saving the largest one for the housekeeper who at first refused the drink, then reluctantly agreed with some coaxing from the big man.

Vincent knocked back his shot in one, but it did nothing to take away the vile taste in his mouth. Had he have come clean earlier on about what Jasper had told him, perhaps by now Mathew and his team could have vanquished the vampires, and poor Father James would still be with them.

The blame for the evil which had permeated his town had to be his to shoulder.

Regardless of his original ignorance at his father's involvement he was the laird of the manner, and as such it was his responsibility to oversee the safety and protection of his people.

Vincent swore to himself that he would do all in his power to ensure that Father James was the last victim of this monstrous plague which had swept through his district.

Eventually, Mrs Oakes' weeping subsided to little more than a sniff. The poor woman had obviously cried herself dry, and whether as a result of the brandy or not, she had calmed down enough for Vincent to suggest that she return home to grieve for Father James with the love and support of her family.

He did not have the heart to ask her not to repeat what she had seen when she arrived at the presbytery that morning. That would have been too much for the woman to bear and would doubtless have led her to believe that he was nothing more than a heartless brute trying to cover up his own inadequacy at keeping his subjects safe.

Ned and Gregory agreed to take the poor woman home, and make sure that she was safe and warm before returning.

Once they had left, Vincent and Mathew made their way across to the cottage where they found Stuart and Tom washing the priest's body.

Neither man had the stomach to complete the ritual they normally afforded a victim of a vampire. After all, Father James was no ordinary man, he was one of God's own, and they feared that to plunge a stake into his heart and remove his head might bring a judgement upon them which dared risk.

When Vincent and Mathew entered the cottage, they both stopped what they were doing and stood back to allow the men to inspect their handiwork.

Mathew moved forward and tilted the priest's neck to one side.

There he saw the familiar marks of a vampire's fangs, as he had expected.

He turned the priest's neck the other way and was surprised to find no marks on that side, whatso ever. He peered down for a closer look just to make sure.

"They got 'in on his wrists," Tom offered.

Mathew checked and found the marks as his man had indicated.

"So, there were three of 'em," he confirmed, turning towards Vincent. "No doubt the last three left in your cellar. Now we know for sure that they 'ave another escape route besides the cellar."

"But 'ow did they know we were there?" asked Stuart.

"What d'yer mean?" replied Mathew.

"Well, if they didn't know we were keeping watch in the cellar, why didn't they use that way out to attack someone in the house? It would've saved 'em trekking across country and risking being caught. So, if they knew not to use the cellar, an' to use their other escape route, 'ow did they know? Someone must've told 'em we were there, lying in wait."

Mathew mulled over his man's theory.

It did make sense that the vampires used their alternative route because they knew his men were in the cellar. So, it begged the question 'how did they know?'.

"We're the only ones who knew," Mathew insisted. "Me, you lot, the priest, and his lordship 'ere, so who else could have told 'em?"

He turned to Vincent as if for confirmation.

Vincent wacked his brains, then shook his head. "No one. I told my family, naturally, and I told Hobson my head servant, so that he could make the preparations for you all in the cellar. Other than that, no one else knew that you were coming."

Mathew kept his gaze on him. "And you're sure you can trust this man?"

Vincent paused, then continued. "Yes, I'm sure of it. Besides, he would have to be in league with these creatures, otherwise why would he help them?"

"Are you sure 'e's not?" asked Tom suspiciously.

"God, I hope not," Vincent admitted. "Jasper was the only one my father took into his confidence, and I'm positive that he never told anyone except me on the night he died."

"Then 'ow did they know we were there?" insisted Stuart.

"Maybe, they have some way of seeing into the cellar from their secret entrance," offered Vincent. "Some secret panel in the wall." He looked at the men's faces and could see at once that his suggestion met with scepticism. "I'm only surmising of course, I can't say it with any certainty," he added.

Mathew nodded. "Tonight we'll 'ave to be smarter than them bastards if we want to catch 'em. But to be on the safe side, I suggest you don't tell anyone, not even yer family that we're coming." Mathew saw Vincent flush red and raise his eyebrows, so he held up his hand to stop the Viscount from exploding. "I'm not sayin' they're responsible, just that one of 'em might let it slip to the wrong person, then we'll be right back where we started, with more corpses to deal with tomorrow."

Vincent calmed down once he heard Mathew's explanation.

I did make perfect sense, and after all, none of them knew him or his family particularly well so they were well within their right to act with suspicion.

"Okay," Vincent agreed. "Let's keep this between us alone."

They all nodded their agreement.

"What are we gonna do with the father 'ere?" asked Tom sheepishly, almost as if he feared the answer.

Mathew scratched his beard. "I'll 'ave to send word to the Archbishop about Father James, but there's no tellin' 'ow long it'll be before 'e sends in a replacement priest."

Tom looked at his colleague. "'e means what're we gonna do about 'is body," suggested Stuart. "I mean, do yer want us to stake 'im and..." He trailed off whilst making a cutting movement across his own throat.

"Can't see like we 'ave much of a choice," ventured Mathew. "He may well 'ave been a man of God while 'e was alive, but now those monsters may 'ave changed 'im into one of them. We can't afford to take the risk."

"What about a proper burial?" asked Vincent. "Surely, we owe him that much, at least?"

"Aye, but who's gonna do the ceremony?" replied Mathew. "None of us has been ordained."

"Well even if we just say a few prayers over him, it'll be something," added Vincent. "Once the new priest arrives, he can always conduct a more formal ceremony, but we cannot just dump his corpse in the ground and leave it."

Vincent was sorely aware that that was exactly what they had done with several of the townsfolk the previous day, including his loyal servant, Margaret. But somehow, this was different.

"Carpenter called by this mornin' with the first of the new coffins Father James ordered," said Tom. "We could always use it for the father. Especially since we already buried all the other corpses."

Mathew nodded. "That'll do then. We'll wait fer Ned and Gregory to return then we'll dig a fresh grave for the father and his lordship 'ere can say a few well-chosen words before we cover 'im over. Agreed?" He glanced at Vincent.

Reluctantly, Vincent nodded.

"An' in the meantime," Mathew continued, "I suppose we 'ave to deal with the preparation of 'is corpse. God 'elp us."

Chapter Forty-Nine

BY LATE MORNING ALL THREE MEMBERS OF VINCENT'S family were finding it difficult to keep their eyes open. Of the three of them, Emily seemed to be the liveliest, but even she had almost dozed off in front of the fire while reading.

Corinne had caught herself twice, and Stella, usually so focussed on her needlework, had managed to drop several stitches when her eyelids grew too heavy to concentrate.

Finally, Corinne decided that enough was enough.

"I don't know what the matter with us is, my little ones, but I think we could all profit from a small nap. What say you both?"

"Mmnn, good idea," agreed Stella, "I'm fighting a losing battle with sleep here."

Emily, who often rallied against being forced to still have an afternoon nap at the age of seven, placed her doll on her chair and jumped down, stretching and yawning.

"Good idea, Mama," she said joyfully. "Let's go."

Corinne sent the girls up ahead while she informed Hobson of where they were going.

"If my husband returns, please tell him to come and wake me up," she added.

Hobson bowed. "Yes, your ladyship. At once."

Corinne took the stairs slowly. She could not understand why she felt so weary, but she clung onto the banister just in case she should topple back and fall.

Her legs grew more cumbersome with each step and her eyelids felt almost as if there were lead weights hanging from them.

Once she made it to the first floor, Corinne had intended to go and check on the girls. But she was so afraid of falling over through her tiredness that she decided to forgo the exercise and just take herself off to her room.

Within seconds of falling on her bed, Corinne was asleep.

As with the previous night, her dreams were dark and heavy.

She imagined herself lying on couch in the middle of an icy wasteland, with nothing to see for miles except white. Strangely, although only dressed in her nightdress, she did not feel cold. The wind whipped across the terrain agitating the top layer of snow, but even this did not seem to bother her.

In her dream Corinne was still very sleepy, and she only had her eyes half-open when Emily suddenly appeared beside her, shivering.

She swept the little girl up in her arms and held her close, trying to protect her from the cold.

Emily too complained of being sleepy, so Corinne turned her towards the backrest of the couch for extra protection from the wind and used her body to block out the cold coming at them from the other direction.

She held the girl as tightly as she could, promising her that she would keep her safe, out of harm's way.

Just before she fell back to sleep, Corinne saw Emily turn over to kiss her goodnight.

Corinne felt a slight pinprick on the side of her neck as

Emily snuggled into her frame, but she thought no more of it. Her prime concern was the safety of the little girl.

As she dozed off, Corinne could hear singing in her head.

It was the sweetest sound she had ever heard and lulled her straight back into blissful sleep.

———

Further down the corridor, Stella was soon lost in the middle of a similar dream, only instead of being out in the frozen waste, she was on s ship similar to the one which had brought them over from France.

She was sitting on the deck enjoying the view as the sun began to set behind the horizon, when she suddenly realised that she was completely naked.

The shock of her predicament caused her to sit bolt upright and look about for something to cover her modesty. Fortunately, there appeared to be no one else on deck, which Stella found strangely perplexing at this time of day.

However, it was nonetheless gratifying that she had not been seen by any fellow passengers or staff.

She wondered if perhaps everyone was changing for supper or enjoying a pre-meal drink. Either way, it allowed her valuable time to cover herself up and find her cabin before she was discovered.

At that moment, Emily arrived.

Her little sister seemed completely bemused by her sibling's nudity and found it hard to stifle her fits of laughter.

Stella tried to chastise her for drawing attention to her nakedness, but Emily appeared totally nonplussed by the reprimand and continued to chuckle.

Ignoring her sister, Stella glanced around for anything that she could use to cover her modesty. The thought of scurrying back to her cabin in such a state filled her with a mortifying sense of dread.

Stella tried to lift herself off the deck, but her arms did not appear to be strong enough for the task. She tried again, but to no avail. Her entire body felt completely exhausted as if it had been drained of every last ounce of energy.

The sun had dipped behind the horizon and the sky had turned to a leaden grey.

Curiously, although she anticipated a sudden drop in temperature, Stella was not cold, which made no sense to her. She was, however, glad for the fact, as the freezing cold wind which whipped across the channel would otherwise have cut into her nude frame, bringing her even more discomfort.

The spray from the channel as it crashed against the side of the ship, splashed over her in a thin sheet of water, forcing her to close her eyes to avoid the stinging sensation from the salt.

Suddenly, Emily was crawling on top of her, covering her nakedness with her own tiny frame and using what little protection her own dress offered to conceal her embarrassment.

At first, Stella could not see what possible difference her sister's efforts would make. For one thing, she was half her size, and her dress did not even seem to be a winter one with multiple lairs.

But to her surprise, Emily managed to wrap her arms around her and shelter her from both the elements as well as prying eyes.

Like a parent comforting her child, Emily began to sing to Stella, a sweet calming lullaby. She had never heard her sister sing before, and was immediately taken by the melodious tune, and the calming tone of her voice.

In a moment, Stella forgot about her predicament, and lost herself in the warm embrace of her younger sister.

When she opened her eyes, Stella was back in bed, with Emily curled up beside her, fast asleep.

Although relieved that it had only been a nightmare, Stella could feel a slight throbbing across her forehead. She sat up for a while hoping that the pain would subside unaided. But after fifteen minutes she decided that she needed a glass of water, and possibly one of the powders she had been prescribed in France when she had a similar ailment.

She was sure she still had a couple of them left in her trunk, so she carefully pulled back the blanket she had covered them with, and, picking up her shoes so as not to make a noise, she crept out of the room, closing the door behind her.

As she walked along the corridor towards her own room, Stella could feel the pounding in her head increasing with every step.

She dropped her shoes on the floor and held onto the balcony with both hands to help steady herself. The landing appeared to be swimming before her, and she blinked several times to try and eradicate the sensation.

"Are you alright, my lady?" A soft voice beside her brought her round. She looked to her left and saw the young footman she only knew as Jonathan, standing beside her.

His expression conveyed his concern at her condition, and her first thought was to ensure him that she was perfectly fine and dismiss him.

But as she gazed into his deep grey-green eyes, Stella felt an overwhelming desire to kiss him. But more than that, she wanted to sink her teeth deeply into his neck and suckle him like a baby calf extracting nourishment from her mother.

"I'm fine, thank you," she assured him. "Just a little woozy. Would you mind escorting me to my room?"

She could tell at once from his flushed cheeks that Jonathan was not accustomed to entering any of the bedrooms of the female members of the household.

Doubtless, he had been tutored against it and even warned

of the consequences which would befall him if he were ever caught in such a predicament.

"Don't worry," Stella assured him. "It'll be our little secret." She attempted a wink, but in her present state both eyes closed simultaneously.

Reluctantly, Jonathan offered his arm, and slowly walked Stella towards her bedroom door.

She could feel his body trembling against her arm, so she held onto him even tighter as if afraid he might escape.

When they reached Stella's bedroom door, she let Jonathan turn the handle and push it open. He stayed put, almost as if he were afraid to cross the threshold, so Stella moved forward dragging him with her. Although she was only alight of frame, she obsessed a strength which Jonathan had not been prepared for.

"Come on," urged Stella, "help me to my bed, or would you rather I collapse here on the floor?"

Jonathan apologised profusely, his voice shaking from the effort.

Once they reached her bed, Stella slumped back, her arms and legs asunder.

The footman stood there for a moment, not sure where to look, so he kept his gaze on the ceiling as if inspecting it for damp, or mould.

Eventually, he spoke up. "Would your ladyship like me to fetch anyone to assist you? Your mama, perhaps?"

Stella replied from her horizontal position. "No thank you, footman. You may go and retrieve my shoes from the landing and bring them into me, then you may go."

Relieved by the command, Jonathan bowed and backed out of the room.

He located Stela's discarded footwear, and carried them back to her room, as instructed. When he reached her door Jonathan was shocked to see that Stella was no longer on her bed. From his angle he could see most of the inside of the room, but she was nowhere to be seen.

"Your ladyship?" he asked, tentatively. "I have your shoes."

"Well don't just stand there like a lemon. Bring them in and place them beside my bed."

He could not distinguish exactly where her voice was emanating from. It appeared to almost vibrate around the room, almost as if she were everywhere at once.

Jonathan took a quick glance up and down the landing, just to ensure that no one was in sight. Even though he was only obeying a command from one of his betters, he knew that to be caught in a lady's room would be the end of his service.

Feeling as if he were in no position to refuse, Jonathan walked into the bedroom and over to the bed, where he placed Stella's shoes on the floor, as instructed.

He stood up with a start when he heard the door slam shut behind him.

He was even more shocked when he saw Stella standing behind the closed door, her hands on her hips and her dress on the floor.

The young man had had a very sheltered upbringing before being taken into service, so he had never seen a lady with so few clothes on before.

Jonathan gulped, loudly.

He wanted to speak but did not know what to say without sounding foolish.

A cruel smile spread across Stella's lips as she walked towards him, her stocking feet padding on the floor hardly making a sound.

His instinct was to flee, but Jonathan knew he had nowhere to go. Stella was blocking his path, and he dare not barge her out of his way in an effort to escape.

When Stella finally reached him, he opened his mouth ready to beg for his release, but before he had a chance to formulate a single word Stella placed her hand firmly in the middle of his chest and pushed him backwards.

Jonathan landed on the soft mattress, his mind reeling. He could feel himself growing hard, but in his heart, it was fear he felt rather than excitement.

Stella moved forward and sat on the bed, straddling him so that her full weight was on the protrusion in his pants.

She began to slide gently back and forth, tilting her head back and moaning softly to herself as she did so.

Jonathan lay back and closed his eyes. Although his mind could not make any sense over what was happening, he could not help himself but be pleasured by the experience.

Stella grabbed his wrists and placed his hands on her breasts as she continued to writhe and grind down on his stiffened organ.

She licked her lips and opened her mouth.

With his eyes still tight shut, Jonathan did not see her elongated fangs until it was too late.

Chapter Fifty

THE MEN ALL WORKED TOGETHER TO ENSURE THAT
Father James received the best possible burial, under the
circumstances.

Although it grieved him particularly, Vincent had to bow to
Mathew's greater knowledge of the resilience of vampires when
it came to them manging to rise from the dead once they had
been *turned*. Therefore, he stood by with his head turned away
while Mathew staked the poor priest's chest and removed his
head.

The rest of the service was far more traditional and carried
out with reverence and grace. Vincent spoke some appropriate
words form the bible as the coffin was lowered into the ground,
and helped the men cover it with dirt.

Everyone felt deflated after the service, and they all
returned to the presbytery to raise a glass in honour of the
priest.

Regardless of the solemnity of the service, Vincent could not
assuage the guilt he felt at being responsible for the priest's
murder. Mathew and the others tried as best they could to
convince him that there was no way he could have foreseen such

a circumstance, but the viscount knew that he would have to live with his guilt for some time to come yet.

On top of the death of Jasper, which he blamed himself for even more than that of Father James, and Margaret who died under his protection, not to mention the deaths of so many of his tenants, Vincent could not help but hold himself culpable as their lord and master.

He had loved his poor father dearly, but right now he could feel his anger at his actions boiling up inside him.

The only thought which kept him sane was that he knew deep down that if his father had thought for a single moment that such tragedy would follow his actions, he would never have gone ahead with them in the first place.

The thought that over time rumour and speculation might point the finger for this horrendous massacre at his beloved father turned his stomach to stone.

It was down to him to finally bring it to an end and eradicate the cause.

Naturally, he could not accomplish such a task without help, and right now he thanked God for the intervention of Mathew and his crew. When he first arrived in Hasterley, Vincent had to admit that he found the presence of Mathew and his gang to be an erroneous and unnecessary decision by the archbishop, and at the time he had every intention of informing him of his feelings in the strongest possible terms.

But there had been so many deaths and so much grief in the las few days that Vincent had to swallow his pride and admit that he would be at a total loss without them.

The thought jogged his memory, and he put his hand in his pocket and removed the purse with the gold crowns he had promised himself he would give to the men for protecting his family the previous evening. Now, more than ever, he felt they needed some reassurance that their presence there was not only appreciated, but vital to the survival of the town.

Vincent placed the purse on the table.

"Forgive me, gentlemen," he said, "a little token from me for all your help thus far."

Mathew took up the purse and emptied the coins onto his large hand.

"There's one for each of you brave men," Vincent continued. "As I say, just a little token of gratitude from me. Without your efforts I dare say this town would have been overrun by these creatures by now."

The men's eyes lit up at the sight of the gold coins. But they could all feel their leader's hesitance at accepting the gesture, so none of them made any attempt to move forward and take their prize.

Mathew turned to Vincent. "The church pays us fer our work," he stated. "What we do, we do fer the church and fer God. We are all willing to sacrifice our lives in the name of God, an' we don't ask fer anything more than what the church gives us."

Vincent nodded. "I understand your sentiment, honestly, I do. But this is my town, and without you gentlemen my people would not be safe in their beds. I am sure that you all value your commitment to the almighty, it is to be commended, but these few coins come with my personal appreciation for having you all here. I would be extremely honoured if you would accept them in the manner in which they are offered."

Mathew thought for a moment, then turned in his chair and held out his hand to his men. Taking his action as meaning his consent, each man in turn took a coin, thanking Vincent for his kindness.

They all took another drink, raising their cups to Vincent.

"So, what's the plan for tonight?" Vincent asked, wiping his mouth. "Last night's actions may have kept my family safe, and I'm very grateful for that, but it proved that the vampires have an alternative escape route which, so far, we haven't been able to locate."

"True," agreed Mathew. "What I reckon is, tonight we'll 'ave to split up. Three of us will camp out in the woods. I'm positive their escape tunnel leads out there somewhere. We won't be able to cover the entire area, obviously, but I still want two of my men in the cellar, just in case they decide to use that exit."

"That will mean just three of you to cover the entire woods?" Vincent noted.

"I know," replied Mathew, "but it's too late now to send fer reinforcements, so we'll 'ave to make the best job of it we can. I don't see 'ow we 'ave any other option."

Vincent thought for a moment, then said. "Right, then tonight I'll stake out the woods with you. With four of us we can cover more ground."

"Are you sure?" Mathew asked. "You know what we're up against, an' with all due respect, you're not trained as we are."

"I know, but I can wield a blade as well as any man, and we'll have pistols as well, so I am more than willing to take my chances for the sake of my family and town."

"You're a brave man, I'll give yer that," said Mathew, smiling. "Right then, we'll see you at the hall same time as last night, an' don't ferget, keep our presence a secret, just in case."

———

Vincent rode back to Mandrake leaving the others back at the presbytery.

Unlike the morning, the afternoon sun had hidden behind slate-grey clouds, threatening rain. Even with the cloud cover, Vincent could tell that the eastern sky was fast turning black, and that soon Mathew and his men would be setting off for the hall.

Before he left, Mathew reminded him to keep to himself the fact that he and his men intended to keep watch in his cellar again tonight, or that they would also be scattered around the surrounding woods.

It was still considered important by all those concerned, that they did not enter the hall until after everyone else had gone to bed. This, however, left a sizeable gap between when the sun went down and their arrival.

Therefore, Mathew decided that he and his men would take up their positions in the woods just before sunset, then two of them would make their way across to the hall when Vincent appeared on the veranda and waved them in.

It seemed like the most plausible plan as it afforded the men total secrecy as Mathew was still suspicious that Vincent might have a mole within his household. Added to which, this allowed them the opportunity to spread out in trying to locate the vampires hidden escape route, should they decide to use it again tonight.

It was by far the best plan they had with the manpower at their disposal.

Vincent was eternally grateful for the fact that Mathew was still prepared to spare two of his men to keep watch in the cellar, just in case any of the vampires used that exit, leaving them free to run amok within his own house.

Mathew had suggested that Vincent stay in the cellar with one of his men, allowing the other to join him and his team in the woods. But Vincent argued that with only two of them in the cellar, it was far better to have two trained vampire slayers at hand, rather than just one and him.

At least in the woods he could help keep an eye out for any suspicious movement and assist the others if they discovered the entrance to the vampires' lair.

Vincent was still filled with trepidation for the night ahead as he reached the hall.

One of the younger servants awaited his arrival, and Vincent handed him the reins after dismounting.

The young man appeared rather vague as if he were still half-asleep as he welcomed Vincent home.

"Are you alright?" he asked, concerned.

The young man snapped upright as if just shaken from a stupor. "Yes, your lordship, thank you," he replied, but his words sounded slurred as if he were trying too hard to expel them from his mouth.

Still not convinced, Vincent let him take his horse back to the stables.

Hobson greeted him inside. "Their ladyships are awaiting your arrival, your lordship. Would you like me to prepare you an aperitif before dinner?"

"Please Hobson, my usual, I think. I'll just go and see everyone before I get changed."

Vincent strode into the drawing room to find all three of his family fast asleep.

He smiled to himself, and hushed Hobson as he appeared with his drink.

Vincent crept over to the fire to warm himself, taking his drink with him. He was careful not to disturb any of the ladies, although, to look at them, they all seemed to be dead to the world.

Corinne was on the couch with Emily asleep in her lap. The sight of them in such close proximity gave him a warm glow inside. He was so glad that Emily seemed to have shaken off that nonsense about Corinne not being her mother.

Stella was asleep in a chair, nearest the fire.

Vincent knocked back his drink and gazed down at his eldest daughter.

He knew too well that very soon she would have to find a suiter and be married off. Not that he believed they would have any trouble in that direction. Stella had grown into a beautiful young lady. Educated, well-mannered, and above all generous of spirit.

He wondered who would feel the wrench more when she left: Stella, Emily, Corinne, or him. He was sure there would be tears come the time, but he hoped that most would be tears of joy, rather than sadness.

Emily would most definitely miss her big sister. She had always been there for the little girl, acting more as a surrogate mother when their own passed away. He had never witnessed a bond so close between siblings, and he knew that he did not deserve any of the credit. Stella had always been devoted to her sibling, and he knew that one day she would make a wonderful mother, too.

Just then, Stella stirred from her sleep. "Papa, how long have you been back?" she asked, rubbing the sleep from her eyes.

"Not long, just long enough to warm myself by the fire."

They looked over as Corinne moaned softly and blinked open her eyes.

She smiled up at Vincent, still half-asleep. She tried to shift her position without waking Emily, but as soon as she moved the little girl opened her eyes.

"Ah, I see that all my sleepyheads are awake, what a fine welcome home."

"I am sorry my love," offered Corinne. "I cannot understand why I am so tired."

"Well, you slept badly last night, it's to be expected. Perhaps you should all have an early night straight after supper? Do you all the power of good."

Emily slipped out of Corinne's grasp and walked over to Vincent, pressing herself against him and wrapping her arms as far as she could around his thighs.

He bent down and kissed the top of her head.

Emily yawned, loudly, excusing herself.

Stella and Corinne followed suit, both managing to place a hand in front of their mouth, before opening them.

"That's if the three of you can manage to stay awake long enough to eat supper," Vincent observed, smiling.

Chapter Fifty-One

VINCENT'S CONFIDENCE THAT HIS WIFE AND daughters would all be tucked up in bed early was soon dashed when during supper they all appeared to perk up and come alive.

He suspected it might have something to do with the extra naps they had all enjoyed during the day, and although their company was both pleasant and stimulating, he could not help but concern himself with the problem of what he was going to do if they were still awake when he needed to take up his post.

Vincent purposely fed Corinne and Stella copious quantities of wine at supper to help relax them, until Emily made a comment about her papa wanting to get them drunk.

He laughed it off, but then both Corinne and Stella started joking about the question, so he backed off, claiming he had not noticed how much they had consumed.

Emily-naturally too young for alcohol-was going to be the real problem, he feared.

Her energy that evening seemed limitless and after supper she insisted that they all play a round of brag before bed.

Vincent could hardly reveal the exact reason why he wanted

everyone to have an early night, although in truth, he had no reason to suspect that any of his family were in league with the vampires, he had promised Mathew that he would keep their pans to himself, so he pretended that he had some important papers to peruse before the morning.

Even so, having listened to all three women beg him to play with them, Vincent relented and agreed to one game, if they all submitted to retiring afterwards so that he could work in peace.

After the game, Stella took Emily upstairs to prepare her for bed.

Corinne insisted that Vincent escort her also, finally feeling the aftereffects of the wine.

On their way up, Vincent informed Hobson that he may excuse all the staff and let them enjoy an early night. Hobson thanked him and rushed away to pass on the good news.

They had to take the stairs one at a time as Corinne was not joking about feeling the wine. Once they were outside her bedchamber, Vincent made to kiss her goodnight, but Corinne opened the door and dragged him in with her.

Although she was no size compared to her husband, Corinne managed to keep hold of his wrist as she slammed the door behind them with her foot and pulled him onto her bed.

Vincent did not fight back as Corinne climbed on top of him and started kissing him all over while simultaneously pulling at his clothing. He never could resist his beautiful wife, but her behaviour that evening took him completely by surprise. Corinne had never refused him intimacy, but by the same token she had never instigated it either.

Her actions made her seem like a completely different woman to the meek, mild-mannered one he had married.

Vincent could feel himself growing hard through his trousers as his wife gyrated on top of him whilst her hands explored his bare torso. Before he had time to react, Corinne was unbuttoning his trousers and feeling for him inside his undergarments.

As excited as he was, Vincent knew all too well that time was of the essence and needed to allow Mathew's men entry to the hall.

Reluctantly, he grabbed Corinne's hands and almost had to fight with her to remove them from his genitals. Her enthusiasm seemed to have given birth to a strength well beyond her means, and Vincent struggled to win the fight.

"What's wrong my love?" Corinne whispered in his ear. "You don't want me anymore?"

"Not at all my darling," Vincent assured her. "It's just that I have some extremely important paperwork which I must complete before morning."

His excuse sounded pathetic, even to him, but under the circumstances he could not think of anything else to say.

"Is it more important than me?" continued Corinne, kissing his bare chest while Vincent still held onto her hands.

"Of course not, but I do need to finish it before the morning, you understand?"

"No!"

"Please, my darling, this is so unexpected."

"You haven't visited my bedchamber since we came here," Corinne pointed out. "Are you sure you have not gone off me?"

"Never my darling, nothing could be further from the truth. It's just that tonight of all nights…I promise I will visit you tomorrow."

"No. Now!" With a power which defied reason, Corinne whipped Vincent over onto his back and held down his arms by the wrists. She began kissing him on his neck, taking little bites of his flesh as she moved her mouth up and down from his ear to his shoulder.

Vincent closed his eyes.

He was unable to resist her allure anymore.

Suddenly, he felt a stabbing pain in his neck where Corinne's mouth had made purchase. He yelled at her to let go, but she continued to cling on like a crustacean.

In desperation Vincent bucked and thrust his body, eventually managing to dislodge his wife from his neck. He heaved with all he had, knocking Corinne off, and rolling her to one side.

Vincent jumped off the bed and slapped his hand against his neck.

When he looked at it, it was spotted with blood.

He held out his hand to Corinne. "What is the meaning of this, madam?" he demanded.

Corinne merely laughed and lay back on the bed, offering herself to him.

"We will discuss this later!" Vincent said, sternly.

He could still hear her laughing to herself as he slammed the door behind him.

Perplexed, Vincent rushed back down the stairs to the main foyer.

He had never seen his wife ac in such a way, and although a part of him was excited and thrilled by the prospect of his wife becoming more sexually promiscuous in the bedchamber, the other part of him could not help but wonder what had suddenly awakened this new appetite of hers.

For now, though, he knew that he had to concentrate on more important matters.

Although Vincent had given word that his staff may retire early, he knew that they would not abandon their duties before doing so. Therefore, he made a quick search of the downstairs rooms to see if anyone was still there.

Their supper things had been cleared away and the table set for breakfast.

The fires in the lounge and the parlour had been seen to, so that, and the general lack of staff milling around, made Vincent believe that the coast was clear enough to invite Mathew's men inside.

Vincent retrieved his key for the cellar from his office and, grabbing a candle from the foyer, he went out onto the veranda to signal to Mathew.

The wind whipped across the grounds as her opened the door. Fortunately, Vincent was protected from the worst of it by the fact that where he stood was set back a little from the rest of the building.

Even so, he used his free hand to shield his flame from blowing out and waved it slowly back and forth.

After a while, he saw two shadowy figures emerge from the trees which surrounded the grounds.

Soon, he recognised them as Ned and Tom. Each man carried a pack on his back, and a pistol on either side of his belt.

Vincent welcomed then inside and led them straight to the cellar.

The men lit torches once they were behind the cellar door, and Vincent apologised for not providing food as he had done on the previous night but explained that as he had kept their presence a secret from everyone, there was no way of him securing them food without raising some suspicion.

He men assured him they were fine, especially when Vincent informed them that they could help themselves to anything they wanted from the cellar's vaults.

Vincent left the cellar door unlocked, returning the key to its usual hiding place, and collected a couple of guns and some ammunition from his office before making his way back outside to join Mathew and the rest of his men.

Ned had already pointed out to Vincent from the veranda where Mathew and the rest of the me were lying low, so Vincent had a strong idea which direction to aim for.

Walking across the grounds, he suddenly felt very alone and

vulnerable, almost as if the vampires could strike at him from all directions leaving his virtually defenceless.

He knew that his guns offered some resistance, but nothing nearly as powerful as a wooden stake plunged in at the right angle. Vincent hoped that Mathew had remembered his promise that afternoon to make plenty of new ones so that there would be enough to go round.

Once he reached the edge of the tree-lined surround, Vincent stopped and tried to concentrate on the area in an effort to locate where the rest of the men were lying in wait.

After a moment of scouring the area, he could still see nothing.

Vincent could feel his anger rising inside his chest. If they had moved off without him, or were playing some childish joke at his expense, he would not be happy.

A slight rustling in the trees directly ahead of him caused Vincent to take up his stance and point his pistol towards where the sound emanated.

"Don't shoot," came a familiar voice out of the darkness. "It's me, Gregory."

Vincent recognised the man's voice, even smothered through the undergrowth, so he stood down and waited for the man to appear.

Eventually, Gregory emerged from the surrounding woodland.

Vincent had to admit, the man was clearly extremely adept at camouflaging himself from unwanted eyes.

Once he was in the open, Gregory signalled for Vincent to follow him back the way he had come. Taking in a deep breath, Vincent did as he was instructed, wishing more and more now that he had insisted on keeping watch in the cellar.

Out here was too vast an area to cover for so few men. Even skilled and trained ones such Mathew would be hard put to fight off a band of vampires converging out of the darkness, unseen until the moment they strike.

By their accounts there should only be here of them left, which helped to even the odds with four of them lying in wait. But what if they had miscalculated? Taking the word of an old man on his deathbed hardly made his revelation set in stone.

Added to which, there was no way that they could possibly account for any victims the original vampires had *turned*. Their main fight thus far had been against ordinary local who had been attacked by the vampires and subsequently turned into one of them themselves.

The entire district could be outrun with them, and here stood Vincent at the head of a band of three, surrounding the woods, their main feeding ground.

He should have insisted on bringing in the militia when he first thought of it.

But then, he had no idea how widespread the potential of these bloodsuckers could be. His main priority now had to be the safety and wellbeing of his family, and if that meant him sacrificing his life to save them, then sobeit.

He only wished now that he had taken the time to kiss his daughter's goodbye.

Not to mention make love to his new wildcat of a wife.

Through a small clearance in the woods, they eventually came across Mathew's point of operations. Looking around, Vincent realised that they had brough enough arms, stakes, crucifies and even holy water for an army.

Mathew explained that from their vantage point they could see Mandrake Hall from the front, so if any vampire opened a tunnel or a trapdoor they would know exactly where they were coming from, which in turn meant that they knew how to block their path, and if necessary, make their return impossible.

He ordered Gregory and Stuart to set up in the same way around the back of the hall, watching out for any sign of them rising from that side. The two men nodded and collected up their arms before setting off to take up their new post.

Feeling even more isolated since the other two men left, Vincent turned to Mathew to discuss their plan of action should anything happen.

"First off we use guns," he replied. "They won't kill them, but they can still stun them and slow 'em down in order for us to get close enough to use the stakes. If we 'ear the boys shooting first, we go to them, and vice versa."

"What if they use the entrance through the cellar?" Vincent offered. "We might not hear anything from out here."

"They'll be working in close proximity, less chance of the vampires managing to escape. Tom and Ned know what they're doing, and if the vampires do manage to make it passed them, chances they'll panic and run right into our trap. We'll get 'em one way or the other."

Mathew's confidence did encourage Vincent, but he could not help feeling deep down the man's words were more from a place of practised bravado than actual military skill.

Either way, they were prepared for the worst, and they were the best that they had.

Even so, Vincent found a prayer slipping through under his breath.

This could prove to be a very long night.

Chapter Fifty-Two

EMILY OPENED HER EYES. SHE COULD HEAR THE distant sound of her mother calling to her.

Carefully, she slipped out of bed, making sure she did not disturb Stella lying beside her, and made her way over to the window to look for her.

But there was no sign of her.

Wrinkling her nose in frustration Emily looked both ways to see if she could see her in the shadows, but to no avail.

She asked her mother where she was, and why she was hiding from her.

Her mother answered her in her usual way.

Emily smiled as she listened and nodded.

Excitedly she ran over to the bed and began shaking her sister awake.

Stella reluctantly opened her eyes and blinked several times. "What's the matter?" she asked, nervously. "Is everything alright?"

"Yes, yes," replied Emily, pulling at her sister's hand. "You have to come with me, our mama is calling for you."

Stella frowned and sat up. She wiped the sleep from her eyes with her free hand and shook her head. The wine from supper was still lying heavily on her head and she realised that she had moved too quickly.

The room began to spin a little in front of her. "Emily, what are you talking about, I can't hear Mama calling to us?"

Emily pulled at her even harder. "She said you might not be able to hear her yet, but I can. She wants us to go downstairs and meet her. She's going to tell us how we can all be together. Come on Stella, she's waiting."

The little girl's enthusiasm was infectious, but Stella was feeling far too worse for wear to share her excitement.

"You're not making any sense Emily, what do you mean Mama is waiting for us downstairs, she'll be in bed, asleep, where we should be."

"No, not that mama, our mama! I told you she had come back for us and now she is ready to meet you. Come on Stella please, before she has to leave again."

Stella gently extracted her hand from Emily's grasp and rubbed it where she had been pulling. Her mind was beginning to clear, and she finally understood what her younger sister was alluding to.

Obviously, she had had another one of her vivid dreams and she was convinced that their departed mother had somehow come back from the grave and was waiting for them downstairs.

Stella patted the bed beside her. "Come here little one," she urged. "Sit beside me for a minute."

Emily pulled away. "But we haven't got time, Mama is waiting," she urged.

Stella held up her index finger. "Just one minute, that's all I'm asking. I'm sure she can wait for a single minute."

She could tell from her sister's expression that she was not impressed with the idea but realising that the sooner she acquiesced the sooner they would be on their way downstairs, Emily reluctantly climbed back onto the bed.

Stella put her arm around her shoulders and hugged her tightly.

"Now then, we've had this conversation before, haven't we? You remember how angry Papa became when you insisted that Corinne was not our real mama?"

"But she isn't!" Emily insisted. "You know she isn't."

Stella sighed. "Well, I realise that she didn't give birth to either one of us, but she has been like a mother to both of us since she met Papa, and you know she loves us as if we were her own."

"I know, I know," Emily agreed, close to tears. "But I'm telling you that our real mama is downstairs right now, in our house. Why won't you just come with me and see?"

Stella realised that her argument was falling on deaf ears and she was beginning to feel guilty at seeing Emily so upset by her reluctance to believe her.

The problem was, what was Emily going to say when they went downstairs, and no one was there. Would she then be willing to accept that it was all as a result of a dream? Or would she then blame Stella for taking too long to go with her.

Either way, Stella predicted that it was going to be a long night.

She kissed her little sister on the head. "Okay, okay, give me a second." She swung her legs out of bed, shivering in the chill air. By the time she had slipped her feet into her slippers and pulled on her nightdress, Emily was already by her side of the bed, urging her to hurry.

The candle on the mantlepiece was still burning, so Stella grabbed it on the way out of the room. She had to remind Emily that they needed to be quiet as the rest of the house was still asleep. Emily nodded her understanding but continued to pull her sister along the landing towards the stairs.

An odd feeling of trepidation swept over Stella as they descended the stairs to the ground floor. She could not explain it, but it left her with a sense of foreboding which made her feel extremely uncomfortable.

Her attack on Jonathan earlier in the day had not escaped her, and she knew that such behaviour was completely out of character. But she could not deny the compulsion which had forced her to act in such a way, nor the pleasure she felt from it.

Whether it was all connected with Emily's strange dreams she could not fathom, but she knew she felt different inside since this afternoon, and it was a difference she could not explain.

As they reached the cellar door, Emily turned the handle and, to Stella's surprise, the door opened. She knew their papa usually kept the door locked so as not to tempt the staff to help themselves to one of his expensive bottles of wine, so the fact that he had not locked it made no sense.

Suddenly, Stella was struck by an awful sense of fear.

She no longer wanted to go any further.

She held back, but Emily pulled at her, urging her on.

"Emily, I think that this has gone on long enough and we should return to bed," she insisted. "It's dangerous down there and who knows what rats or spiders we might encounter in the dark." In truth Stella had no idea what the cellar was really like, but she hoped that her vivid description of rodents and arachnids might just be enough to tip the balance in her favour.

But it was to no avail. "It's fine," Emily argued. "I've been down there to see Mama, and you did promise me."

Before she could respond, Emily grabbed the candle from her hand and began to lead the way down the wooden staircase, instructing Stella to close the door behind them.

Hesitantly, she did as she was told, ensuring that the latch was engaged before moving on.

To Stella's surprise, there were a couple of lit torches in the cellar which, although they did not illuminate the entire area, certainly helped to eradicate her initial fear of venturing down there in the middle of the night.

Once they reached the bottom of the stairs, Emily let go of her sister's hand and ran towards the wall at the far end.

Stella's heart jumped a beat. "Don't run with a lit candle," she chastised her sibling, but Emily was by now in a world of her own.

Following the glow made by the candle, Stella followed Emily and watched curiously as the little girl began pushing certain bricks in the wall.

She was about to open her mouth to ask her what she was doing, when the little girl stood back, and a moment later there came the sound of stone rubbing against stone as a doorway in the wall began to open.

Stella stood there, open mouthed, as the entrance grew bigger, until finally, she saw a woman, dressed in white, standing in the open doorway.

Before she had a chance to react, Emily ran towards the woman, her arms outstretched as if in anticipation of a loving hug, the candle disregarded on the floor where it immediately burnt out.

The woman bent down and swept the little girl up in her arms.

Stella's immediate urge was to run and fetch her father, but she was frozen to the spot, unable to leave her little sister in case she was in danger from the woman.

She took a step forward, prepared to demand that the woman released her sister, immediately. But just as she did, the woman looked up straight at her. In the shadowy glow of the cellar's torches, Stella was shocked at the piercing strength of the woman's gaze which held her captive.

Eventually, the woman placed Emily back down on the floor.

The little girl reluctantly let go of the woman and turned to face her sister, a smile of pure joy etched across her face. "See," she announced triumphantly. "I told you our real mama was waiting for us down here." She held out her hand towards the frozen Stella. "Why don't you come and give her a hug, she's missed you, too?"

Stella tried but found herself incapable of answering.

The woman no longer appeared to be staring at her, but through her. Almost as if she was trying to ascertain something behind Stella in the shadows.

Shaking off the woman's spell, Stella crouched down and held her hand out towards Emily. "Come here darling," she whispered, almost as if afraid that the other woman would hear her.

But Emily seemed defiant. "No, you come here," she insisted, holding out her own hand.

Stella's mind raced. There was no way she was going to leave her little sister at the mercy of this strange woman, even though the little girl seemed adamant that she was not going to leave her.

If Stella left the cellar to fetch help, even if she screamed the house down, by the time anyone arrived the woman could have easily disappeared back behind the secret panel, taking her little sister with her.

Then, what if no one else knew the secret code to open it?

Emily could be lost forever!

Stella stood up and took a step forward. She still had no idea what her plan of action was, but for now he closer she was to Emily the more chance she had of protecting her.

But as she was about to take another step, Stella saw more shadows emerging from the doorway behind the woman.

She stopped dead in her tracks. She could make out at least two, or three of them, emerging from the darkness.

The shock on her face must have registered with Emily, because she turned around, and when she saw the other figures, she clung on tightly to the woman in white, burying her face in the woman's dress.

He three shadowy figures all moved closer as if one, until they stood just behind the woman Emily was clinging to.

Stella could just about make out their shapes. There were two women and one man, and all of them appeared to have their eyes fixed directly on her.

Somehow, Stella cold feel their hunger.

Their desperate yearning for fresh living blood.

Now she no longer feared for her sister alone, but for herself.

There was no way that she could defend herself against four of them.

Her instinct was to turn and run, but she fought against it for the sake of Emily, for she knew deep down that whatever her little sister thought about this strange woman, if she were to leave her at her mercy, she may never see her alive again.

Stella's entire body began to shake. Whether it was from the cold of the dank cellar, or the fear, which was building up inside her, she could not tell.

But she knew that she had to act soon before it was too late!

Chapter Fifty-Three

"Now!" The voice erupted from behind, a man's voice, harsh and rough. Not the voice of a gentleman.

Stella spun round, just in time to see two men rushing at her from the darkness.

Unaware of their intent, she instinctively turned back and made a lunge for Emily, managing to grab her and pull her away from the woman. The pair of them tumbled to the ground, Stella keeping her arms tightly wrapped around her young sister to help cushion the blow.

The force from the fall knocked the wind out of Stella, but she managed to keep hold of Emily, despite the little one struggling to break free from her grasp.

Ned was the first to burst free from the shadows. He raced towards the vampire holding a wooden stake above his head, ready to strike.

But the vampire was too fast for him. She moved at the last moment, avoiding the stake, and grabbed Ned by the arm, propelling him backwards where he crashed into Tom who was bringing up the rear.

Tom grabbed hold of his colleague and together they fell back onto the ground.

The vampire moved in closer, looming over the two men, her arms outstretched, fangs bared, poised to strike.

"Kill them! Kill them both, Mama!" screamed Emily, still fighting with Stella to break free.

Ned rolled off his friend and scrabbled about in the darkness trying to locate his stake.

Tom, now free of the encumbrance, grabbed his gun from his belt and aimed a shot at the vampire. There was a flash of gunpowder and the vampire reeled back, grabbing at her shoulder.

The force of the bullet did little more than stun the vampire who quickly regained her composure and reset her sights on her attacker.

With no time to reload, Tom, still lying on his back, kicked out against the floor to try and put some distance between him and the advancing vampire.

Before he had a chance to blend into the darkness, she was upon him, pinning his arms by his side with her thighs. In a split second the vampire lifted her head back and lunged forward, sinking her fangs into his neck.

There was a scream of rage, but it did not come from Tom.

Out of nowhere Ned sprang forward, stake held aloft, and drove it into the back of the vampire as she fed on his friend.

Ned drove it in, putting all his weight behind the effort.

The vampire reared up, the point of the wooden stake just protruding through her chest. She fell off Tom and rolled to one side desperately trying to reach behind her to remove the sharpened object.

Tom, blood squirting from his neck, slapped a hand over it to staunch the flow, as he staggered back to his feet.

Before the vampire managed to dislodge the stake, Ned

raised his boot and slammed it down hard on the end, forcing it even further into the hapless creature.

"No!" Stella felt her little sister tear herself free of her hold with a power that belied her years. Before she had a chance to react, Emily flew at Ned, jumping on his back and sinking her fangs into his neck, tearing at hm like a terrier.

The guttural noises the little girl was making as she tore at his flesh sounded more like they belonged to some savage beast than a seven-year-old girl.

Ned fell to his knees, reaching behind him to dislodge his unwanted passenger and swinging his body back and forth in an effort to free himself from her violent grasp.

With his strength ebbing slowly away, Ned's entire body began to shudder as Emily continued with her monstrous feast.

Seeing the fate of his companion, Tom staggered backwards until he located the stash of weapons which they had brought with them. Still holding his hand fast against his neck, he grabbed a fresh stake and lurched towards Emily.

Leaping across the floor, Stella charged at Tom knocking the stake out of his hand.

Without stopping, she pulled away his hand from the wound in his neck and sank her own fangs into the holes left by the female vampire.

Tom's legs gave way almost immediately. He had no strength left to fight Stella off, and she sank to the floor with him, draining away his life's blood as she continued to suck on his neck with renewed vigour.

After a while, both Stella and Emily pushed their victims aside and savoured the taste of the blood in their mouths.

Stella was somewhat taken-aback by her actions. Her initial intention had been to protect her sister from Tom's advance, but once she had reached him and seen the blood oozing from his neck, she found herself unable to resist the temptation of biting him.

Now that her lust had subsided, she felt less guilty than she imagined she would and convinced herself that she acted as any protective sibling would, under such circumstances.

Wiping her mouth with the back of her hand, Emily suddenly remembered her mother, and dragged herself across the floor to her motionless body.

Like a child unable to fathom the certainly of death, she began shaking the woman, pleading with her to wake up.

Although Stella knew that the woman had not been their mother, she still felt the grief that her sister was suffering.

Picking herself up, she walked over to her and gently held her by the shoulders, lifting her back to her feet. Emily turned towards her and buried her face in her nightshirt, sobbing uncontrollably.

Stella held her close until her tears subsided.

Suddenly remembering the other three vampires, Stella glanced over her shoulder towards the entrance they had been standing in moments before, but the doorway had been closed and they were nowhere to be seen. Doubtless, she surmised, they made a break for it when they saw the two men charge out of the shadows, ready to attack.

Eventually, Emily's tears began to subside and were replaced by a dry sobbing.

Stella desperately wanted to help relieve her sister's pain by telling her that the woman lying dead before them was not their mother. But right at that moment she was not sure how well the news would be received.

Emily had obviously convinced herself that she was their birthmother so she knew she would have to pick her moment very carefully.

Finally, Emily moved away from her sister and dried her eyes with the sleeve of her nightshirt.

Stella rubbed the back of her head and smiled down at her.

"We showed them," Emily announced, indicating towards Tom and Ned's bodies.

"We certainly did," confirmed Stella, still feeling a twinge of guilt at the pride she felt at her sister's actions.

Emily walked over to Ned's corpse and began stamping on it, her carpet slippers making little impact, but she continued anyway until Stella moved in and told her to stop.

"He killed our mother," Emily pouted. "I want to hurt him some more."

"Darling, I think he's beyond feeling pain anymore."

Emily looked back at the two corpses on the floor. "They deserved to die," She stated.

Stella took Emily by the hand and led her over to the stairs. She sat on the bottom step and pulled Emily onto her lap, wiping away some drops of blood with her own sleeve.

"Now then," she began, "you're getting to be a big girl now and one of things you have to understand is that sometimes you must hear things which you don't like, even if there're the truth."

Emily frowned. "Such as what?"

"Well, for instance, that lady on the floor, what makes you think that she was our mother?"

"She told me so. Didn't you recognise her?"

Stella smiled. "Darling, you know I'd never lie to you. Our mother was a lovely lady called Charlotte. She was very pretty, with beautiful long hair the same colour as yours, and a smile which could light up a room. But that lady over there was not her."

Emily looked up at her sister, genuinely startled. "But..."

"I know, darling, sometimes people lie, usually for their own benefit, but other times just to try and see whether you'll believe them or not. It's cruel and mean, but that's just how some people are. As you grow older, you'll learn who to trust and who not to," Stella assured her. "It just takes time."

Emily looked over at the dead vampire, then back up at her sister, pouting.

She buried her head back in Stella's chest and stayed like that, not speaking.

Stella wrapped her arms around her and kissed the top of her head.

With her speech muffled by her siter's gown, Emily asked. "You'd never lie to me, would you?"

"Never, my darling. Never."

Chapter Fifty-Four

VINCENT STOOD UP AND STRETCHED OUT THE CRAMP from his legs. In hindsight he realised he should have brought something out with him to sit on, squatting was obviously something which hunters and poachers became accustomed to, but in his case the spirit was willing but the legs themselves had other ideas.

The sound of a fallen branch being trodden underfoot made Vincent spin round.

He could see the shadow of what appeared to be a woman several feet in front of him.

"Who's that?" he demanded, levelling his pistol in her direction.

"Your lordship," came a shaky response. "It's me, Hetty Stobart. I've just returned from visiting relatives in the next town and I'm looking for my husband. I wondered if he might be with you at the hall."

Vincent felt his heart freeze.

He lowered his pistol so as not to alarm her.

The poor woman clearly had no idea what had happened to her husband, and this was hardly the time or the right circumstances in which to break the news to her, but what choice did he have.

He considered taking her back to the hall so that at least he could offer her a brandy and sit her down in front of the fire to break the awful news to her. But that would mean leaving Mathew out here alone to face the vampires if they happen to come this way.

Hetty moved in closer. "Have you seen my Cedric, your lordship? I feel so lost without him."

Vincent glanced over to his right just to check if he could see Mathew in the undergrowth. He needed to signal to him without making too much noise so that he could at least warn him that he was leaving he area for a while.

But Mathew was nowhere in sight.

As Vincent turned back to face Hetty he suddenly noticed two other figures behind her. They were in shadow and too obscured by the darkness for him to tell who they might be.

Hetty moved in closer. "Don't worry about them your lordship, they're my cousins from the next town. The ones I went to visit. I'll introduce you to them."

It seemed like an odd thing to suggest, especially considering the circumstances, but Vincent surmised that the woman was merely being polite in front of her squire.

Vincent tucked his pistol back in his belt. "Pleasure to meet you," he said. "Welcome to our fair town."

He almost apologised for the circumstances in which they were being acquainted, then realised that they were none of his making, so stopped himself.

At least Hetty was with some of her own kin which should hopefully, make breaking the news about her husband a little easier.

As Hetty moved closer out of the shadows, Vincent saw the vacant look in her eyes.

Before he could react, Hetty opened her mouth baring her fangs and sprang at him.

Vincent released a cry just before she hit him with her full weight, sending him flying backwards to the floor. His landing knocked the wind from him and before he had a chance to recuperate Hetty was sitting astride him, her hands gripping his wrists, pinning him to the woodland floor.

She hissed at him, spittle drooling from her fangs.

She lowered her head until they were close enough to kiss.

Vincent tried to turn his head away to avoid the awful stench of her fetid breath, but something kept his gaze focussed on her dead eyes.

He could hear the rustling sound of crackling leaves and twigs as the two figures behind Hetty shuffled closer until he could see them both towering over her, eagerly gazing down at him as if he were nothing more than defenceless prey, waiting for the kill.

Vincent tried to buck and kick Hetty off him, but she held on tightly with her thighs, crushing his upper torso until he found it difficult to breathe.

From out of the darkness a shot rang out.

Hetty raised her head and looked around her, trying to discern from which direction the noise had emanated.

One of the shadowy figures behind her screamed out in agony and jerked to one side.

Mathew was a big man, but without making so much as a sound he suddenly appeared behind one of the figures and rammed a stake deep into his back, forcing it through all the way.

The male vampire hit the ground, roaring.

The female vampire who had been shot, recovered her composure, and leapt forward, slamming into Mathew, and sending them both crashing to the floor.

The pair of them seemed to climb back to their feet together, and they stood there for a moment facing each other, ready to pounce.

From out of nowhere another shot rang out hitting Hetty in the throat.

She immediately let go of Vincent's wrists and clasped her wound, releasing the stranglehold she had on his waist just enough for him to take advantage and knock her off.

Once he was free of her, Vincent shuffled backwards along the ground until he felt he had enough room to regain his feet.

The vampire who had been facing Mathew was also shaken by the shot which hit Hetty, and she spun around ready to attack whoever had shot her companion.

Seeing no one, she turned back to concentrate on Mathew just in time to see him lunge at her with a fresh stake.

Fast as she was, the vampire could not move out of the way in time, and Mathew managed to pierce her heart with the sharpened end. The woman screamed so loudly that Vincent feared his entire household would hear her and venture down to investigate.

The vampire staggered backwards holding the protruding weapon, then a sudden *swish* from out of the darkness sliced her head clean off.

It hit the ground with a dull thud and rolled away before ending up against the nearest tree.

Vincent looked over to see Gregory standing there, a sword in both hands, his breath coming in heaving gasps. He had obviously run all the way from where he and Stuart had been lying in wait, aroused no doubt by the sound of Mathew's gunfire.

Seconds later, Stuart appeared by his side, a pistol in one hand and a sword in the other. He too was heaving for breath, and Vincent nodded his thanks to him, surmising that he must have been the one to shoot Hetty.

The male vampire, was still writhing around on the floor, desperately trying to remove the stake from his body.

This time Stuart moved in and decapitated him with a single blow.

From behind them, Mathew grabbed hold of Hetty by her hair and hosted her back to her feet. Even with the gaping in her neck, oozing blood, she still managed to swing her arms about in an effort to free herself.

Mathew held her at arm's length from his body, whilst Gregory approached them.

He lifted his sword and held it aloft, waiting for Mathew o give him the signal.

One second later and Hetty's severed head joined the others on the ground.

The men all stood around for a moment catching their breath.

After a moment, Mathew looked over a Vincent and asked. "Did she manage to bite you?"

His enquiry shocked Vincent, and for a split second he could not be sure of his answer. Tentatively, he rubbed both his hands around his neck and throat before holding them out before him to inspect for blood.

To his relief, there was nothing there.

Vincent let out a huge sigh of relief.

Gregory went round the back of the hall to fetch the cart, and the four men loaded the decapitated bodies onto it.

"We can go and get the lads now," suggested Mathew. "Now that we've accounted for the last three vampires, I reckon our work 'ere is done, by an' large."

As they made their way back to the hall, a thought struck Vincent.

He stopped in his tracks. "Just a minute," he said, turning to face Mathew. "One of those vampires was Cedric's wife, Hetty. She was never one of the original six, so if my calculations are accurate, we've still got one more to find."

Gregory and Stuart groaned in unison.

Mathew turned to face them. "Okay, you two stay out 'ere and keep 'em peeled. Jus' in case the last one comes out this way." He clapped Vincent on the shoulder. "We'll go an' see 'ow Ned an' Tom are farin'."

Mathew and Vincent walked back to the hall together, neither one concerned about what they might find in the cellar. If the last vampire had tried to exit that way, both men were confident that Ned and Tom would have dealt with it, without too much trouble.

When they entered Mandrake, Vincent was pleased to see that no one was awake. He felt sure that when the female vampire had shrieked, she was sure to have woken at least some of the staff.

Fortunately, that did not seem to be the case.

The two men made their way down to the cellar.

Vincent took the lead as they descended the stairs. The area was in semi-darkness, but one torch still burnt over by the far side of the room, casting a shadowy glow across the floor.

Vincent stopped in his tracks when he saw the bodies come into view.

Mathew, behind him, called out 'No' when he saw his two men lying dead on the floor. They inspected the bodies for any signs of life, but if they were being honest, they both knew they were already dead before they reached them.

For a moment, Vincent believed that the big man was going to break down at their discovery. But his grief soon turned to anger against himself for not being here when they needed him.

Vincent tried his best to assure him that there was no way he could have foreseen such an outcome, but Mathew refused to be convinced. They were his men, his team, and as far as he was concerned, he should have put his life before theirs.

The one saving grace from the whole debacle was the discovery of the last vampire.

It was clear to both men that Tom and Ned had fought the

woman together, both dying in the process with one of them managing to stake her before their final breath left his body.

At least this counted for the last of the original vampires, and Vincent could not help but breathe a huge sigh of relief for that.

Mathew stayed with his men while Vincent went back outside to inform Stuart and Gregory of their fallen comrades and the final vampire.

Vincent helped the dejected and heartbroken men carry the three bodies out to the cart. They made a point of leaving a gap between the four vampires and their friends.

Once they were loaded on, Vincent shook hands with all three men, thanking them for everything they had done in order to save his town, and the people therein.

Vincent stood on the veranda and watched until the cart rolled out of sight.

Chapter Fifty-Five

VINCENT SLUMPED BACK INSIDE MANDRAKE HIS
entire body drained from the evening's campaign.

He desperately needed a stiff drink to help with his aching
limbs, so he took himself into the drawing room and poured
himself a large glass of whiskey, raising it to his fallen soldiers
before downing it in one.

The fire coursed through his body causing him to shudder,
involuntarily.

Against his better judgement, he poured himself another
large measure and downed that too.

Placing his glass back on the table, Vincent went into his
study and grabbed the key to the cellar. With all the spilt blood
on the floor he did not want anyone to venture down there until
he had arranged to have the area cleaned.

The less awkward questions asked, the better.

Dragging himself up the stairs, Vincent noticed that his
wife's bedroom door was slightly ajar. In truth, with everything
else that had happened since, he had quite forgotten his
encounter with her earlier, and her strange behaviour towards
him.

Even so, he was feeling guilty that he had been neglecting her lately, so he made a promise to himself to be more receptive to her charms the following evening.

Vincent walked along the corridor until he was outside her room.

He listened at the door for a moment, but could hear no sound coming from inside, so he presumed that Corinne had simply forgotten to close it properly before she went to bed.

The last thing Vincent wanted to do now was disturb her. But still, he decided to poke his head around the door, just to make sure that everything was as it should be before he retired.

He gently pushed the door just far enough to allow him to see inside.

In the light from the solitary candle which still burned on the mantelshelf, Vincent could see Corinne sitting on her bed with her back to him.

Her head was bowed so she did not see him when he entered the room.

As she was still awake, Vincent decided that he would make his apologies and assure her that things would very much be back to normal from the now on.

He was surprised that she did not hear him as he crept up on her, but her concentration seemed to be focussed on something in front of her.

From his vantage point Vincent could not see what it was that so engrossed his wife, so he crept along until he reached her bed, then edged his way around the side to surprise her.

The sight of Corinne sucking at the neck of their young footman Jonathan was something which he had not anticipated.

Vincent felt his blood run cold as he stood there taking in the scene, his mind rebelling against the sight before him.

As if suddenly conscious of his presence, Corinne withdrew her mouth and turned to face him.

Even in the half-light, Vincent could see that there was fresh blood dribbling down her chin as she licked around her mouth, as if afraid she might miss out on some.

"Sorry, my darling," she said, casually. "I didn't hear you come in."

Vincent stared in abject horror his mouth unable to form the words he wanted to say.

From behind, he heard the door close.

Still in a daze, he turned to see Stella and Emily emerge from their hiding place behind the door.

"Papa," squealed Emily, running towards him.

Instinctively, Vincent scooped her up in his arms, afraid of how she would react when she saw what her stepmother was doing.

But she wriggled in his arms until she could have a better view at the debauched feast Corinne was engaged in.

"Mama was very hungry," Emily announced, matter-of-factly. "So, Stella suggested Jonathan as he was already almost done."

Vincent could hear his youngest daughter's words, but still they refused to register in his mind.

"We've been waiting for you, Papa," added Stella from behind him. "Now we can all be together as nature intended."

Vincent glanced down at Corinne as she casually pushed Jonathan's spent body onto the floor. As she stood up, he noticed for the first time the fangs which protruded from her mouth as she smiled at him.

He reeled back in horror, but Stella put out her arm to stop him in his tracks.

Vincent turned to look at her and saw that she too had vicious-looking fangs which she proudly displayed to him.

"Come my love, let's be together from this night until the end of time." It was Corinne's voice he heard from behind, but try as he might, he could not tear his eyes away from Stella's hypnotic gaze.

"Come, Papa," Stella added, holding out her arms to him.

Vincent heard a soft murmur escape from Emily's mouth. But before he had a chance to respond, she leaned in closer and sank her fangs deep into his neck.

The End.

About the Author

 I have dreamt about being an author of horror fiction for as long as I can remember. Few other genres ever captured my interest enough to keep me engrossed and I have always been inspired by those whom I consider to be the greats in this field, the likes of Richard Laymon, Guy N. Smith and James Herbert to name a few. I have a law degree from the University of Westminster, and was a semi-pro wrestler until my body screamed NO MORE! I now work in the legal section for the Ministry of Justice and live in Kent (the garden of England), with my six adorable rescue cats.

To learn more about Mark L'Estrange and discover more Next Chapter authors, visit our website at www.nextchapter.pub.

Tormented
ISBN: 978-4-82418-468-9

Published by
Next Chapter
2-5-6 SANNO
SANNO BRIDGE
143-0023 Ota-Ku, Tokyo
+818035793528

14th July 2023